moms of MAYHEM

MAYHEM HOCKEY CLUB BOOK 1

AIMEE VANCE

Revel Books
Paperback ISBN: 978-1-963848-15-1

Edited by Brittany Corley

Cover art and Illustrations
Copyright © 2025 Chelsea Kemp

Cover and Interior Formatting
Copyright © 2025 Aimee Vance

www.aimeevancebooks.com

*To the moms knee-deep in the messy middle,
and the friends who wade through
the mayhem right beside us*

Emmy

Nothing triggered me faster than a crowded parking lot in the middle of December. I circled the lot of the ice rink for what must have been the tenth time, my back teeth grinding together and my faith in humanity dwindling by the second.

"Make this next inhale slow and exaggerated," the guided meditation said through my brother's fancy SUV speakers. I unclenched my jaw long enough to breathe in through my nose, but the sound was nothing like the calm breath the narrator had. "Exhale through the mouth, letting all of your negative thoughts go with it."

"I've got plenty of those," I muttered. My hand rested over the horn, ready to unleash at the next idiot who dared cut me off in this endless waiting game. But I did as the narrator said, letting my shoulders sag with each exhale.

"Picture yourself on a beach, gentle waves lapping at the shore. Breathe in and out in time with them."

Now that one was harder to follow. The beach was a long way from Linwood, Colorado, a tiny mountain town nestled deep in the Rocky Mountains, about two and a half hours from Denver. This was the heart of ski country, but here in Linwood, hockey was our blood.

The steady voice came through the speakers again, "Are you picturing the beach?"

"Nope." I glanced up at the snow-tipped peaks around me, white flurries just beginning to fall. Pink touched the mountains as the sun set, washing the world with a glowy haze. The snow on the ground outside the parking lot was fresh enough to sparkle, and deep enough to make the parking lot a muddy, slushy pit.

"Good," the narrator said again. "Now repeat after me. Today is going to be a good day."

A stuttered "Ha!" ripped out of my throat.

"I am a good person."

I wiggled my head back and forth, repeating that one.

"I deserve good things."

My chest tightened, this one harder for me to believe, despite a year's worth of therapy under my belt. Did I *deserve* them? Maybe. But the last 16 years had squashed that expectation, and sometimes it was difficult for me to remember.

A mom walked through the rows of cars toward me, and I sat up straighter. She carried a huge hockey bag over one shoulder and a baby on the other hip. Two more little boys followed her like unruly ducklings, jumping in every puddle they came across. We made eye contact, and she nodded her head toward a minivan a row over. I waved her across, then hurried down the lane to follow her.

I wasn't sure about the whole *deserving good things*, but I definitely deserved a parking spot. It was past time I got inside the rink in time to see Jace play in his first high school hockey game.

"And my happiness is in my contr—"

A loud ringing cut off the narrator's voice, and I glanced down at the massive touch screen to see my ex-husband's name scrolling across. Bile rose in my throat the longer the phone rang, but I couldn't bring myself to hit that big, taunting green button to accept his call.

Today was going to suck.

I knew it from the moment I woke up.

Six months ago, with my divorce finalized, I'd up and left Connecticut with my son and everything my old Jeep Grand Cherokee could hold. That day in June was a year to the day after finding out my ex-husband had not just been having *multiple* ongoing affairs, but one of his mistresses had a baby on the way. With shaking hands, I'd called my brother, who'd hired the best divorce attorney money could pay for, and I changed the locks on the house.

The following year had been terrible for all of us, but finally, the divorce settled, custody was arranged, and I stuck Jace in a car, headed west.

My intention had never been to return to Linwood but home called me. Plus, being near my brother was like having a security blanket, and I needed him, even if I didn't like admitting that.

"Please tell me you have seats," I answered, all the calm I might have found in that stupid meditation guide flying out the window at the thought of seeing Ryan for the first time in months. Flipping my blinker on, I waited just to the left of the mom loading her minivan. "I'm in the parking lot, but it's packed, and I haven't been able to find a spot."

"Not even a, Hi, Ryan. How are you, Ryan?" his deep voice rumbled. Even though it wasn't a video call, I could see the disappointed look on his face, the image painted on the inside of my eyelids from the number of times he'd pointed it my way in our 16 years together. "As cold as ever, I see."

I inhaled through my nose, puckering my lips to keep the thoughts roiling through my head in my mouth.

"Where are our seats?" I asked, not letting him bait me like he had so many times before.

Minivan mom was struggling to get everyone in the car and looked up at me with a frustrated sigh. I waved, offering her my best smile, even though I was ready to scream. But not at her. Moms in parking lots got every inch of slack I had to give—that shit was hard.

"—your fault you moved across the country and made this so hard on me."

My brow creased, trying to replay whatever Ryan had said that I must have tuned out. "Wait, you're here, right?"

"And you say it's me that's a terrible listener. Honestly, Emmy."

"That didn't answer my question. Tell me you're fucking here."

"We're on in five!" someone called in the background of Ryan's phone, and my hands tightened on the steering wheel.

"You're still in *Connecticut*?" I nearly hissed, my eyes flashing to the rink across the parking lot. "Tell me you're not still at the studio."

"I don't know what you want me to say," Ryan responded. "He was here with me two weeks ago for Thanksgiving—we had our time together. And you know how busy my job is. It's not like I can take days off during hockey season."

My mouth opened and closed; words lost to me. I dropped my forehead to the steering wheel, trying to picture that stupid fucking beach and its stupid fucking waves.

"How did Jace get to the rink? Why didn't he call me? Why didn't *you* call me?" I said, my heart racing with every passing second. "You were supposed to fly in this morning, pick him up from school, and get him here. Tell me he's not missing his first high school game because you didn't think to tell me until 15 fucking minutes before puck drop."

Oops. So much for not letting him rile me up.

"He said Ty picked him up."

I slammed my hand down on the steering wheel, the horn firing off when my palm slipped. The piercing sound was the equivalent of the streak of cusswords I wanted to unleash, but my head snapped up.

The minivan was half out of the spot, and I made eye contact with the mom again. Guilt overwhelmed me as she glared at me, and I waved apologetically, wishing for a way to explain it wasn't her but my stupid ex.

In the time it took her to move out of the way, a huge black truck swept in and took the spot.

A bitter laugh rumbled in my chest. "Oh, you have got to be kidding me."

"Text me the score of the game," Ryan said. "Video it if you can."

I ground my teeth together, wanting to scream and hang up, but Jace was more important than Ryan would ever be, and my son wanted his father in his life. "Fine."

"You really should work on your temper," Ryan said.

Not trusting myself to respond, I hung up, done with his shit for today.

My SUV rolled forward, and I fumbled with the buttons on the door, trying to roll down the window and give this asshat parking lot spot-stealer a piece of my mind. The doors unlocked and locked, the seat reclined, and the trunk opened and closed, but no freaking window button. I let out an aggravated snarl, the car's spasmatic motions feeling like a perfect depiction of the anxiety and frustration bubbling under the surface of my skin with nowhere to go.

"Why is your car so freaking fancy, Ty?" I growled, cursing my brother and the luxury SUV he insisted I borrow while he fixed my Jeep.

The truck door opened, and a pair of crutches came out first, followed by the dark sleeve of a sweatshirt. The hairs on the back of my neck stood up, and I watched a mountain of a man closing the truck door, a hip brace over his left leg and a crutch under each arm. He wore a black Denver Yetis hat low over his eyes, a dark beard covering the rest of his face, and I hated him instantly.

Injury aside, who the hell stole a parking spot when someone had their blinker on?

He moved to walk toward the rink, and I let out a long exhale, circling the parking lot again.

After all, today was going to be a good day.

I was a good person.

I deserved good things.

And my happiness was in my control, dammit.

2

BECKETT

I weaved my way through the crowded parking lot of the Linwood Rink, trying to place my crutches just right to avoid any icy spots. With each step, pain shot up my left leg like it had for the last four weeks since my hip surgery. These crutches were the bane of my existence, a constant reminder how quickly my career had gone up in smoke.

Being back in Linwood was just the cherry on my shit sundae.

My phone vibrated in my pocket, and I glared at the Land Rover as it drove by again. The woman in the driver's seat stared, but my mean mug and grizzly beard were enough to make her look away. Moving to the sidewalk, I reached into my pocket and pulled my phone free.

TY

Meet me inside, center ice. Last row.

I shook my head. That asshole knew I was on crutches and still chose the last row. Sliding my phone back in my pocket, I looked up at the rink in front of me.

It had been over a decade since I'd been back in Linwood, and the rink showed every single day of those years. Everything here was the same as I remembered, just a downtrodden version of the picture in my mind. One glance at the crutches in my hands and maybe I fit that bill too.

I squinted against the setting sun, taking in the dirty red brick walls in desperate need of a power wash. The sign above the door had several letters with lights out or broken, now reading *inood nk*. Massive icicles hung from the gutters along the side of the building, dangerous if one fell on a passerby below. Coach Mikaelson never would have allowed such a thing in his prime, but his death had hit us all hard.

Well, not *everything* was the same.

With a grunt, I crossed the slippery sidewalk to the front walkway and toward a statue of three hockey players, posing together with Coach Mikaelson. Coach stood in the middle, his signature whistle around his neck, arms crossed over his chest. My heart lurched at the sight of my mentor, feeling guilty I hadn't had the guts to come to his funeral six years ago. That phone call had hurt worse than hearing my father had passed away, and even now, I wasn't ready to face the fact he was truly gone.

I cleared my throat, looking at the other figures frozen in time. Each wore a Mayhem jersey, like the players inside still did, looking like a moment stolen from my memory, smiling out at the parking lot.

The one on the left had hair swept back from his face and trailing his neck, a mullet like Ty had worn every day for most of his teen years and NHL career, no matter the hair trends. The grin was wrong as my best friend hardly ever smiled, but the rest was spot on.

The one on the right was a little shorter, but not by

much. How the artist captured Mason's mischievous streak, I wasn't sure, but even the statue version of my brother looked like he was ready to blow up a barn or try skijoring on a whim.

I frowned at the face next to Coach, the tallest of the four. A bronze version of me smiled out at the parking lot, a smirk plastered on his cocky face. That part was right, but the rest of it... Fuck, why did they make my ears stick out like that?

A heavy sigh slipped free, and I crutched my way toward the door. *Thunderstruck* boomed over the speakers inside, a tune I'd heard so many times my heart pumped in time with it. Coach would have hated to see his beloved rink in disrepair, but he would have loved knowing his legacy lived on in the team's warmup song.

I struggled with the door, more likely to throw my crutch through the glass than ask for help and finally got it open.

Despite having played professional hockey for 16 years, there was nothing like the first Mayhem game of the season. Linwood was a small town in a valley of small towns, nestled in the Gore Range. Our high school wasn't big enough to justify its own team, so the other local towns joined in to create one. Being a Mayhem was a legacy carried with you your whole life, or at least it was at one point. Now, I wasn't so sure.

The arena was packed, a few hundred people milling about in front of the concession and walking toward the stands. Tiny kids walked around in little black-and-green Mayhem jerseys, and parents wore a wide variety of Mayhem gear.

Tate stood behind the concession counter, serving food at a rapid pace I couldn't keep up with. She wore her long red hair braided and hanging down over her shoulder under a backward Mayhem cap with a green hoodie showing *Mikaelson* across her shoulders. It was jarring to see Coach's daughter grown, and yet still the same. A testament to how long I'd truly been gone.

She looked my way and tipped her chin up in recognition, but didn't draw any attention to me, which I appreciated. So far, the incognito look was working for me.

"Watch out!" someone called, and I looked down in time to see a dad scrambling to keep his toddler from running right into my knees.

I gritted my teeth, reining in any response at what could have set my recovery time back weeks. "All good."

"I'm so sorry," the guy said, meeting my eyes. I saw the moment he recognized me, his head jerking back a little and eyes expanding. "Hey—"

"No," I cut in before he could even ask. My name. For an autograph. How I was feeling. I wanted none of it.

"You're Beckett Conway," he continued anyway.

My crutches squeaked across the rubber floors and up the walkway to the rink as I booked it away from him. Screw Ty for insisting we meet here instead of his hardware store. If I didn't need the key to my own house, I wouldn't have come at all.

The temperature dropped with each step toward the ice, and my heart thundered to the beat of the song. I turned toward the stands—something I'd never done in Linwood— and looked for Ty in the crowd.

Like his message said, he sat right smack in the middle of the rink, elbows resting on his knees. He was alone in a stretch of the only empty seats in the crowd, nodding to everyone who stopped to acknowledge him. Not a hint of a smile showed, but he was as polite as I'd ever seen him be. At his feet, Rowdy lay sprawled out like he owned the place—Ty's three-legged black lab mix with a white patch on his chest and the kind of soulful eyes that made even the grumpiest rink rats stop and scratch behind his ears. The missing back leg didn't slow him down, but it sure added to the legend.

"You look like shit," Ty said when I worked my way up the narrow steps to him, and Rowdy barked his agreement.

"Not as shit as that caterpillar on your upper lip." I dropped into one of the seats next to him, sliding the crutches under our feet. "This Tom Selleck look is way worse than the mullet. You trying to actively repel people now?"

"Was working 'til you sat your ugly mug down next to me."

I chuckled, adjusting on the cold metal seats. My hip still hurt like a motherfucker, and I'd skipped painkillers today so I could drive up from Denver. Maybe that was a mistake.

"How are we looking this season?" I nodded toward the ice, leaning down to pet the dog I hadn't seen in years, then hit the underside of Ty's Mayhem hat. "Festive."

"Jace is on the team this year."

I looked over at him, but Ty's gaze was glued on the ice where twenty kids warmed up in their black-and-green Mayhem Hockey Club jerseys. "Who's Jace?"

"Emmy's kid."

"Emmy?" I frowned. "Like, your sister Emmy?"

"No, the other Emmy."

"Is her kid like the ice boy or something?" I looked back at the teens going through pre-game stretches, trying to remember how old they were. "I remember you saying she had a kid, but he's gotta be, what, six? Seven?"

"Fifteen."

My jaw dropped, looking back out at the ice again. "How the fuck does your *little* sister have a fifteen-year-old?"

Ty looked at me then, his dark eyes squinting underneath his hat. "Sometimes I forget how hard you checked out of life the moment you were called up to the NHL."

My jaw worked. Fuck, that stung a little, but he wasn't wrong. "We're 37, so Emmy's what, 35?"

Ty hummed, his hand brushing over his mustache as he looked down at the ice once more. "Glad to see that concussion wasn't enough to knock out basic math skills. We both know you never would have made it out of Algebra 1 without cheating on my tests."

I smirked, holding back a laugh. "Fuck you." Elbowing his side, I said, "Alright, which one is our kid then? Who am I watching?"

Ty pointed to a right winger wearing number 61—*my* number. His face mask covered most of his features, so I couldn't see the kid, but his footwork was great if a little choppy, and his wrist shot went right past the goalie, into the net.

"He any good?"

He grunted, but something about his stiff posture made me look back at the kid again. "Yes, unfortunately."

Jace skated over to the bench, grabbed a water bottle, and looked out over the stands. He stared right at us, and I glanced over at the empty seats to my right. "Where are his parents? I haven't seen Emmy since high school. Wait, do I know his dad?"

Ty chuckled, the sound ominous from a man who hardly ever laughed even as a kid.

A woman stormed toward us, fire in her stride and zero

regard for how hard she was hitting my nervous system. Black puffer vest over a Mayhem hoodie, leggings clinging to strong legs that moved like she had somewhere to be and no intention of apologizing for it. Her dark brown hair curled softly beneath a green beanie with a ridiculously large pom-pom on top—adorable, infuriating, and somehow sexy as hell.

I couldn't look away. Couldn't stop the way my gut twisted like I'd just taken a slapshot to the stomach. Every inch of her was pure, unbothered confidence wrapped in curves and attitude.

My gaze dragged upward, slow and hungry, not because I meant to be a jackass, but because my body reacted before my brain could catch up.

Then I reached her face and froze. Honey-hazel eyes, sharp and unblinking, locked on mine with the same heat I'd felt earlier in the parking lot.

Shit.

"I should have known it was you." She dropped into the seat next to Ty like gravity had kicked in. "Of course it was you. Like this day could get any worse."

I froze for half a second, then leaned over Ty and a tail-thumping Rowdy to get a better look, even though I already knew it was her. That same simmering scowl. That same quick-fire presence that made the room feel smaller.

And Jesus, she was gorgeous. Even pissed off. *Especially* pissed off.

"Do I know you?" I asked, unable to stop the smirk tugging at my mouth. "Aside from your wildly misplaced parking lot aggression?"

"*Misplaced?*" She threw her hands in the air, but her eyes were glued to the ice as the players headed back to the locker room one more time before the game. "I'd been waiting for that spot. I had my blinker on and everything. You swooped in with your Napoleon truck that might as well have testicles dangling from a trailer hitch you've probably never used and *stole my spot.*"

"Funny, because I didn't see your name on it. Maybe you should give it to me."

She cackled. Head thrown back, *cackled,* and I couldn't help but grin in response.

Ty crossed his arms over his chest, a hint of a smile showing beneath his mustache. "It's been a long time since I've heard you two bicker."

My eyes flicked to him, then back to the woman now scowling at the ice. "Oh shit. Little Emmy Hudson is all grown up."

"It's Emmy Meyers. Has been for a long time, asshole."

I reeled back, looking at Ty. "As in—"

"Yep."

Forget my crutches—they weren't the bane of my existence. No, that place was held by Ryan fucking Meyers, my former teammate, my loudest hater, and now host of Hockey Tonight.

3

Emmy

My knee bounced constantly, nervous energy coursing through me as the players took the ice. Jace came out with the first shift and bile rose in my throat.

"This is U18, right?" Beckett asked Ty, and I squeezed my eyes shut. "AAA?"

"Yeah," Ty answered. "The best we have."

"And he's a freshman? On first string?"

I could hear the surprise in Beckett's voice, and part of me wanted to reach across and slap him for doubting Jace, but I was too keyed up to move.

"I told you he's good."

Brother of the year, right there. As much as I hated letting Ty swoop in to save the day for me, he was more than half the reason I'd moved back to Linwood, the support system and role model I wanted for Jace that he'd never had in Ryan. Sure, he wasn't his dad, but as today proved, Ty showed up far more than Ryan ever did, even when we'd lived in the same house.

The music in the arena stopped, and I held my breath,

watching the players take their positions. Jace leaned down on his stick, his gaze laser-focused on the ref standing in the middle of the ice, ready to drop the puck. Between Ty, then Ryan, then Jace, I had been to thousands of hockey games in my life, but this one mattered more.

"Come on, buddy," I muttered, my hands steepled in front of my mouth. "Show them what you're made of."

I felt Ty and Beckett looking at me, but I could hardly breathe, let alone care about what anyone thought of my crazy mom vibes. No one loved my son more than me, and my son loved hockey more than he loved anything. He had been pissed when I moved him across the country this summer, but it was a mother's job to do what was best for their kids, and Ryan was not it.

The puck dropped, and I shot to my feet. Thankfully, Ty knew this about me, which was why he chose the last row. No one behind me was going to ask me to sit down.

"Let's go bud!" I screamed, unable to keep the words in my mouth.

Jace took off after the puck, faster than anyone else on the ice despite being younger than all of them. He caught the puck on a pass, then cut to the right, flying past a defender and toward the net. The game moved fast, the way all good hockey did, and I gasped and screamed in turn.

A kid twice Jace's size flew toward him, and Jace dumped the puck to a teammate, but it was intercepted. Jace stood upright, frustration evident as he took off back down the ice, chasing it again.

"I'm going to puke," I mumbled, adrenaline sending my heart into overdrive like it was me down there instead of my son.

"Careful, Jace," Ty said next to me, and I shot my

brother a look that said, *talk shit about him, and I'll murder you in your sleep.*

Before Jace could catch up with the puck again, his shift came off the ice and he sat down hard on the bench. I sagged down onto my own seat, my shoulders dropping.

"He's off tonight," I said to no one in particular. "Dammit, Ryan."

Ty patted my leg, then stood when the ref blew the whistle for an offsides call. "I'll go get you a pretzel. Need anything else?"

"Fireball?" I suggested. "Xanax? A tranquilizer, maybe?"

Beckett chuckled, and I shot my brother's best friend a look. "Long game ahead of you for you to be losing it this quickly."

"Once you push a 9-pound baby out your nostril you can tell me how to mother. Until then, keep your mouth shut."

He held his hands up, and Ty slapped me on the shoulder. "One hot pretzel, coming up. Diet Coke too?"

"Does a bear shit in the woods?"

My brother shook his head, then walked down the aisle, Rowdy hopping along at his heels.

The game moved on, and I tried to remember the names of the other players on the Mayhem, but this was his first season with this team, and I'd been too busy moving and setting up Elevation Pilates, my studio in town, to attend as many practices as I usually would have.

The Bruins had a shot on goal, and our goalie dropped, blocking the puck with his stick. Beckett let out a long whistle at the save, and I glanced his way.

It had been years since I'd thought seriously about Beckett Conway, but the moment I saw him, it hit me like a freight train of memories and pheromones.

Damn.

He was even more gorgeous than I remembered—bigger now, broader in the shoulders, all adult muscle and quiet confidence, but still carrying that same effortless magnetism that used to make every girl in town lose her mind.

We'd grown up under the same roof more weekends than not, with him raiding our fridge and roughhousing in the yard with my brother. He left for Juniors at 16 and never looked back. The last time we were in the same room, I had braces and a bad attitude, and he was already halfway to becoming the town's collective heartbreak.

Now he looked like the universe had given him an upgrade just to mess with me.

The scruffy dark beard clinging to his jaw had no business being that hot—messy enough to look effortless, trimmed just enough to know he cared. His Denver Yetis hat was pulled low over his brow, but I didn't need to see his eyes to remember their exact shade. Unfairly blue, like the brightest summer day, warming you to the core. They used to sparkle when he laughed, and I *hated* that I still remembered the sound.

Worse, I was suddenly hyper-aware of every nerve ending I had.

I didn't want to notice. Didn't want to feel anything.

But there he was, real, magnetic, and hotter than sin, and my lungs forgot how to work.

My brother didn't talk about Beckett much—then again, my brother didn't talk much at all—but I knew the space Beckett had let stretch between them hurt more than he let on. And honestly, that was enough for me.

Beckett Conway was a selfish, self-absorbed hothead who

clearly cared more about his precious NHL dreams than the people he'd left behind.

Sure, he was hot. Like, *infuriatingly* hot. But I was stubborn and petty, and more than capable of holding a grudge. I had a whole list of reasons to dislike him—number one being the fact that he stole my parking spot and did it with the smug confidence of a man who was sure he deserved *all* the good things.

By the time Ty got back with a hot pretzel and a Diet Coke, Jace was back on the ice. I shot to my feet again, this time clutching the pretzel and shoving chunks into my mouth like a rabid chipmunk.

"What'd I miss?" Ty took the seat between Beckett and I again and flipped his hat around backward, adjusting it several times in what I knew was a nervous tick. Rowdy settled between his legs, curling up like he had a thousand times.

"Our goalie is quick," Beckett answered. "Reflexes are great, but his glove hand was nowhere near where it needed to be."

Ty hummed, and I chewed, savoring the salty, buttery pretzel. Tate made the best ones in town—it was a shame all she ran was a bougie concession stand and not a restaurant. She'd make a killing.

Jace got the puck again, and I clutched the pretzel to my chest, swallowing as fast as I could. He raced down the ice; the countless hours he spent conditioning with Ty this summer showing in how fast he moved. I bounced in place, my calves screaming after today's Pilates classes, but things like physical pain didn't register in the delirious state I resided in while watching my kid play.

"She always like this?" Beckett asked.

My head snapped his way, and if this had been any pretzel but Tate's, I would have chucked it at his head. My mouth was too full to shoot off the sassy retort I had planned, then the sound of bodies slamming against the glass ricocheted through the arena.

I sucked in a breath, damn near choking on the last of the pretzel in my mouth as I looked back toward the ice. Jace was on his knees, scrambling to get back up, and the Bruins had the puck again.

"Get up, get up," I mumbled, my eyes trained on my son, reading every furious line of his body. "Keep it together, bud."

Before Jace made it down the ice, the buzzer sounded, and the Bruins scored.

"Shit," Beckett said, and I sagged back onto the bench. The shift changed and Jace came off the ice again, except this time he knocked the water bottle off the bench, sending it flying.

"He's going to lose it," I said to no one, dropping my head in my hands, dread coursing through me.

Even from across the rink and separated by layers of glass, I could feel the frustration pouring off my kid in waves. He'd always had a temper, but every time Ryan broke a promise to him, it got worse. Unfortunately, we had a lot of experience with unfulfilled promises.

I pushed my head down between my knees, unable to watch the rest of the game, knowing how this would go.

"He's back on," Ty said.

I gave him a thumbs up but kept my head down. The buzzer sounded again, and no one around me cheered.

0-2.

I peeked at the game between bouts of panic attacks,

munching on my pretzel and sipping the Diet Coke when I could, but by the time we were down 0-4, it was hard to watch.

The third period started, and you could feel the energy in the rink deflate. Lots of families left, and I could hardly blame them. Hockey was a fast game, and every second mattered, but this one felt like a runaway train.

I didn't bother texting Ryan or sending any videos—the last thing Jace needed after this beating was a phone call from his absent father dissecting everything he'd done wrong.

Jace was on the starting shift again, and even behind his mask I could see the anger on his face. He hated losing, but I knew it was Ryan's absence that was the real problem.

Teen years meant my son acted indifferent about almost everything these days, but their Thanksgiving visit had gone well, and Jace was excited to show Ryan Linwood.

He'd talked about maybe staying at the hotel in Vail with his dad, and where they'd eat this weekend, and the video game he wanted to show him. He'd even worn a University of Michigan shirt to school today—Ryan's alma mater.

Beckett's too, but the last thing Jace needed was to know his idol was watching him lose this bad.

Jace got the puck off the tip off and shot toward the net like a bat out of hell. But the Bruins' defender had his number now, and raced forward at the same time, slamming him into the boards. Jace's head snapped back from a high stick, then crumpled. He was back up in an instant, but his stick was gone.

I shot to my feet as Jace flew toward the defender with control of the puck, his shoulders dropped. "Oh shit, oh shit, oh shit."

In an instant, Jace threw himself into the defender's

abdomen, dragging him down to the ice. He sat on his chest and slammed a glove into his face, and I turned my back. "Tell me when it's over."

The ref blew the whistle, and—I knew it was coming—ejected my son. "Bruins' Number 12: five-minute major and a match penalty for intentional high sticking. Mayhem's Number 61: two minutes for instigating, five for fighting, and a game misconduct. Number 12 and Number 61 are both ejected from the game. Penalties will be served as assessed."

I dropped my head, then sighed. Ty bumped my shoulder, and I shrugged him off, not ready to hear whatever he had to say. Grabbing my purse, I stormed down the steps toward where my son was coming off the ice.

So much for a great day.

4

BECKETT

The final horn blasted, ending the game with the Mayhem losing by six. The crowd shuffled down the ramps and out into the atrium outside the rink, headed for the exit.

"That was painful." I leaned down to grab my crutches from under Ty's and my legs, ready to leave. "A shutout to start the season."

Ty grunted, but didn't get up, still staring out at the ice while the teams left. Several other parents lingered around the rink, and I glanced at my friend for any hints as to what was going on.

The garage door at the far end of the rink housing the Zamboni opened, and Tate stood there with several shovels. Ty walked down to where she opened the gate. One by one, the parents who had stayed back grabbed shovels from her, then moved out onto the ice. In practiced motions, they worked their way around the rink, smoothing over the surface.

I crutched my way over to them, putting light pressure on my leg. "What are you doing?" I asked Ty, glancing through the garage doors for a Zamboni that should be doing this job for them.

"Zamboni broke last summer," he answered, taking a shovel from her and following the parents out onto the ice, scooping up the shavings the kids' skates had left behind. "Hey Tate."

Tate smiled, then raised her brows when she looked at me. With hockey skates on she was up to my chin and the spitting image of her late father, freckles dotting her pale skin. "I thought that was you before the game. Long time, no see, Conway."

I nodded, trying to come up with what to say. In that "long time" was her dad's funeral I hadn't attended, unable to come face to face with the loss of my mentor and friend. "You're all grown up now, aren't you?"

She rolled her eyes, then took a bucket of water held on a sled and pulled it onto the ice. With a quick hop, she skated over the frozen surface, her homemade contraption spreading water in an even layer by the mop extending behind the sled.

There was a pond behind my mom's house that froze over every winter, so I was no stranger to manually smoothing and caring for an ice rink, but seeing this in a frequently used commercial rink was jarring.

Ty came off the ice and stored his shovel on a rack against the wall as the other parents finished up. But he didn't walk away like the others did; Ty grabbed a set of skates and the second sled contraption, following Tate out onto the ice. Rowdy climbed up onto the sled, tail wagging like he'd done this a dozen times.

I leaned against the glass, hands resting on the metal boards separating the rink from the stands, the ache in my hip a sharp reminder that I wasn't cleared to so much as tie my own skates, let alone help.

I hated standing on the sidelines.

Watching instead of doing.

But this was my reality now—four weeks post-op from a hip labral tear that started with a dirty hit and ended with years of wear and tear catching up to me.

A month into the season, and boom—down for the count.

The surgery was one thing. The aftermath was another. So were the conversations that followed. Could I come back from this at 37? Everyone seemed to think I was a relic. They talked like I needed to hang it up and start practicing my golf swing.

Sure, I was a veteran. Sixteen seasons in the NHL. Tried and tested with four Stanley Cups to show for it. I'd earned every bruise, every scar, and I sure as hell wasn't letting some hotshot rookie with too much ego or a washed-up NHL Tonight talking head decide when I was done.

I'd decide. No one else.

"Don't break my boards," Tate said as she came off the ice.

I looked down at where my hands clutched the metal, my knuckles white. Loosening my grip, I turned to watch Ty finish up and put his sled away.

"Is there a reason you haven't replaced the Zamboni yet?" I gestured toward the sleds. "This seems like a lot of work."

Tate clenched her jaw, her eyes turning to slits. "I'm working on it. I won't let Dad's legacy die like this."

My gaze flicked to Ty's, and he met my eyes with a shake of his head. "Well, let me know if you want help."

She threw her hands up. "Not you too. First Ty, now you just ready to swoop in and save the day."

My eyebrows hit my hairline under my hat. "Is that such a bad thing? I mean, it's not like either of us are hurting for cash. How much can a Zamboni cost? Couple grand?"

A laugh ripped out of Tate's mouth, her head tipping back. "Oh God, I forgot how out of touch hockey players are." She shook her head, cleaning up the rest of the garage and muttering, "*Couple grand*, I swear."

Ty put his skates back, then reached up above Tate to pull the garage door down for her. She slid the lock in place, then slapped him on the shoulder. "Thanks, Huddy."

"Always."

"Good to see you, Conway. Maybe stop by more than once a decade. The kids would love to see their hometown hero."

I waved, resting my weight on my crutches as she walked off. Ty put his hands in his pockets and strolled down the bleachers toward the exit, Rowdy at his heels, and I moved to follow.

"Something going on between you two?" I asked. Ty was a loner, never one for many friends or relationships outside his family and the shadow of a rescue dog. Once upon a time, we were inseparable, and I would have already known the answer to that. Now, I had no idea what his life was like.

"Aside from me trying to keep this place from going under without her realizing I'm doing it?" Ty said, not turning to look back at me. "No."

"Would you like there to be?"

This time he did turn. "For so many reasons, no. Coach asked me to take care of her before he died, which you'd have known if you came to see him. Or to the funeral. Or anytime in the last 20 years."

I jerked back, the words hitting like a slap. And fuck, I deserved it.

"But also, when was the last time you talked to your brother? Because Mason has had a thing for Tate since they were in diapers."

Ty pushed open the doors to the parking lot, and I followed him outside. It was snowing harder now, coming down in big, lazy flakes that made the mountain scenery look like a snow globe.

Linwood hadn't changed much in all the years I'd been gone. The mountains still loomed like guardians around the town, evergreen trees dusted in white. The cold bit at my cheeks, but the air was clean in a way Denver never quite managed—crisp, quiet, sharp enough to make you feel something.

The rink behind us buzzed with laughter and skates carving into the ice with the Beer League guys starting up soon. But out here, it was just the hush of snowfall and the crunch of boots on packed snow. My breath puffed out in clouds, and I stood there for a second, letting it hit me.

I was really back.

Back in the town where I'd spent every winter morning freezing my ass off on a backyard pond. Where Ty and I would race to see who could skate fastest before school, then ditch homework to do it again after. Back in the place I'd left at 16 with stars in my eyes and a stick in my hand, convinced I'd never look back.

And yet here I was—older, bruised, busted-up—and somehow the mountains still looked at me like I belonged, even when I'd left everything important behind.

Guilt sat heavy in my chest as Ty approached a royal blue vintage F-150. Before he got to his truck, he turned back toward me, his keys in his hand. With quick movements, he pulled one key free from the ring and held it out to me.

"I haven't been by in a week, but everything is pretty much the same since before the accident. The heater was working last I checked, but if it's not, check the furnace in the basement. The flame might have gone out again. Call me if you need help getting it going."

He dropped the key into my hand, and I glanced down at it. This was the key to *my* house, the childhood home where my mom had raised my brother and I, and yet it was Ty who took my mom to the hospital after her fall, who watched out over the property, who fixed all the messes I left behind.

"I'm sorry." The words slipped out before I thought too hard about it. I looked up at my best friend, my fingers closing around the cold metal. "For a lot of things."

Ty nodded, then opened the door for Rowdy to jump inside the pickup cab. "Do better. That's all the apology I need."

I watched him back out of the lot, headlights shining in the dark sky, then made my way to my own truck. It rumbled to life when I hit the ignition, then slowly backed out onto the road.

My windshield wipers flicked back and forth, clearing the window as I drove down the dark roads away from town. My mom still owned a farmhouse on her grandparent's property, sprawling acres of land butting up to the mountains. Even after so many years away, I knew these roads like the back of my hand.

A text message came through, lighting up my touch-screen display, and I pushed the button on my steering wheel to read it aloud.

MASON CONWAY

Did you make it? Is she okay?

Showering and post-game interviews,
then I'll call you

I sighed, not ready to call my brother yet anyway. With both of us wrapped up in our NHL careers, neither of us had been around to see just how much things had changed.

Mom had always been tough. Quiet, self-sufficient, and proud to a fault. She never asked for help, never wanted to be a burden. And maybe that's why I'd convinced myself there'd be time later—time after I retired, time to come home and reconnect, to finally be the son she deserved after all those years she held it together on her own.

But that phone call from the ER shattered that illusion in seconds.

"Shit." I slapped my hands against the steering wheel, jaw clenched as I replayed every word. She'd slipped, hit her head, and broken her arm. The concussion was mild, but the doctor had sounded hesitant. Like there was more going on than just a bad fall.

They were worried about her mobility, her balance. Said she'd likely been struggling longer than any of us knew.

And I'd been so wrapped up in my own life—my injury, my career, my ego—that I hadn't seen it. Hadn't even thought to check.

After a flurry of calls between Mason and me, we knew one thing for sure—she couldn't go back to that house alone. I'd looked into assisted living, but she'd shut it down before I could finish the sentence.

So here I was. On injured reserve, benched indefinitely, and suddenly faced with a version of my mom I wasn't ready for. The strong, unshakable woman who raised us was slipping through our fingers—and I hadn't even seen it coming.

The old cattle guards rattled under my tires, useless now that the ranch had been out of business since my grandfather died. I leaned forward over the steering wheel, looking up at the farmhouse at the top of the hill. The driveway would be plowed in the morning by the crew we'd hired to maintain her property, but tonight it was snow-packed. Luckily, my 4x4 made the slippery drive, and I parked in the detached garage next to the house.

Everywhere I looked, I could see Ty's efforts—a new safety rail along the front porch steps, a ramp from the driveway to the porch, and string lights hanging along the path to the frozen pond. I'd bet good money Ty had even prepped it for skating.

In fact, I hoped he had. I hoped he used it, maybe with that nephew of his. It was the least I could offer for everything he did for me and my family.

The door squeaked when I pushed it open and went inside, my crutches creaking on the old wood floorboards. Even in the dark, everything felt the same. I stopped to work my way out of my coat and hang it on the hooks behind the door, then sat on the bench like I had a thousand times before and took off my shoes. Old habits died hard, and even without my mom's scolding, I tucked them under the bench and out of the way.

After a day of driving and the hockey game, the thought of climbing the steps to my bedroom was entirely too much, so I left my crutches by the front door and lifted my foot, hopping on one leg down the hall and into the living room.

Heavy cream curtains hung beside the wide windows, a little sun-stained at the edges, framing a view of the mountains and the frozen pond where we'd learned to skate. Moonlight spilled in across the hardwood floors, catching on dust motes and the edge of the old wooden coffee table that still bore a ring from Dad's forever-missing coaster.

A brown leather couch sat along the far wall, creased and softened by years of use; the cushions slightly sunken on the right side where Mom always sat. A small table beside it held her daily lineup: pill bottles in neat rows, a half-drunk glass of water, a box of tissues, and a Sudoku book with a cracked spine she hadn't touched in days.

The heat clicked on with a familiar groan, and the whole room felt like it exhaled. I let myself breathe deep, inhaling the woodsy scent this house always had. There was a layer of must mixed in now, but the house was better than I was expecting after hearing her health had declined. I probably owed Ty for that, too.

I dropped my keys and phone on the coffee table, then sat down on the sofa. My phone lit up with incoming texts, and I picked it up to click through them. One from Coach, asking where I was, another from our head trainer, reaming me for missing a doctor's appointment today. And then one I wasn't expecting.

MIKKO

It gets better, veli. You won't feel like this forever.

I stared at the screen, throat tight. Mikko Laaksonen, the Yeti's star defender and one of my best friends, wasn't the type to drop serious stuff unless it mattered. He'd gone through his own hell, missed nearly a full season after an

ACL tear, and clawed his way back to the top. I wasn't alone in wondering if he'd ever look like himself again, and thank God he did.

Our injuries weren't the same, but he was throwing me a rope.

My phone buzzed again, this time from the far-less-eloquent Logan Parrish—our line's forward and hands down the cockiest Alberta farm boy I'd ever met. The kind of guy who grew up chasing moose on a snowmobile and thinks duct tape can fix emotional trauma.

LOGAN

> Bro, you dead? Or just being a duster and ghosting the boys?

I shook my head, half-smiling.

ME

> Not dead. Just dealing with some stuff. I'll catch up tomorrow.

LOGAN

> Atta boy. We'll save you a Gatorade and a warmup fight with the vending machine. Don't get soft on us out there, Grandpa.

The phone landed on the table with a soft thud, and I leaned back against the couch, the quiet pressing in on me like a heavy blanket.

I knew Mikko meant it when he said it got better. I just hoped he was right. Because right now? It didn't feel like it ever would.

5

Emmy

My thumbs drummed on the soft leather steering wheel, and I peered out into the dark, snowy night. George Strait crooned a 90's love song in the background, the sound low enough to make the tension in the car feel loaded. "Ready to talk yet?"

Jace kept his headphones around his neck, which told me he *did* want to talk, but he'd turned his whole body away from me. I flicked my gaze toward him, staring at the golden-brown curls I'd always loved—my color and Ryan's waves. It was an absolute mop lately, but wet from the shower and shoved under a backward Mayhem hat, it curled at his nape.

"The snow is pretty tonight. Maybe we can go sledding on Sunday." I tried to steer the conversation toward neutral ground, shoving all my anger and frustration down. The last thing we needed was for me to elevate Jace's anger, even if I was disappointed in how he'd chosen to handle it.

Jace grabbed for his headphones, and I reached across the center console, resting my hand on his arm. "I can't let this go, bud. You know that wasn't okay."

He dropped his hands back to his lap and made a grunting noise that told me he'd spent a lot of time with my brother in the last few months.

"You do know words, I'm positive. How else would I know about every Pikachu?"

My sarcasm finally caught his attention, and Jace shot me a bored look. "It's Pokémon."

I bit the inside of my cheeks to keep my smile from showing. "That's what I said, isn't it?"

He rolled those pretty hazel eyes, and I silently high-fived myself for getting him to talk to me at all. "Want to get out your cards and tell me all about them like you used to? We can order a pizza, and I won't even get mad when you leave them all over the living room."

With a shake of his head, Jace said, "I thought being a young mom meant you were supposed to be cooler than other adults. Turns out you're also lame."

I shrugged, then patted his shoulder. "I hate to be the bearer of bad news, but I wasn't cool even when I was your age."

"Then how'd you end up with Dad?" he asked. "Wasn't he the hockey star everyone wanted?"

I drew in a breath, thinking through my answer. No matter my frustration with Ryan, he was Jace's dad, and he wasn't *all* bad, even if my memories were now tinged with his betrayal. There was a time when I thought we'd been a happy family, or, at least, happy-ish.

Glancing his way, I pondered whether Jace was old enough to know the truth of how his father and I came to be, or if I should keep feeding him the same "college sweethearts" line we always had.

Jace tipped his head back on the headrest, then tilted his

face my way. "I already know you got drunk at a hockey party you weren't supposed to be at."

A nervous laugh bubbled out of me, and my hands tightened on the steering wheel. "It did go something like that, yes. Who told you that?"

"Ty," he answered, fiddling with the strings of his hoodie, pulling them back and forth.

Don't hide your own problems from him, my therapist's words rang in my head. *Show him it's okay to make mistakes, own them, and learn from them. That you can be better because of them.*

I puckered my lips, trying to think through my words. Because no matter the circumstances his life came about, nothing about becoming Jace's mom was a mistake, and I never wanted him to think that.

"You understand the whole birds and the bees thing," I said, settling on a partial truth.

Jace cringed, his whole body recoiling into the chair. "God Mom, no."

This time I did laugh, the sound genuine as it rumbled out of my chest. "Relax. I'm not giving you the blow by blow."

Jace put a hand over his mouth, fake gagging.

I laughed harder. "Stop. I promise."

His attention was on me, and his hands settled in his lap. If it took me opening up to Jace for him to want to open up in return, then I could do that.

"I was 19, a freshman at Arizona State, and homesick as all get out. A month in, and I regretted not following Ty out east. Then, at least I would have known someone, even if I didn't want to follow in his footsteps. We were playing Michigan in one of the early season games, and I went, thinking at least being in the same building as Beckett was a taste of home."

"Beckett Conway?" Jace asked, his eyes alight with hero worship the way they were every time he talked of our hometown star. "You were friends with him?"

"Not really." I shrugged. "He was Ty's best friend, so we spent a lot of time together over the years, but I wouldn't have called us *friends.* He was a piece of home though, a connection to Ty, and I was grasping at straws."

Jace sighed, looking out the window again, and my heart hurt for him. Unfortunately, our cross-country move meant he understood what it meant to feel new and lost.

"Anyway," I started my story again. "I heard the Michigan hockey team was going to a house party after, and so I got it in my head I should go too and find Beckett."

"And that's how you met Dad."

I nodded, my mind replaying the memory. I hadn't just met Ryan that night; I'd given him my virginity and gotten pregnant, all in one fell swoop.

"Underage drinking is bad"—I shot my son a look, and he smirked—"but I was nervous and lonely and drank too much. Your dad rescued me before I could make any terrible decisions and walked me back to the dorms. After that, we were inseparable, and I transferred to Michigan to be with him. Then you came along."

"You hate him now, don't you?" Jace asked, his voice quieter as he studied his hands in his lap.

I turned right onto River Street toward our row house, my headlights shining on the sparkling snow. "Hate is a strong word, and I don't like it. So, no, I don't hate him."

Jace sighed, then pulled his headphones over his head and put them in his backpack. "Well, I do."

Tires crunched over the packed snow in our driveway, and I pulled into the carport Ty had put up behind my house. The moment it was in park, I reached both hands across the center console and grabbed my son's cheeks, pulling him toward me until our foreheads touched.

"I love you so much it's absolutely stupid." He started to pull back from me, and I held tighter, needing him to hear my words. "Like, redefined the word for me. The moment I saw that little pink line saying you were on the way, my life changed forever. And for the better. But knowing you, watching you grow, seeing who you're becoming"—my face tingled, a mixture of nostalgia for the little boy he once was and rage-fueled tears burning my eyes for the pain my son was in—"it's the best thing to ever happen to me."

"Please don't cry."

I laughed, then pulled back and opened my car door. "Okay. I won't. But even on our worst days, Jace, I love you more than anyone in this entire world. Throwing punches in a hockey game doesn't change that."

"Yeah, yeah. Love you too." Jace got out of the car, then opened the trunk and pulled his hockey bag out, heading for the shed to unload it.

"Get your gear aired out, then come bring me your Play-Station remotes and your headphones."

He turned back to me, his forehead creased under his hat. "I thought I wasn't in trouble?"

I hummed, then held out my hand, palm up. "I said throwing punches and getting thrown out of a hockey game didn't make me love you less, not that you weren't in trouble."

With an eye roll fit for Sisyphus, Jace reached into his bag and grabbed his headphones, slapping them into my open palm.

I took them, then walked up the back steps to the kitchen door. The alarm beeped when I opened it, and I reached over to turn it off. Ty had insisted on installing one since I refused to live with him, and it did offer me peace of mind sleeping in an empty house when Jace was with his dad.

Flicking on the lights, I headed toward the fridge on the far side of the kitchen, refilling my water cup before heading upstairs. After living a sad beige life with Ryan for so long, my house looked like an explosion of color. The cabinets were a deep magenta, the dishes a mismatched collection of sapphires and florals, and there was a vintage bread tin that made me happier than it probably should have. The open shelves were full of hand-painted mugs, brass accents, and spices I'd mostly bought for the pretty jars. It was a little chaotic and a little cozy, but it felt like *me*, something I craved after 15 years of trying to fit a mold I was never made for.

Jace came in and locked the door behind him, not making eye contact as he stomped down the hallway toward the living room. He yanked open the bin I stored his video game gear in and tossed a remote my way. With quick reflexes, I caught it. "A week."

He shook his head, then went toward the stairs. The old floorboards creaked with every step, and I leaned against the kitchen counters, listening to the movements above me.

As temperamental as my son was, he was a good kid. I braced myself for the door slam, but it didn't come. It clicked closed, and his speakers turned on, the windows rattling with the bass blaring from an angry rock song.

My phone vibrated in my vest pocket, and I pulled it out

to a text from my brother. I flicked the lights off, then reset the house alarm and headed upstairs to my room.

TY

Make it home safe?

EMMY

Yes, Dad. We're good.

TY

Need me to talk to him?

EMMY

Not your job.

TY

Not what I asked.

I sat on the edge of my bed and rubbed the ache forming between my eyebrows, hating the idea of leaning on Ty even more than I already did. He was fixing my Jeep, had cosigned the rent agreement on my Pilates studio, and was Jace's backup ride anytime I got caught up with work. And yet, here he was texting me to check in on us. Aside from asking the final score of the game, Ryan hadn't texted at all.

EMMY

We're good tonight. But I offered to go sledding with him this weekend. Can we come to Copper Ridge?

TY

The ranch is yours. You never have to ask.

Grabbing Jace's headphones, I put them over my ears and turned on the sound canceling feature, blocking out the music blaring from my son's room.

It helped, sort of.

What didn't help was the knot of guilt and frustration tightening in my chest—the constant push and pull of trying to be everything at once: the calm parent, the cool parent, the one who enforced boundaries without becoming the villain in his teenage coming-of-age story.

I lay back against the pillow and stared at the ceiling, the weight of the day finally settling into my bones. Some days, being a single mom felt like juggling knives while walking a tightrope in a windstorm. Tonight, I was fresh out of balance.

But Jace hadn't slammed the door, hadn't fought back about the headphones or PlayStation. And I was holding onto those little wins like they were lifelines.

Maybe sledding would help. Maybe Ty's ranch would be a reset. Or maybe it would just be loud and cold and full of awkward silences.

Either way, I'd show up. Because that's what moms did, even when I was exhausted and just as lost as he was.

I'd always show up.

6

BECKETT

I jerked awake Monday morning to the sound of music blaring from outside. After the laziest weekend I'd had in years, it took me a minute for my brain to come online, blinking into consciousness against the early morning sun streaming through the windows to my right.

Even though it had been over 20 years since I'd last lived here, my childhood room was mostly the same—a hockey stick for a curtain rod, pennants from every tournament I'd played in with the Mayhem, trophies on every available inch of shelf space, and a three-foot-tall orange teddy bear Mason and I had won at a summer carnival when I was a teen still sat parked in the corner. It had seen better days, and from the state of my back pain, so had I.

The windows rattled with the bass line of *Welcome to the Jungle*, and I dropped my legs over the side of the full-size bed, ready to investigate. My mom's house was in the foothills with no neighbors, but I'd gifted her a speaker system out by the pond several Christmases ago. My crutches sat across the room, so I put my good leg down, pushed off the mattress, and hopped to the window.

Pulling apart the cheap blinds, I squinted through the dirty glass at the fresh snow that had fallen over the weekend. It sat heavy on the evergreens surrounding our property, painting the peaks behind in white.

Plans to go see Mom in the hospital were trashed when the snow had closed Vail Pass for two days, locking us all in place. So, I'd spent the weekend on the phone with the Yeti's team administration, my training staff, and every doctor involved in my recovery to figure out how I could manage to be here for my mom this week *and* not mess up my recovery to be back by March in time for the end of the season and be ready for playoffs.

I wasn't sure what I expected to find outside, but a kid skating around my pond by himself wasn't on the list. I leaned against the windowsill, the glass cold against my bare arm, and watched him set up cones, then push a net out onto the pond. Snow was piled three feet high all the way around the ice, a giant mound separating it from the trees and mountains behind.

A shovel rested on top of the heap, and I glanced back at the kid, my head tilting to look for anyone else out there. A bike with fat snow tires rested in my cleared driveway, but I hired a service to handle that for Mom every time there was a snowstorm. However, I did not pay them to make a path to the pond, and I sure as shit didn't pay them to clean off the ice.

I let out a low whistle, staring down at the shovel-wide path this kid must have done himself to get to the pond before he could even begin to clear it off.

"Damn, son," I said aloud, my voice gravely with sleep but full of awe.

Shoveling snow was a hell of a workout, and that was without riding a *bike* in the *snow* here. Add the way he was moving around my backyard with a comfortable familiarity to tell me this was certainly not his first time out here? This kid was something else.

I wasn't mad he was trespassing. Hell, I was glad it got some use. Anyone willing to put in this much work for some free ice time deserved it.

Once everything was set up the way the kid wanted it, he sat on the stump Ty and I had left for exactly that reason, tightened his laces, then pulled out a phone from his pocket, fiddling with the screen until the song switched to *Enter Sandman*. His head bobbed along to the Metallica song for a few seconds, then he pulled on a pair of hockey gloves and hopped on his skates, flying across the ice in a warmup.

My phone vibrated on the nightstand nearby, but I ignored it, arms crossed over my chest as I watched the kid move. He was quick, skating laps around the outside of my little pond, before switching and doing it all backward. His stick dragged across the ice as he moved, then eventually grabbed a puck from the pile he'd dropped in the middle of the makeshift rink.

With quick flicks of his wrist, he pulled the puck back and forth between the cones, holding perfect control of it before launching it into the top right corner of the net. Over and over, he did the same moves, hitting different invisible targets, and I watched with rapt attention.

I hadn't seen Ty's nephew without a helmet at the game, but I could tell by the way he moved, this was the same kid. Emmy's son.

The last time I'd even seen Emmy, she was a freshman in high school—the same age as her kid down there on the ice. Fuck, that was a weird thought. Then, she'd just gone through a huge growth spurt, all gangly legs and braces. She had a penchant for oversized 90's country band tees and an obsession with everything peach, right down to the color she constantly painted her fingernails.

With her so close in age to Ty and me, our friend groups crossed often, but she was perpetually my best friend's little sister. I'd never seen her as anything but a target for our stupid teenage pranks just to hear her fiery comebacks, so it was hard for me to reconcile that version of her with the one I'd seen at the rink on Friday night.

That one had been full of the same sassy soul I remembered, but I did *not* remember the curves she had on her. No, those were new, as were the not-so-PG thoughts about my best friend's little sister. After everything Ty had done for me, that was the last place my mind needed to go.

I cleared my throat, looking back down at the ice at Emmy's son. Like his mom, he had brown hair that seemed to catch the sunlight, glowing with a golden hue where it peeked out from under his green Mayhem hat. Here in my bedroom preserved in time, it was easy to picture Ty, Mason, and I out there instead of him, a snapshot of a past that seemed so very long ago.

My phone buzzed again, and I hopped across my bedroom to retrieve it, not so much wanting to talk to whoever was trying to get ahold of me, but desperate for a connection to my long-lost friend again.

When Ty's name popped up on the screen, I grinned. Maybe he was thinking the same, too.

TY

Motion sensors are going off at your
pond. You home?

TY

Shit. Jace skipped school again,
didn't he?

I glanced back out the window at the kid circling the ice, his face shuttered of all emotion except for sheer focus.

BECKETT

He's here. Guessing he's not supposed
to be?

TY

That sneaky fucker. I'll come get him.

BECKETT

I'll handle it.

TY

You sure? I can be headed that way in 10.

BECKETT

I got it. Take him to school?

TY

Yeah.

And thanks

Grabbing the black sweats from the top of my suitcase, I awkwardly got myself dressed, then reached for my crutches and headed downstairs. Luckily, I'd remembered to set up the coffee pot last night, so I filled a stainless Denver Yeti tumbler with coffee.

I could still see Jace working his way around the ice through the window over the kitchen sink, endless energy driving his moves. Once upon a time I'd been that way too—

unable to stop—but watching him made me realize how *old* I was.

Sure, aside from my hip injury, I was in peak condition, but I was still in my mid-thirties. Still a veteran player. Still a constant topic of discussion on Hockey Tonight about if I can even come back from an injury like this "at my age".

The black coffee was as bitter as my thoughts, burning its way down my throat like the dawning realization that the kid out there was the future, and I was the past.

With a sigh, I grabbed a crutch and limped my way out onto the back porch, watching my footsteps to make sure I didn't eat shit and set myself back several months. The music was loud, scaring off any stray predators nearby, but also keeping this kid's head down. I stood there for several more minutes, watching him skate, before I swiped across my phone to the sound system's app, and killed the power.

The silence was deafening after the volume he'd had it at, and the kid's body jerked upright as if electrocuted. He glanced around the driveway, then to the storage shed where the sound system was housed, before I put two fingers to my lips and whistled. It echoed through the mountains, the sound as piercing as a gunshot, and Jace's head snapped my direction.

"Trespassing is illegal, you know," I called out.

"So is breaking and entering," Jace answered, pointing at the house behind me. "Pretty sure that's way more jail time, pal."

A low chuckle rumbled through my chest. I shouldn't have been surprised Jace was just as quick-witted as his mom, but damn, I hadn't expected that. "Hard to get me on breaking and entering when my name is on the deed."

Jace jerked upright, the butt of his stick slapping against

the underside of his hat. "Holy fucking shit, you're Beckett Conway."

"Manners, son. Watch your mouth."

Any of the awe that was there a second ago disappeared, his gaze hard once more. "I'm 15, not 8. You can't tell me what to do, and I'm not your son."

"Really?" I raised my brows, pointing at his setup out here. "Should I check with the Sheriff about that? I'm pretty sure he'd agree with me, considering you're on my property illegally, pal."

"Ty said I could use it whenever I wanted," Jace shot back. "And I'm also not your pal."

"Damn, what a shame." I mock-frowned, holding a hand to my chest. "And here I thought you might want to be friends with an Art Ross Trophy winner."

"Manners, pops," Jace shot back. "Watch your mouth."

A laugh burst out of me, and I shook my head. "Aren't you supposed to be at school?"

"I don't know." He shuffled back and forth on his skates, gloved hand resting on the top of his stick. "Aren't you supposed to make it past the first round of the playoffs?"

Hot damn, this kid had fire. Without thinking, I shot back, "Says the kid who was ejected out of the first game of the season, and let his team lose 0-6."

That must have been a step too far. Jace looked down at his skates, his jaw ticking.

"Let me take you to school. They'll make you miss practice if you're caught truant, right? Is that still the Mayhem's rule?"

"Can't practice for a week, and I'm sitting out the game on Friday, anyway." Jace turned his back to me, skating around the ice again, obviously done with this conversation.

The snow on the deck had been cleared along with the driveway, but it was still covered in a thin sheet of ice. I grabbed the railing and slowly inched my way to the stairs, headed toward the garage. "Missing school will just add days to that sentence, won't it?"

Jace shrugged. "If Coach even shows up, maybe. He doesn't care about us."

That gave me pause. The Mayhem Hockey Club under Coach Mikaelsons's leadership had been a tight-run ship, demanding the most from its players both on the ice and in the classroom. Hell, if I hadn't been required to attend in order to play, my high school years would have looked a lot like this.

"Does your mom care?" I asked, hedging my bets.

Jace whipped his last shot into the net, then turned to look at me. "Why do you care?"

I shrugged, pushing the garage door opener in my pocket and then the remote start on my truck. "I don't. But she probably will."

"You know my mom?" he asked, opening the shed door and pulling out a backpack. He dropped to a squat just above the ice, unlacing his skates in a move that I wasn't sure my old and broken body would allow, even healed. Once they were off and a pair of unlaced Timberlands were on his feet, he stored the gloves, stick, and skates in the shed, then padlocked it once more. "Why has she never mentioned you before last night?"

Well, that cut in an unexpected way, but Emmy's and my relationship was non-existent these days. I breathed in the crisp mountain air, the smell of pine overwhelming me with its sense of familiarity and comfort even though it had been years since I'd been home. "Small town, kid. We all know everybody. But it's been a long time since I've seen her."

"That's right." Jace snapped his fingers, then hurried past me toward the garage. He spun around and stared at me with a hard set to his jaw. "Because you're a washed-up has-been who abandoned everyone you ever cared about. *Now* I remember."

Of all the cheap shots this kid had taken at me, that one hurt, and he knew it would. Maybe he expected me to leave, to call the Sheriff like I'd threatened, to turn my back on this grumpy, smart-mouthed kid. From what I'd seen on Friday, he had a dad who didn't show up, and I knew how shitty that felt. Like it was easier to keep everyone at a distance so they couldn't hurt you like that again.

But he also didn't *know* me. He didn't understand that, like him, I refused to give up. Every single newscast, especially those led by Jace's daddy dearest, said I was done. Cooked. Finished. A washed-up has-been. But I wasn't done until I said I was done, and I'd do anything to prove it.

"Get in the truck," I said, limping my way into the garage with these stupid crutches.

The door slammed as he climbed into the cab, but I'd take it.

Beckett: 1.

Jace: 0.

7

Emmy

"Order for Emmy!" the barista shouted, then pushed a cardboard tray of drinks across the counter toward me. A little brown box sat next to it with a handful of pastries and breakfast wraps, ready to treat my staff to a Monday morning pick-me-up. After Friday's game and then the silent treatment Jace had given me for two days, I needed it.

"Thanks, Luca." The barista raised his chin as I reached for my order. "God, I'm starving."

"Yeah." Luca's tongue peeked out to lick the corner of his lip as his eyes raked over my body, rubbing his hands together like some cartoon villain. Tattoos covered his hands and forearms, giving off a *don't fuck with me* vibe that clashed spectacularly with his fuckboy haircut and overall personality. "You ever get tired of carrying all that weight by yourself? You know, your drinks, your business, that perfect ass? Let me take care of you sometime. I can hold it for you."

I gave him a flat look. "Hard pass. I'd rather get a root canal from a raccoon."

Luca laughed, unbothered, then swooned with a hand to

his chest. "What can I say? I love it when you bust my balls. It'll make it that much sweeter when you finally admit you feel this connection."

"The only thing I feel is secondhand embarrassment." I grabbed the drink carrier and the box of food, then balanced my large, iced coffee on top with surgical precision. "You're exhausting."

"Can't win on a shot you never take."

"The last man who said that gave me a wedding ring and a big fat therapy bill," I muttered. "I'm in my post-men, post-pick-me, Pilates era. You're about 15 years too late."

He grinned. "Need me to help you carry those down the street?"

"If I give you an inch, you'll take a mile."

"Oh, I can give you a lot more than an inch—"

"Gross!" I barked, shouldering open the door with my hip. "I'm telling your mother when she comes in for class this afternoon."

"Do it!" he called after me through the jingle of the bell. "She loves you too, so she'll be thrilled about this love affair!"

If my hands hadn't been full to bursting, I would've flipped him off. Instead, I rolled my eyes, muttering to myself as I stalked toward the studio.

Linwood was a picturesque mountain village, doing its best to preserve the town's history rich with Wild West culture. River Street was the main business core, home to our local sporting goods outfitter, hardware store, grocery, a restaurant, a bar, the coffee shop, and then my newest addition: a Pilates studio. Each building on the strip was painted a different color, most with an apartment above, and it gave the whole thing a very Norman Rockwell feel.

After living in suburban and modern Connecticut for a

decade, it was both strange and wonderful to be back in my little hometown.

Trees dotted the sidewalk, draped in twinkle lights, and covered in snow. Most of the cars on the street were either Subarus or Jeeps, and almost all of them had a ski rack on the roof. Living in a town that was blanketed in snow from October to May wasn't for the faint of heart, but there was nothing like the morning after a snowstorm.

The sun was shining bright in the sky, making everything glitter. The roads weren't quite brown sludge yet, like they would be later today, and everything was just... quiet. My breath fogged in the morning air as I walked toward the Pilates studio, mentally mapping out my day.

A horn honked in the street to my right, and I jumped, losing my grip on the drink tray just as a woman and child turned the corner. Between one breath and the next, every-thing went flying.

"Oh no!" I yelled, scrambling to catch the drinks. Appar-ently, I was also moving slower this morning. I reached for the flying food, trying to save the woman and child from the carnage but was far too late.

Luckily, the hot drinks splattered on the ground, the flimsy paper cups bursting open and across our snow boots. But my iced coffee went right down the front of this poor woman's chest.

"I'm so sorry," the woman said, her baby crying in her arms. She bent to help me salvage the rest of the breakfast pastries.

"Girl, why are you apologizing? This was my fault." I looked up from where I hovered in a squat, the crushed box in my hands, and frowned, trying to recall where I'd seen this woman before. "Do I know you?"

The woman's hands stopped, two empty coffee cups in her hands, and met my inquisitive stare. Dark circles painted her under eyes blue, her dark blonde hair in a messy topknot that looked more utilitarian than intentional chic. The baby cried again, her little body squirming in her mom's arms as their down jackets rubbed against each other, making the hold this mom had on her child impressive. It had been so long since Jace was that little, but immediately I was catapulted back in my mind to the days where I'd looked just as tired and worn down as this woman.

"I didn't get her with the coffee?" I nodded at the little girl quickly escalating to a full tantrum.

"No," the mom answered, looking over at her baby, then to me with a sheepish smile. "She's teething, and just permanently mad."

I grabbed the last of the trash, stacking the now-empty cups as best I could. "Man, I remember those days."

"You're a mom too?" she asked, looking around for a toddler trailing me.

"He's a teenager now"—her eyes snapped back to my face, calculating my age like everyone did—"but he had colic. I'm well acquainted with a pissed-off baby." I lifted the empty cups in a wave. "I'm Emmy. Are you new to town?"

"Oh." The mom bounced her daughter on her hip until the little girl stuck her thumb in her mouth and rested her head on her mom's shoulder. "I'm Stevie. And yeah, my husband took a job with a custom home builder up here this fall, so we're still getting settled. Are you from Linwood?"

"Born and raised." I grinned, then pointed to the hardware store across the street. "Hudson Hardware. I'm Emmy Hudson Meyer. Well, I guess just Emmy Hudson now, but that's a new development. My son Jace and I moved back here this summer after my divorce."

"Oh, I'm sorry." Stevie shrugged, a tentative smile pulling up one side of her mouth. "Welcome back, I guess? Or are we not happy about this change?"

I chuckled. "It's a good thing for both of us. I just need Jace to come to that conclusion too."

The door to my Pilates studio opened and closed behind Stevie, attendees beginning to arrive for the next class.

"I need to head to the studio," I said, waving what was left of the crumpled pastry box at the door. "But let me make up for drenching you in coffee with a free class."

Stevie's eyebrows hit her hairline, and she looked over her shoulder at the studio. When she turned back to me, I could see the *no* in her eyes, but something about this woman made me want to make this work.

"I have a private lesson spot tomorrow night at five. Just you and me, so we can get you acquainted with it all. Unless you're already familiar with reformer Pilates?"

"I'm not, and I can't." Stevie frowned, bouncing her daughter again. "My boys play hockey on Tuesday nights, and my husband is helping coach this season, so I don't have anyone to watch Harper."

"Bring her," I said before I thought too hard about the words coming out of my mouth. My Pilates studio wasn't exactly kid-friendly, but my mind was already working in overdrive to make this work. "We have a playpen in the back" —no, we didn't, but I could get one—"and Shannon loves kids. I'm sure she'd love to watch Harper to give you a break." That part was at least true.

"Oh." She looked down at the little girl, now closing her eyes. "Well—"

"No pressure." I held my trash-laden hand out to stop what surely was another excuse. "Just show up if you want to try it. If not, no worries. I'll leave a free pass at the front desk you can redeem whenever."

"You really don't have to," Stevie said. "Accidents happen, and I'm used to being covered in random food thanks to three kids. But thank you."

I nodded, my head bobbing all over my shoulders, knowing I was trying too hard but also unable to stop myself. "Have to and want to are two different things. This is me, wanting to. You're new, I'm new-again. You're a mom, I'm a mom. We both have hockey bo—" My eyes expanded, suddenly realizing why I recognized her. "Ah, shit. I honked at you in the parking lot as you were trying to load up the kids on Friday night, didn't I?"

"I mean, they were taking forever, so I get it."

I squeezed my eyes shut, wishing I had a free hand to rub my hand across my wrinkled brow. "No, that's a total misunderstanding. My hand slipped and landed on the horn. It's my brother's car and way too responsive. That was *not* you, and now I feel extra bad. Mommin' is hard enough without anyone giving you shit when you're just trying to do your best. Now you *have* to let me make it up to you."

Stevie laughed, her gaze shifting to the coffee shop and back to me. "Really. It's okay."

The timer on my watch started beeping, and I dropped my shoulders. "I have to go but think about tomorrow. We'll make it work at your speed."

She nodded, and this time her smile seemed more genuine. "I'll let you know."

I smiled back, watching her walk away, Harper half-asleep against her chest, the weight of motherhood settling into her posture the way it used to settle into mine.

As I turned toward the studio, juggling the crushed pastry box and what little dignity I had left, the ache hit me square in the chest. That old familiar loneliness. The one I thought I'd outgrown once Jace got older—once I could sleep through the night and hold a full adult conversation without a baby monitor in my hand.

But the truth was, those early years with him had been so isolating I sometimes forgot who I was. I became a mom at the same time my friends were getting their first legal drinks, focused on nights out and casual hookups. Meanwhile, I'd married Ryan when I was five months pregnant, holding onto the naïve hope that if I loved him and our baby enough, I could make us all happy.

So, I buried myself in diapers and daycare drop-offs, all while taking college courses to get my Bachelors in kinesiology, and finish *most* of my Doctor of Physical Therapy courses. But between my second and third year, Ryan went to the minors, and I had to walk away from it all.

I'd tried to tell myself I was fine. That Jace was enough. That being a mom was everything I'd ever wanted.

And he was. He *is*.

But that version of me—the one who used to sit in the dark while he cried himself to sleep, the one who didn't know how to ask for help—she was still in there somewhere. And sometimes, on days like this, I felt her panic echoing just beneath the surface. That familiar clawing need for someone who gets it. For connection. For friendship that wasn't laced with small talk and forced smiles. For someone to see me and all of my mess and stay anyway.

I glanced back toward the corner Stevie had disappeared

around, and something tugged at me—a hope I hadn't felt in a long time. A tiny thread pulling me out of my bubble, toward someone else who might understand this strange, messy middle of motherhood.

One thing I'd learned over the last 15 years, parenting didn't get easier—it just changed. The newborn years weren't more difficult than the teen ones; they were just *different.* And the loneliness didn't leave; it just got better at hiding in the cracks between responsibilities.

Maybe I'd come on too strong with Stevie, but I recognized that same slightly chipped and a little bit broken spirit, held together with glitter glue and an unhinged adoration for your children. If she was anything like me, she was white-knuckling her way through the hard parts and smiling through the mess.

So, I wasn't *asking.* I was just *giving.* No strings, no expectations.

This wasn't about coffee or Pilates or even making up for a flying iced latte to the chest.

This was about not wanting to do it all alone anymore.

If offering her a free class and a moment's respite was what it took to start—somewhere, *anywhere*—then so be it.

Hope welled in my chest, a flicker of lightness threading through the chaos, like maybe I'd done something good today. Something younger me would've latched onto in a heartbeat.

I drew in a steadying breath, squared my shoulders, and turned toward the studio.

That's when I heard the low rumble of a truck behind me. Two short honks followed, like I wouldn't immediately recognize the only set of tinted windows in a small-town radius.

I didn't even turn around, just peered over my shoulder. "What do you want, Beckett?"

The window rolled down, and he leaned out, all smug confidence and stubble. I kept walking toward the nearest trash can, wrestling with the bear-proof lid.

"Hell of a way to greet a man after he just caught your kid trespassing."

The heavy metal lid crashed back down, narrowly missing my fingers as it slammed back in place. My eyes squinted, and then I slowly turned back toward his truck. "Run that by me one more time."

"Jace was out on the pond this morning, but I just dropped him off at school. He left his bike at my house though, so we'll have to get that back to him another day."

I pinched the bridge of my nose as someone called my name from down the street. "Jace"—I pulled in a deep breath —"was at your house this morning, instead of school."

"Hell of a skater. Too bad he can't seem to obey rules like no fighting in hockey, no skipping school, no tresp—"

"He's a good kid." My head snapped up; my jaw set as I glared up at his obnoxiously large truck. "Actually, he's a *great* kid. He's just had a shitty year."

Beckett held his hands up from the steering wheel, then put it in park and opened the door. I'd almost forgotten how tall he was until his foot touched down on the snow-covered ground, hanging on the door frame to keep the leg he was babying out of the snow. He towered over me, at least a head taller, but I got caught staring at his arms bulging under his fitted tee.

Now was not the time for me to notice the forearm candy in front of me, covered in black ink tattoos. Unlike Luca's whimsical designs that seemed a patchwork of half-baked ideas, the designs on Beckett's skin seemed intricate, planned out, and purposeful.

By the time I remembered I was pissed at all the men in my life, Beckett was wearing a sly grin, one that said he saw what had snagged my attention. I stabbed a finger into his chest, and dammit, it was so hard, my hand nearly bounced off.

"You know, I could always call the Sheriff"—I poked him once more for good measure—"on you. Mention that I finally figured out who brought a cow into Linwood High and led it up the stairs during homecoming week."

"That was never proven."

"Oh, please. I found the ear tag two weeks later in the janitor's closet. It had your granddad's ranch name on it."

His mouth twitched. "That could've been any Conway."

"Sure," I deadpanned. "Because your cousin Maggie was definitely the one in the security footage wearing an inside-out Mayhem Hockey hoodie."

He rubbed a hand over his face, laughing under his breath. "And who's to say the ear tag wasn't a plant? What if I was framed?"

"Uh-huh. *Sure.* On the night before you left for Juniors" —I scrunched my nose, giving a little sarcastic nod—"I believe it."

Beckett grinned, and I had to shut my eyes to block out how unbelievably gorgeous he was. "Did you know it took the fire department three hours and six boxes of Little Debbie cakes to coax that poor cow back down? I'm sure the Sheriff would love to finally close the case on Linwood's cow caper."

He chuckled, leaning harder on the truck door. "You blackmailing me, Hudson?"

I shrugged. "Just keeping my options open."

Beckett leaned forward into my space, close enough to whisper, "Pretty sure that's illegal."

"Pretty sure you're a jackass," I whispered back. "And I'd do anything to protect my kid."

He shook his head, smiling like he didn't hate it—and still standing far too close. "Remind me again why we never dated?"

I poked him in the chest, a little harder than necessary. "Because I liked my brother too much to visit him in prison for burying your body behind the rink."

Beckett caught my hand, pinning it against his chest. The moment our skin touched, it was like sticking a fork in a socket. Heat jolted up my arm and set up camp somewhere low in my stomach. His chest was solid beneath my palm, his pulse steady. Of course it was. Mine, meanwhile, was doing a full gymnastics routine.

"Easy, Mama. I'm already injured. Don't make me explain the tiny bruises dotting my chest at my next checkup. Your fingers are basically shivs."

I rolled my eyes and tried to pull away, but he held on, his grip gentle but firm. His head dipped until I had no choice but to meet his gaze again. Those stupid blue eyes sparkled like mischief and morning sunlight had a baby.

"I'm not pressing charges," he murmured, his voice dropping just enough to make it feel dangerous.

Finally, he let go. I dropped my hand like it burned and flexed my fingers, hoping the air would erase the memory of him.

Beckett reached up and grabbed the top of his door frame, leaning into the stretch, and lifting his shirt just enough to flash the carved V of muscle that led right below his waistband. My eyes flicked down on instinct.

I didn't look.

Okay, I looked. *Briefly.*

"In fact," he said casually, "he's welcome to use my pond anytime. Least I can do after Ty's kept us all afloat."

I squinted at him, forcing my gaze away from his abs and up to his maddeningly perfect face. "Why the hell didn't you call me when you saw my son?"

Beckett shrugged, the kind that said *I know exactly what I'm doing.* "He asked me not to. And I remember those days. If he thinks I'm in his corner, that's one less person he's itching to defy."

I ran my tongue along my front teeth, trying to argue with logic that, annoyingly, made sense. "So, he's at school."

"He's at school." Beckett nodded. "Watched him walk through the front doors. Was headed to the hardware store, hoping I'd find you."

"So, you could tell me all about what a delinquent my child is?" I raised an eyebrow, ready to unleash my full Mama Bear if he so much as hinted at judgment. "Or remind me what a mess of a parent I am?"

He stepped closer, his face now inches from mine, voice low and dark. "Nah. You want to pick that fight, Peach. Give yourself a target for all that simmering rage you've been bottling up for, what—five years? Ten?"

I held my ground, but my breath hitched when his eyes dropped—just for a second—to my mouth.

"And yeah," he said, voice dropping to a whisper. "I can think of much better ways to let off steam."

Unlike with Luca, this didn't feel gross. It didn't feel

performative. It felt like I'd been caught, clothes stripped away, heart exposed—and the worst part?

I didn't hate it.

"Figures your little pea brain would go straight to sex," I snapped, flustered, my cheeks blazing.

His eyes sparked. "I was talking about kickboxing. But I'm flattered."

He straightened, that damn smirk still tugging at the corner of his mouth, and looked across the street at Hudson Hardware. "You're Ty's little sister. Alas, kickboxing's all I can give you."

I gestured to his bum leg and raised a brow. "Yes, well, beating the elderly is generally frowned upon."

A deep laugh burst out of him, the kind that made my stomach clench for reasons I refused to examine. "You haven't changed at all, have you, Little Huddy?"

"Me and my childbearing hips beg to differ. And don't call me that—I'm 35. The nickname can die now."

He didn't respond, just stepped in close again and reached out, his fingers brushing the edge of my jaw.

I froze.

My brain screamed *don't you dare lean into that*, but my body had other plans.

"Those leggings Friday night," he said, voice like warm bourbon, "showed off all your curves."

His thumb skimmed just beneath my jaw, and a shiver ran down my spine.

"Not a complaint in sight," he added, gaze burning into mine.

I couldn't breathe. Couldn't think. Couldn't do anything except feel the heat rising from my chest, flushing my cheeks, melting something I hadn't let myself feel in years.

Mercifully, or cruelly, my watch alarm blared.

I jumped back like I'd been electrocuted, my hand clutching my chest.

Beckett rubbed the back of his neck, eyes dropping to the snow. "I promised Jace I wouldn't call you. But I never said I wouldn't *tell* you."

I nodded, still trying to remember what the hell we were even talking about. "Right. Then... thanks, I guess."

He reached for his truck door. "That boy of yours has a hell of a mouth on him."

I opened mine to fire back, but Beckett got there first.

"I know exactly where he got it. Just forgot how pretty a mouth it is. Thank God for braces."

That snapped me out of it. I rolled my eyes so hard I nearly saw my childhood. "Shoo, hotshot. Don't you have something better to do?"

He grinned. "I can think of a few things."

I turned and walked away, doing my best to shake off the aftershocks still humming under my skin. Beckett Conway was trouble, and my body needed to get the message.

Fast.

8

BECKETT

The steady *ding, ding, ding* of the truck—door open, engine running—wasn't nearly enough to pull me back to reality. Wrapped in a ridiculous knee-length puffer and still managing to short-circuit my entire nervous system, Emmy disappeared into that new Pilates studio like she hadn't just flipped my world upside down in under five minutes.

And somehow, I was still standing there, stunned like a kid seeing fireworks for the first time.

What the hell had just happened?

She'd always been Ty's little sister—mouthy, fearless, off-limits. But now? Now she was all woman, all fire, and that five-minute conversation had more heat in it than any of my previous relationships. My heart was racing like I'd just taken a hit on open ice, and my brain... yeah, it was *useless*.

Where the hell had *that* come from?

Had she always been this sharp? This electric? Had I just been too wrapped up in hockey and my own ego to notice?

Suddenly, every memory I had of Emmy as a teenager was being overwritten by the woman who'd just knocked the wind out of me with nothing more than a glare, a smirk, and a few cutting words.

I swore under my breath and finally reached for the door, my hand still tingling from where she'd touched me—where *I'd* touched her. That look in her eyes when I brushed her jaw, like she'd felt it too, wasn't my imagination.

And, God help me, I wanted to feel it again. Whatever this was, it was dangerous. No matter how gorgeous Emmy had grown up to be—how much heat pulsed between us just standing on a sidewalk—she was Ty's sister. I couldn't go there. Not when I'd be out of this little town and back with my team as soon as I got Mom settled into something resembling a routine.

Once she was out of sight, I grabbed the handlebar above the door and hoisted myself back into the truck. With a hand braced on the passenger seat, I glanced over my shoulder and reversed out onto River Street, needing to put a little distance between me and the wildfire that woman had just lit in my chest.

A few taps on the screen sent a message to Ty:

Jace made it to school. Talk later.

Originally, I'd planned to swing by the hardware store and tell him that in person but doing it now with a semi over his sister felt like a bad call.

I cruised through town, past the brightly painted buildings and crooked wooden storefronts that had stood here longer than anyone still alive. Linwood always felt frozen in time, like a snapshot of an age long ago. And yet, it didn't feel stale. Somehow, even with the changes, it still felt like *home.*

I turned down Second Street, slowing at the familiar

curve past the elementary school and letting my hand rest on the gearshift, like muscle memory alone could steer me through a town I hadn't lived in for 20 years.

I didn't belong here anymore. Not really.

But damn, for the first time in a long time, I missed it.

My phone rang as I made it out of town and onto the highway, my manager's name lighting up the screen. I hit the button to deny the call like I had been all weekend but hit a pothole and accidentally accepted it instead.

"He lives!" Gavin York's voice came over the speakers in my car. "About time you answered your damn phone."

"Tried to hang up on you but wasn't quick enough."

"Yes, well, maybe your reflexes would be better if you actually showed up to your PT appointments."

I could practically hear him pinching the bridge of his nose, so I let him sit in silence for a moment.

"You there?" Gavin said, and I chuckled. "Dammit, Conway. You make my life difficult."

"Okay, I'll take that plane you just bought then."

Gavin sighed. "What's going on, man? Why did you skip town without telling anyone? And where are you?"

"Linwood."

"Oh, shit. Really? Everything okay?"

"Yeah," I said, unsure if that was actually true. "Mom had an accident, and since I'm laid up, felt it was time for a visit."

"Sure, sure." The sound of keyboard clicking filtered through the phone, and I knew Gavin well enough to know he was already handling the mess I'd made for myself. "So how long are you staying? Or are you headed back now?"

"Don't know yet." I checked the rearview mirror, the white-tipped mountains filling my vision, and the thick clouds above them heavy with more snow. "Headed to see her now, and then we'll go from there."

The keyboard clicking stopped, then started again. "Okay, so a few days. Let me get your doctors and trainers on the phone, and we'll get a plan in place. No time for setbacks, and you'll be back in Denver by, what, Wednesday? Two days? Does that work?"

"Sure." I wasn't even kind of sure, afraid of what I'd find when I saw Mom, but that wasn't a conversation I was ready to have. "I gotta go."

"Talk soon," Gavin said. "Quit ignoring my calls."

"Never." I hung up, and the radio switched back to the early 2000's rock blaring over the speakers.

The mountains flew by in a blur, each little town in the Vail Valley looking the same. Luckily, this area was home to some of the best doctors in the country. It was one of the main reasons I hadn't already insisted she move down to Denver or to Dallas with Mason. Also, no one told Lori Conway what to do.

My tires crunched as I pulled into the valet circle at the front entrance to the hospital. A kid hopped up from just inside the sliding doors and ran around the front hood, there by the time I opened the door.

"Morning, sir," he said, holding his hands out for my keys. "Are you here for an appointment or to visit?"

"Just visiting." I dropped the keys in his palm, then grabbed the crutches from the passenger seat and slid them under my arms. Another week of babying my hip, and hopefully I'd be rid of these for good.

The kid handed me a ticket, and I walked inside. Soft piano music filtered through the lobby, painting a serene picture for a building that housed the sick and dying. Sure, maybe miracles happened here too, but all I could think about was my mom somewhere in the maze of these halls, all alone.

"Shit," I mumbled, guilt rising in me that I hadn't tried harder to get here over the weekend. I handed my ID over to the receptionist, and watched as she read my name, then did a double take.

"You're Beckett Conway. From the Denver Yetis."

I nodded, offering her a brief smile, even though I wasn't in the mood. "Here to see Lori Conway."

Her mouth snapped shut, and she turned back to the screen. A paper badge printed out with my ID picture, a time stamp, and her room number.

"Third floor. Elevators are to your right, and down the hall." She handed it to me, her hands slightly shaking. "We're huge fans of yours in my house. Your comeback this year is all we can talk about, especially with this six-game losing streak right now. No way can we make it to the Cup with you out for the season. Will you be back?"

I grunted, then took the badge from her. "Trying my best."

My crutches echoed on the tile floors as I made my way down the sterile hallway and to the elevator, then up to the third floor. With a quick glance at the sign, I found my way to her room and rapped on the door.

"Come in," she said, her voice groggy, and I pushed the door open with my good hip, then spun to walk inside. I wasn't exactly sure what it meant that I was getting good with my crutches, but it couldn't be anything good.

Mom's room was dark, light leaking in through the crack in the blinds on the sides of her windows but otherwise lit only by the many machines beeping and blinking around her. "Didn't mean to wake you."

Her head jerked in my direction, her mouth spreading into a wide smile. It had been far too long since I'd seen my mom, but she was just as stunning as always, her white-blonde hair pulled back in a ponytail, face creased with laugh lines from a life well-lived. "Well, hey stranger! What are you doing here?"

I shook my head, and she held her arms out for a hug. One arm was bound in a cast from her thumb to her elbow, and a bruise lined her cheekbone, but otherwise she looked okay. Frail, but okay.

"What the hell do you mean, what am I doing here? How about, why didn't you call me?"

"Language, son." She swatted at my back with her good hand as I leaned in for the hug. "I know you have manners."

I chuckled, careful of the wires and IV tubing as I hugged her gently. "You know, I had this exact conversation this morning with Emmy's son."

She let out a laugh that quickly turned into a wince. "Oof. Don't make me laugh. My ribs hate me right now."

"Sorry," I said, settling onto the chair beside her bed.

"What were you doing with Jace?" she asked. "He out at the pond again?"

I hummed. "I take it he does that a lot."

She waved a dismissive hand, a tremor in her fingers barely there—but there all the same. She noticed the flicker of my gaze and tucked her hand beneath the blanket. "That boy's been through it. If sneaking onto my pond gives him a bit of peace, I'm not about to chase him off. Don't you go doing it either."

"Uh-huh. And what about the part where he's skipping

school?" I lifted a brow, knowing my retired teacher mother would have something to say about that.

She rolled her eyes. "School first, always. You better have told him that. Though," she added, eyes twinkling, "I doubt he listened. That boy thinks the sun rises and sets on you."

"Really? Because he went toe-to-toe in a verbal sparring match this morning. Weird way to talk to your idol."

Mom shook with laughter, wincing once more as she leaned back into the pillows. I moved to help adjust them, but she lifted a shaky hand and shot me a look that said, *don't hover*, clear as day.

So, I stayed seated, my hands gripping the edge of the chair to keep them still.

"Don't make me laugh," she said once she was settled. "My ribs hurt like a little bitch. And don't you dare say anything about my language. I'm hurt."

I waved a hand over my bum leg and the crutches. "But I don't get a pass?"

Her head tipped to the side, giving me that same stare that had gotten me to confess many wrongdoings over the years. "You're my son. Can't have anyone thinking your terrible behavior is a reflection of my parenting skills."

"Even when I'm 37?"

"Even when you're 87, I'll still be your mother."

I nodded, my lips pulling up in a smile. "Missed you, Mom."

She reached forward, her trembling hand brushing my long hair off my face. "Not as much as I've missed you, my boy."

"Knock knock," someone said from the doorway.

A short woman in a white lab coat stepped in, clipboard in hand. Her dark hair was pulled back in a no-nonsense clip, and her expression matched—sharp, efficient, like she didn't waste time or words. As far as doctors went, she looked about as trustworthy as they came.

"Oh, good. You must be one of the sons." She extended a hand. "I'm Dr. Miriam Navarro, head of Neurology."

I stood awkwardly, crutches balanced under one arm, and shook her hand. Firm grip, calm eyes. I didn't miss the quick glance she gave my leg brace before turning her attention to my mom.

"Lori, how are we feeling this morning?"

"Better now that Beckett's here." My mom beamed at me like nothing was wrong. Like this was a routine check-up and not a damn hospital room filled with machines and bruises. "Ready to break out of here."

"Glad to hear it." Dr. Navarro flipped through her notes. "Concussion protocol is complete, and your CT scans came back clear—no brain bleed, which is exactly what I wanted to see. Any changes in memory or mobility?"

"Other than this cast, no." Mom held up her arm, the tremor in her fingers impossible to miss.

It wasn't subtle. Wasn't occasional. It was constant now.

My throat tightened.

I'd noticed it when she came down to Denver this summer—a shaky hand when she poured tea, a slight stiffness when she walked—but I brushed it off. Told myself it was age, maybe arthritis. I didn't ask. I didn't want to see it.

"Good. And how are your ribs this morning?"

Mom tilted her head, wincing slightly. "Sore, but I'm okay. Ready to move."

"Let's not get ahead of ourselves. I've got orders for inpatient rehab for the next week. Slow and steady is the goal," the doctor said, then turned her attention to me. "And what is your plan for her care after she's discharged?"

I leaned forward, trying to shift the weight off my hip. "Well... she'll go back home, right?"

Dr. Navarro pressed the clipboard to her chest and looked at me the way you look at someone who's about to get a dose of reality they didn't ask for.

"She'll go home, yes. But that house needs to be retrofitted from top to bottom to make it safe. No stairs, no rugs, grab bars in the bathroom, cleared walkways, lighting upgrades—the works. And more importantly, I can't recommend her living alone anymore. Or driving."

"Well, I'm not *that*—"

"Lori," Dr. Navarro said, holding up a hand, and somehow, miraculously, my mother went quiet.

"Don't get me wrong—you're still sharp as ever. But you're also one of my most stubborn patients, and it's time for a serious conversation. Your Parkinson's is progressing. Right now, I'd say we're at Stage 2, possibly even Stage 3 if this fall is to be taken seriously, which I very much think it should be. Living alone in a big ranch house miles outside the nearest town and almost an hour from the closest hospital is not advisable long term. You need home health, if not a full-time caregiver."

My mom inhaled slowly, eyes falling to her lap, her fingers curling slightly as they trembled in her cast. "I hear you," she murmured.

But I didn't.

I sat there frozen, the rest of the room blurring at the edges, words floating around me like static.

Parkinson's.

She had *Parkinson's*?

My brain scrambled, searching for evidence—something, anything—that should have clued me in. The tremors. The stiffness in her shoulders. The way she'd trailed off during a phone calls like she was trying to find her words. I thought it was just age. I thought she was tired. Hell, I thought maybe she was bored up here in the mountains alone. But this?

She never told me.

Not once.

She had Parkinson's Disease, and I didn't know.

My stomach dropped, a hollow, sickening weight settling behind my ribs. How had I missed it? How had I not asked more questions? Why hadn't I seen it?

This woman raised two sons on her own, taught middle school English for 25 years, and still found time to bake pies for the church bake-off. She was tough as nails and always had been. The kind of woman who didn't break, who didn't bend. And now she was sitting in a hospital bed, hiding her shaking hands in a blanket and swallowing pain behind a smile, while I stared at her like a stranger.

I barely heard Dr. Navarro as she continued, flipping through her notes with practiced calm.

"For now," she said, "I'm willing to clear you for inpatient rehab to work on your balance. Let's give your ribs a week to heal before I release you into Beckett's care."

I blinked. "Wait, what? Into my care?"

She looked up, pushing her glasses onto the top of her head with a calm, too-knowing smile. "Yes, Beckett. I know exactly who you are and what's going on. NHL vet. Big comeback. Busted hip. Crutches today, walking in a week if you're lucky."

I opened my mouth again to protest, to explain that I was

leaving in two days, but she kept going, steamrolling right through my stunned silence.

"In fact," she added, "I think these next three months together could be good for you both. Mobility is top of mind for you, Beckett, so you can make sure Lori here is doing all her exercises right alongside you."

Three months?

I was supposed to be rehabbing in Denver. Getting cleared for playoffs. Fighting for one last shot at the Cup.

But as I looked at my mother—her hands trembling beneath the blanket, her face turned toward the window like she couldn't meet my eyes—something shifted.

I hadn't been there for her. Not really. Not for a long time. And when I finally showed up, I'd missed the signs.

I'd completely missed everything.

She'd always been the strong one. The reliable one. The steady ground beneath everyone else's chaos. And she hadn't even told me she was falling apart.

Suddenly, the list of things I'd get to after retirement glared at me like a giant to-do list written across my eyelids, unable to be cleared. And top of that list had always been, *take care of Mom.*

No more excuses. No more running.

I nodded, my jaw tight as I swallowed the guilt and the heartbreak and the sharp burn of anger, mostly at myself.

"Yeah," I said quietly. "We'll figure it out."

Because we would. Because I couldn't leave. Not now. Not when it was finally my turn to be the one holding her together.

Mom sucked in a breath, her blue eyes shining with unshed tears, and Dr. Navarro barreled on like she hadn't just upended both of our worlds. They continued talking about what the recovery process would look like, and I pulled my phone from my pocket to fire off a text.

BECKETT

Change of plans. I'm staying in Linwood.

GAVIN

...ok. For the week? How long are we talking?

BECKETT

Til I'm cleared to skate. Make it happen.

My phone vibrated with an incoming call, but I slid it back in my pocket. Of all the things I'd thrown at Gavin over our long careers together, this might have been the biggest wrench, but also the most important.

"Sound good?" Dr. Navarro said, tapping her clipboard on Mom's blanket-covered feet.

Before I could think through the implications of what I said, the words were out of my mouth. "Sounds great."

9

Emmy

"Who was that guy?" Shannon asked as I ran through the studio doors, unzipping my coat and throwing it at her. She caught it, then hung it on one of the hooks along the wall for me. "And why is your coat all wet?"

"Tried to buy you coffee, and it backfired," I said while hopping on one foot, unlacing my boots and sliding into my grip socks. This was the one class of the day I could actually teach Pilates and workout at the same time, and I didn't want to miss it. "And no one. Can you figure out how to get a playpen by tomorrow night?"

Shannon looked down at my stomach, then up at my face, one black eyebrow lifted. "Something you forgot to share with the class? And that didn't look like *no one*. That looked like Beckett Conway, which that paired with the playpen ask is raising a lot of questions. You do know he's trouble, with a capital T, right?"

"Well aware of exactly who Beckett is. And were you watching with your face pressed to the glass?"

She let out an indignant huff. "Of course, I was. This

town is boring as hell, and you went from looking like you were picking his grave plot to debating kissing him in the blink of an eye. It happened so fast, my neck hurts from the whiplash." She shook her head, her black hair cascading down over her pale face. "Shame, because I have just the spot to hide a body, but here you are talking about playpens instead."

"Lots of things need to happen before I'd need a playpen, like break my year-long dry spell"—Shannon's brows shot up and looked to the parking lot—"*not* with Beckett. It's for a friend."

"You don't have any friends." The complete straight face she delivered the insult with made me chuckle, used to Shannon's no-nonsense attitude after the last few months together.

"We're friends."

"We're not friends." Shannon propped her checkered Vans on the counter as she blew a bubble with the gum in her mouth. "I can't be friends with someone who listens to country music unironically."

I gasped, my hand over my heart. "How dare you talk about our lord and savior, Shania Twain, like that. I could fire you for this."

"But you won't. Because I'm your only friend."

"But we're not friends, remember?"

She pointed a long black nail at me. "Now you're getting it."

"You're ridiculous," I chuckled. "And I'm trying to change the *no friends* thing. Hence, playpen."

Her dark eyes studied me, then her long black nails tapped on the keyboard at the front desk. "Best I can do is Thursday delivery."

I shook my head, grabbing the headset I wore to project my voice through the gym. "Needs to be tomorrow. Find one I can go pick up, even if I have to drive for it."

She dropped her feet to the ground and pulled at the black plaid flannel over her Alice in Chains T-shirt. Every outfit she had was some version of this punk-goth vibe she committed hard to, and she had the slightly bored and disinterested vibe to go with it.

Most people knew her as the small-town rebel and the younger sibling of the two biggest troublemakers in town. Despite her brothers' bad reputation and her slightly intimidating *get-fucked* attitude, I loved Shannon. She was the hardest worker I'd ever employed and motivated to get the hell out of Dodge. And despite what she said, we *were* friends, no matter what little we had in common.

"What are we using this for? And don't think I'm not going to circle back to Conway."

"I'll explain when class is over. Just make it happen." I adjusted the knobs on the speaker pack I clipped to my waistband, then tapped the counter. "Find me some 90s country, please."

Shannon shook her head. "You do this to torture me, don't you?"

"If we were friends, maybe I'd be nicer." I waved over my shoulder and walked behind the partition wall separating the lobby from the studio beyond. The overhead lights were dim, bright enough to see where you were walking and cast in a purple hue from the LED strips above the mirrors.

Twelve Pilates reformer machines lined either wall of the long and narrow room with mats and other accessories to their side. Each reformer was long and low, a sleek stretch of metal and wood with a movable carriage atop. Springs and attached to the foot bar, and pullies above the shoulder block, forcing my students to use controlled motions to survive the ruthless machine.

Every single one was occupied this morning, and I grinned at the sight. Nothing better than a full class of people willingly signing up to suffer quietly while I counted down ten-second holds with a smile.

When I'd pitched Ty on the idea of opening the studio, he'd gone all in with me, but I didn't think he really understood the vision I had—just blindly supportive the way my big brother always was.

Tell Me Why by Wynonna drifted through the speakers, and I shook my head, smiling at Shannon's song choice.

"Alright everyone, let's get started. Set your springs to one red, one green, one blue, and lay on your back. Feet on the bar in Pilates stance. Heels together and toes apart, then push away for a count of six."

An hour passed in a flash, and I walked away from the reformer with a satisfying burn in my muscles, waving goodbye to my patrons. Before I knew it, I'd taught six classes in a row to a wide variety of attendees, and the day was over for me.

"Playpen is ready for pickup in Glenwood Springs after 5 p.m. tonight," Shannon said as I leaned against the front desk.

A low groan slipped out of me, and I dropped my head to the counter. "Nothing closer? Did you check the ski towns? I'll pay more to not have to drive that far."

"Sold out." Shannon tapped the back of my head a little

harder than necessary, and I looked up at her with a scowl. "Maybe I would have tried harder if you'd explained yourself."

With a sigh, I reached down and slipped off my grip socks, then reached for my snow boots in the bottom cubby. "It's a long story, but I met a woman who I invited to class tomorrow night at 5."

Shannon frowned, then clicked around on the screen for a minute. "You don't have a class at 5 tomorrow, and Michael doesn't work Tuesday evenings, so we're closed. You told me not to schedule you during dinner hours so you can go to the rink to watch Jace."

"I know, I know." I puffed out my cheeks, trying to think through how to explain why this felt important. Something about Stevie pulled me in, or maybe I just recognized that *slowly drowning in what everyone says is supposed to be magical* expression she wore. "I feel like she needs me."

My not-friend shook her head, then grabbed my coat from the hook behind the desk and tossed it to me. "You're just like Ty, you know that? Needing to swoop in and rescue everyone."

I slid my arms into the jacket. "He does love a damsel, doesn't he?"

"Says the woman currently driving his car." Shannon arched a brow and gave me a pointed look.

"Listen." I grabbed my purse and swiped open my phone to a text from Jace letting me know he was practicing with the team tonight after all. "Pick your battles, Shannon. He wants me to drive his fancy car while mine won't start when it dips below freezing and it's the beginning of winter? That one wasn't worth stubborn independence. And besides, you should see the Christmas haul I bought for Rowdy and the chickens."

"You bought the chickens presents." Shannon delivered it with such little inflection, I chuckled at the non-question.

"Not like he'd let me buy anything for him, so yes, I bought the chickens presents. Well, really, my plan is to decorate the coop for them."

Shannon shook her head and waved me off. "Your family is weird as fuck."

"Darn." I patted her cheek, then grabbed my keys and remote started the car, wearing a smirk. "Guess I'll return your presents then."

Her dark eyes flicked up to mine. "What did you get me?"

"Well, now I can't tell you since I have to return it."

"It's weird to buy presents for your not-friends."

"So weird." I pushed the door open to a blast of cold air, then waved over my shoulder. "See you tomorrow!"

Lee Ann Womack blasted over the speakers as I got in the warm car, settling into the heated seats. Of all the ways Ty had forced his way into my life over the past year, this car was the thing I felt like arguing the least over, especially as my hands curled around the heated leather steering wheel.

I'd made a decent living as a physical therapist assistant in Connecticut before the move and did okay off the Pilates studio income. Between my paychecks and Ryan's divorce settlement, I lived comfortably, but I didn't have future NHL Hall of Famer money. If my brother insisted on doing things like fixing my car and giving me his as a loaner then I wasn't going to complain.

My fingers tapped along to the beat of the song as I drove through the snowy town toward the rink, passing the colorful row houses and shops littered along River Street. Between the bright colors, the softly falling snow, the setting sun, and the cheery music, I couldn't help but smile. Life wasn't perfect, but when was it? Every time I thought about my interaction with Stevie this morning, I got a little more excited, hoping she'd show up.

All day I'd thought about younger me, back when Ryan was playing minor league hockey, trying to make it to the NHL. I'd spent my days home alone with a cranky baby, wavering between awe that this was my life and despair that each of his little breaths was all my existence boiled down to.

In the 15 years since then, I'd come to terms with the fact that motherhood was like that—violent waves of emotion as you floated between feeling lost at sea and buoyed by love for your children that was so all-encompassing it was all you needed to survive. Not food, not water, and definitely not sleep—just caffeine and pure adoration for the little life you created.

But, of course, that wasn't sustainable either. At some point, I came to the realization I had to take better care of myself to be the mom I wanted to be. It was hard to show up and be present and happy when you were drowning.

Maybe I was projecting my journey on Stevie and she didn't need me, but on the off chance she did, I wanted to reach a hand out and let her know she wasn't alone.

I passed the last row of houses in town and crossed through the wide expanses of ranch land that backed up to the Gore Range mountains. Ty had renovated my parent's ranch house over the last decade and now lived on their property, surrounded by large expanses of nothing but his animals and the one neighbor he tolerated. It was a far cry from his high-rise apartment in Chicago when he'd played for the

Storm, but the peace and solitude our mountain town brought him suited my brother.

Living in a valley between two mountain peaks meant the roads were long and twisty, weaving alongside the Eagle River. It had been a long time since I'd spent a winter here in Linwood, but I knew these roads like the back of my hand.

The rink sat about two miles outside of town, backing up to the water. Every night here was busy with multiple age groups using the same rink, and the parking lot was full yet again. I turned on my blinker, listening to the steady *click* as I circled for an open spot close to the entrance when a black truck turned into the row from the other end, nose pointed at me.

I grinned, hand resting lightly on the horn and ready to fire. "Not today, Conway. *Not today.*"

10

BECKETT

The second I saw the name flash across my screen, I cursed under my breath.

I hit accept and braced myself. "Coach."

He didn't waste time. "Before we get into anything else—how's your mom?"

That question hit harder than I expected. My throat tightened. Not because I had an answer, but because I didn't.

"Honestly?" I stared straight ahead, the mountains a blur outside my windshield. "I don't know."

It was the truth. I'd just found out about the Parkinson's diagnosis myself—something my mom had been hiding for God knows how long—and the words still felt foreign in my mouth.

"Gavin mentioned the diagnosis," Coach said after a beat. "I'm sorry to hear it."

"She fell last week. Broke a couple ribs. ER visit, hospital stay. Recovery at home's not an option, not without help. She shouldn't be living alone."

"I'm sorry," he repeated, a little gruffer this time. "That's a tough one."

I grunted in response, my hands locked tight around the steering wheel. What else was there to say?

"I can't say I'm thrilled about the way this all went down, Conway. The front office has been in meetings all morning combing through your contract for a breach."

There it was.

My stomach knotted, and I pulled the car over, needing solid ground under me.

"I'm in your corner, though," Coach added, voice steel-edged but solid. "Hockey's not forever. You've paid your dues. You've thrown a wrench in the recovery plan, yeah, but—"

"You know me. I'll be back as fast or—"

"I wasn't done," he snapped. "You'd think by now you'd have learned when to shut up."

I clamped my mouth shut. "Yes, sir."

"I do know you, Beckett. You're reckless, but you're smart about it. Calculated. You push the edge harder than anyone I've ever coached, but you always know the line. That's why I'm going to fight for this. Because I believe you've still got more to give."

I let out a slow breath, some of the weight lifting off my chest. "Thank you."

"Don't get soft on me now. This isn't going to be an easy sell. Management's pissed you left without clearance, missed appointments, blew off check-ins. But I told them—family's family."

"I know I handled it wrong. I'm sorry, Coach."

"I'm not your priest. I don't need an apology. I need you

to remember that we're a team, and you matter—to this franchise and to me."

My jaw clenched, emotion burning hot behind my eyes. I dropped my chin to my chest and tried to breathe it down.

"I watched Mason light it up in Dallas last night," he said after a pause. "Guessing he's not with you?"

"No, sir." I'd watched the highlights too—my little brother's hat trick in the third. "Didn't make sense for both of us to miss games. I told him to stay."

"Alright." Another sigh, one I could practically see as him pinching the bridge of his nose. "Sit tight. I'll be in touch with next steps. And Beckett?"

"Yes, sir?"

"Answer your damn phone."

A laugh slipped out despite everything. "Will do."

The line went dead, and I sat there a minute longer before pulling back onto the road. Each mile forward felt just a little lighter. Maybe I wasn't done yet.

Getting Mom settled at the rehab center didn't take as long as I'd planned, so I'd gone home. Before I even made it inside, I noticed Jace's bike still parked by the garage. Without much thought, I'd carefully loaded it into the bed of my truck, ready to hunt down the kid to return it.

My first stop was the hardware store, but Ty's SUV Emmy had been driving wasn't parked on the street anymore. I didn't know where she lived, but my first guess was one of the little row houses she'd always loved as a kid.

Trying not to be a total creeper, I cruised down River Street looking for her car and a Mayhem Hockey Club sign in the yard—she seemed that type of mom—but struck out. I'd forgotten just how many kids in this community played for the Mayhem, so that didn't narrow it down at all.

Next stop, the rink. My phone rang again, and I rolled my eyes at the sight of Gavin's name.

"It's bad," he said as soon as I answered.

"Could be worse," I replied, mostly to annoy him. "Just hung up with Coach."

"Oh, good. He's still speaking to you, then. Management isn't on the same page."

I bit the insides of my cheeks, turning into the rink's crowded parking lot. "Make it work, Gavin. This is what I pay you for."

"Not enough. Not fucking enough, Beck." Gavin sighed, and I waited him out. "You can't argue any of their plans. You understand? This was the only ask they're going to allow."

Snow crunched under my tires sounding an awful lot like my back teeth dissolving with this tension. "I get it."

"Alright. Going to go get you not-fired."

I turned into a new row just as a car began backing out, right next to Emmy's SUV. Even from a distance, I could see her glaring at me through the windshield, her blinker ticking an irritated rhythm.

Remembering how mad she'd been Friday night, I flipped on my own blinker, a grin tugging at my lips for the first time all day.

The Subaru slowly began to angle out, its bumper swinging in my direction. From this side, I had the advantage. Emmy gave a sharp honk, then pointed two fingers at her eyes and one directly at me.

I laughed and waved, enjoying her attention more than I probably should. I'd been thinking about her all day—about our conversation this morning, how close I'd come to kissing her. That wasn't like me. I wasn't exactly celibate, but I'd quit chasing women years ago. Hockey had always come first, second, and third. Hell, I hadn't even noticed my own mom's health slipping, let alone had time for a relationship. Especially not with my best friend's little sister.

She crept her SUV forward and I matched her, both of us crowding the poor Subaru like wolves circling prey. The driver looked terrified, his head swiveling between mirrors as he eased out at a glacial pace.

The second he cleared the space, I slid forward and blocked the spot.

Emmy's window rolled down. Her eyes were slits of pure fury. "That was *my* spot."

I glanced at the empty space, then back at her. "Weird. I didn't see your name on it."

Her nostrils flared. I grinned and then pulled forward just enough to let her have it.

She pulled in and parked, then hopped out of the car, stomping through the slush toward my truck. Her brown hair was pulled back in a little ponytail, bouncing with each step she took, and damn, I liked it too much.

Without hesitation, she yanked the door open, shivered once, and climbed in.

The second it shut behind her, her eyes widened, like she was just now realizing how close we were. Barely a foot between us. Her mouth opened, then closed again, and all I could do was stare at it like it held the answer to every question that had been rattling around my head all day.

Seconds stretched. I tried not to look at the way her chest rose and fell behind that white cropped top—tight and ribbed and clinging in all the right ways. The layers she'd worn outside had kept her curves a secret, but now? Now, I was screwed. Pink cheeks. Heaving chest. Eyes locked on mine like she was daring me to do something stupid. My brain short-circuited into territory it had no business being in.

"You can't just steal parking spots like that."

She crossed her arms under her chest, and Jesus—nope, that didn't help. My gaze snapped to the dashboard as I shifted the truck into gear.

She shifted too, angling toward me. "Where are you going?"

"To park."

I pulled into the nearest open space—handicap right by the front doors—and threw it in park.

Then, because apparently, I was a glutton for punishment, I reached between her legs to pop open the glove box. My shoulder brushed her thigh, and she sucked in her stomach like it would give us an extra inch of space. Unfortunately, all it did was make both of us painfully aware that if I turned my head just slightly, I'd be face-first in her lap.

I didn't, but it was a near-death experience for my self-control. Instead, I grabbed the hang tag, sat back up, and clipped it to the mirror.

"Coming, Peach?"

Her blush deepened from irritated pink to a slow, burning crimson, hazel eyes locked on mine like she wasn't sure if she wanted to slap me or kiss me.

And holy hell, I was gone.

She scrambled out of the car and stomped up onto the sidewalk, snow catching in her dark ponytail under the streetlights. Her shoulders were hunched against the cold, and I couldn't stop watching her.

"Why are you even here?" she snapped, waving a hand

toward me as I eased out of the truck with one crutch under my arm, the other still in the backseat.

"Shouldn't you be back in Denver for doctor's appointments and trainers?" Her eyes dropped pointedly to my hip brace, strapped over my joggers. "And are you even supposed to be down to one crutch crutch yet? Recovery after a labral tear isn't a joke, Beckett. No way are you cleared."

I braced a hand on the truck and stepped up onto the curb beside her. "You sure do know a lot about me."

Then, naturally, my foot slipped on an icy patch.

Emmy moved before I could catch myself, her arm wrapping around my waist, steadying me. My hip flared with pain as I righted myself, and I groaned.

"Are you always this stupid?" she muttered, breath visible in the frigid air.

Her hand landed on the sliver of skin between my hoodie and waistband, and nope, I could not remember a time I'd ever been quite as stupid as this.

"Five-week appointment is tomorrow," I said, voice lower than I meant it to be. "I didn't say I was cleared."

She tilted her face up toward me, snowflakes dusting her lashes. "So, you're just out here risking re-injury in a snow-covered parking lot, because...?"

I didn't have an answer. Not one I could say out loud.

She was shivering, still wearing only those painted-on leggings and that tiny, cropped tee. Without thinking, I tucked her into my side and started walking. She stayed close, as if her little frame could keep me upright, and I let her. Everywhere our bodies touched lit up like static, and suddenly, my hip pain didn't seem quite so important.

We made it inside without another slip, and the second we crossed the threshold, Emmy pulled away like I'd burned her. Arms crossed tight under her chest, she turned away, giving me zero chance of not staring.

I leaned my crutch against the wall, tugged my hoodie off, and dropped it over her head.

"Wha—"

"You're freezing," I said, tugging it down until her face peeked through. The hood framed her flushed cheeks like a damn portrait.

"I left my coat in the car," she mumbled, sliding her arms into the sleeves. "I got a little distracted when someone stole my parking spot."

My hoodie swallowed her frame, hanging past her ass, and I turned quickly toward the concession stand before I made another bad decision. "I'll buy you a pretzel to make up for it."

Her stomach growled in response.

I grinned and looped an arm around her neck, rubbing my knuckles into her scalp. "Still such a menace."

"A noogie?" she huffed, batting me away. "Really?"

"That's what bratty little sisters get."

"I'm not your sister."

She glared up at me, hair wild from my noogie, cheeks flushed, lips parted just enough to wreck my focus, and damn.

She wasn't my sister.

She was a walking complication with killer curves, eyes that could cut glass, and a mouth I was dangerously close to remembering in far too much detail.

"Mm. But you are a brat, aren't you?" I said, my voice lower, rougher.

Her nostrils flared. For a second, I swore she was going to

close the distance between us and say something that'd undo the last sliver of restraint I had left.

Instead, she spun on her heel, hips swaying, and stormed toward the concession stand.

I followed, jaw clenched, pulse pounding, and very aware I was losing the war between logic and every damn cell in my body screaming for more of her fire.

"Pretzels," she told Tate when she approached the snack bar, holding up her fingers. "He's buying."

Tate's brows rose as she grinned. "Back so soon, Conway?"

"Jace left his bike at my pond," I said. "Figured I'd drop it off. Maybe catch practice. Kid's good."

Emmy's stare was back on me, but I kept mine forward. I didn't trust myself to meet it.

"Don't know if there's a practice," Tate said. "Coach didn't show. Again."

Emmy tensed. "Seriously?"

Tate shrugged. "I'd help, but I'm stuck here. Concessions make more than anything else in this place."

Well, that wasn't a good sign.

"They can't free skate?" I asked.

"Insurance won't allow it without a certified adult on the bench."

Emmy cursed under her breath and turned to stare at the ice. "We need a new coach. This can't keep happening."

Tate sighed. "No one wants to take on a losing team, history or not. And at the level these kids play, it's a huge commitment for little to no cash."

They exchanged one of those silent conversations women seem to have: raised brows, tiny shrugs, mutual sighs.

Emmy pulled at the strings on my hoodie, biting her lip. "Are you thinking about disbanding the team?"

"What?" I nearly reeled back. "You can't shut down the Mayhem."

Tate's face fell. "I'm running out of options."

I raised a hand, heart pounding harder than it should've been. "Okay, no. This rink? This team? It's our past. Mine. Ty's. Mason's. Hell, Emmy's. You don't just erase that like it never mattered."

My voice caught, chest tight. Everything I loved about growing up here—this rink, this team, the people who built me—was falling apart in real time, and I couldn't do a damn thing to stop it.

"And I can solve one problem right now," I said, gripping the crutch under my arm like it could anchor me. "I got certified last summer for a kid's camp with the Yeti. I'll take the bench tonight. And while I'm rehabbing... I'll help. I'll run practices."

"What?" they both said, eyes wide.

Yeah. That definitely wasn't supposed to come out.

But the words just kept coming. "I'll rope Ty in too. You know he'll do it."

Emmy let out a sharp exhale, but Tate looked like I'd handed her a miracle. "You've got the bench tonight. We won't tell the kids yet, but for now—they're yours."

I looked at Emmy. I didn't know what I was searching for —approval, backup, someone to stop me before I committed to more than I could handle—but I needed something.

"Emmy?"

She had the sleeve of my hoodie pulled up over her mouth, her gaze fixed on the ice like she was trying not to feel any of it. Not the rink falling apart. Not *me* falling apart.

"It's your call."

She finally looked at me, steady and unblinking. "You disappoint him," she said coolly, "and I'll bury you. Got it?"

A grin tugged at the corner of my mouth. God, I loved her fire.

"Crystal," I said, not even a little afraid, just completely, utterly gone for her.

We walked side by side toward the bleachers, our arms brushing briefly as we split—she veered left, I went right. I shifted my crutch under my arm again, the cold metal biting into my side, grounding me in the chaos of it all.

The kids hadn't noticed me yet.

So, I whistled—loud and sharp, two fingers in my mouth like I had a hundred times before—and every head turned.

I shoved open the bench door with my free hand and stepped inside. "Playtime's over, Mayhem. Time for sprints."

11

Emmy

"Mom, Beckett Conway coached us tonight," Jace said as he threw himself into the passenger seat of my car. "*Beckett Conway.*"

Even though he'd showered, his hockey bag sat in the trunk smelling like a gym sock married a wet dog whose diet consisted solely of rotten cheese and they honeymooned in a landfill. I plugged my nose, then cracked the windows before backing out of the parking lot. Who cared if it was snowing —I could not sit in this car with the stench wafting through the air.

"That's so exciting." I tried to keep my voice light, tamping down how nervous this whole thing made me. The last thing Jace needed was another male role model to fall flat in his life. "But it was just for tonight."

"Still." Jace tipped his wet hair back on the headrest, looking at me with a huge grin. "Did you see the pointers he gave me? He said I was weak on my left cuts, and *he was right.*"

I chuckled, driving carefully down the winding road back

into town. A black truck tailed me home, and I looked in the rearview mirror at Beckett behind us. "So, you like being told you're not doing something good enough? Because for the thousandth time, your clothes go *in* the hamper, not on the floor in front of it."

Jace rolled his eyes. "Mom. Stop."

"If I had Beckett tell you to do it, would you?"

A slow smile spread over Jace's face. "If he told me it'd help me make it to the NHL, sure."

I reached across the center console and slapped his belly that was far harder than I remembered from my little boy. "Where'd you learn to be such a smart ass?"

Jace looked at me pointedly, and I shoved a finger in his face.

"Don't answer that."

"I said nothing."

With a shake of my head, I turned off River Street and into the narrow driveway behind my little row house. Jace was out of the car before I came to a full stop, rushing toward Beckett's truck as it pulled in behind me. I stayed put, hands on the wheel, heart thudding like I'd just sprinted the last mile home.

I didn't know what made me feel so pulled to him—like I was stuck in his orbit without realizing I'd started drifting. Maybe it was old familiarity, a comfort I didn't know I'd missed. I'd known Beckett Conway since I was six years old.

But whatever this was now—it didn't feel familiar.

It didn't feel safe.

It definitely didn't feel like harmless teasing with my brother's best friend.

I parked under the carport and grabbed my water bottle, coat, and bag from the backseat, watching Jace roll his fat-tired bike down the snowy driveway with a grin that nearly knocked me over.

"He said I can come skate at the pond tomorrow morning."

I squinted against the headlights of Beckett's truck. "You have school in the morning."

"Before school," Jace said, already bargaining.

"It's dark before school, bud. I don't want you riding your bike in the dark."

"I'll pick him up," Beckett called from the truck, his voice cutting clean through the still night.

I straightened, pulse jumping as I looked between my son and the man I barely recognized anymore. His voice was warm, easy, like this was all so simple. But it wasn't.

"Besides," he added, "I could use the help setting up some gym equipment being delivered this weekend. We'll call it a trade."

"Come on, Mom." Jace clasped his hands together like a prayer. The way his bottom lip popped out nearly undid me —it was the same look he'd given me when he was four and wanted a puppy. "I promise I'll finish my homework."

I pointed a finger at him. "No more skipping school."

He looked back over his shoulder toward the truck. "Okay, Brutus."

"I didn't call her." Beckett leaned out the window with his hands up in mock surrender. "But don't keep secrets from your mom, kid. Bad move. They know everything."

I tugged at the sleeves of my shirt, trying to stay grounded. "You remember what I told you earlier?"

Beckett laid a hand over his heart like he was reciting a vow. "Loud and clear, Mama. I got it."

The smirk on his face made my stomach flip—and I

hated that it did. Hated that I liked the way he said Mama like a nickname, not just a title. Like it meant something more.

"Fine," I said, even though it wasn't fine at all.

Jace whooped, then darted to my trunk for his hockey bag, lugging it toward the shed to let it air out.

I walked to Beckett's truck, the gravel crunching under my boots, and leaned in close so Jace wouldn't hear me. The scent of him—pine and spice and winter air—hit me like a sucker punch.

"You get one chance. Understood?"

His blue eyes caught mine, and it wasn't just the cocky gleam that got me—it was how much he meant it when he said, "Pinky promise," holding up his hand like a goofball.

I batted his hand away before I could do something even dumber than I already had, then turned and marched back to the house.

"See you in the morning, Jace!" Beckett called. "Goodnight, Peach."

I flipped him off without turning around, because it was that or let him see the smile that was tugging on my lips.

Inside, Jace collapsed dramatically on the couch, replaying every second of practice like it was the best thing that had ever happened to him. And maybe it was.

That thought twisted something sharp inside me.

Because he already had a father who let him down at every turn. The last thing he needed was another man who'd vanish when things picked up again—especially one who was only in town because of a blown hip and a ticking clock.

I brushed my fingers through Jace's shaggy hair. "He's only here for a little while."

"Duh, Mom." Jace rolled his eyes, then walked toward

the kitchen. "The Yeti don't stand a chance without him. I know he won't be here forever. But he's an NHL star—I'd be stupid to pass up this chance."

I smiled, but it was tight.

"You do remember your uncle played in the NHL too, right?"

"Yeah, but Ty played defense," Jace said, his voice muffled as he rooted through the fridge. "Beckett plays right wing. Like me."

"Finish your homework," I said, peeking over the banister.

"I *know*, God, Mom." His arms were full of sandwich ingredients.

I climbed the stairs slowly, the warmth of the house doing nothing to ease the chill that had settled in my chest.

Once in my room, I closed the door behind me and leaned against it like that would keep the panic out. Like it would hold everything in place just a little longer.

But the buzz of Beckett's voice still echoed in my ears. The fire of his gaze didn't fade. And I was starting to think this might be the worst idea I'd ever had.

With shaky hands, I fished out my phone from my leggings side pocket.

EMMY

Send me Beckett's number?

TY

... why?

EMMY

Jace is skating with him tomorrow morning at the pond. I just need to confirm plans.

TY

Before school?

Conway's getting up that early?

EMMY

Hence the need for me to confirm this.

Another text came through with Beckett's contact card, which I saved.

EMMY

Thank you. Also, he volunteered you and him to take over coaching the Mayhem.

My phone rang, and Ty's picture lit up the screen. "Beckett's going back to Denver tomorrow. What do you mean he volunteered us to coach the Mayhem?"

"I know about as much as you do." I sat on my brightly patterned duvet. "He said he's here for the winter and wanted to help. Also, did you know how bad the rink's finances are?"

Ty sighed. "I've asked Tate about it a few times, but she doesn't seem interested in my help."

"And that has stopped you, when?" I chuckled, leaning back on my hands and stretching out my sore calves. Between Pilates this morning and being on my feet all day, I was ready for bed.

"I'll talk to her," he said, and Rowdy started barking in the background. "I gotta go—someone's at the door."

He hung up, and I stared down at my phone, unease settling in over all the unknowns in Jace's world right now. With no coach and no hockey team, I was terrified of what

Jace's after school life would look like. It was just about all he cared about, and his only dream was to make it to Juniors, then the NHL beyond, just like Ty and Beckett had.

I threw myself back on the bed, staring at the ceiling. Everyone warned you that the newborn years would be exhausting, and the toddler years filled with frightening adjectives, but no one talked about these later years. I wasn't worried so much about my son choking on a stray toy or jumping off the roof anymore—though that one wasn't completely out of the realm of possibilities either.

Now, what kept me up at night was worry that even when I'd done everything I could to make sure my kid turned into a mature, kind, and happy adult, it wouldn't be enough. That the beating the world around us dealt was out of my control, and he'd end up damaged because of it.

I grabbed my phone, firing off a text before I could think twice about it.

EMMY

> I need to set some rules before you're allowed to spend time with my son

BECKETT

Wow, confident move texting me with no name

EMMY

> Hanging out with many other women's sons lately?

BECKETT

Alright, so you're a woman. Thank you for narrowing that down. Maybe a selfie would help jog the memory.

EMMY

Does that work for you? Do women
actually send you selfies?

BECKETT

Sometimes. Maybe you're lying and are
actually a man. Before I get too flirty, best
to find out how to tailor my approach.
Like should I lead with complimenting
your beautiful eyes or your Adams apple?

I snorted a laugh and grabbed my phone, headed for the bathroom to change. A yawn slipped free, so I hit his number to call him, too tired to type.

"It's me, you idiot," I said as soon as the phone stopped ringing.

"Miss me already?" Beckett asked. "It's only been, what, 15 minutes?"

I rolled my eyes and propped my phone on the stand I used for skincare videos, wedged between a jade roller and a half-empty bottle of retinol. With my back to it, I started lining up the products for my very basic nighttime routine—cleanser, serum, moisturizer, the works.

"Considering I never once missed you in 15 years, no, I'm good," I said, grabbing a headband to push my hair back.

"You and your son with the sick burns." Beckett laughed. "At this rate, I need to invest in some aloe just to survive hanging out with you two."

I smiled, walking across the bathroom to toss my socks into the hamper. "As I said, I need some ground rules if you're going to be around Jace more."

"I'm listening."

"Number one. Clear expectations." I peeled off Beckett's hoodie and hung it on the hook behind the door. "If there's even a chance you'll have to cancel on him, you tell him in advance. No last-minute disappearances. He's had enough of that."

"Makes sense," Beckett said. "And yeah… I hate that for him. What else?"

"Number two. No bullying." I reached for the waistband of my shirt, dragging it and my sports bra off in one motion. "He's got a sharp tongue and can take a joke, but don't push too far. Ryan is…"

I paused, trying to find the right words.

"He hard on him?" Beckett's voice had dropped, rough and low. There was something sharp underneath it—protective, maybe. Dangerous.

A shiver danced across my skin at the sound, heat blooming low in my stomach despite the chilly bathroom air. I was still facing away, my bare back to the phone. A few feet of distance shouldn't have made his voice hit me like that.

"He's critical," I said quietly. "Jace needs structure, but he's still a kid. He needs to feel like someone's proud of him. Like someone sees him trying."

There was a pause, then a throat-clearing on the other end.

"Got it. Any more rules, Mama?"

"Yes, about that." My fingers slid beneath the waistband of my leggings. "I can't do this flirty thing."

"Emmy—"

"No, let me finish." I pushed the leggings down and kicked them into the hamper, now standing in nothing but my underwear, still turned away. "I'm a divorced mom with a son who comes first. I'm not looking for anything. I don't want the lines getting blurry."

"Hey, wait—"

"Just let me say it." My voice was shaky, but I needed to get it out. "Whatever this is—it feels flirty. I can't do flirty."

A low groan slipped out of Beckett's mouth, and I slid my thighs together at the sound, wishing it was for other reasons. And hell, when was the last time I'd thought about sex? Unwilling to go there, I reached across and pulled his hoodie back off the hook, sliding it back on.

"Oh, *fuck*," Beckett said, his voice nearly guttural now. "Tell me you didn't just put my hoodie on over your naked body. Is that what you're sleeping in?"

My knees nearly buckled.

Heart hammering, I whipped around and froze at the sight of Beckett's face lit up on my phone screen.

Video call.

FaceTime.

I slapped both hands over my chest, the sleeves of his hoodie falling halfway over my fingers. "How long have you been *watching* me?"

He winced, one hand over his eyes with just the smallest gap between two fingers. "The whole time?" he said, then laughed. "I tried to stop you. I *swear* I did. Luckily—or unluckily—you didn't turn around until now. Rear view only."

I dragged my hands down my face, mortification setting my skin on fire. "Oh my God."

"You have a *fabulous* ass, for the record," Beckett said, grinning. "But I won't say that because—what was it? No flirting? Good thing it's just a *fact*."

My whole body pulsed with embarrassment, as well as something hot and totally inappropriate.

"I was about to bend over and put my hair in a bun," I muttered. "You would've gotten the full show."

Beckett leaned back in the frame, lacing his hands behind his head like he was settling in for Pay-Per-View. "Don't let me stop you. I'm learning so much about divorced single moms. This is extremely educational."

"Is there a way to turn back time five minutes?" I groaned. "Delete this entire call from your memory?"

"Over my cold, dead body." He leaned closer again. "When I'm old and senile and can't remember my name, I'll *still* remember the finest ass I've ever seen on little Emmy Hudson."

"Meyers."

Beckett's head tilted. "I don't think Ryan has a claim on you anymore, *Peach*."

His voice dropped even lower, threaded with something darker. Something dangerous.

"In fact," he said, "I think you're ripe for the picking."

My breath caught, fingers clenching in the hem of the hoodie. Everything inside me went still.

"Beckett..."

"Go to bed, Emmy," he said, voice soft but commanding. "Slide under those covers in nothing but my hoodie. Sleep tight knowing I'll be there to pick up your kid in the morning."

His eyes sparkled, and then, "I promise to be a good role model *if you* promise to tell me when you touch yourself wearing my clothes."

My jaw dropped.

Beckett just smiled, cocky and unrepentant.

"Goodnight, Emmy."

The screen went dark.

I stood there, staring at the phone in stunned silence, my entire body thrumming.

By the time I crawled into bed and turned out the lights, all I could think about were his parting words. I tossed and turned, trying to force them out of my head—but the second my hand slid beneath the covers, his smirk came rushing back.

I refused to picture those blue eyes, that lazy grin, that infuriating, gorgeous man.

Two sharp knocks at my door had my hand jerking away like I'd been burned.

"Goodnight, Mom."

"Night, buddy!" I called back, way too loud.

I turned on my side, heart still racing, Beckett's voice replaying in my head like a broken record.

He was off-limits, even to my imagination. And I was going to remember that, starting now.

12

BECKETT

The sun was just beginning to rise over the mountains when I pulled into Emmy's driveway. I sat in the idling truck, eyes fixed on the soft glow behind the upstairs curtains of that little blue house. Just hours ago, I'd seen more of Emmy Hudson than I ever expected to.

The smart thing would've been to apologize and back off. She'd laid down boundaries. Hell, she'd made a *list*. But every time I saw her, every time I remembered her pulling that hoodie over bare skin, my brain turned to static and something possessive curled deep in my gut.

"Bye, Mom!" Jace called, bounding down the steps with his backpack slung over one shoulder, gloves dangling from the other. His Carhartt jacket and Mayhem hoodie combo made him look like a mini-Ty, and I didn't know whether to laugh or panic.

Emmy stepped into the doorway behind him, cradling a mug of coffee. She leaned against the jamb, backlit by the warm house lights, somehow managing to look casual and knockout gorgeous all at once. Even from here, I could see her gaze shift to mine.

Not a word. Not a smile, but that same tension tugged at me anyway.

I popped the passenger door open for Jace to climb in. "Morning."

He tossed his backpack into the backseat like he lived here. "Cool if I sync my phone?"

"Make yourself at home," I muttered with a laugh, glancing back at the house one last time before reversing out of the drive.

The air in the truck felt heavier than it should have. Maybe it was the weight of last night. Maybe it was knowing I'd already crossed a line I wasn't supposed to touch.

"Ready to skate?" I asked as we turned toward the road back to the ranch.

Jace stayed quiet, scrolling through his phone, his mouth puckered the same way Emmy did when she was concentrating. Finally, he set it in the cupholder and hit play.

The opening chords of *Sound of Madness* by Shinedown filled the cab, and Jace started air-drumming like he was on tour.

"You know Shinedown?" he asked.

"Do I—" I gave him a look. "Yes. I'm injured, not ancient."

He shrugged. "I don't know. You're pretty old. That's my dad's favorite thing to point out on ESPN."

"You don't pull punches, huh?"

He shrugged again, then smirked. "Why? You getting sensitive in your later years?"

A laugh broke from me before I could stop it. "Between

you and your mom, I'm not going to have an ego left by the time I get back to Denver."

At the mention of her, Jace's expression shifted. His arms folded, and his eyes dropped to the window.

"What do you care about my mom?"

I winced. "Calm down, bud. We're just friends."

He didn't respond—just turned forward and kept his eyes on the road ahead. The music played on, but the energy in the truck had shifted, and I knew better than to push it.

We pulled into my driveway a few minutes later, the lights around the pond already on.

Ty was waiting, leaning against his pickup with arms crossed, a familiar scowl painted across his face. Rowdy sat in the passenger seat, head out the window, tail wagging slow and steady.

Jace hopped out with a fist bump for his uncle. "You skating with me this morning?"

"Planned on it," Ty said, eyes locked on me. "Need to talk with Conway here first."

I let out a slow breath, reached for my crutches, and eased out of the cab one leg at a time. The pain in my hip pulsed as soon as I hit the ground.

I hadn't called Ty last night—hadn't had the guts—but I should've known Emmy would. Those two had always had each other's backs.

"Didn't know you were coming," I said as I approached, moving slowly on my crutches.

"Didn't know you volunteered me to coach," Ty replied.

We knocked elbows, and he bent to grab his skates. Rowdy jumped down and did his little trot-hop beside him, tongue lolling to the side.

"You want to tell me what that was all about?" Ty asked, his voice low and even as we headed toward the pond.

"What part?"

Ty glanced back, one brow raised. "The coaching thing. Why? What else do we need to talk about?"

I stepped slowly down the plowed and salted path, crutches clicking against the wooden steps.

"Because I saw what those kids needed last night," I said. "And I saw what Tate was carrying alone. You and I built our lives out here on that pond, and now it's slipping away. I'm not going to just stand by and watch it fall apart. Coach would hate us for it."

Ty shook his head but didn't argue. He turned and led the rest of the way down, Rowdy at his side, leaving me to move at my own painfully slow pace.

My hip burned with every shift of weight, and I was starting to second guess the whole damn plan. First doctor's appointment was in a few hours—I needed to get through this morning in one piece.

By the time I reached the pond, Ty and Jace had nearly finished clearing it. The shovels were put away, skates laid out. I took a seat on the stump by the stairs and let out a long breath. My leg throbbed, my shoulders ached, and my brain still hadn't stopped replaying that damn video call with Emmy.

But as Rowdy curled up beside me, and I watched Ty knock off Jace's hat, a familiar kind of peace settled in.

This was still home.

It just didn't look the same anymore.

"What's up, little buddy?" I scratched behind the black dog's ears, and he leaned into my touch. "Think we can turn

Jace into an actual Juniors contender instead of just a smart-mouthed asshole?"

"Heard that." Jace slid on his gloves and grabbed a stick from the shed.

"I fully intended you to."

Ty's mustache twitched, the closest I'd get to a smile from my friend, and I leaned forward, resting my elbows on my knees. "Alright, warmup first. Ty, run him through some drills."

My old friend took over, and I watched Jace's every move. He had great instincts on the ice—read the play well, handled the puck with confidence, and wasn't afraid to take risks, even against a much bigger opponent.

But time and time again, Ty beat him to the puck, battling it away from his nephew in one-on-one. As Ty shot it into the right post for his fourth goal, he held his hands out to the side. "You want me to autograph that puck before I do it again?"

"It's fine, your knee will give out soon enough. I'll win the long game, Grandpa."

I shook with laughter as the chirping began, glad this kid's barbs were aimed at someone other than me for once. They flew around the ice, playing posts in one-on-one, Jace ducked low, and snapped the puck right into the crossbar.

His hands shot into the air, a loud whoop echoing through the valley as he celebrated. But it was his little hop as he changed directions, pointing his stick at his uncle, that caught my attention.

I whistled, pointing at his skates, and both Ty and Jace turned to look at me.

"That. Right there. Do that again."

Jace frowned, looking down at his skates, then up at his uncle. "Score? I told you I'd win the long game."

"No, you cocky dipshit. The hop."

Ty started skating backward, then grabbed some cones off the top of the net, throwing them out onto the ice. "Transitions?"

"Exactly. He needs some juice."

Ty nodded, and laid out several drills, intent on making Jace change directions fast, and be explosive off the drop.

Before I knew it, an hour was up, and Jace lay in the snow next to me, chest heaving and cheeks pink from the cold and exertion.

I stood over him, then gently kicked him in the shoulder. Jace frowned, but I could see the excitement in his eyes.

"Find the juice, bud. You've got the raw talent, now we just need to dial up the pace to match your skill level. And maybe tamp down the attitude."

Jace rolled his eyes, and I turned away from him, making my way back up to the house. "Good job, kid. Put your stuff away, then come inside and shower before school. You smell like a trashcan."

Jace put away his gear, then grabbed his backpack from my truck, headed toward the back door. He disappeared inside, clearly familiar enough to help himself. The door was unlocked, and he didn't hesitate.

Ty shut the shed door and locked it. "You serious about coaching?" he asked. "What's this about you staying in town?"

I scratched the back of my neck, the truth sitting heavy in my gut. "Yeah. I think I am. Mom is worse than she's letting on. Did you know she has Parkinson's? I only found out a few days ago."

"Shit, man, I didn't know. You just found out?"

I nodded slowly. "She never said anything. The doctors told me when they were discussing her discharge to the rehab center. Otherwise, I'd still be clueless."

Ty exhaled hard, running a hand down his face. "I wondered, but she never confirmed it. If she had, I would've told you."

"She made it sound like she didn't want anyone worrying. But after the fall, the doctors said she can't be alone, not right now. And I just... I don't feel right leaving."

Ty gave a single, understanding nod. "What about your contract?"

"Coach is trying to keep me out of trouble." I took Ty's outstretched hand to help me stand. "Gavin's working on it too. I might still be screwed, but I'll deal with that later."

Ty jerked his chin toward the house. "And the kid?"

"I know Emmy will skin me alive if I screw this up." I smirked, remembering her threats as my breath fogged in the cold air. "Trust me, I'm aware."

Ty's long strides skipped steps as he went up to the back porch, Rowdy right behind him. I did my best to follow at a much slower, safer pace.

"What's the deal with Meyers?" I asked as we stopped by the back door.

He let out a long sigh. "Ryan Meyers is a piece of shit. Always was, and he just grew up to be even shittier."

"Did he hit them?" I asked, rage lighting a fire in my chest at the thought of anyone putting hands on Emmy or Jace.

"If he had, I'd be in prison and he'd be dead," Ty said flatly. "No. But he's a narcissist. Everything's always about him. If it isn't, he finds a way to make it a problem."

That tracked with the arrogant loudmouth I'd shared ice time with in Michigan before entering the draft. Couldn't stand him then either.

"Cheater, then?"

Ty shot me a dry look. "Jace has a two-year-old little brother that they all learned about a little over a year ago. Emmy found the paternity test results in the mail, and it blew everything wide open. Cheating implies he was ever playing by the rules, so that word doesn't even fit for a fucker like him."

"Damn," I muttered, glancing toward the house. "How much does Jace know?"

"Plenty. You can't hide a scandal when your dad is on national TV. Emmy tried to protect him, but once the ink was dry on the custody agreement, she packed him up and got him out of that bullshit Connecticut suburb. The kids there made his life hell. He was getting in fights every week."

I remembered too well what it was like to be the kid in town with a dad everyone whispered about. How badly I'd wanted out and to never look back.

"They both needed a reset," I said.

"They did." Ty leaned back against the railing while Rowdy laid across his feet. "So do not screw with them. That kid's finally starting to feel like himself again. And Emmy? She's barely gotten her feet under her."

I stiffened. "That a warning?"

Ty raised a brow. "Does it need to be?"

Footsteps thudded inside, and Jace burst out the door, hair damp, backpack slung over one shoulder and a protein bar dangling from his mouth, wrapper still on.

"Kid's got talent," I said, eyes still on Ty. "I think I can help. That's all I'm interested in."

Ty clapped a hand on my shoulder, then turned toward his truck. Rowdy trotted ahead, hopping easily into the cab like the three-legged badass he was.

Jace adjusted his backpack strap. "Ready?"

"Come on, Juice." I reached out and gave him a light swat to the back of the head. "Let's get you to school on time so your mom doesn't murder us in our sleep."

I snapped a selfie of Jace and I at the front doors of the school, then sent it to Emmy to let her know I'd kept my side of the deal. When she texted back, I couldn't help but flirt even though I knew I shouldn't.

Today was my first checkup with my new doctor the team had assigned. I sat in a different wing of the same hospital Mom had been in, this one decorated with portraits of famous athletes who had been treated at the state-of-the-art sports medicine clinic. Thankfully, whatever Coach and Gavin had worked out with the team meant this was possible at all.

A monitor on the wall that was probably used to inspect imaging was instead lit up Brady Bunch style, showing Coach Tremblay, the Yeti's head trainer Frankie Rhodes, Gavin, and even some of the Yeti's front office staff. I sat buck-ass naked under a hospital gown, but after decades in a locker room, that didn't bother me as much.

There was a gentle knock on the door, followed by a young doctor entering the room, flipping through my chart. He looked up, a small grin taking over his face as he held out a hand.

"Beckett," he said, his handshake firm. "I'm Dr. Carter. I'll be taking over your recovery alongside your team's staff."

I nodded, then glanced up at the screen of faces all watching this, feeling like a goldfish in an aquarium.

Dr. Carter looked back at my charts. "Five weeks out," he said. "How's the pain?"

"Manageable," I said, glancing at Frankie's face on the screen across the room. "Better every day. I've only been taking Tylenol the last few days."

Frankie nodded, leaning away from the camera with his arms crossed. The screen light shone off his brown skin, a glare coming off his bald head. His shoulders barely fit in the screen, the former linebacker turned trainer just as broad as he'd been in his college days.

Dr. Carter's little hum seemed pleased too. He gestured to the table, urging me to lay back. I did, and his cold hands gently inspected my incision, then guided my leg through a few movements. I gritted my teeth once or twice but didn't stop him.

"You're right on track." He stepped away from the exam table and typed notes into the laptop across the room. "Are you still using the crutches?"

"Down to one, but I feel good enough to be done with them."

He looked back up, leaning against the counter. "I agree, based on your mobility today. You can be done with the crutches, but take it slow, especially in this weather. I know you want back on the ice yesterday, but if you rush this, you're looking at setbacks, not speed. Let's stay patient."

I stared at my hands, trying to keep my thoughts to myself. Hell yes, I wanted back on the ice yesterday. Hockey was all I'd ever dreamed of, and being sidelined like this was killing me.

"What's the plan for PT?" Dr. Carter asked.

"We've got it worked out," Frankie said. "I made some calls and found a few options. Since Beckett has room for equipment in his mom's basement, that's the first step. We'll do virtual workouts, but I also am going to work with someone local in Linwood."

My attention snapped up to the screen, and I frowned at Frankie. "Who?"

"A woman in town was a physical therapist for a clinic back in New England, working with a buddy of mine. He swears up and down she's great and can do the in-person checks for me. We can probably knock two birds out here too and have her check on your mom's recovery when she's out of rehab."

"Who?" I asked again, racking my brain for anyone that fit that bill. As far as I knew, we didn't have any PTs in Linwood. It was a small town, but I'd also been gone for a long time.

"Emily Meyers," Frankie said, and I let out a sharp laugh. "Goes by Emmy, I think."

I scrubbed a hand across my face, then pinched the bridge of my nose. Of course it was fucking Emmy.

"Problem, kid?" Frankie asked.

I looked up to see every single face on the screen studying me. Gavin's little face stared daggers at me, looking like he was about to blow a gasket.

"Nope." I popped the P, trying to think through how I was going to go about avoiding Emmy when I was contractually required to see her daily.

"Good," Dr. Carter said. "You're working on everything Frankie went over before you left town last week?"

"Yes, I've been keeping up my stretches like you showed me."

"Great," Frankie said. "Just remember you're five weeks out of hip surgery, not auditioning for Cirque du Dumbass. Nothing risky."

Dr. Carter let out a snort, then held up a hand in apology.

Frankie barreled on, immune to everyone laughing at his odd quips. "Apparently Emmy owns a Pilates studio in Linwood now. Starting next week, let's add some Pilates into your rehab. It's excellent for stabilizing the core and reactivating those deep hip and pelvic muscles."

My brows hit my hairline. "Pilates?"

"That's a great idea." Dr. Carter pointed at the screen, and suddenly I hated that he and Frankie seemed to be on the same team. "If you start with mat work, I've seen it work wonders with athletes post-op."

Frankie nodded. "We're aiming for precision and control, not reps. If you're compensating or shaking, you're doing too much."

I nodded slowly, still trying to picture myself in a Pilates studio. "But—"

Frankie didn't even slow his stride. "The only 'but' I want to hear is yours *on the Pilates mat,* doing your clamshells like God intended."

Several of the people on the screen chuckled. One even wheezed. I just sighed like a scolded puppy, keeping my thoughts to myself.

"Depending on how you're doing at your next physical,

we'll add some light resistance work in the next week," Dr. Carter went on, "but still no skating or running."

"When can I get back on the ice?"

"If everything stays on track, maybe around week 12. No contact drills until closer to 16 or 20. We'll reassess as we go." Dr. Carter stood and gave me a firm look. "Stay smart and we can get you back in time for the Stanley Cup, if the Yeti make it that far without you."

"Sooner," I said through gritted teeth. "I need to be back for playoffs."

"You try to shortcut this, Conway," Frankie said, and I glanced up at the screen to see him leaning in, "and the only thing you'll be back for is a second surgery and a front-row seat in a suit."

He raised a brow, waiting a beat to let his words sink in. "You don't rehab faster by cutting corners. You rehab faster by not screwing it up."

I opened my mouth, ready to argue, but Coach Tremblay cut me off before I could say a word.

"You heard them, Conway. Follow Dr. Carter's instructions, do your clamshells like a man, and stop pretending your hip isn't ready to send you into retirement if you don't listen."

I scowled at the screen, but Gavin's wide-eyed expression and flared nostrils reminded me I didn't have much leeway here. "Fine."

Frankie gave me a look that was a mixture of pride and exasperation. "Good. I'll see you back here in a week. Don't make me send a team of clamshells to your house."

"That's not even a thing," I mumbled, sounding an awful lot like the teenager I'd dropped off at school a few hours ago.

"Act like a dipshit and it can be."

Dr. Carter chuckled, then shook his head before handing me a slip of paper. "See you in a week."

13

Emmy

Once Jace left with Beckett for the day, I poured my coffee into a to-go tumbler and got in my car, headed to pick up the playpen in Glenwood Springs.

Luckily, rush hour wasn't exactly the same in mountain towns—the highway was mostly clear, more people headed toward the ski towns east of Linwood than the larger city nestled in the mountains.

Michael taught the morning classes on Tuesdays, so I didn't have to be at the studio until after noon, but I couldn't stop glancing at the clock, wondering how this afternoon would go.

The playpen was ready for pickup at the front desk of the store, but I grabbed a cart and headed toward the baby aisle, my mind snagging on how I could make life easier on Stevie.

It had been over a decade since I had a baby, but some things never changed. If I were going to make my studio more accommodating to Stevie, and maybe other moms who needed it too, then I needed a changing table in the bathroom.

I slid the large box off the shelf and onto my cart, then grabbed a basket I could fill with diapers and wipes. A mixture of excitement and nostalgia got to me, and before I knew it, I had a cart full of baby necessities and toys. Everything was so cute and small, it was hard to say no.

I had a tiny pink coat that looked like a teddy bear in my cart and was already mentally planning joint family vacations to the beach. Jace could make sure her kids didn't die inside while we read romance novels on the porch with steaming cups of coffee we didn't have to reheat, and her husband... shit, I didn't even know her husband's name.

With a sigh, I put the coat back, reminding myself that I had known Stevie for approximately six minutes. This wasn't a friendship yet; it was barely a handshake, and she hadn't even agreed to come tonight.

No matter how excited I was at the prospect of a new friend in town, I had to reel it in. This was the equivalent of a first date—something I hadn't done in a long, *long* time.

My phone dinged in my pocket, and I opened it to a selfie of Beckett and Jace in front of the school, both of them giving the camera thumbs up with a broad smile. I grinned back at the screen, zooming in on Jace's face. His eyes were focused more on Beckett than the camera, but his whole face was alight with happiness. Tears gathered in the corners of my eyes as I looked at his big smile, something he hadn't done nearly enough lately.

With a sniff, I wiped at my eyes, then saved the photo before I could overthink it.

EMMY

Thank you

BECKETT

Practice after school at the rink tonight

EMMY

I have to miss tonight, but I'll ask Ty if he can take him for me

BECKETT

Hot date? Make sure you wear my hoodie.

I stood in the middle of the aisle, smiling like an idiot at my phone.

EMMY

That seems like a faux pas, right? Wearing another man's clothes?

BECKETT

Nah. Just sends the signal that you're not as available as he thought.

EMMY

Am I not available, Beckett?

BECKETT

You tell me, Peach.

And I can take Jace. I'll pick him up from school and get him to and from the rink.

The smile on my face disappeared, and I swallowed down the lump in my throat. This thing with Beckett seemed dangerous. My son was smiling like an idiot while staring at him lovingly, and I wasn't far behind him.

Maybe it was best if I kept my distance from my brother's best friend—we all knew this was temporary, and Beckett would be gone again soon enough.

Even if he planned to stay in Linwood to recover and help his mom, that didn't mean I had to see him regularly. I'd never spent much time talking to any of Jace's coaches before now, so that didn't matter either.

I could be aloof.

I could separate myself from this.

I could focus on finding friends like Stevie and not on the hot as hell man that was currently weaseling his way into my son's and my life. Hell, I could even lean on my brother like he kept begging me to if it meant avoiding Beckett.

EMMY

Don't worry about it. I'll ask Ty.

Nodding to myself, I pushed the cart toward the register and checked out with far more baby items than I probably needed.

I loaded it all into the trunk with a smile on my face, then headed back to Linwood, firing off a text to Shannon that I'd need help unloading when I got back into town. She sent back an emoji with an arched eyebrow, but I ignored her and cranked up the music, feeling good about today.

"Oh, my God," Shannon said as we stared at the open trunk full of baby items. "Did you buy the whole store?"

I scrunched my nose, then picked up the little dragon toy on top. "How was I supposed to say no to this, Shannon?"

Holding it in front of my face, I wiggled the toy's little arms until Shannon rolled her eyes and took it from me. "You're ridiculous."

"Aren't you the one taking all these classes to be a child therapist?"

"Speech therapist," Shannon clarified. "And yes, but this is a lot for a woman you don't even know is going to show up tonight."

"Positive thoughts." I tugged the large box with the changing table out of the car, then carried the awkward box into the studio. "If a man can build a baseball field in the middle of a corn field to coax ghosts of baseball players to join him, then maybe I can lure lonely moms into the studio with a playpen full of toys."

"You're talking in weird sports metaphors again," Shannon said. "I understood none of that."

"Yes, well, as the little sister to an NHL player and the ex-wife of a sportscaster, *Field of Dreams* was entry level knowledge required."

"Oh no, I've failed Sports 101. Someone revoke my woman card and replace it with a foam finger."

I huffed a laugh while readjusting my grip on the box, then pushed my way inside the studio. Michael's voice sounded above the hip-hop music, so I put the box up against the wall and went back to grab the rest of the items I'd bought.

"Next time you shop for kid's toys, tell me," Shannon said when I snapped the trunk closed. "There's a resale shop in Avon we can go to, and I can look for ones that are stimulating for little brains."

"Careful." I grinned at her, holding the door open. "That almost sounded like you care."

"About little developing minds? Yes. About you? We're not friends."

"Right, right. How could I forget?"

Class ended, and my patrons filtered out, each casting glances at all the baby items littered around the small entryway.

Michael leaned against the wall, staring at me with a raised brow. He wore a New York Sentinels hat over his black close-cropped coils. "What's all this?"

"Making the studio more accommodating to reach young moms who don't have childcare."

"We *also* don't have childcare," Shannon said, arms crossed as she stared at me. "Does your business insurance even cover this?"

"Yes, actually." I dragged the changing table box down the aisle between the reformers. "I checked on it last night to make sure I wasn't violating my policy, and we're all good."

"Except for the whole *who's going to watch the babies* part."

"I've got it covered." I dropped the box with a loud thump outside the bathroom. Luckily, it was large enough to accommodate the new piece of furniture, so I grabbed the toolbox from my office and sat down on the floor, ready to assemble it.

By *got it covered,* my plan was multi-faceted. Shannon was on the schedule until six tonight, and I was secretly counting on the fact that this tough as nails woman actually loved children. Like, had a hard time walking past a baby on the street without stopping and talking to them, never in a baby voice, always teaching. Stevie's little girl was adorable, and I had no doubt Shannon would crack the moment Stevie walked in the door with her. If all else failed, I was prepared to hold the baby myself for an hour.

Now I just had to hope Stevie actually showed up.

Between setting up the little play area in the studio and

teaching classes, the day flew by. Pink light filtered through the front windows as the sun set over the mountains, and I looked at my watch every ten seconds or so while I wrapped up my last class of the day.

"If you enjoyed today's class, I teach the same level at four on Thursdays, and it fills up fast, so make sure you're on the list!" I said to my class as they wiped down their equipment, then hurried to the front desk. "Any word from her?"

Shannon shook her head, casting a glance at me. "You going to be okay if she doesn't show up?"

"What?" I scoffed, trying to play off how disappointed I already was that we hadn't heard from Stevie at all. I'd told her to just show up but had been holding out hope that she'd call to confirm. "Yes. I'm fine. If she doesn't show up, I'll go watch Jace practice like I was planning to. But I'm staying positive. If a team of Jamaican track runners can make it to the Olympics for bobsledding, then I can make a new friend as an adult."

"I swear you live to annoy me."

I pointed a finger at her, barely containing my smile. "*Cool Runnings* is as classic as Shania Twain. I'll allow no Sanka slander."

Shannon held up her hands, then stepped away from the desk to go through closing activities for the night like she normally would.

I stood at the desk, flipping through my phone. Ty had picked up Jace like I asked, and my son's little tracking bubble showed he was at the rink like he was supposed to be. Even though I was dying for this to work out with Stevie, I was also curious to know how practice was going.

Ty had agreed to coach with Beckett like I knew he would. I might have fought harder against this idea if I didn't secretly think it would be great for Ty to pick his head up from all the responsibility he carried for literally everyone in town.

Yes, coaching was another huge responsibility, but Ty loved hockey in a way he did not love the hardware store or any of the multitude of things he signed up for. Retirement had been an adjustment for him, and I still felt like he was scrambling to fill his days so full he didn't allow himself time to miss it.

And besides, Ty loved my son. Adored him, even. I might have struck out for my kid on the whole, *sorry your dad is a piece of shit* thing, but at least I'd given him the best uncle to ever exist.

I fiddled with the sound system until soft piano music played over the speakers, something that would be relaxing for both Stevie and her little girl. A wave of nostalgia hit me as the soft tunes played, and I picked up my phone, looking back at the picture of Jace from this morning.

When I went to zoom in on his happy face again, my thumb slipped, and suddenly I was staring at Beckett up close instead.

God, he was stunning.

That scruffy-but-suspiciously-well-groomed beard framed a jaw so sharp it could probably cut through my better judgment. And those bright, impossible blue eyes holding a hint of mischief had me so flustered I let out a tiny moan.

"You okay?" Shannon stuck her head out from behind the partition.

I scrambled to minimize the picture, clicked the wrong button, and somehow opened my own camera instead. So now I stared at an unflattering version of my panicked front-camera face while still thinking about his stupidly perfect one. "Yep. I'm good."

Shannon's brow scrunched, then movement on the street caught her attention, and I followed her gaze to the front door. Stevie stood outside, carrying a red-faced baby girl and a worn-out expression.

I hurried out from behind the desk to get the door for her, my smile big enough to blind a NASA satellite and maybe distract from the fact that I'd nearly cried over a man's jawline ten seconds ago.

"Hi!" I chirped, my voice two octaves too high.

"Hey," I tried again, this time channeling my bored teenage son mid-eyeroll, then cringed.

"I'm so glad you made it!" Third time was the charm, and this time I sounded only *slightly* like a Pomeranian who might pee on your foot at any moment.

Stevie rocked back and forth, staring at her daughter who had stopped crying long enough to give me the stank eye, as if she remembered I was the one who'd thrown coffee on her.

Harper had deep brown eyes and blonde hair peeking out from under a tiny beanie. She had little snow boots on over what looked like a fleece one-piece pajama set with snowmen on it.

"I almost didn't come," Stevie said. "Teething is killing us this week, and Harper is on one today. She wouldn't even let me get her dressed."

A soft squeak sounded from behind me, and I turned to see Shannon standing behind the partition with a hand over her mouth. "That is the cutest fucking baby I've ever seen."

Stevie laughed, and I turned back to her. "So, that's Shannon. She's in school to be a speech pathologist and great with kids, if Harper doesn't have stranger danger."

"It's fine," Shannon said with a sniff that didn't cancel out her previous reaction at all. "I'm patient. She doesn't have to like me."

As if Harper carried a little bullshit detector, she wiggled out of her mom's arms and toddled over to Shannon, looking straight up. Her hat slipped off her head and fell on the floor behind her. Shannon let out a giggle that did not fit with the Goth vibe she wore like a suit of armor. I bit the insides of my cheeks as Shannon squatted down in front of Harper with a wave.

"Hi Harper, my name is Shannon." She pulled the little dragon toy out from behind her back, shaking it gently until Harper looked at the toy. "Would you like to see what other toys I have?"

Harper looked over her shoulder at her mom, then followed Shannon into the studio toward the playpen in the back.

"Holy shit," Stevie said, peeking around the corner of the partition wall into the dimly lit studio. Shannon held the gate open to the playpen, and Harper sat down on her bottom, trying to pull off her little boots.

"What a smart girl." Shannon squatted down to help Harper take off her shoes, then took off her own. "We take off our shoes when we go inside, don't we?"

Harper said nothing, but Shannon kept talking as if Harper was responding, never babying her, but also speaking in short enough words to show me she'd be absolutely fabulous as a speech pathologist when she finished her degree.

"She just—" Stevie looked back at me with wide eyes. "Harper hates everyone."

"Yes, well, kindred spirits, I guess. So does Shannon."

Stevie chuckled, then let out a sigh a sigh. "Maybe I

should be slightly more alarmed that my toddler was so willing to leave me for a complete stranger, but also, she hasn't let go of me in days. So, thank you for this. I'm already happier than I've been all week."

I shrugged my shoulders, trying to tamp down the excitement bubbling up in me. "Well, welcome to Elevation Pilates." I nudged her shoulder, then clapped my hands in quick succession, unable to contain my excitement. "I'm so glad you're here."

Stevie nodded, then returned my smile. "Me too. Although, I have to warn you, I haven't exercised regularly since I had my second kid. Who is five."

"That's okay." I led her back into the studio, gesturing to the reformer closest to Harper, then the one farthest away. "You tell me where works best for you."

Stevie glanced over at her child happily clapping along to a song Shannon sang, then pointed at the reformer farthest away. "Out of sight, out of mind, maybe."

I bent down to adjust it for her, pointing out the basics of the machine. Stevie took off her jacket, listening intently, casting glances up at her daughter every few minutes. "You ready to try it?"

Stevie opened her mouth to answer, and the cutest belly laugh sounded from the back of the room. Shannon laughed in return, and Stevie grinned at me. I swear some unhealed part of my own motherhood journey stitched itself closed at the sight, my chest squeezing. I was so happy to offer even this tiny slice of peace to a mom in need.

"Let's do it."

I smiled, then helped Stevie get in position lying flat on her back on the reformer, feet on the bar. "Close your eyes and focus on your breathing for a minute, and I'll go grab my phone. I wrote out a list of exercises that are great for post-partum moms, no matter how long you've been post-partum."

She yawned and gave me a thumbs up, so I headed for the front desk.

My phone still sat face-up, and I grabbed it, glancing down at several excited texts from Jace. Seemed like we were both having a good day.

"Alright." I tapped the little heart emoji on Jace's text, then went back toward Stevie's reformer. "First, we'll start with some warmups. Put your heels together, toes about three inches apart, and slowly push away from the bar until your legs are straight."

When no movement came from my peripheral vision, I looked up at Stevie only to find her passed out asleep, mouth slightly ajar and a soft snore filtering through the room.

I bit the insides of my cheeks to contain my laugh, then glanced back at Shannon and Harper playing contentedly at the back of the room.

When I'd imagined this class, I wanted to create a "take what you need" vibe, and apparently what Stevie needed was a nap.

Tip-toeing away from her reformer, I left Stevie to sleep and went back to the front desk to retrieve my laptop. She was still asleep when I came back into the studio, so I sat on the reformer next to her and began answering emails I was behind on.

Most were bills I quickly paid, only slightly sweating over the balance in my business checking account. Things were going well, but I still had about $16,000 in start-up costs to pay off in addition to my regular operating costs, and the last thing I wanted to do was ask Ty for another loan.

Avoiding the rest of the bills for today, an email from my former boss caught my attention, and I clicked on it.

Subject: PT Check-Ins – Linwood Athlete

Hey Emmy,

Hope you're doing well. I heard you've got your studio up and running in Linwood—congrats!

Quick question: I got a call from an old contact about an athlete currently staying near you during his recovery, and the Denver Yeti would like someone to do daily PT progress checks while he's there. Nothing too intensive—just eyes on mobility, pain management, and adherence to the plan they lay out for him.

Would you be interested in taking that on? They're offering $1,750 a week, but I think you can ask for even more, and they'll say yes. Seems like a desperate situation. This athlete is insisting he won't go back to Denver until he can practice with the team, so you'd be looking at eight weeks, at least.

Let me know your thoughts, and I can send you the details.

Best,
Jordan Riviera, DPT

I brushed a hand over my face, reading the email again, then again. There was no doubt in my mind Jordan meant Beckett, unless some other Denver Yeti player was insisting on recovering in teeny, little Linwood, Colorado.

"*Fourteen thousand dollars,*" I whispered, and Shannon

lifted her head to look at me with a quizzical look. I waved her off, then looked up at Stevie, still sleeping peacefully, and back at my computer.

My finger hovered over the reply button, unease eating me alive. Avoiding Beckett would be a lot harder if he wasn't only coaching my son's hockey team but also required to check in with me daily for his PT progress.

I hit the button, still not sure how I was planning to answer. Professional? Friendly? Emotionally dead inside? Because there was no version of this where I'd survive watching Beckett do slow, controlled hip work every morning while I pretended to take notes instead of experiencing a full-body spiritual crisis.

Labral tear rehab was basically just a 10-week thirst trap, and I was one deep breath away from prescribing ice and celibacy.

Yeah. Totally fine. Definitely qualified for this. Very above it all. Probably.

Subject: RE: PT Check-Ins – Linwood Athlete

Hey Jordan,
Great to hear from you, and thanks!
See if they'll up their price to $2,000 a week, and I'm in.

Sincerely,
Emmy Hudson Meyers
Elevation Pilates

My computer made a little *whoosh* sound as my email was flung into the virtual ether, and a high-pitched delighted squeal sounded from the back of the room.

Stevie jerked upright like she'd been electrocuted, her hand over her chest. "Oh, my God. I fell asleep. *I'm so sorry.*"

I grinned, then put my computer to the side. "The way I see it, you just tapped into that deep breathing like I told you to. So, job well done."

Stevie chuckled, then covered her face with both hands. "This is so embarrassing. We were supposed to be on a first friend date, and I *fell asleep.*" Her hands dropped and her eyes went wide. "Shit, I just said we're on a date out loud, didn't I?"

I snorted and walked around her reformer to sit on the mat beside her, curling my legs under me like we were at a sixth-grade sleepover. "If it makes you feel better, that's how I've been thinking of it in my head too. I even considered bringing matching friendship bracelets but figured I should play it cool."

"That actually does make me feel better." Stevie laughed, then looked toward the playpen, where her daughter and Shannon were having what could only be described as a tiny rave—butts were shaking, hands in the air, while knees bounced to a beat of a song about bananas.

"Don't tell my husband, but this might be the best first date I've ever been on."

I dropped my chin to my chest, trying not to grin like a lunatic. "Your secret's safe with me. But fair warning—I'm the clingy type. You fall asleep on me once and I'm already giving us a couple's name. Stemmy has a nice ring to it, don't you think? Or maybe Evie?"

Stevie's hands shot up, her face lit up with excitement. "How about the Moms of Mayhem instead?"

A little gasp came out of my mouth, and I bounced on my knees. "Yes. That. Should we make shirts?"

"Absolutely, we should."

"Consider it done." I stuck my hand out, ready to shake, and Stevie slapped her palm in mine. "Welcome to the club."

14

BECKETT

On Tuesday afternoon, I went straight from Dr. Carter's office to my mom's rehab center, just down the street. The front desk clerk waved me through after checking my ID, and I walked slowly down the hall toward the room she'd been assigned. Moving without crutches felt a little awkward, but the hip brace still restricted my range of motion—as long as I didn't do anything stupid, I would be okay. Or so I kept telling myself.

Mom's door was propped open, the low sound of a soap opera drifting out into the hall.

"Knock, knock." I rapped on her doorframe.

She sat in a recliner on the other side of the room, her casted arm in a sling. The bruising on her cheek had turned green, but her smile was as bright as it always was. "Well, look what the cat dragged in."

She patted the armrest of the sofa next to her, and I walked into the room, taking in the very basic surroundings. Her room here in the rehab center wasn't quite as clinical as the hospital, but it still bore the unmistakable stamp of impermanence.

The walls were soft, muted beige, going for homey but not quite there. A framed print of a watercolor landscape hung slightly crooked above the dresser, and a vase of artificial daisies sat on the windowsill. The bed was neatly made with a pale blue quilt tucked tight, and someone had folded a cheerful pink blanket at the foot of it.

A tray table sat beside her chair, half-covered in the Sudoku books I'd brought from home, a plastic cup with a straw, and a small bag of peppermints she always kept in her purse.

Not home but trying.

I sat down on the couch, stretching out my leg, not thinking about the pain after being poked and prodded all morning.

My mom didn't miss a beat, pointing a trembling hand toward my leg. "No crutches. That's good. How are you doing?"

I raised a brow, then pointed back at the bruise still covering most of her cheek. "How are *you* doing?"

She waved me off, then put her hand back in her lap, turning her attention to the TV. "Don't you worry about me. I'll be out of here in no time."

"Then you don't worry about me either."

She *tsk*ed, but I saw the smile on her face. "You may be old, but I am still your mother. I'll worry about you until I'm six feet under—and maybe even after that if I get bored."

I sighed; she sounded an awful lot like another mom I couldn't quite escape.

"That was a loaded sound." My mom reached across her

side table to the TV remote and muted it, then turned toward me with that knowing look. "Want to talk about it?"

"*It?*"

She shrugged, then her brow pulled together as if the small movement had caused her pain. "Whatever it is that makes you look like you'd be running your fastest mile away from here if it weren't for your bum leg and my bum face."

I scrubbed a hand across my face, then scratched at my jaw. Even though my mom was never one to judge, I didn't think it was a good idea to repeat Emmy's and my conversation last night, then finding out today I'd be reporting to her daily for PT updates. That is, if she agreed to the team's plans. If she didn't, I was extra screwed.

"Is it about Emmy and her boy?"

I dropped my hand, giving her a flat look. "How do you always do that?" I waved in her general direction, and my mom grinned. "Know things."

"I know my sons." Mom took a slow sip of her water. Her blue eyes sparkled, like my life was as juicy as the trash TV she loved to watch. "And Emmy has always been a pretty girl. You mentioned her boy, so it was only a matter of time you ran into her. You'd be blind not to see that Emmy has grown into quite the woman, and an even better mother than I am."

"Well, I don't know if I'd go *that* far. You're pretty great."

She waved me off. "We're beyond flattery, and you were a little shit. Still are."

I laughed, dropping my head to the wall behind me. "The team okayed me staying in town for rehab."

"Is that what you want?" Mom asked, and I rotated my head to look at her. The mischief in her gaze was gone, replaced with a melancholy I hated seeing there. "You have a whole life I'm keeping you from, and I don't want that."

I lifted my head up, adjusting my hip until I could sit on the edge of the couch. "This is what I want. We can beat around the bush and pretend like they didn't tell me you have Parkinson's and won't be getting better, or we can do our best to fix the rift that's formed in our family since Mason and I left you to chase our dreams."

Mom scoffed. "Listen to me and listen good." Her hand reached across to lay over my arm, and the trembling was more obvious. "I am your mother. Chasing your dreams is *exactly* what I want you to do."

She tightened her grip on my arm, and I put my hand over hers, squeezing back.

"Don't just chase them," she said. "*Catch* them. Grab them by the reins and hang on until a new dream comes along that's even bigger and better than the last one. Then, and only then, do I want you to let go. Don't let me get in the way of that."

I dipped my chin, my face tingling with emotions I tried and failed to keep at bay. "I don't want to lose you."

"Well, I'm still here, aren't I?" She patted my arm, then let go. "And so are you."

"I want to stay." This time the words sounded surer than they had any time I'd said them before. "I want to be here with you and rehab this shit together."

"Language."

"I'm 37 years old."

"And I'm your fucking mother, so watch your mouth."

I chuckled, then stood up and put my hands in my pockets. "While I'm here, I want to fix things with Ty. Being back has made me realize what a mistake letting that friendship drift away was."

My mom nodded, a bright smile on her face. "Ty is such a good boy. You really did win the lottery with that one."

"I know I did, so it's time I make sure he knows it too. Retirement is hard on all of us—walking away from a sport that becomes our whole personality is never easy. I can be here for him during this."

"Good." Mom's eyes crinkled at the corners when she smiled. "So, what's your plan other than wooing his sister?"

I snorted, then shook my head. "I'm not *wooing* Emmy. And dating my best friend's sister hardly seems like a way to support a friend."

"You should absolutely woo his sister. And sure, it is. Ty wants her taken care of, so you do it. You show him that you can be that type of man, set that example for Jace. The boy I raised knows how to do it, even if you've never met a woman worth trying for before."

"Mom." I held out a hand in an attempt to stop this conversation from hemorrhaging. "It's not like that. The team has mandated I work with her for PT check-ins once a day. And I may be coaching her son."

She grinned, her smile turning slightly diabolical. "Oh, perfect. Make it so she can't avoid you even if she tried. I love it."

"I think you're getting the wrong idea," I said, attempting to pull her back down to earth. "I can't be interested in her. Hell, she told me we can't even flirt."

My mom's white eyebrows shot up. "And how did that conversation come about, Beckett?"

I blew out a breath, staring at the crooked watercolor instead of her. "You're not going to let this go, are you?"

My mom clasped her hands together in front of her face as much as the sling and cast would allow. "It would make your dying mother so happy to see you happy."

"I thought you weren't dying?"

"Aren't we all?" My mother shrugged, and I couldn't help but chuckle. "I'm not saying you have to marry the girl, but she and that boy of hers deserve a slice of happiness, and so do you, my son. Be the bright spot in their lives."

I exhaled deeply, turning back to my mom. "Alright, well, when Emmy is kicking both our asses in Pilates, we'll see if you change your tune."

"You're taking Pilates?" A soft laugh emanated from my mom, and I shook my head. "That should be fun to watch. I'll have to call the knitting group so we can all go with you."

"Yes, because a group of women in their early seventies watching me do sun salutations is every man's idea of a good time."

My mom laughed harder. "Beckett, have you ever done Pilates before?"

"No?" It came out more of a question than I'd anticipated, but my mom's reaction caught me off-guard. "How hard can it be, though? I get paid millions of dollars to play sports professionally."

This time, her laugh turned into a full belly laugh until she was gripping her side. "Don't go without me. I need to watch this."

A rap on the door sounded, and I turned to see the therapist come in the room. "I'll let you go, you mean woman. See you tomorrow?"

My mom waved, then blew me a kiss. "Woo her, darling. Do it for me."

I pinched the bridge of my nose, then walked back out

into the hallway and to my truck. I wasn't sure about the *wooing* thing, but my mom wasn't far off the mark with her evaluation of Emmy. Everything I'd seen so far from her pointed not just to her being a good mom, but a *great* one.

And fuck, she was beautiful. Not in some polished, high-maintenance way, but in the kind of way that snuck up on you and settled under your skin. And those sharp hazel eyes were always watching, like she saw more than you were saying out loud.

Then there were the freckles on the bridge of her nose. Just a few. Barely there, even. But every time I was close enough to see them, I had to stop myself from staring. Like they gave her away somehow—told a quieter truth about a vulnerable woman behind all that fire.

Yeah. She was something else.

And I was in trouble.

It was a good thing Emmy had insisted on not letting me pick up Jace from school today since I was cutting it close making it from the rehab center to the rink. I pulled in just as Ty and Jace were getting out of his truck, Rowdy on their heels.

The sun was setting behind the mountains, and I stared up at the dilapidated building.

"It's falling apart," I said to Ty as we walked side by side into the rink.

It didn't escape my notice that Ty had slowed his strides to match mine, Jace practically running into the building in front of us even with the weight of his equipment bag slowing him down.

Ty hummed, squinting up at the dirty brick walls. "I've

tried talking to Tate about a donation to help get it fixed up, but maybe that's the wrong tactic."

I put my hands in my pockets, turning slightly toward him. "What else do you have in mind? Fundraisers?"

"Maybe." Ty looked away from the building and toward the statue of the two of us and my little brother with Coach. "I think I'll ask her if I can have ad placement too, not that I need any advertisements when we're the only hardware store in a 30-mile radius. Or maybe we can talk to Mason, and the three of us honor Coach by becoming investors in his dream."

I nodded, imagining his smile at the idea. "He would have liked that."

"Yeah." A hint of a smile hid under Ty's bushy mustache. "He'd be thrilled to see you back here on the bench too. You always were a bossy fucker."

I scoffed, then walked into the building. "Too bad you never listened to a word I had to say."

"Someone had to put you in your place."

"Your whole family seems pretty great at that. Speaking of." My mom's words haunted me as I stopped, and Ty turned to toward me, any hint of a smile long gone. This was probably a really stupid fucking idea, but the words slipped out of my mouth before I could stop them. "Is Emmy dating anyone?"

Ty's nostrils flared, then he adjusted the Mayhem hat on his head, lifting it and bringing it back down again. "Why, Conway?"

I shrugged, playing it off. "Nothing. She just said she was busy tonight, so I was curious."

"She took on another Pilates class tonight, I think."

"Oh." Well, that made sense considering it was her *job*.

Me and my one-track mind had jumped straight to conclusions there.

"I don't like that *Oh*. Or the look on your face right now, like you'd been contemplating rearranging someone's face."

I smirked. "I wasn't going to rearrange anything. It was just a little flicker of irrational jealousy in a brotherly sort of way. It passed."

Ty narrowed his eyes. "You sure? Because I'd never refer to my sister dating anyone as *jealousy.*"

"Relax. I'm not pursuing it."

Ty crossed his arms, leaning against the hallway that led to the locker rooms. "Good. Because if you so much as hurt a hair on her head, I'm legally obligated as her brother to set your truck on fire."

A laugh ripped out my throat, and Ty's mustache twitched again. "Jesus, man. It's not that serious."

He pushed off the wall but stopped just outside the locker room doors. "It is exactly that serious. Emmy's not a weekend kind of girl, Beckett. And she has Jace to consider, too. You know that."

I rubbed the back of my neck, suddenly feeling 12 again and on the receiving end of a lecture from Coach. "I know."

His dark eyebrows rose until they were hiding beneath the brim of his hat. "You sure you know?"

I met his eyes, then nodded. "Yeah. I'm not going to screw it up, especially now that we're probably working together on my PT too. But damn, the way she pushes my buttons."

Ty sighed, loud and theatrical, then slapped a hand against my shoulder. "Well, hell. If you're going to fall, at least try not to face plant in the process."

"No promises." I chuckled, then waved down at my hip brace. "Bum hip and all."

"In all seriousness, brother, be careful. She's tough as hell, but if you're going to make me choose sides, I'm choosing her every time."

I swallowed, then met his gaze. "Got it, loud and clear."

With a quick jerk of his head, he went into the locker room. "Good."

Emmy

By the time Stevie and Harper had left, Shannon was on cloud nine, and I was right there with her.

"It went so well, don't you think?" I clasped my hands in front of my chest, a huge smile on my face as Stevie backed her minivan out into traffic.

"She slept through the entire class," Shannon said, a hint of laughter in her voice. "You have weird standards."

I dropped my hands down at my sides, turning away from the window. "You can't rain on my parade today. She's coming back next Tuesday."

"For naptime, sure."

I chuckled, then went behind the desk, finishing out the last of the closing tasks for the night. "Are you going to stand there and tell me you don't want her to bring Harper back for another hour?"

"I mean, I'm a bitch, not a liar."

The drawer snapped closed as I pulled my purse out, shaking my head. "So, I'll keep you on the schedule for next Tuesday night, then."

Shannon pulled on her black puffer jacket, then tugged a burgundy beanie down over her brow, her long black hair hanging down beneath it in a chic way I could never figure out. "Absolutely, you will. Harper and I are best friends now."

I flicked off the lights, grabbing my coat too. "I'm going to choose not to be insulted that *we're* not friends, but a toddler who can't talk *is* your friend."

We walked outside together, the evening air carrying a bite to it despite the sunny day we'd had. Shannon shoved her hands in her coat, then turned to me with a hint of a smile. "She's way cuter than you, and I get little kids. Life is simple, in the best way." She shrugged. "Sometimes you're pissed because your sock is turned wrong, and that's worth being pissed over. She doesn't know yet that society is going to tamp her down until she's just a remnant of who she once was, and throwing a fit over a sock is frowned upon."

"Geez, Shannon." I locked the door, then turned back to her with a shiver, my coat still slung over my arm. "You're just a ray of pitch black."

She smiled, the dimples on both of her cheeks popping outright, making her look every day of the ten years younger than me she was. "Someone needs to balance out your sunshine."

"Right, because that's what friends are for," I called as she moved toward her car down the street.

She turned, walking backward as her little car's front headlights blinked when she unlocked it. "Except we're not friends."

I pointed a finger at my nose, then at her. Shannon shook her head, then climbed in her car. I waited until the engine turned over, always worried about how her old hatchback would handle the cold weather and snow up here. She seemed more worried about getting through college with as little debt as possible, so a better, more appropriate car was not on her list of concerns. I couldn't help the motherly instincts that kicked in as I watched her pull out onto the road, back tires slipping before catching and propelling her forward.

Once she was gone, I climbed into Ty's SUV, enveloped in warmth and luxury I couldn't help but soak in. With a quick glance at Jace's location, I headed to the rink, hoping I could catch the last of the practice.

The parking lot wasn't nearly as full tonight, so I found a spot quickly, then grabbed Beckett's hoodie off the front seat where it had sat all day, reminding me to return it.

Not until I got inside the building and it wasn't any warmer than outside did I realize that once again, I'd forgotten my coat in the car. I waved to Tate as I walked down the hallway toward the rink, spotting Beckett on the bench across the ice. He stood with his arms braced on the boards, and I saw the wince as he shifted feet, taking the pressure off his hip.

A shiver raced down my spine as my breath fogged in front of me, and I slipped on Beckett's hoodie for an extra layer. Like his gaze was magnetized to the movement, I *knew* his eyes would be trained on me when I settled the hood over my head. I looked across the rink, and just as I predicted, that blue gaze was staring right back, one eyebrow hitched high on his face.

"Ty." He still looked at me as he called to my brother out on the ice with the players. "What's the goalie's name?"

"Miles?" the kid in question answered, pointing at his

chest where he stood between the posts with his helmet up on the top of his head. "Miles Claussen. You mean me?"

"Yes, you." Beckett's attention broke from mine, but not before a wash of heat went through me at the memory of last night. "How many fingers am I holding up, Pickles?"

Beckett held four fingers in the air, and Miles looked from the players back to Beckett. "Uh."

"Pickles!" another kid yelled. "Hell yeah, fuck yeah. That's great."

"Language," Ty and Beckett said at the same time, and I bit the inside of my cheeks to keep in my laugh.

Ty slowly skated closer to the kid who stood in front of far too many pucks in the net. My brother slid off his glove, holding up the same four fingers as Beckett. "How many fingers, kid?"

I walked across the bleachers and took my seat, watching this whole thing play out.

"You see it too?" Beckett said to Ty, and my brother nodded in answer.

"Would make so much sense. His reflexes are great, just his timing is shit."

"I can hear you," Miles said, looking up at the stands, but I was the only parent here tonight. "And didn't you say we weren't allowed to swear?"

"Answer the question." Beckett leaned forward until his elbows were propped on the boards and his back was flat, trying to relieve pressure on his hip.

"Son of a," I muttered to myself, then stood up and cupped my hands over my mouth. "SIT DOWN, CONWAY."

Every head snapped my way, and Ty bent at the waist, his chest shaking with a laugh. Beckett stared at me, his eyes amused and his lips tipped up in a smirk. Slowly, he lowered his ass to the bench, sitting down before looking back at the players on the ice.

"When was the last time you had your vision checked, kid?" Ty asked, and Beckett crossed his arms over his chest.

"Couple years ago?" Miles answered, his inflection going up on the end. "I have glasses, they just fog up out here when my body temperature's elevated, and then I can't see."

"You mean you're hot?" Jace said, and several kids on the team chuckled until Ty waved his hand to quiet them down.

Beckett hung his head, and his chest heaved with a sigh. "Ty, are there any eye doctors in town?"

Ty shook his head, then scooped up another puck, passing it to the players all forming a line to his left and right. "I'm on it."

I leaned my elbows back on the row of bleachers behind me, a slow smile taking over my face as I watched the two boys I'd spent my whole life with turn into men right before my eyes.

One by one, Beckett called out weaknesses with each kid on the team, highlighting not only what he saw they were doing wrong, but minor tweaks they could help each kid improve. And each time, he gave them more and more ridiculous nicknames, including Jace's very own *Juice.*

In the 30 minutes of practice I got to watch, the improvement in the Mayhem players was shocking to see.

Now that I was watching for it, I didn't know why no one noticed Miles' vision problem sooner. He was always in the right spot, doing everything he was supposed to. But every time the puck flew at him, there was this tiny delay, and it was just enough for it to slip past.

Miles wasn't falling short because of effort or attitude—

he was trying harder than anyone out there. He just quite literally couldn't see the full picture.

My phone buzzed in my pocket, and I looked down to see an email from Jordan, with one word on it.

Subject: PT Check-Ins – Linwood Athlete

Done

Jordan Riviera, DPT

I twisted my hands in my lap, a riot of emotions flooding me. Taking Beckett on as a client was a smart move. Eight weeks with him and the mountain of debt that had been sitting on my chest like a brick would be gone. It meant forward motion, instead of just treading water.

But it also meant Beckett. Up close. Hands-on. Every single day. And that was complicated.

I was already too aware of him. Of the way he moved, the way he watched people when he didn't think anyone was watching him. The way his voice dropped when he told me to touch myself and think of him.

There was no professional distance when my pulse kicked up every time the man so much as looked in my direction. Any walls I'd normally have against a man like him were gone because, deep down, I *knew* Beckett, or at least who he once was.

And the man sitting across the ice, coaching my kid through speed drills, was exactly who I remembered. Always wanting the best for everyone and determined to push them until they achieved it.

This wasn't a crush. It was a full-blown problem, and I was signing up for a front-row seat.

Soon enough, practice was over, and Tate lifted the garage door that housed the equipment to clean off the rink for the next team. Our kids had done this enough times, they knew the drill. One by one, they grabbed sleds and shovels, circling the ice in a pattern to get it cleared.

Ty stood in the center of the rink, directing them, and Beckett left the bench. I stood up, his hoodie hanging down to just above my knees and my hands lost to the sleeves, making my way toward him.

"Cute hoodie," he said as I stopped in front of him.

"Cute limp." I gestured toward his leg he wasn't standing on, and the lack of crutches in the vicinity. "Didn't think you were this stupid."

Beckett grinned, then shook his head. "Cleared today. Did you hear the news?"

"That you're mine for the next eight weeks?"

The grin on his face morphed into something different, and he licked his lips, eyes moving slowly down over my body still covered in his hoodie. "Just say the word."

I rolled my eyes and pushed his chest, but that was a mistake. He was warmer than he had any business being, and his body was as rock solid as I should have expected. With a quick move, I yanked my hand away, but not before Beckett's eyes snapped back to mine, playfulness mixing with pure lust.

"Can't wait to hear what you have to say about my pelvic thrusts," Beckett said, then walked down the hallway away from me, trying his hardest not to limp. "See you Thursday."

A weird stutter-laugh left me, and I pulled my hands inside my sleeves, only now realizing I'd forgotten to return his hoodie.

Eight weeks of Beckett being cocky and hot and entirely too close might just kill me.

I was so screwed.

Wednesday went by in a blur, and I signed the contract with the Yeti to oversee Beckett's rehab. Frankie, the team's head trainer, had sent over a long list of exercises and things he wanted me to watch for. I was impressed with how thorough his list was, even if he insisted on far more clamshells than I thought necessary. Maybe it was a hockey thing.

To my surprise, a deposit of $8,000 hit my bank account Thursday morning, the day we were set to begin working together. I'd texted him the night before asking him to come to the studio for a check-in before my Core Connection class, which was the slowest, easiest class at Elevation Pilates. If all went well, then he could stay for class and try a modified version of it.

Beckett had picked up Jace to skate before school the last two mornings, and they practiced together with my brother last night at the rink. Despite the way he'd so quickly woven himself into my life, I'd done my best to avoid him yesterday.

Did that make me a chicken shit? Absolutely. But I didn't know how else to survive this growing attraction to Beckett other than avoid him like I avoid folding laundry—I knew it was there and it stressed me out, so I pretended it didn't exist.

Like the laundry, I knew it would get to a point when it

couldn't be avoided any longer, and the balance of my bank account staring back at me was a reminder that today was the day.

I paced the back of the studio, bouncing lightly on my feet as I checked the clock for the thousandth time this morning. I tugged the hem of my shirt down, then up again, then smoothed it flat like it was personally responsible for my emotional stability. The front door opened and closed, and I looked up at the entrance, finding Shannon staring back at me in surprise.

"You're early." She peeled off her coat and hung it on the hooks beneath the neon Elevation Pilates sign. "Did I know you were opening this morning?"

"New routine."

I pulled at the sleeves of my plum tee, hooked my fingers through the thumb holes, then immediately pulled them out again to rub my palms down the front of my leggings. This shirt was form-fitting across my chest, stopping just above the waistband of my matching leggings. I had on white grip socks that came just above my ankle bones, then black slides I could ditch if I needed to demonstrate something to my class.

"How was your night?"

"Fine?" Shannon studied me, then wiggled the computer mouse to wake up our system. "I hate even asking this, because it'll seem like I care, but are you good? You seem weird."

I stopped fidgeting, ready to dismiss her comment when movement outside caught my attention. Beckett walked down the sidewalk toward the studio in black shorts despite the snow on the ground, a hoodie that looked a lot like the one hanging on my bathroom door, and a backward hat over his brown shaggy hair. He was a little scruffier this morning, like maybe he'd woken up late and hadn't had time to clean up his beard. Which was interesting, since he was right on time to pick up my kid before the sun was up.

Realizing my mouth hung slightly open, I snapped it shut and straightened my spine.

Shannon looked from me to Beckett and back, her eyes squinting. "You didn't."

"I did nothing." I cut my hand through the air. "Well, I agreed to oversee his PT progress, and I think they want him to take some classes here. But that's all I did."

She sighed long and deep, then began fiddling with her phone as the front door opened and Beckett walked inside. The moment our eyes met, I felt transparent, like he could see exactly why I'd been avoiding him.

"You made it," I stated the obvious, and Beckett smirked. My knees damn near buckled at the sight, taken aback by just how stunning this man was. Remembering what I was supposed to do, I shoved a tablet into Beckett's chest with more force than I intended. His smile faded as he looked down at the screen. "Questionnaire. Pain points, progress, all the things the team wants me to be tracking."

"Got it." Beckett took it from my hands. His attention flicked up to me, then around the studio. "Nice place."

"Thanks!" My voice was doing that whole wrong-octave thing again, and I glanced over my shoulder at Shannon before introducing her.

Beckett held out a hand to shake, and Shannon just stared at it, squinty-eyed. "Oh, I remember you."

He looked at me questioningly, then finally dropped his hand. I let out a weird laugh, trying to dissolve the tension, and both Shannon and Beckett looked at me. "Sorry." I jabbed a thumb over my shoulder into the studio. "I'll just be in here. Come on back when you're done with that form and bring the tablet with you. Shannon, get music going for me please?"

Shannon watched me scurry away, her gaze about as pointed as they came, and I hurried into the dim-lit room, needing a minute to breathe before I had no way to escape everything that was Beckett Conway.

16

BECKETT

Emmy practically jogged out of the entryway of her studio and behind the partition wall out of sight, and I was left standing there with the tablet and a scowling Shannon.

I sat on the bench just inside the front door, looking down at the form full of questions about my pain levels, where things hurt, and other general health questions. Little sounds of disapproval came from behind the desk until I finally looked up at the grumpy receptionist.

"Do we know each other?" My brows raised in question. Linwood was a small town, so the chances I knew her were pretty high, but she also looked a lot younger than me, so my mind was blank.

She scoffed, then shook her head. "Figures."

I frowned, thinking harder about everyone I'd known my whole life, trying to decipher what that even meant. "I apologize, it's been a long time since I spent any time in Linwood, and I've taken more than a few shots to the head since then."

It was meant to be a self-deprecating joke, but Shannon just squinted harder. "Shannon Wilder."

"Wilder." I pursed my lips, thinking of the only Wilder family I'd known in Linwood, then my eyes expanded in shock. "Oh, shit. Ray Wilder's Shannon. The Wilder twins' little sister?"

Shannon crossed her arms over her chest, and suddenly I could see it. The dyed black hair was different from the tee-head blonde little girl I remembered from my childhood. She was all sharp angles and had the kind of pale skin that looked like it actively rejected sunlight.

Aside from the hair, she was the spitting image of her father, Ray. The man who'd done time for vehicular manslaughter after driving drunk with my dad in the passenger seat after they'd gone on a bender together.

As much as that day had changed my life forever, it had hers, too. Cash and Colton had been promising defensemen on the Mayhem before our world came crashing down around us in a flash of red and blue lights, but they had gone the way of our fathers in their absence.

"It's been a long, long time," I said, not sure how to come back from this awkwardness. The last time I'd seen her had been at my dad's funeral, 21 years ago. She wasn't her father, just like I wasn't mine, but hell. "You good?"

Shannon held her hands out to the side, indicating the space around her. Her grey eyes were clear, no sign of using like her brothers and dad, which I was glad to see. "Grand."

"How's your dad?" I asked, even though that felt weird to say aloud.

She raised her brows, then let out a little laugh. "Alive, so I guess better than yours. If you're asking if he's still in jail, then no. He's back home, and the same as ever."

I sighed, then tapped the tablet, finishing my questionnaire. "I'm sorry to hear that."

She hummed, and I pushed my hands into the seat to help myself stand. I winced only slightly as I pointed at the studio, ready to get the hell away from this uncomfortable trip down memory lane. "Good to see you again."

Shannon shook her head, then glanced down at her phone, fiddling with something on the screen.

After 21 years of playing semi- or professional hockey, I'd been in a lot of gyms all around the country. Heck, I'd even seen a Pilates reformer before, but this was my first time in a true studio.

Twelve reformers were arranged in two neat rows with a wide aisle between them. Each one had a mat next to it on the floor with a basket of accoutrements that all looked very girly. Not a single weight bench was in sight, no machines; nothing except for the strange reformers that looked a lot like a medieval stretching table.

"Back here." Emmy peeked her head out from a private room in the back. I followed her with careful steps, minding not to bump my hip on any of the equipment.

She stood in a brighter room with overhead lights, and a simple table, just like Frankie's, sat in the middle. She patted it, and I sat down and laid back, knowing the drill.

Her back was to me, fiddling with something on a small table, and I took the opportunity to study her. Her purple top hugged her in a way that made it impossible not to look —fitted across her toned shoulders and down the curve of her waist, stopping just above the waistband of her matching leggings. Her white socks peeked above her slides, grounding her in this everyday moment that still somehow knocked the breath out of me. She didn't know I was watching—didn't see how easily she pulled all my focus just by existing in a quiet room.

"Morning, kids." Frankie's voice snapped me to attention, and I blinked, looking for the source.

Emmy moved out of the way, and a screen sat where she'd been standing, Frankie's bald head and bright smile filling the monitor.

"Didn't know you'd be here, too." I stared up at the ceiling so Frankie couldn't see how much I wanted to stare at Emmy, not him.

"Just to get you two started," Frankie said. "Then you're all hers."

I swallowed, liking the sound of that a little too much.

Without further ado, Frankie called out things he wanted me to do, and what he wanted Emmy to pay attention to.

Emmy stepped close to the table. "I'm going to touch you."

I looked up at her, and our eyes connected when I gave her a brief nod. Her little fingers touched down on my hip between the bars of my brace, and I sucked in a breath.

"Does that hurt?" she asked, breaking our eye contact as she looked down at my injured joint.

"No," I answered. "Not more when you're touching me, at least. But your hands are cold, even through my shorts."

She pulled them away from me, rubbing them together. "Sorry."

"Felt good." I grinned, and Frankie's deep exhale was enough to remind me that we weren't alone.

"Should I give you two a minute?" he said, and Emmy's cheeks flushed pink. "I can go alphabetize my spice rack or teach my cat to skateboard. Either sounds more enjoyable than being a third wheel to whatever this is."

I brushed a hand across my face, trying to hide my laughter. "Since when do you have a cat?"

"I don't," he said, and Emmy giggled.

"Don't encourage him." I pointed a finger at the monitor, and Emmy looked over her shoulder at Frankie grinning back at her. "Once you laugh at his jokes, he never stops. Then they get weirder by the minute."

"Alright, I don't have all day, kids. Sit up on the table for me, Conway."

Emmy held her hand out to help me sit up, and I took it. A little shock zapped us both with the contact, and it jerked both of us to the present. She flexed her bicep to help me curl up, and I let go once I was upright, even though my hand still tingled from the contact.

"Sit tall, don't slouch, and move your leg outward, just a little," Frankie said. Emmy stood to the side, watching me closely. "We're not opening a dance studio here—just get that hip moving."

I did as he said, going through several movements. My hip and back were tight, but nothing was painful as long as I didn't push it.

No, the only painful thing about this was trying to tamper my semi every time I looked up at Emmy chewing her lip in concentration.

A commotion behind Frankie caught my attention, and two familiar faces leaned into frame over his shoulder.

"Hey, Conway," Logan called, flashing a grin when he saw Emmy on the screen. "Oh, *hello* little Ten. You're way hotter than Frankie. Definitely an upgrade from his busted mug. No offense, Frank."

Frankie didn't even blink. "None taken. I've seen a mirror."

Mikko tossed a lazy wave, his voice more subdued. "Boys

miss you, man. Team's soft as Logan's handshake without you chirping us during drills."

Logan shook his head. "I've worked hard to perfect the dead fish grip. It's memorable."

Emmy tried her best to stifle a laugh, her back turned to me.

"Thanks, boys."

"Nah, he's serious," Logan chimed in. "Rookies are asking for video on your penalty kill setups. Told 'em its classified. They can suck it and get back on the wall."

"You tell them I'm coming back?" I asked.

"Every damn day," Mikko said.

"Okay, boys." Frankie clapped his hands. "On that note, this lovefest is over. I gotta run. Emmy, you got this?"

"Yes, sir," she said.

I squeezed my eyes shut, needing to forget the sound of those words coming out of her mouth if I had any chance of making this not awkward as hell. Frankie ended our call, and I breathed through my nose in a sharp inhale, trying to ground myself before I lost it entirely.

"Does that hurt?" Emmy asked, and I opened my eyes to find her standing right in front of me. The way she looked at my hip, so focused, so close, felt like a personal invasion.

But I was staring at her, memorizing every single freckle across the bridge of her nose, the soft curve of her lips, the way her dark hair fell just right around her face. Everything about her felt dangerously close, like if I took one more breath, I'd cross a line that could never be uncrossed.

"No, Peach." My voice came out lower than I meant, gravelly and rough. "You can touch me however you like."

When she looked up to meet my gaze, everything shifted.

The air between us thickened, and I wasn't sure what she saw there, but I knew exactly what I felt. A pull, like gravity had taken over, and no matter how hard I tried to fight it, I couldn't stay away.

Violin music blasted through the speakers above us, and Emmy jumped away from me, her hand over her chest. The tune changed until I recognized the beginning notes of *Bust Your Windows*.

I chuckled, then looked over my shoulder toward the entry to the studio where Shannon stood, eyes mere slits on her face as she stared at us both.

A timer on Emmy's watch went off, and she tapped the screen. "I think that's enough for today. I have a Pilates class starting here in 10 minutes. I can walk you through some of it as a starting point if you want to stay."

She kept talking, but my brain was lagging, still trapped in a lust-filled spiral. I nodded, willing to agree to anything she said right now.

Emmy beamed, then patted me on the shoulder, walking backward into the main studio space. "This is great. I'm glad you're open to it."

I gave myself a minute to recover, willing my body's reaction to her proximity to dissipate with thoughts of the least sexy things I could think of: Coach Tremblay's locker room speeches, the time I got hit in the face with a puck and had to pick my tooth out of my mouthguard, the smell of the Mayhem's locker room after a game.

It helped. Barely.

I adjusted the waistband of my shorts and muttered, "Get it together, man."

Voices filtered in as other patrons came into the studio,

and I got up, headed that way. I didn't know what I was expecting to find, but a dozen geriatrics that made my mom look spry was not it.

I stared slack jawed as, one by one, they took their places on the reformers. Most of them had silver hair and several wore sparkly grip socks. All of them looked like they made a mean funeral casserole and had literal war stories, but when they started adjusting straps and tightening springs like pros, I realized I was the one out of my depth.

One of the ladies shot me a wink and cracked her knuckles. Another flexed her bicep at me, and she had *definition*.

"Pick a reformer, hotshot," Emmy said, her smile so big I could tell she was barely containing her laugh. "Hope you're ready. Ruth gets competitive."

I swallowed hard and shuffled my feet, trying to ignore the smug little grin on Emmy's face.

This wasn't just Pilates.

This was initiation.

I took the spot Emmy pointed to between two-guns Ruth and a lady in a neon tracksuit who offered me a Werther's Original from her pocket like we were about to board a cruise ship.

Emmy clapped her hands from the front of the room, then adjusted her little headset microphone. "All right, everyone! Today's focus is hip mobility and pelvic alignment. We'll be starting on the mat. Beckett's joining us for the first time —be nice."

A chorus of greetings echoed around me like I'd just walked into a very supportive cult. I nodded, trying to keep the nerves off my face, but this was the weirdest thing I'd ever done.

Emmy led us through some preliminary moves to warm up our lower body, pacing between the center aisle and fixing our posture as needed. I did okay, proud of my ability to keep up, even if it was with eleven octogenarians.

"Let's start with some basic pelvic tilts," Emmy said from the far side of the room. "Feet flat, knees bent, back pressed gently into the mat. Inhale to prepare, exhale to tuck the pelvis."

Sounded easy enough.

Except my abs didn't seem to remember how to work, and my hip protested even that small movement.

"Good, now slowly roll your back off the mat, one vertebra at a time, until you lift your hips up."

I tried to copy Ruth without looking like I was copying Ruth, but she caught me staring. "Breathe through it."

Fuck me, I tried, but my breath stuttered out like a deflating balloon. The playlist switched to *That Don't Impress Me Much,* and the song choice felt more than a little pointed.

Emmy walked past, eyes scanning my body in a way that 20 minutes ago would have given me another semi, but right now all I could focus on was how low my ego could go before I imploded.

"Good, Beckett. Don't force it. Just move within your pain-free range."

Pain-free range? Was that some sort of a sick joke? I wasn't exactly in pain, but even the smallest movements were activating muscles that I, a paid professional athlete, had never used this way before.

We moved into hip extensions and abductions, on our hands and knees. Emmy showed us how she wanted to straighten one leg back, then tap it outside the mat, and bring it back. She came to check my position, ensuring I didn't push my range of motion past what my brace allowed.

Her gentle hands on my back would have been tempting if I hadn't started sweating by the second rep, trying to keep my back from arching like she said. It didn't help that Neon Tracksuit was chatting casually with her neighbor while powering through the moves like it was nothing. Meanwhile, I had a river forming down my back, dripping into my waistband.

Next up, Emmy instructed the class to move into clamshells. On their sides, knees bent, lifting the top leg like they were auditioning for *an X-rated version of the Little Mermaid: Boomer Edition*. Most of the ladies did it with a resistance band, but my hip wasn't ready for it yet, and that was its own canon ball to my ego.

"Skip this one, and let's have you move on to adductor squeezes instead." Emmy handed me a blue Pilates ball and showed me how to put it between my knees, laying on my back.

After over 16 years in the NHL, lifting my legs off the mat without dropping the ball should have been simple. But I felt every damn muscle in my hip fire like it had been years instead of weeks since I'd last used it.

Ruth was knocking them out like a metronome, making me feel worse as I grunted through mine, legs shaking by the eighth rep.

"I'm feeling this in places I didn't know had places," I muttered, earning a snort from Emmy as she passed by.

By the time we hit planks, my whole lower body was vibrating like it had caught an electrical current from hell, even though I got to cheat and keep my knees on the ground, only lifting them a few inches off the ground.

"Last one," Emmy called cheerfully. "Let's finish with a hip opener. Lay on your back, one knee up. Ankle over opposite knee, then gently pull on your knee until your foot leaves the mat. Breathe into the stretch. Beckett, only hold it for ten seconds, but do ten reps for me."

I followed along, groaning as I pulled my leg in one after the next.

And then it happened. Sweet, *glorious* release. My hip loosened, and my body melted into the mat. The sound that came out of my mouth was part moan, part exorcism, and it echoed off the walls.

Heads turned.

Neon Tracksuit cackled.

"Jesus." I covered my face with my forearm and let the other arm rest on the floor under the reformer. "Sorry. That was involuntary."

Emmy just grinned, hands on her hips where she stood in front of my mat. "You good?"

Ruth reached a hand over to pat mine. "You survived, sweetheart. I can't wait to tell your mother about this when she comes back to the knitting club meetings."

When the hour was up, Emmy passed out sanitizing wipes and instructed us all to wipe down our equipment.

"What did you think?" she asked when it was just the two of us left in the studio. "That was one hell of a moan."

I laughed, even though my whole body felt like it had been stretched and pulled in a hundred different directions. But for the first time in what felt like forever, the pain felt productive, and I was overjoyed.

Emmy's hazel eyes were still on me, so I leaned down until my mouth was just above her ear. "Seemed fair for you to hear my sex moan when I know exactly what you look like wearing nothing but my hoodie."

She pulled back with a little inhale, her cheeks flushed and eyes alight. I ran my hand down her back, then stepped by her, both sore and feeling better than I had since my injury.

Damn. I was *never* underestimating Pilates again.

17

Emmy

Beckett left right before noon, and I sat on the front bench in the entryway with my head in my hands. Shannon cast a look my way, and I knew if I wanted to talk, she'd stop and let me. She took two classes at the local community college on Thursday afternoons though, so today was not the day to delay her.

The studio emptied for 2 hours in the middle of the day to give my staff time to clean and eat lunch. Normally, I used the time to catch up on paperwork, but my leg bounced, restless energy coursing through me.

Instead, I grabbed my coat and slipped my arms in the sleeves, then went down the street to the grocery and ordered two sandwiches from the deli counter. Paper bag in hand, I crossed River Street and went inside Hudson Hardware.

No matter how I'd changed in the last 15 years, my dad's hardware store stayed the same. It smelled like sawdust, garden soil, and the faintest whiff of popcorn—comforting in a way only a small-town hardware store could be. The little bell above the door chimed when I walked in, and the worn wood plank floor creaked underfoot.

My brother stood behind the counter with his back to me, rearranging a cluttered corkboard plastered with flyers for firewood deliveries, community events, and a Free Kittens sign that had been up since Halloween. "Welcome in. Let me know if I can help you find anything."

"It's me," I said, and my brother looked over his shoulder. I held up the bag of food, then shook it. "Hungry?"

"Yeah, let me finish this, and then I'll meet you in the office."

He turned back to the board, pulling off the outdated flyers, and I walked through the narrow aisles crammed with shelves stacked high with everything from screws and paint cans to snow shovels and gardening gloves.

My hand ran across the shelves, not a single fleck of dust in sight, just how my dad always kept it. Everything had its place, even if that place didn't make much sense to anyone but him.

It wasn't fancy, and it wasn't trying to be. Hudson Hardware was dependable—just like the town that kept it running and my brother that had taken over when my dad suddenly retired after a heart attack had taken him by surprise. From the looks of it, Ty hadn't changed a single thing in the year and a half he'd been running the store.

The rustic space was so different than my Pilates studio across the street, I couldn't help but think about everything my brother had given up to pick up my dad's mantle here in town.

Had anyone even asked him if this was what he wanted, or had my parents just assumed he'd take over since Dad's heart attack had coincided with Ty's NHL retirement?

I sat in the wooden swivel chair behind the desk and laid out our food, twisting back and forth while I stewed over that depressing thought. How much would my brother give up for the people he loved? I wasn't sure there was a limit.

A few minutes later, Ty walked in and took the chair across from me, grabbing his chicken bacon ranch sandwich and barbecue chips without asking which one was his. "You good?"

"Yeah." I nodded, because for the first time in a year, I was. "You?"

Ty nodded in return, then bit into his sandwich. Ranch caught in the edge of his mustache, and I threw a napkin at him. "Caught in your mustache. Or what was it the kids called it? Lip lettuce?"

My brother chuckled, then wiped at his face. "Jace good?"

"Are we this bad at talking that we just ask each other if everyone is good until we die? Next thing you know, you'll be asking when the last time I changed my oil."

He tugged on his hat, readjusting it over his hair he'd let grow out lately. "Since it's my car, I already know when the last oil change was. Now, the weather? We could definitely talk about the weather. Real barn burner of a topic."

I raised an eyebrow. "Yeah? Got strong feelings about clouds today?"

He took another bite, chewed, then shrugged. "They exist."

God help me, this was his version of emotional vulnerability.

"Game tomorrow," Ty said.

I tipped my forehead down to the wooden desk, staring at the spot where I'd spilled an entire can of neon pink paint when I was 10. My dad had sanded the wood floors and restained it, but you could still see little flecks of color. I wasn't entirely sure he hadn't done that on purpose.

"Is my son going to get thrown out again?"

Ty crumpled his empty chip bag into a ball and tossed it at my head. "Not if I can help it. Beckett's good with him."

The longest sigh of my life slipped free, and I picked my head up, resting my chin on the desk so I could see Ty. "I know. I hate it."

Ty's mustache twitched, then he shook his head. "Shit. Not you too."

I sat up straighter, fixing my posture. "What does that mean? *Not me too?*"

He groaned but didn't elaborate. "Is Jace still flying out to spend New Years with Ryan?"

"Yeah, unfortunately. After Ryan didn't show up for the home opener, it's been more than a little tense though." Dread filled me at the thought of my son flying across the country for a week, but our custody agreement specified a rotating holiday schedule, and this was how it fell. "He leaves the day after Christmas, and I'm alone for a whole week."

Ty scrubbed a hand across his face, then took his hat off completely, setting it on his knee. His hair was long, curling at the nape of his neck from wearing a hat over it so much, but it had the same slightly wavy texture as my own. We were only 16 months apart in age, and people often confused us for twins growing up.

He twisted his neck to the side, then grabbed at it, as if something was bothering him. "Why don't we go out for New Years then?"

My brows shot up. "What did you say?"

"We should go out, maybe just to The Lantern here in town. Get a drink or two, since we've never done that."

I chuckled, realizing what he'd said was true. "How are we now in our mid-thirties and have never gone out for a drink together? You are my favorite brother, after all."

"You know I love a stacked competition," he said, then put his hat back on. "Let's do it."

I finished the rest of my sandwich, then folded the wrapper and put it in the trashcan under the desk. "I'll think about it."

Ty nodded and stood up. "Take a bag of candy from the counter if you want one."

I did a little fist pump, glad that some things never changed. Without hesitation, I grabbed a bag of sour peach dots, then waved them over my head as I went back outside.

The plastic crinkled as I ripped the bag open and plucked a little candy out, then shoved it into my mouth. The flavor exploded like a ray of sunshine, and I grinned up at the sunny sky.

Unlike my lifelong obsession with everything peach, this infatuation with Beckett would fade. He'd be gone in eight weeks, and my life would go back to normal here.

I could do this.

"I can't do this," I said the next night, hands over my eyes. It was Friday, and the Mayhem had another home game. Unlike the last one, the Mayhem were tied 2-2 at the end of the second period. With Ty and Beckett both on the bench across the way, I was left sitting alone.

Well, not *alone*. I sat with Rowdy, Ty's dog that went

everywhere with him, and Juniper, his neighbor's daughter. When he'd introduced us before the game and asked if she could sit with me, I stared at him with a dozen questions, but Ty asked for nothing *ever*, and this was the second thing he'd asked of me in as many days.

"Statistically speaking, the likelihood of us winning this game is almost zero," Juniper said.

I looked down at the 8-year-old who had talked almost the entire game using words that I only understood half the time. She wore a Mayhem hoodie that looked like it might be Ty's it was so big on her, black sparkly leggings, and snow boots I knew Ty sold at the store. Her unbelievably thick dark blonde hair was pulled into a haphazard ponytail, cheeks pink from the cold rink, and no parent in sight.

"The Summit went to the State Championship last year. Sure, their captain went on to play Juniors and is no longer with them, but the Summit have a long line of recent successes that suggests their coaching style both attracts talent and develops it. On paper, we are much worse."

"Well, that's good to know, I guess."

She looked up at me, pale blue eyes magnified behind her thick glasses. "Would you like to know their record from the last five years?"

"What about the statistical rates now that Miles has new glasses and is playing like he's on fire?"

A beat of silence went by before she finally said, "I don't know that yet. But I could start tracking the shots on goal."

As if he could hear us, Miles dropped and blocked a shot headed straight between his legs, slamming his glove down over top of it. The stands exploded in excitement, and I reached a hand around Juniper's shoulders, squeezing her tight to my side. "Look at him!"

The little girl stiffened under my touch, so I quickly let her go. "Sorry."

She shook her head, staring at Ty across the ice. "I like hugs."

"Me too." I nudged her shoulder with my hip, then leaned down. "You let me know anytime you want one, and I've got one ready for you."

She nodded, not taking her eyes off my brother. I looked back and forth between them too, trying to figure out the relationship here. Prior to his retirement, Ty had spent little to no time in Linwood, so there was no way he had a secret daughter, but something about their unusual relationship screamed father-daughter.

"You spend a lot of time with Ty?" I asked, curiosity getting the best of me.

Juniper grinned, her teeth a little too big for her face and more than a few missing. "Yeah. We live next door. My mom has headaches, and I like hanging out at his farm when she's sick. The chickens are cute, as long as you don't try to steal their eggs. Then they peck you."

"Especially Nugget."

Juniper nodded vigorously, her glasses nearly slipping off her face. "Nugget isn't very nice. But Cluck Norris is the meanest."

A laugh ripped out of me at my brother's stupid names for his chickens. "He's so mean, isn't he? Almost as mean as Ty."

Juniper shook her head, then looked up at me. "Ty's not mean. He's the nicest person I've ever met. I like Beckett, too."

The second period ended, and I stared at the two men in question, wondering when they'd grown up to be such decent men. They ushered the kids off the ice and into the locker room to regroup before the third period while several parents got up and cleaned the ice with the sled contraptions Tate used.

"You've met him?"

Juniper stood up to let someone by, and Rowdy shuffled until he stood directly between her legs, like he was guarding her. "He stopped by the ranch last night while I was playing with Dolly Pawton. Ty says she's going to have babies, and then we'll have new barn kitties."

I looked toward the locker room, wondering just how much time my brother spent with this little girl between working and taking care of his animals and now coaching my son's hockey team. "Oh, yeah? What were they talking about last night?"

Juniper sat back down and shrugged. "Something about New Years? I wasn't really listening. Dolly got stuck in the hay bales again, so I was helping get her unstuck. OH!" She bounced in her seat, and I raised my brows to match her excitement. "They were talking about *Christmas presents*."

"Oh, yeah?" I asked, wondering what two grown ass men were doing have a conversation about presents in a barn. "For whom?"

Her little hand shot out and poked me in the arm. "For *you*, silly!"

My head jerked back toward the lockers in time to see the players march out, my son in the lead. Beckett and Ty walked out last, shoulders almost touching and their heads together while they stared at a clipboard.

Once upon a time the two of them were always this inseparable, and I loved to see it again. But what the hell were they scheming up presents for me for?

"What were their ideas?" I asked, staring at Beckett so hard he must have sensed my attention. His eyes met mine, then flicked over to the little girl at my side. He winked, and we both blushed, as if his attention was enough to drive us both out of our minds.

"I can't tell you," Juniper said. "My mom says it's no fun to spoil surprises."

I hummed, my mind racing in a hundred different directions.

The game started again, and I stood on the bleachers, needing a better view. The difference between last week and this was shocking to see, the sloppy formations and stupid mistakes all but gone under new coaching. Beckett and Ty had switched up lines so the players on the ice were better matched, and everything just seemed to *jive*.

Jace hopped over the boards for a line switch, and I pulled my hands inside my sleeves, cupping my hands around my mouth. "LET'S GO JACE!"

Juniper stood up next to me, mirroring my words and motions, casting sideways glances at me every time. I grinned, loving having a little sidekick who didn't yet think I was lame. Rowdy barked in answer every time I yelled, and together, the three of us were one chaotic cheering section.

With a minute left in the game, Jace got the puck and hopped, changing directions faster than I'd ever seen him move.

"GO!" I screamed, my heart slamming against my ribs with each beat.

With a snap of his wrist, the puck sailed over the goalie's glove and hit the back of the net. My hands shot into the air, and a yell ripped from my throat. The buzzer sounded, and Jace dropped to one knee, fist-pumping before his team tackled him to the ice like they'd just won the Stanley Cup and not the second game of the season.

Juniper's arms clamped around my waist, and I hugged her to me while we bounced up and down. "He did it!"

My gaze found Beckett across the ice where he shook hands with the other coach, then looked up at me. His grin was wide, and his eyes sparkled with excitement. Like if it weren't for his bum hip, he'd be right in the middle of the kid pile trying to unfold themselves in the middle of the ice.

Before everyone had even left the ice, the garage doors at the corner of the rink opened, and the sound of an engine rumbled toward us.

A green-and-black custom painted Mayhem Zamboni rolled out onto the ice, a man almost the spitting image of Beckett driving it while standing up. One hand was on the steering wheel, the other in a parade wave as he rode out onto the ice. LED lights lit up the rink green as he moved and *Turn Down for What* blared from a speaker somewhere on the Zamboni.

Tate stood in the garage bay with her hands on her hips, looking as shocked by this turn of events as everyone else. As if sensing the attention had drifted away from him, Mason Conway looked over his shoulder and saw Tate behind him.

In quick movements, he stopped the Zamboni and turned it off, hopping down onto the ice. The LED lights in the machine's undercarriage still blinked bright colors and the music still blared from the speakers rumbling on the side of the hood as Mason slid across toward her with a microphone in hand, then dropped to a knee.

"Tate. Tater tot. My sweet potato pie. Make me the happiest man alive and marry me."

18

BECKETT

My attention was split between my brother, kneeling on the ice in front of Tate Mikaelson for what had to be the 20th time, and the new Zamboni parked in the middle of the rink.

Mason held his hands in front of his chest like a prayer, and Tate stared down at him with a look that could kill. I couldn't see his face, but I knew he'd be smiling broad and his blue eyes would shine bright with hope and more than a little mischief.

There was nothing Mason loved more than attention; proposing to Tate had been a long running joke since their high school years. First, it started for laughs from their friend group, then he realized they could get free dinners if he did it publicly.

But somewhere along the line, I'd forgotten that my brother had had a crush on Coach Mikaelson's daughter since elementary school. Once upon a time they'd been best friends, but now... I wasn't so sure.

"He's still doing this?" Ty said at my side, his voice holding a hint of amusement.

"Apparently." I shook my head, then looked back across the rink for Emmy. The Mayhem had left the ice, high off their first win of the season, and with the new Zamboni here, the rink was clearing out fast.

Emmy was gone, but since she had Rowdy and Ty's neighbor kid with her, she couldn't have gone far.

I glanced at Ty out of the corner of my eye. "Where are you meeting up with Emmy?"

He sighed, then shook his head. "This is a thing, isn't it?"

I grinned, then patted him on the back. "Nah. We're just friends."

"Sure." Ty ducked out from under my touch, then walked toward the locker room. "And I'm running for Miss Congeniality."

My hip had felt a little better after only a few days working with Emmy, but I still wasn't willing to push it to hurry after him.

"Emmy?" I called, and Ty turned around.

"She took Rowdy and Juniper home for me. I'm taking Jace so she wasn't stuck here as long."

"Oh." My shoulders dropped, then I looked back over at my brother leading Tate out to the Zamboni. "Pizza at my place, then? Invite the team?"

Ty nodded, then spun back around to head into the locker room. With one last glance at the rink to make sure she really was gone, I followed him inside.

Boxes of half-eaten pizza were spread across the coffee table, and my mom's living room smelled faintly of sweat and victory. Several players on our team sat scattered around the kitchen and living room, and it threw me back in time so hard it was almost jarring.

Jace had ditched his hoodie somewhere on the floor, hair still damp from the post-game shower. He was halfway through his second slice and talking with his mouth full.

"Did you see that guy from Summit face wash me? Glove right to the face, just one big swipe."

Miles snorted, reaching over to grab the last slice of Meat Lovers from where he perched on the brown leather couch next to Jace. Without the goalie pads, the kid was on the scrawny side, his glasses perched on his freckly skin.

Ty raised an eyebrow, then pointed at Jace. "And yet he still managed to land you on your ass in the second period."

"Technicality." Jace waved him off. "The ice was extra slippery tonight. But dude"—he reached over and slapped Miles on the arm—"I still can't believe your glove hand, Pickles. That last save at the end of the second period was sick."

"Thanks, bro," Miles said, adjusting his new glasses. "Helps that I could see."

Mason let out a loud burp, then crushed the orange soda can in his hand before launching it through the air and into the trash. "Great game, boys. Almost looked like you knew what you were doing out there."

"And girls," Molly added from where she lay stretched out on the floor, her long brown braid laying out to the side. "Or, girl, I guess. Just me."

"Can't forget the Mollinator." Silas Delgado tossed a football into the air and caught it repeatedly. "Money Moreau. The Mayhem's own Molotov cocktail."

"So, what should we call this goon, then?" Mason said, pointing at Delgado.

Without hesitation, Ty and I both answered, "Smash."

"Hell yeah, fuck yeah." Delgado pumped his fist in the air, delighted by the nickname.

"Fitting since the only way you're stopping on skates is by using someone as a cushion between you and the boards," Molly said, and the kids all howled with laughter.

Jace swallowed, then stared at my brother practically heart-eyed. The whole team was having a little bit of a meltdown being in the room with three former and current NHL players, and I couldn't blame them—Ty, Mason, and I would have had the same reaction when we were in their shoes.

"You never did say how you got me on the active roster for tonight." Jace looked from Beckett to me, then back to Mason.

"Don't ask me." I held my hands up, looking over at Ty. "That was your uncle over there."

Ty cleared his throat, then picked up the empty paper plates littered on the floor around him. "I made some calls."

"Oh, this sounds juicy." Mason slung a leg over the armrest on my mom's favorite chair, his chin on his fist. "Do tell."

Everyone quieted down for the first time since we'd left the rink, waiting for Ty's answer. "The kid you fought, Jack Donovan? His name is *Johnathan* Donovan, and he was thrown out of the league last season for repeated misconduct. Since he's not allowed to play even under a new name, your game misconduct against him was also thrown out."

Jace's jaw hung open in shock, and I just grinned. "How'd you figure that one out?"

Ty shrugged, then grabbed a Gatorade off the coffee table. I held my hands out, and he tossed me one too. "I didn't. Junie did."

Emmy's son frowned. "The neighbor kid?"

"Yep." Ty sat back on the couch, adjusting his hat, not elaborating further than that.

"You fu—"

I whistled loudly, slicing a hand across my neck in a *stop* motion, and Mason tipped an imaginary hat at me.

"—*dating* her mom?"

Ty shook his head, then put his hands on his knees, ready to leave. "No. Just helping out. Jace, grab your stuff. It's late."

Jace did as he was told, shoving one last slice of pizza in his mouth as he grabbed his backpack and hoodie, then waved.

"Tomorrow?" I asked as they were headed toward the front door. "New furniture and gym equipment should be here, if you can help set it up. I'll pay you in food."

Jace did a fist pump, then gave me a thumbs up, his cheeks stuffed like a chipmunk, exactly how his mom ate pretzels in the stands.

Mason stood to help me clean up the rest of the boxes as the rest of the team left, until it was just the two of us in our mom's kitchen.

"When I asked if you knew how to find a Zamboni, I didn't realize that meant you were finding one and driving it onto the ice yourself."

Mason laughed, his dark hair a little longer than mine and far more styled. Despite both playing professional hockey and having the same brown hair and blue eyes, we were wildly different in just about every way. "Honestly, I love the idea of investing in Tate."

"In the rink," I clarified with a raised brow. "It's a business."

Mason turned and leaned against the counter, his arms

crossed and his smile wide. "Yes, but Tate *is* the business. She's the heart of it all, isn't she? It's not Linwood Rink without a Mikaelson in charge. We're just giving her a nicer ship to fly."

I chuckled, tossing the last pizza box into the bin. "Pretty sure Zambonis don't fly. And a Zamboni is not a ship nor a plane."

"Honestly, it might be. The features on that thing are unreal—I pulled out all the stops. The chair is a massage seat with memory foam, perfect for those long, grueling five-minute laps. And I forgot to show you the fog machine."

Pulling one of the barstools out from the counter, I sat down, my hip tired after a long day. "What did Tate say?"

"To the proposal?" Mason asked, his eyebrows jumping up and down. "You ready for a sister-in-law?"

"No, dipshit. I know she said no to that, just like every other time."

Mason pointed at me, then winked. "One day, brother. One day I'll get her to say yes, and she'll realize exactly what she's been missing out on."

"A cocky son-of-a-bitch who's missing a few teeth and a whole lot of brain cells?"

He laughed, then shook his head. "She was pissed about the Zamboni until she climbed up and felt that massage chair. That changed her tune—I knew it would. I like the investors angle though, and Tate's the smartest girl I've ever met. I bet she'll go for it."

"Good Are you headed back to Dallas in the morning?"

"Yeah." Mason looked out at the now-empty living room that hadn't changed much in at least two decades, even though everything else had. "The bye weekend worked out so

I could come see Mom when she gets home tomorrow, then I fly out after lunch."

"How are you dealing with the whole Parkinson's diagnosis?"

My brother scratched at his jaw, then let out a long sigh. "I don't know. It always felt like she was invincible, right? Like, after everything Dad put us through, she was just the toughest woman on the planet."

I didn't say anything, because I didn't need to. I felt the same way.

"I'll come spend the off-season up here with her," Mason said. "Summer feels like a long way off, but it's time, I think. We've been running for a long time."

"I forgot how much I love this little town."

Mason smiled, one half of his lips tipping up in a slow, crooked grin. "Especially when the hockey moms are all tens, right?"

I shook my head, laughing as I made my way carefully to the stairs, headed up to my room.

Tomorrow, my new mattress was scheduled to arrive, the least of the changes happening around here if I was staying in town.

I had eight weeks to prove I still had what it took to make it in the NHL and get my mom set up for a healthy and happy life here at home.

Eight weeks to get the Mayhem back on the right track and pick up all the responsibilities I'd left behind so many years ago.

Eight weeks to stare at my best friend's sister, thinking things I'd never thought before.

Even if the Yeti renewed my contract, I wasn't an idiot —retirement was on the near horizon. And maybe, for the first time in my life, I had an idea of how I'd like to spend it.

Ty let out a low whistle as he helped the movers get down the basement steps, guiding a stationary bike with a screen so large it was almost comical.

"Conway," he called over the movers' heads, "are you training to ride in the Tour de France or build a new hip from scratch?"

"Both." I tugged on the grab bar we'd just installed next to the front door, making sure it was secure. "Mom gets a house that she can move around safely in. I get a basement that might let me get back on the ice before playoffs. Win-win."

Jace stood at the top of the stairs, holding a box labeled *Recovery Crap* in Frankie's scribbled handwriting. "This stuff better work. It's heavy as fu—"

I raised a brow, and he grinned.

"Fluff. You'll get me tickets to the Cup, right?"

"Maybe if you focused on protein and not just junk food, you could carry more," Ty yelled up the stairs. "You're going to need to bulk up if you want beat me on the pond this winter."

Jace rolled his eyes, then hopped down the stairs to drop off his boxes. I followed him down at a much slower pace, taking in the new setup.

The basement had transformed in a matter of hours. New rubber flooring covered the old concrete, the once-bare cinderblocks had been painted a fresh white, and a full corner was dedicated just for rehab.

Frankie lived up to his promise to get me setup: there were adjustable dumbbells, a cable trainer, resistance bands, a muscle stim unit, and—God help me—an actual ice bathtub that hummed quietly in the corner like it was judging me.

Ty walked around it and gave me a look. "Can't believe you bought one of these. You hated them."

"Still do," I muttered, stepping gingerly around the boxes yet to be unpacked. "But I hate not skating more."

"Mom was doing this study on Hyperbaric Oxygen Therapy before we moved." Jace dipped his hands into the frigid water circulating in the tub. "Something about it speeding up recovery. You could ask her about it. Maybe you can get one of those, too."

I cast a glance to the side at Ty. He stood with his arms crossed but bobbed his head back and forth as Rowdy appeared at his side, tongue out. "Not the worst idea. I don't think it could hurt."

"Did she do a lot of sports medicine in Connecticut?" I asked, watching for Jace's reaction.

Since he'd shut down several days ago when I mentioned Emmy, I had purposefully avoided talking about her again. He knew she was helping me with my hip, and I was leaving it at that, as far as the kid was concerned.

"Yeah." Jace moved on to testing the new bike like he couldn't help but touch everything in the room. "She worked for Dr. Riviera, who did a lot of PT for the Sentinels."

"Baseball, huh?"

Jace moved on to push-ups on the new rubber flooring, showing off after Ty had called him out about bulking up.

"Dad hated it. He said baseball players were all showboaters with too much money and no morals, and that Mom had no business wasting her time around guys like that."

Ty let out a sound that was halfway between a growl and a curse, and I couldn't help but agree with him.

Emmy's son hopped up far easier than I could, then brushed off his hands before shooting us a fake smile. "Weird, coming from a guy with six mistresses and a secret baby, huh?"

"Jace." Ty reached out a hand to stop his nephew as he headed for the stairs, but Jace walked right past, his shoulders tense and body language telling us we'd touched on a topic he wanted no part of discussing.

"Well, that was fun," I said. "Do we need to go after him?"

Ty sighed, then turned back to me. "No. Emmy told me this morning she can tell he doesn't want to go to Connecticut for New Years. But Ryan has threatened to take Emmy back to court if he refuses. Worst part is, I don't even think Ryan cares if he sees Jace or not. He just wants to control Emmy, even now. And Jace knows it."

I crossed my arms, hating that for them. "He really is a dick, isn't he?"

"He really fucking is."

Ty headed for the stairs and I followed, switching off the lights on my new home gym as we went.

Upstairs, the living room was mid-transition, movers and contractors Ty helped me find getting everything ready. The old couch was gone, replaced by one that was much higher and easier to get off. The new coffee table was round with no sharp corners and no water ring reminder of my alcoholic father. We even took down the old curtains, replacing them with shades on a remote timer so she didn't have to open and close them on her own.

We laid down textured floor runners in every hallway, removed anything that was a tripping hazard, and redid the doors on the downstairs shower to make it walk-in, complete with a grab bar and a stool.

I'd even had the movers bring Mom's bedroom furniture downstairs, and two guys were busy finishing the install on new French doors over what was once our dining room. Now, she was on the first floor and had no reason to go up and down the stairs.

Subtle changes, but important ones. The kind of things you didn't think about until you had to. The kind that might let her come home from rehab without worrying what might knock her over next.

I paused in the living room, then turned to Ty. "You think she'll like it?"

He pulled off his hat, then put it back on his head, taking it all in. "She'll notice every single change we made, but I think she'll like it."

I nodded, swallowing around the lump in my throat at the thought of *why* all of this was necessary.

Mom was coming home today, and I wanted it to feel like home—not a hospital, not a halfway place. I wanted her to know how much we loved her.

A car pulled in the driveway, then honked three times. I looked out the front window to see Mason behind the wheel of a flashy SUV I had no idea how he'd acquired on such short notice. It was lower to the ground than my truck and would be much easier for her to get in and out of, so I didn't plan on asking many questions.

He parked as close as he could to the ramp over the front

stairs, then ran around the car to help Mom out. Jace came out of the garage and grabbed her other arm, and I smiled at the sight.

The bruising on her face was almost gone, and someone had combed her hair into a neat ponytail, right above her neck. Mason had just signed a new sponsorship deal with Adidas, and she was wearing a new pair of pants and a loose tee she could fit her cast through—one of about eight sets my brother had brought for her.

Together, Mason and Jace helped Mom across the short walkway, then up the ramp into the house. Ty grabbed the door, holding it open. "Welcome home, Mrs. Conway."

"How many times have I told you to call me Lori?" Mom nudged him with her shoulder as she walked by, holding on to Mason's arm. "You're old, I'm old. We can be friends now."

Ty's mustache twitched, but I held my breath, waiting for Mom's reaction to the changes I'd made.

She stopped in the foyer, staring at the new door frame in the dining room entrance, then leaned in to see her furniture within.

"Did I do okay?" I asked, nervous as hell for her answer.

She let go of Mason long enough to hold her good arm out for a hug, and I stepped into her embrace. Her hands trembled on my back, and I fought not to tear up at the feel of it, but she just held me tighter. "Thank you, my sweet boy. What a wonderful idea."

When she let go, her head bobbed in a little nod, then she pulled Mason forward.

"Geez, Ma, take it easy on me," Mason said, and Mom giggled.

Her laugh was one of my favorite sounds, so light and

airy. It had the same lilt it always had when we were kids—like nothing in the world could touch her in that moment. Like for just a second, everything was easy again.

Mason led her to the new sofa, then helped her sit down. She let out a sigh, then rubbed her hands across the soft but supportive off-white fabric. "You kids would have destroyed this couch so fast."

Jace's laugh caught me off-guard, but I turned to see him walk inside too. "We had a white couch at our old house, and my dad insisted we couldn't eat on it. Couldn't even put our feet on it."

Mom lifted her socked feet until I was staring at the little grip marks on the bottom, then settled them on the couch. "You only live once, kid."

I ducked my head, loving the sound of her little contented sigh. Jace kept talking, now perched on the edge of the sofa next to Mom talking about God knew what.

Mason nudged me with his shoulder, leaning against the wall. "Have we been replaced?"

"He's shockingly nice to her," Ty said from my other side. "Way nicer than he is to everyone else."

"Yes, well, she's used to asshole sons rebelling against their terrible fathers," Mason said, eyebrow raised as he stared at me.

I shoved him in the side, then went into the kitchen looking for food. "Who's hungry?"

Jace hopped up, already circling the couch. "What's for lunch? And if you say chicken and veggies, I'm calling Child Protective Services."

Mason didn't miss a beat. "Good. Tell them we've got a minor in need an attitude adjustment."

Ty smirked. "Make sure they bring a rib-eye steak. Rowdy and I aren't trying to stay lean."

The black dog barked at his side, and Ty reached down to pet his head.

I opened the fridge and grabbed one of the dozens of pre-packaged meals that had been delivered this morning, tossing it at Jace's chest. "Survival of the fittest, kid. You want to make it to the pros? Then eat like it."

Jace caught it with a scowl, and my mom laughed. "This is abuse."

"Document it," Mason said, dropping onto the couch and resting his head on Mom's shoulder. "But make sure you spell 'whiner' right in your report."

"Don't worry, Jace." Mom leaned into Mason's hold. "I'll show you where I keep the cookies later."

Jace pointed at her, then stood to walk toward the microwave, ready to heat up his meal. "I always knew you were my favorite."

She looked over the back of the couch, grinning at me. Tears shimmered in the corners of her eyes. "It's so good to be home."

Her fingers trembled where they rested on Mason's arm, but the smile was the same as it always was. And for a second, I didn't care about the new gym equipment or my busted hip or any of it.

All I cared about was a second chance to do this right, to be a good son and friend, not just a good hockey player.

19

Emmy

"Oh, fuck, right there," Beckett groaned as I rolled the pair of lacrosse balls over the tight line of muscle running from his low back into his hip on Sunday morning.

We technically weren't supposed to see each other today. But the SOS text he'd sent this morning—*Overdid it. Dying. Please help*—and the noises he was making now told me exactly how badly yesterday's move-in had gone.

I leaned in, repositioning the balls beneath his glutes, and pressed into his piriformis. "Let me know if I need to ease up."

His response was a long, guttural sound that vibrated somewhere low in my spine. "Don't stop," he murmured, voice thick and wrecked. "This feels incredible."

My fingers paused just for a second. *Focus.* But God, the way his shirt clung to the muscles of his back, how the heat of his body radiated through the cotton—how was I supposed to ignore any of that?

I turned my gaze to the wall, trying to keep my mind clinical. I was a professional, dammit. But all I could think about was the way his breath hitched when I pressed just a little deeper.

"You're ridiculously tight," I said, then immediately regretted the words. "Sorry. I should just keep my mouth shut."

Beckett laughed, low and unguarded. "This is so much better than Frankie abusing the shit out of me. You can say anything you want, and I'll just tell you *more.*"

My hand stilled again. He looked over his shoulder, his eyes catching mine with a heat that nearly undid me.

I cleared my throat and reached for the next spot on his glute and pressed harder, focusing on the task at hand. "I hold all the power here, hotshot."

His head dropped and a loud groan escaped him, then his chest shook with laughter. "Just how it should be, Peach."

I didn't answer. I couldn't. Not with the way my hands were already trembling.

Beckett let out one more exaggerated moan just to mess with me, and I rolled my eyes, stepping away from the table.

"You done putting on a show?"

He glanced over his shoulder again, still grinning like he got entirely too much satisfaction out of teasing me. "Depends. Are you going to go to The Lantern with us?"

I blinked, surprised by the question. "What?"

"New Year's Eve. You, me, Ty. Small-town chaos, mediocre beer, and shitty line dancing. You in?"

I tugged the sleeves of my shirt down, just for something to do with my hands. "I didn't know you were invited."

"Should I not be?"

Beckett pushed himself up slowly, arms straining a little as he sat upright on the table. I didn't move fast enough, and suddenly, we were nose to nose.

His knee brushed my hip as he settled, and a zap of electricity shot through me, snapping my gaze to his. He smelled like spearmint gum and some sort of woodsy soap. My fingers twitched, aching to reach for him.

I cleared my throat. "Ty didn't mention you were coming, too."

Beckett's smirk deepened. "I mean, I own a cowboy hat. It seems a shame to waste it."

I snorted. "You do not."

His hand lifted off the table and a finger landed under my chin, tilting my face up so I couldn't look away. His voice dropped just a little, and the dare in it made my breath catch. "Don't test me, Peach."

I moved back abruptly, trying to put distance between us, but Beckett rose to full height, moving slower, favoring his right side.

"You good?" I rested a hand lightly on his waist to steady him, a justifiable move. Totally clinical. Except his skin was warm under my palm, and his breath hitched when I touched him.

Somehow the space between us shrank again, like the room was conspiring against my self-control, and I realized just how alone we were in the studio this morning.

"Getting there." His gaze dropped briefly to my mouth before flicking back up. "So? New Years?"

I stepped away from him and grabbed the tablet to input our session notes. "Well, with the promise of seeing you in a cowboy hat, I have to go now."

Beckett tilted his head, eyes narrowing just a little. "So, you'll dance with me?"

I tried and failed to look away, my cheeks burning with a blush I had no way to hide. "If you're lucky, sure. But I'd suggest working on your exercises, bud. You won't be able to keep up."

He grinned again, wicked and easy, like he already knew luck had nothing to do with it.

I scurried back to the front door, unlocking it and putting my coat on. Beckett followed at a slower pace, but already he was standing taller than he had when he'd come in.

"What are your plans for the rest of the week besides abusing me every morning?"

He pushed the door open then held it for me. I clicked the button to remote start the SUV, then turned to lock the door when it closed behind me. "Pilates as normal this week, then Christmas is Thursday, then Jace leaves. As much as my everyday life with him is exhausting, I hate when he's gone. I'm too sad to be good company, and too lonely to be alone, so I read and do puzzles and take baths and all the things I otherwise don't have time for."

The words were out of my mouth before I realized how pathetic they sounded, and I blushed for what had to be the tenth time this morning despite the chill breeze blowing my hair around like a tornado.

"Sorry, that was depressing."

Beckett shook his head, then looked out over the mountain town. "No, I get it."

"Is your mom settling in okay?" I asked, stalling just a little longer.

His attention came back to me, and this time his smile was softer than when he teased. It wasn't the same as the sexy grin when he was flirting—no, this one was a little distant and held a level of sadness I hated seeing there. It made me want to rise on my toes and kiss him, just to pull him back from wherever his mind had gone.

"Yeah. She's good. I'm going to bring her to Pilates after the new year."

I must have looked like a bobblehead I was nodding so much, then jabbed a thumb toward my car, needing to end whatever this was. "I've got some last-minute errands to run, but I'll look up rehab plans for her that will be perfect for Parkinson's."

"Thank you, Emmy." Beckett brushed a stray hair off my face, then let his warm palm rest on the side of my neck. "I haven't said that yet, but I keep thinking it."

I swallowed hard, his gentle touch sending heat down my spine, even as the bitter wind bit at my cheeks.

"You don't have to thank me," I said, though my voice came out quieter than I meant. "It's nice. Helping you. I like it."

His thumb grazed my jaw before he dropped his hand, and the absence of his touch was its own kind of ache.

"I'll see you tomorrow." He backed away a step. Still watching me.

I nodded again, sure my head was about to roll right down the street. "Yeah. Tomorrow."

He turned toward his truck and limped the few steps to it without looking back. I watched him go anyway—watched the way he moved, slower than usual, the way his broad shoulders rose and fell like he was carrying more than just a healing injury.

I hated how much I wanted to be the one to ease that weight.

Sliding into my car, I sat there a moment longer than necessary, fingers curled tight around the heated steering wheel. It wasn't just that he was stupid hot or made me laugh with his never-ending flirting.

It was how he looked at me—*really* looked at me, like I wasn't just Jace's mom or Ty's sister or the girl running the studio on fumes, and that was terrifying.

I exhaled hard and pulled out onto the street, telling myself I was imagining things. That whatever this was would burn itself out. But even as I drove away, I could still feel the echo of his hand on my neck like it belonged there.

I did my best to keep things professional on Monday and Tuesday morning, focusing on Beckett's hip and his recovery timeline. Jace had told him about my research study with Dr. Riviera investigating healing times for professional athletes when incorporating Hyperbaric Oxygen Therapy, and that gave us something other than sexual tension to discuss.

Luckily, I could tell he was following all of Frankie's and my instructions, and his progress was coming along well. I, on the other hand, was having a mental breakdown over the idea of going out with him and Ty on New Year's Eve next week.

By the time Tuesday evening rolled around, I'd worked myself up so much, I was pacing in front of the studio window, looking for Stevie. We'd exchanged numbers and had texted throughout the week, but with school officially out for winter break, I wasn't sure if she'd show.

Shannon stared at me through squinted eyes, but she'd been too focused on finals to ask about why my hands were practically pretzel-shaped I'd wrung them so many times since Beckett left this morning.

Headlights flashed in the studio window, and I clapped

when I saw Stevie's minivan. My new friend climbed out, then opened the sliding door.

"They're here," I said, and Shannon clicked the computer off, coming around the desk to stand next to me.

The moment Stevie opened the door, Shannon held her arms out and Harper damn near flew into them. "Hey, bestie. How have you been?"

Harper smashed her little hands on either side of Shannon's face, then leaned in until their foreheads touched.

"Tell Mommy to have fun!" Shannon said, then put Harper down on the floor. The little girl waved to her mom, then toddled down the aisle holding Shannon's finger.

"That is still unreal," Stevie said, her hat and coat still on where she stood just inside the door. "I'm not even sure she likes my husband that much."

I chuckled, then helped her out of her coat. "Pilates today? Or a nap?"

"I actually napped while Harper was down today. The boys destroyed my living room but everyone was still alive, so we'll call it a success."

As I was turning away from the window, I caught sight of a black truck parked across the street at the hardware store. Like he'd been summoned from my thoughts, Beckett walked out of my brother's store. He looked across the street and our eyes met.

"Shit." I practically dove down out of sight, even though it was too late.

"Uh." Stevie looked between the window and me. "Everything okay?"

I peeked around the bench, but Beckett was already gone.

"Yep. Totally fine. Everything is great," I said, voice about two octaves too high. I stood and brushed imaginary lint off my leggings like that would somehow restore my dignity.

Stevie arched a brow, then followed me behind the partition and to the closest reformer. "You just hit the floor like they were passing out a PTA signup sheet. Who are we avoiding?"

"Beckett Conway," Shannon said from the back where she and Harper were stacking blocks into a makeshift castle.

I glared at her, but Stevie slapped my arm, getting my attention. "Why do I know that name?"

"Because there's a statue of him outside the rink?" Shannon said, putting her hands around Harper's ears. "You should hear the noises coming out of the back room when he's here every morning, Stevie. Like amateur porn."

Unfortunately, Stevie was mid-sip of her water when Shannon decided to add that tidbit of information. Water sprayed out of Stevie's mouth and down her shirt, her eyes wide.

"It's not like that." I handed Stevie a towel, helping her clean up while I glared at Shannon. "He's on long-term injured reserve for the Denver Yetis and is in town only as long as it takes to get him back on the ice. I'm overseeing his physical therapy."

"Is that what the kids are calling it these days?" Shannon said.

Stevie sat down on the reformer, and the shuttle slid away from the springs. She reached out to grab the foot bar, then turned to look at Shannon. "How old are you? Surely, we're older than you."

"Oh, you are." Shannon added another block to the top of Harper's tower. "Please get her to talk more about this though, Stevie. Drama feeds me."

I sighed and rubbed the heel of my palm over my forehead. "I mean, it's nothing. Beckett's is Ty's best friend. He's also Jace's hockey coach. And he's not even staying in town."

Stevie blinked. "Okay, so naturally you're flirting with him."

"I'm not—" I groaned. "Okay. Maybe. But I didn't mean to. It just sort of *happened*."

I recapped Sunday's piriformis massage, and they both cackled in delight until all three of us were crying over how easy it was to make sexual innuendos out of everything he and I were doing.

"So let me get this straight." Stevie wiped the corners of her eyes with the sleeve of her hoodie. "He's hot. Helpful. Bonding with your teenage son. Taking care of his mom. You know he's a good guy, *and* you get to put your hands all over a professional athlete's body in the name of science? And you're mad about it?"

"I'm not *mad*." I sat down on the mat next to her reformer. "I'm terrified."

Harper squealed with joy at whatever tower she and Shannon had just built and then immediately knocked it over like Godzilla. Shannon clapped. "Good job, Harper! Can we do it again?"

Stevie leaned down until she was right in front of me. "Emmy. We don't know each other very well yet, but I think you're allowed to be into someone, even if it's a little messy. *Especially* if you make each other feel good, and I don't just mean in the 'rolls two balls over your piriformis' kind of way."

"Don't say balls in front of Harper," I whispered. "She'll repeat it and make it sound dirty."

"Girl, you have a son. No way is my daughter coming out

unscathed with two older brothers talking about poop or balls at every possible turn. She's fine. You, on the other hand…"

I pointed at my chest, not sure what I believed anymore, so I stuck with the facts. "I'm a divorced single mom, and I can't afford a temporary distraction. Beckett is so much more than a hot body and a pretty face. He's kind. And good with Jace. And loves his mom. And he listens to me. And that's exactly the problem."

Shannon's head popped up over the tower, apparently still listening. "Wow, you're down bad. That's not even crush talk. That's commitment talk."

"Stop helping," I said.

"I'm just saying," she muttered, "the last guy you went on a date with wore toe shoes unironically."

"Toe shoes?" Stevie said, her face rightfully twisted in disgust at the mention of my one and only attempt at online dating since coming back to town.

"We were never going to talk about that again, Shannon," I deadpanned my not-friend.

"*You* weren't," Shannon said as the tower tumbled again to the sound of Harper's little *"Yay!"* "I'm for sure going to talk about it again."

"But Beckett?" Stevie poked me in the leg, and I looked up at her. "He sounds like he might actually be worth the mess."

I groaned and flopped onto the mat, staring up at the ceiling fan like it might know the solution to my problems. "I don't want to drag Jace into something that isn't real. I can't let him get attached to someone who's only temporary and will forget about him the moment he leaves."

"But what if it is real?" Stevie slid to the floor next to me until our shoulders touched. "He stayed when he didn't have to, stepped up to help your kid, showed up even on days you're not scheduled to see him... That doesn't seem *temporary* to me."

I opened my mouth, then shut it again, because hope was something I didn't have room for. That thought cracked something open in my chest that I wasn't ready to face.

"I'm not putting my life on hold for a man again," I said, thinking back to the years I'd spent on the sidelines of my marriage to Ryan. "I can't do that to Jace or myself."

Steve turned her face toward me. "Has he asked you to?"

"You know"—I squinted at her through slitted eyes and a reluctant smile—"I was so excited to be the friend you needed. When did you decide to be the friend *I* needed?"

Stevie shrugged, then grinned back. "When you apologized for honking at me in the parking lot days after it happened, like it had been haunting you. I recognize a girl's girl when I see one."

I looped my arm through hers, once again doing anything but Pilates in our hour together. "I think I like this Moms of Mayhem thing."

"Me too." Stevie leaned her head on mine, and we laid there for a moment, listening to the soft piano music filtering through the overhead speakers. I hadn't listened to it until now, but once I was paying attention, a chuckle left me.

"Is this a piano rendition of *Pony?*"

The sound that came out of Stevie was more wheeze than laugh, and we both laid there shaking with laughter realizing every single song Shannon had on her playlist was some PG version of horny as hell songs. *Pony* gave way to *Hands to Myself*, then *Sex on Fire*, then *Hips Don't Lie*. With each new song we laughed harder, turning this into one heck of an ab workout after all.

When the hour was up, Shannon strolled over, staring down at us while holding Harper on her hip. Her grey eyes twinkled with mirth, even though the rest of her expression looked bored as always.

"Diabolical." Stevie pointed at Shannon, then stood up to take her daughter back. "That was good."

Shannon smoothed Harper's hair down but looked at me. "If you don't go to The Lantern on New Year's and wear something slutty to tease the Hockey God, I'm quitting."

Stevie laughed again, holding a stitch in her side, then nodded in agreement.

"So, what? You'll go back to taking orders at Slice and Spice?" I got up to stand next to them. "I thought they were dead to you after they tried to coin the term Zaco—pizza and tacos."

She breathed a long, exasperated sigh through her nose, lightly shaking her head. "Don't even get me started on how stupid that is. But that tells you how serious I am."

"I don't know, it's kinda catchy," Stevie said, and Shannon shot her a flat look that sent me into a fit of giggles. "You don't have to decide anything tonight. But I agree with Shannon. Be open to something good happening, even if it's just for a little while."

Harper leaned over from Stevie's arms and patted my cheek, then said, "Balls!"

Everyone froze.

Stevie shriek-laughed, pinning Harper to her chest.

Shannon pressed her hands into her eyes, but her chest shook with laughter.

I covered my face with both hands. "I'm never going to survive New Year's."

20

Emmy

One of the best parts about moving back to Linwood was a white Christmas was almost guaranteed. I woke up that morning to snow on the ground and sunlight bouncing off the mountains like someone had wrapped the whole valley in gold foil.

Inside, it looked like a bomb had gone off, like any house with kids should on Christmas morning. Wrapping paper everywhere, stray pine needles in my coffee mug, and a huge grin on my son's face.

Jace sat cross-legged in front of the tree in a new hoodie, holding up one of my gifts. I'd gone a little overboard with the wrapping—velvet ribbon, tiny pinecones, and a hockey skate ornament tied on top that was quickly ripped off and flung across the room.

"This one looks like a Martha Stewart fever dream," he said, squinting at the tag.

I grinned from the couch, a steaming coffee cup in my hands. "Thank you. I stayed up all night hand-lettering that.

Glued part of my hair to the bow in the process, but it's festive. Adds texture."

He snorted, but his smile was soft when he opened the box. Inside was a vintage Chicago Storm pennant and a framed picture of us at his very first NHL game, standing next to the glass with Ty on the rink. I held Jace on my hip, and he had his little hand pressed to the glass to give Ty a high five. Our backs were to the camera, Hudson written on our Storm jerseys with Ty standing between us.

It wasn't lost on me that I had no version of this photo with Ryan, even though Jace's dad had also been playing in the minor league then. Even before he'd given up on his dream of making it to the NHL and settled into sports broadcasting, hockey had come first, and Jace and I ranked somewhere much lower on his priorities list. Things like asking for family pictures before a game would have set him off, insisting it threw off his focus.

And then there was my brother. Even when we were states apart, Ty had always gone out of his way to be in Jace's life. Summers spent right here in Linwood, flying us to Chicago for home games, even setting up a spare bedroom in his penthouse just for my little son.

"Dude." Jace held up the frame, then pointed in the background of the photo. "I totally forgot Ty was playing against the Yeti that night. That's Beckett."

I leaned forward, taking the frame from his hand, and really looked at it.

There in the background was Beckett—mid-stride, stick on the ice, eyes locked somewhere off-camera with that intense, *do-not-mess-with-me* expression I saw every morning while he battled through Pilates classes for the last week.

My finger trailed across the glass, wondering how many other times we'd circled each other, just out of reach.

"How's his therapy going?" Jace asked, and I set the photo down in my lap. "We watched the last Yeti game at Ty's house with him, and I can tell he's dying to be back on the ice."

My head bobbed back and forth far too many times to be considered a nod while I tried to tamp down any reaction to the mention of Beckett. "Good. He has a long road ahead, but he's committed to it. You still like skating with him?"

Jace flopped back on the floor, staring up at the ceiling and tugging at the strings of his hoodie. "Yeah. He's amazing. He's not mean, but he's tough—pushes me harder than anyone ever has but always points out when I did something right too. I don't know that I've ever had someone pay that much attention before, you know? Makes me want to work harder, to be like him."

I stared down at my hands while he detailed everything the two of them had worked on each morning at the pond over the last two weeks, a riot of emotions flooding me: anger, that Jace has never once said anything like that about his own dad; awe, that my son was so motivated to work his ass off for his dreams; and more than a little empathy, because yes, I *did* know.

"I thought it might look good on your Juniors' dorm wall someday." I pointed at the pennant, aiming for casual and missing by a mile instead of answering Jace's rhetorical question.

Jace's head tipped my way, his hazel eyes soft. "Are you okay?"

"Me? Thriving," I said. "Absolutely love sending my only

child off to Connecticut the day after Christmas to live off protein shakes and passive-aggression. Think of all the things I'll get to do *alone*, for once. No shoes to trip over, no wet towels on the floor, no trash on the coffee table."

He rolled his eyes, then climbed up on the couch next to me, laying his head in my lap. His legs dangled over the armrest, way too tall for the little boy I still saw in flashes. I ran my hands through his messy hair, trying not to count how many Christmas mornings like this we had left.

Ty and Rowdy showed up an hour later to find us in the exact same position, watching *Christmas Vacation* with paper and ribbon still strewn across the floor. He stopped in the doorway, seeing the tears shimmering in my eyes, and gave me a soft smile.

"Breakfast?" Jace looked back over the sofa and snapped his fingers for Rowdy, who jumped up into my son's lap.

Ty held up a carton of eggs fresh from his farm, and a pack of bacon. "On it. Want to help?"

Jace got up, and Rowdy followed him into the kitchen. I pulled my knees to my chest, staring at my two favorite boys, wondering how I'd gotten so lucky to win the genetic lottery.

My brother topped off my coffee to warm it back up, then got to work making a smorgasbord of breakfast food meant to feed a small army or a singular teenage boy—take your pick.

Together, we FaceTimed my parents in Arizona, the cacti in the background looking festive with a red Santa hat on the top like a tree-topper. Originally, we'd planned to fly them out for Christmas, but with Jace leaving tomorrow, it just hadn't worked out. After 15 years of us all living in different parts of the country, a video call holiday wasn't as weird as you'd think. It was good to see them, but I wasn't longing for home, not with Ty and Jace right here.

The doorbell rang, and I frowned, looking over at the only guest I'd planned on seeing today.

"I'll get it," Jace said, walking toward the entryway with Rowdy at his heels.

I peered around the corner, watching as he opened the door and picked up a package from the front steps. He closed it again, staring down at a wrapped present.

"Tag says it's for you, Mom."

He handed it to me, then disappeared back into the kitchen.

I stared down at the messily wrapped package. The paper was plain red and folded a little wonky. An excessive amount of tape held everything in place, looking like it had been applied in a fit of stubbornness rather than strategy. The bow was more than a little lopsided, like someone had tried to make it look pretty, then given up halfway and hoped the effort would count for something.

The tag was simple. Just *To: Emmy*. No sender, no handwriting I recognized for certain.

But still, something fluttered in my chest.

It felt intentional. Not in the way someone might toss a gift into a bag and call it a day, but like this person—whoever they were—had genuinely tried. Like they'd stood at their kitchen counter with too much tape and not enough skill and thought of me the whole time.

I peeled the paper back carefully, my heart fluttering. Inside was a puzzle—soft winter colors, a quiet cabin scene tucked into snow-covered pines. A little folded note rested on top, written in messy, slanted handwriting.

In case the house feels a little too quiet this week. Hope it makes you smile.

No signature.

I sat there for a long moment, holding the note in my lap, heart tapping a little faster than usual. There was only one person I'd mentioned I sometimes did puzzles when Jace was gone. It wasn't proof, but I couldn't help thinking of Beckett.

Because Jace was right—Beckett made me feel seen. Not just looked at, not just noticed—but truly *seen* in a way that was both comforting and a little terrifying.

I wasn't used to that.

Maybe the puzzle wasn't from him. It could be a kind gesture from a thoughtful neighbor, or a well-meaning friend. But if it *was* Beckett...

I found myself wanting it to be.

Maybe there was something there. Something worth exploring, even if it didn't last forever. But like Stevie said, it didn't have to.

Some people come into your life not to stay forever, but to make you feel something again. To remind you that you're still capable of soft things—hope, wonder, and leaning into someone new.

I traced my finger over the edge of the note, then set it gently aside.

Tomorrow, the house would be quiet. The kind of deafening quiet that screamed loneliness, if I let it. But when I opened the puzzle box and began sorting through the pieces, I wouldn't feel alone this time.

No, this silly little puzzle made me feel *chosen.*

And for the first time in a long time, I let myself imagine

what it might be like to choose someone back. Even if just for a little while.

The terminal drop-off was fast, and Jace barely looked back as he wheeled his suitcase toward security. I smiled and waved until he disappeared around the corner, then sat in the car for a solid five minutes, willing myself not to cry.

It didn't work.

By the time I walked into the studio for Beckett's PT session, my eyes were puffy and red-rimmed, and I was clutching my coffee cup like it contained the last drops of my emotional stability.

He was already there, leaning against the reception counter in his usual hoodie and backward ball cap. Six and a half weeks post-op, and he was finally starting to move like he trusted his hip again. Still stiff, still cautious, but steadier. Stronger.

His gaze met mine, and something in his expression softened.

"You okay?" he asked, voice low and quiet like he already knew the answer.

I offered a smile that felt too wobbly to pass as casual. "Yeah," I lied, setting my bag down a little too hard and pulling off my jacket. "I'm fine."

Beckett didn't press. He just gave a small nod, the kind that said *okay, but I'm still here,* and followed me into the rehab room without another word.

We went through the exercises, and I corrected his form once or twice, but mostly I just watched him move. He still wore the metal brace over his hip that restricted his movement, but if he kept up with his progress, this was probably the last week of it.

Beckett caught my gaze between reps like he was checking in without ever asking too much, only adding to the *I feel seen* thing.

"Hey, um... weird question," I said after he finished his bridges on the mat. "Any chance you left a puzzle on my porch yesterday?"

He looked up at me, something unreadable flickering across his face before he shrugged. "What a nice gift."

My stomach flipped. Not a *no,* but not a *yes* either.

Just enough to keep me wondering.

I nodded, pretending that didn't make my heart twist more than it should, and went back to my job. But I couldn't help it—every time he looked at me, I swore there was something in his eyes. A tenderness. A question he wasn't sure he had permission to ask.

After he left, I cleaned up the studio in silence, glad I'd made the decision to lighten my work load this week. I drove home, telling myself to get a grip. To be grateful Ryan hadn't bailed on Jace again, that I had a whole week to myself, and that crying at the airport was just part of the gig.

But when I pulled into the driveway, I spotted a little basket sitting on my doorstep. I parked my car, then hurried to the porch, picking it up. Inside was a soft coral blanket, still wrapped in ribbon, a little stack of paperbacks, and another note.

> *For cozy nights, swoony stories, and a reminder that some men know exactly what their women are worth. You deserve all three.*

Once again, the note wasn't signed, but it was the same handwriting as yesterday's package. I stared down at it, fingers trembling, and felt the same warmth bloom in my chest as the night before.

It was him. I was almost sure of it.

I brought everything inside, set the books gently on the coffee table, and unfolded the blanket across my lap as I curled up on the couch. The house was quiet, only the gentle hum of the appliances to keep me company, but I didn't feel as alone.

Reaching forward, I grabbed the book off the top and flipped it over to discover it was a hockey romance about a single mom. I let out a quiet laugh as I read the blurb about her falling for her son's coach.

The next one was another variation: small-town romance with a heroine falling for her brother's best friend.

Then childhood friends to lovers.

All different titles, all the same gentle nudge.

Someone knew *exactly* what they were doing.

Without thinking too hard about it, I pulled my phone from my pocket and snapped a picture—my lap covered in the soft coral throw, the first book centered neatly in the middle. I texted it to Beckett.

EMMY

Thank you.

BECKETT

Looks like a good book. You'll have to tell me about it in the morning.

Still no confirmation. No admission.

But I couldn't stop the smile that took over my face, slow and warm and certain.

Beckett was giving me the space I asked for while making sure I knew I wasn't alone.

No one had ever done that for me before.

21

BECKETT

"Another present?" my mom asked one morning, her eyes glistening with excitement. "I taught you well, son."

I rubbed the back of my neck, clutching the terribly wrapped box to my stomach. "I don't know what you're talking about."

She let out a little laugh, adjusting the blanket over her legs on the new couch. "What did you get this time?"

My gaze slid down to the box in my hands, this one full of self-care items I'd purchased based on the guidance of an Instagram reel. "Stuff."

This was the fifth day of presents I'd left on Emmy's doorstep, hoping to brighten her day while Jace was gone. But then I saw the shy smile when she'd asked if the puzzle was from me, and I was addicted.

Each day I'd left something I knew she'd like on her doorstep, never extravagant but always picked with intention. But then Emmy started trying to catch me, and it became a game.

Two days ago, I barely made it back to the truck before

her porch light clicked on. I peeled out of her driveway, heart pounding like I'd toilet-papered her house instead of leaving a gift basket with one of Tate's hot pretzels and a case of cold Diet Coke cans.

Luckily, I had a misspent youth in Linwood that gave me plenty of ideas as to how I could do this and remain stealthy.

The next day, I parked two houses down, cut through a backyard, and hovered behind her recycling can for a full two minutes while her neighbor walked her dog in slow motion.

How an injured six-foot-four NHL hockey player hid behind a bin of flattened cardboard boxes was a mystery even to me. But I did it, all so I could leave a big bag of peach candy tied with ribbon and a note that read,

For when the week gets a little sour.

It was a good thing I was on long-term injured reserve— if the Yeti boys knew I was sitting here leaving presents on my crush's doorstep, I'd never hear the end of it.

"She's onto me," I muttered as I grabbed my keys.

Mom didn't even look up from her tea, enclosed in a stainless steel tumbler with a lid. Her hands shook, but she didn't stop trying, and that was a victory itself. A home healthcare worker had been stopping by every day, helping me with the last of the changes we needed to make to the house to make it safe for her, as well as doing routine checks.

"Maybe it's time you just tell her."

I opened the door and paused, glancing down at the small package in my hands, heart beating faster than it had any right to.

"Maybe," I said.

But not yet.

Not until I was sure she wanted it to be me.

My appointment with Emmy was at 10 this morning, so I left early enough to park down the street from her house, yet again. She backed out of the driveway, headed to the studio, and that was my cue.

Seven weeks post-op, and I was out here limping through a suburban snowfield like a one-man rom-com mission. All to drop off a box with fuzzy socks, a pack of face masks, and a bunch of beauty gadgets I had no idea what they were for, all without getting caught on camera.

Yes, *camera*.

To my dismay and utter delight, she'd installed one last night right above her porch, the world's tiniest blinking red light daring me to try something stupid.

Challenge accepted.

I cut across the neighbor's yard, boots crunching through day-old snow. My hoodie was pulled up, face turned away from the camera like I was starring in some amateur spy movie called *Operation Bubble Bath*.

By the time I reached her front walkway, my hip protested every step. Not full-on pain, but a slow burn that screamed, *You're not cleared for tactical crouching, dumbass.*

"Just drop the box, Beckett," I muttered. "Place it gently. No limping. No slipping. Definitely do not eat shit."

A quick glance at the camera, then I ducked my head again.

"Fuck." Thank God home security cameras weren't a thing when I was a teen.

I set the box carefully on the welcome mat, note taped on top, and backed away like it contained an actual bomb, not a bath bomb. A gust of wind blew across the yard, and the note fluttered.

"No, no, no—" I half-launched, half-hobbled toward the porch, grabbed the note, and slapped it back on the box. My palm left a wet handprint right on top.

The camera beeped. A red light blinked back at me.

Frozen in place, I hoped the camera would lose interest. Emmy wasn't standing in her studio with her phone in hand, watching a man in a hoodie fumble with a pastel gift box. Right?

With a grunt that sounded anything but stealthy, I straightened up and shuffled down the street like a half-melted snowman with a bad hip. One hand on my thigh, the other struggling to keep my hood up.

By the time I reached my truck, breathless and covered in sweat, I knew the box was on the mat and the note was in place.

Maybe she'd read it before rewinding the footage, or maybe I'd just lost every ounce of mysterious charm I had left.

"You're late," Shannon said as I walked through the door to the Pilates studio a few minutes later. One dark eyebrow was arched, but she'd become far less hostile toward me over the last two weeks.

"Traffic." I pointed over my shoulder toward the mostly empty street behind us, glad I'd stopped panting on the drive over.

Shannon shook her head and glanced down at the phone in her lap. "She's waiting for you."

With a little salute, I walked into the studio and through the rows of reformers. Ruth was in today's class and waved as I walked by.

Dirty Little Secret began playing over the speakers, and I stifled a laugh, wondering just how much Shannon knew of my escapades.

"Hi," Emmy said as I turned the corner into the rehab room. "You're here."

I held my hands out to the side, trying not to look guilty. "I'm here."

"Oh, good," Frankie's voice said from the little iPad in the corner, and my shoulders sagged. I wasn't sure whether it was with relief that I could avoid this conversation a little while longer or disappointment that I wasn't alone with Emmy today.

The screen flickered, and Frankie's bald head shimmered under the lights of the Yeti training room. Someone behind him was submerged in an ice bath.

"You made it," Frankie said. "Look at you! Standing tall. Not waddling. There's almost a pelvis-shaped glow about you."

"Modified lateral step-ups," Emmy said as she walked past me, snapping a resistance band between her fingers like a warning. "He crushed them yesterday."

"Crushed is generous," I muttered. "I did them without swearing. That's progress."

"Hell yeah, it is," Frankie said, slapping the whiteboard behind him. It was chaos as usual—half a diagram of the hip joint, a meme about pain tolerance featuring a screaming goat, and the phrase *your labrum is your legacy.* "You saw the surgeon again, right?"

"Yesterday," I said. "And the brace is off. Still no high-impact but cleared for resisted mobility work and maybe some light on-ice edge drills soon if PT keeps going smooth."

Frankie threw his hands in the air. "That's what I like to hear! We'll have you slicing ice like a hot knife through buttah by February. Assuming you don't dislocate yourself trying to put on socks."

"There was a close call," Emmy said dryly.

"That was one time," I grumbled.

Frankie leaned into the screen, smirking. "Well, the boys miss you. Sort of. Krieger's got your locker now and keeps blasting alpha wave meditations while foam rolling. I'm ninety percent sure he's summoning forest spirits."

"Is he still trying to copy my shot?"

"Oh, he is, and it's tragic," Frankie said. "It's like watching a duck try to ride a bicycle. Determined, but deeply wrong."

I couldn't help laughing. Emmy didn't look at me, but she smiled as she walked past with a Pilates ball.

Frankie clapped once, startling whoever was behind him. "Anyway. You're doing great, Beckett. New Year, new hip, no excuses. This is your comeback arc, baby. Just remember: stretch your hip flexors, hydrate like it's a part-time job, and if you think clamshells are easy, you're doing it wrong."

"Thanks, Frankie," Emmy said, still not looking up.

"Bye, Emmy! Don't let him fake cramp out of bridges again!"

"I didn't!" I called, as the screen went black.

She turned to me slowly, eyebrow raised. "Did you?"

I lifted my hands. "I had a leg spasm yesterday afternoon while we were going over my workouts. Technically true."

She chuckled, and the sound was pure evil. "Technically, you're doing extra now."

And just like that, my hip and I were back in the seventh ring of hell disguised as Pilates.

But if it put a smile on Emmy's face, I wasn't even sure I cared.

This was a terrible idea.

Emmy never mentioned this morning's stealth moves, but she had to know, right? I agonized over it all day, trying to decide if it was worth remaining anonymous.

By the time dinner rolled around, I couldn't stop thinking about her.

I shifted my weight on the porch and stared at the little blinking red light that had caught me this morning, not bothering to hide my face this time. Despite the chill in the air, the bag of tacos in my hand from Slice and Spice was sweating. Or maybe that was me.

In all of my 37 years, I couldn't remember a time when a woman had ever made me this nervous, but the more I saw of her, the more I wanted her to smile.

And fuck, I loved being the one to make it happen.

When she didn't immediately react to the motion sensor on her porch going off, I rang the bell and immediately regretted it.

Then the door opened, and—

I forgot how to breathe.

Emmy opened the door in an oversized T-shirt that read *Hurtin' for a Squirtin'* across her chest, making me lose track of every rational thought I'd brought with me. A bright yellow cartoon lemon smirked beneath the text like it was thrilled to be complicit in her crimes. She wore matching lemon-print knee socks and tiny shorts that barely stuck out beneath the shirt on those long, bare legs. I swear to God, it took every shred of restraint I had not to visibly short-circuit.

She had her hair twisted in a loose bun, soft brown

strands escaping near her temples and along her neck—places I now desperately wanted to kiss just to see if she'd shiver. Her cheeks were flushed from laughing, or wine, or maybe the warmth of the house. Whatever it was, it made her glow like sin and sunshine at the same time.

I knew I was staring, and I tried to look away, to act normal, like she wasn't currently the most dangerous thing I'd ever seen. But it was useless. She was legs and curves and soft skin and sass, and holy hell, I'd never wanted someone more in my entire life.

"Oh." Her eyes went wide. "You're not the delivery food."

"No," I croaked. "Nope. Not delivery."

I was staring. Definitely staring. I wanted to stop, but my brain was now buffering in lemony heaven.

"I, uh—Well, I guess I'm kind of delivery. I brought food," I managed, lifting the bag an inch like some kind of peace offering. "For you."

Giggles erupted from behind Emmy's door, and I realized she wasn't alone.

"And your girls' night," I added, staring at the siding above her head. "If—if you want. I just thought... I figured you might like company and maybe... tacos? Queso?"

The door pulled open to reveal Shannon, wearing a grin that was entirely too happy for someone wearing a purple T-shirt that said *May I suggest the roast beef?* with an arrow pointed straight down at her crotch. "Quit staring at her lemons, Conway."

"I'm not—" I started, but Emmy was turning red, and so was I.

A third woman popped up behind them.

"Hi, Beckett!" she called, then dumped a bag of children's fruit snacks into her tipped-back mouth. "Ignore the shirts. It's a thing. Mine has semen on it."

A choked sound escaped me, then I saw hers said *Covered in Seamen*, surrounded by tiny sailors.

"I have children," she added, as if that explained any of this.

"I don't even know what's happening," I muttered.

"That makes two of us." Emmy bit her lip like she was trying not to laugh. "You, uh... want to come in?"

Did I want to come in?

Into a house full of half-drunk women in explicit T-shirts, one who might be my dream girl and another one carrying 20 years of unspoken resentment?

Every instinct said run. Get back in the truck. Pretend I left the tacos on the porch and vaporized into thin air.

But Emmy's little smile seemed to say she hoped I'd say yes, and I couldn't say no to that.

I nodded, swallowing the lump in my throat. "Yeah." I stepped forward. "Sure. Why not?"

As soon as I crossed the threshold, Shannon's eyes narrowed like a hawk spotting prey. She stared at me in silence, a Diet Coke in one hand, the other resting on her hip like she was waiting for me to flinch.

Instead, I held up the queso like a white flag.

For one long second, she said nothing, then finally gave a single nod.

"Good," she said. "You brought cheese. You can live."

She turned and walked away, and I exhaled so hard I almost deflated.

Emmy looked up at me with a smirk, taking the other bags of food from my hands. "You passed the Shannon test."

"I didn't know I was taking it."

"Oh," she said, already leading me into the kitchen, "you've been taking it since the minute you showed up in town."

And just like that, I was in.

Still terrified. Still turned on. Still very much in over my head.

But in.

22

Emmy

Tuesdays were quickly becoming my favorite night of the week.

After Beckett's many doorstep deliveries—candles, face masks, a freaking weighted eye pillow—Shannon, Stevie, and I had decided to host girl's night at my place instead of at the studio. It felt cozier here anyway, especially with my kitchen lit up like a Hallmark movie had run off the rails.

Stevie's husband Luke had picked up Harper after practice, and it was just the three of us to exchange our tacky holiday tees. Never in our original planning did I think the night might also involve Beckett Conway, sitting in my kitchen with a bottle of Topo Chico and looking devastatingly attractive in a backward hat.

"I'm looking for an edge piece with snow on it." His brow was furrowed, gaze flicking across the chaotic mess of puzzle pieces spread over my table.

Between the puzzle, the half-drunk wine bottles, and the crumpled Mexican takeout wrappers he'd both brought and

I'd had delivered, the whole table looked like the aftermath of a bachelorette party hosted by someone's grandma.

Shannon didn't even look up from her side of the table as she said, "That's like asking me to name which person I said I don't like. You're going to need to be *way* more specific than that."

Beckett froze, mid-reach.

Stevie cackled. I pressed my forehead to the table, laughing so hard my ribs ached. It wasn't even *that* funny, but the whole night was so unexpected, it hit me just right.

Beckett shook his head, grinning like he was actually enjoying himself, which might've been the biggest surprise of the night.

Hockey played on the muted TV across the room, and Beckett's attention was split between it and the puzzle, but he didn't get up. Didn't leave. Didn't even ask me to turn it up so he could hear it over the 90's country that was playing on my speakers.

"Why did you get such a big puzzle?" Stevie asked, leaning back in her chair with a sigh. "Who has time for 1,000 pieces?"

"We don't have to finish it," I said, resting my cheek on the table as I stared at the half-finished puzzle I'd been working on all week.

Shannon slapped her hand on the table so hard, my wine splashed over the rim. "We are *not* quitters. That's what the patriarchy wants."

"Yeah!" Beckett cried, and I looked at the TV to see what he was cheering for.

Except it wasn't the game.

His glass bottle clinked against Shannon's own Diet Coke can, neither of them drinking with Stevie and me.

"I might be," Stevie said through a mouthful of tortilla chips. She was leaning slightly to the right in her chair, her eyelids drooping. "It's so far past my bedtime, it's practically tomorrow."

"Fine," Shannon said, then pushed away from the table. "Let's get you home."

"I can drive myself," Stevie said, standing with her hand resting on the table.

"No," Beckett and Shannon said in unison.

I picked my head up, staring at them. Linwood was a small town, and we all remembered the car accident that had taken Beckett's dad, David, and sent Shannon's dad to prison for vehicular manslaughter while driving drunk.

Beckett had around a decade on Shannon though and had a fantastic mom that was left behind to carry the load. Shannon... she didn't have that. I'd already moved away, but from what I'd heard around town, Shannon had lived with her grandma until her teen years, and then had done her best to survive on her own after she passed away.

"Let's go." Shannon dipped under Stevie's arm and lifting her like she was all too familiar with taking care of drunks.

"Motherhood has made me such a lightweight," Stevie whined, leaning into Shannon's side and resting her head on her shoulder. "I think I'm more delirious than drunk. But this was the best night I've had in years. I just love you girls so much."

Shannon chuckled, then leaned her head down too. "You're not half bad."

I gasped, my hand over my chest. "Are... are we *friends* now?"

Shannon shook her head, her nose scrunched up but a

smile spreading as if it was against her will. "Not yet. But closer."

Gathering Stevie's and Shannon's things, I followed them to the door, already mentally planning out next Tuesday. I stood on the stoop as they got into Shannon's little car, waving goodbye.

Stevie rolled down the window, half hanging out of it as she pointed the door and whisper-yelled, "Beckett's hot as fuck, Emmy. You should bang him."

A choked laugh sounded behind me, and my cheeks flushed with warmth.

"Goodnight, Stevie." I drew out the words as they drove away, Stevie's hand out the window even though it was freezing outside.

I went back inside, suddenly aware it was just Beckett and me in my house. He stood at the kitchen sink, rinsing out cups and looking far too comfortable in my space. Crossing my arms, I leaned against the wall and watched him, noticing the way his biceps flexed on each pass of the sponge.

Stevie was right—Beckett was probably the hottest man I'd ever seen, and the little buzz I had going was just enough to make me admit it to myself.

He looked up at me while he rinsed the next dish. "Did you have fun?"

"Mmhmm," I mumbled, staring at the bubbles clinging to his forearms.

He dried his hands on a dish towel, then turned and leaned against the counter, arms crossed casually like he hadn't hijacked all the air in the room by existing.

"I like your friends." A slow grin tugged at the corner of his mouth. "Even if one of them wants to launch a public campaign for us to hook up. Actually, maybe that makes me like her more."

I groaned, pressing my hands to my face. "You weren't supposed to hear that."

"I was standing right behind you."

"Still."

His little laugh was enough to make me peer through my fingers, and his gaze lit with a warmth I felt all the way to my core.

"Was she wrong?" There was no teasing in his voice. Just quiet curiosity, layered with heat and something I wasn't ready to name yet.

I swallowed. "I don't know what I'm doing."

He slowly stepped closer, like giving me time to bolt if I needed to. "That's okay," he said. "We don't have to know."

God, he smelled good. Clean and warm and like the spearmint gum he chewed. He stopped a few feet away, close enough to feel but not touch.

"Can I kiss you?" he asked, voice low and careful.

I stared up at him, meeting his bright blue gaze. My breaths came quick, my heart racing as I looked up at the boy I'd known my whole life, grown into a man I liked far more than I was comfortable admitting.

"Yes."

One word. Barely louder than a breath.

In an instant, he was there, one hand cupping my cheek, the other brushing the curve of my waist like I was something delicate. His mouth met mine soft at first, but when I leaned into him, it deepened, slow and sure and so full of want I nearly melted against the wall.

It wasn't rushed. It wasn't frantic.

It was *everything*.

When we finally pulled apart, I blinked up at him, dazed and breathless.

"Well," I said. "Stevie's going to freak out when I tell her."

He laughed, the sound rumbling through my chest, then kissed me again.

Neither of us spoke for a second. I could still feel the kiss on my lips—soft, warm, a little dizzying. His forehead rested against mine, and the silence between us was its own kind of intimacy.

Beckett exhaled slowly, brushing his thumb across my cheek. "I should go."

"Yeah," I said, even though every part of me wanted to tell him he didn't have to. "Probably."

He stepped back, eyes sweeping over me like he was trying to memorize this exact moment—the wine-flushed cheeks, the ridiculous lemon T-shirt, the mess of puzzle pieces on the table behind me.

"I'll see you tomorrow?" he said, already reaching for his hoodie on the back of the couch.

"For New Year's Eve," I confirmed, heart beating way too fast. "Don't be late."

He grinned and it was more than a little smug. "Not a chance."

Before I had time to change my mind, he slipped out into the cold. I stood there for a long time after the door shut, lips still tingling, toes curled into my socks, and absolutely no idea what tomorrow might bring.

But God, I couldn't wait to find out.

Stevie added Shannon to the group chat

STEVIE

My head

EMMY

Lol, you doing okay?

SHANNON

Where am I?

Stevie changed the name of the group chat to Moms of Mayhem

STEVIE

Hell?

Is this hell?

It might be hell.

SHANNON

Drink a Gatorade, and have some breakfast. You'll be right as rain in no time.

EMMY

I've never understood that expression, right as rain. Is there wrong rain?

STEVIE

Don't ask me these questions. The kids all got up at 6. I know nothing.

SHANNON

Ouch. Naptime soon? And why am I in the club? I'm not a mom.

STEVIE

Shh. You're one of us now. Go with it.

I'm hiding in my closet, sipping a Gatorade through a curly straw because lifting my head seems like a lot of work.

SHANNON

So… are you coming out tonight? Ruth said she'll come watch the kids.

EMMY

What?! Is that a possibility? PLEASE come tonight! I need moral support.

STEVIE

Only if you promise to make out with Beckett in front of me.

SHANNON

Nope. I don't need to see that.

STEVIE

Are you kidding me? I do. That man is so hot I could cook an egg on him.

EMMY

Okay, well, now I'm blushing and also weirdly craving eggs???

STEVIE

You're welcome.

Also, Luke says he'll wear flannel and pretend to know how to line dance.
We're in.

SHANNON

I hate all of you. I'm going to smell like beer and despair by 9 p.m.

EMMY

That's the spirit!!! We're ringing in the new year with rhinestones and regrets.

SHANNON

Can I wear black? Is that allowed in a country bar?

STEVIE

If you also wear a pair of boots and a bad attitude, sure.

SHANNON

Perfect. I've got both in spades.

EMMY

What do I wear?

STEVIE

The sluttiest thing you own. I need you to bang that man and report back.

SHANNON

Do you own anything slutty or is it all leggings? Do I need to come over and choose for you?

STEVIE

Yes, do that. I'm saying yes for you, Emmy, because this is my personal mission now.

I'm wearing sparkles. Shannon, bring your black eyeliner and general rage.

SHANNON

Done.

EMMY

As our lord and savior Shania Twain once said, Let's go girls.

STEVIE

LONG LIVE THE MOMS OF MAYHEM

SHANNON

God help us all.

I rolled over in bed, grinning as I stared at my phone for a multitude of reasons. It had been a long time since I'd had as much fun as I did last night. And that kiss?

I couldn't stop thinking about it.

Butterflies took flight in my belly at the thought of seeing him again tonight.

Since Beckett had a doctor's appointment this morning, we'd canceled our normal training session, and the studio was closed for two days to give my staff some much-needed vacation time.

Jace had been texting me off and on while he was in Connecticut, and last night he'd even gone to a New York Empire game. The picture he sent was a selfie of him in a new hockey sweater and matching hat.

He was alone, but I could see the chubby little leg of his half-brother in the photo, as if my son had tried to shield me from the reality of our circumstance.

A year ago, I'd been crushed about Ryan's infidelity. Knowing I wasn't the only woman in his life wasn't as devastating as it should have been—I think deep down I knew it, even before it was confirmed. The late nights, the text messages, the trips away that didn't quite line up with his work calendar.

But the baby—that hurt far more than I wanted to relive. I'd wanted more kids our entire marriage, and Ryan had always said no, that our lives were too full, as it was.

That paternity test in the mail was the slap in the face I

needed. The reminder that I'd put my life on hold for a man who wasn't present, who didn't love me, and didn't prioritize my son.

Ryan had a way of spinning things to make everything seem like my fault—if I hadn't been so demanding, maybe he would have stayed. If I'd just smiled more, complained less, stopped needing so much, maybe I could've held his attention.

For a long time, I believed him. I twisted myself into knots trying to be easier, quieter, more agreeable. I thought if I could fix myself, I could fix us.

Then came the anger—slow-burning at first, like a pilot light. It flared every time I remembered the gaslighting, the deflection, the way he dismissed my concerns like I was crazy for even having them.

I grieved the life I thought we were building, the future I'd imagined for our family. I grieved the version of me that believed love meant shrinking myself to fit him.

But now... now I could see it clearly.

It wasn't me. It was *never* me.

He was never going to show up for me the way I deserved. And that wasn't my failure—it was his.

I pulled the covers tighter around my shoulders and stared at the ceiling, the faint morning light filtering through the curtains. It felt strange not to hear the soft thump of Jace's feet on the stairs or the blender whirring up a morning shake. The silence was bittersweet. Peaceful, but empty.

And yet... not entirely.

Because for the first time in a long time, I didn't feel hollow. I didn't feel like I was just going through the motions. Beckett had a lot to do with that.

And that kiss... God. It wasn't just good. It was a shift,

like the ground had tilted a few degrees, and suddenly, I could see a whole new horizon.

I pressed my phone to my chest and let out a long sigh.

Maybe it was reckless to let myself hope for something. But wasn't that what New Year's Eve was for?

A clean slate.

A fresh start.

A little bit of magic if you were brave enough to believe in it.

Tonight, I was going to wear something that made me feel good. I was going to put on lipstick and laugh too loud and drink something bubbly. And if Beckett looked at me like he did last night?

I wasn't going to talk myself out of it this time. I'd spent enough years playing small. Playing safe.

This year, I wanted more.

23

BECKETT

The Lantern hit me with a wall of sound the second we stepped inside—guitars, stomping boots, and a chorus of voices singing along to Alan Jackson like it was the national anthem. Neon signs buzzed overhead, casting everything in a haze of electric blue and red. The floor stuck just enough to remind me this place had history—years of dancing, drinking, and bad decisions sealed into the wood.

Ty clapped me on the back, his mustache twitching with a withheld grin. He'd traded his normal T-shirt for pearl snap button down that fit his whole rugged Mountain Man thing he had going on. "Cute little cowboy getup you've got there."

I tugged the brim of my hat lower, half to hide my grin, half to feel like less of a fraud. The cowboy hat in question hadn't seen daylight since a wedding a few years ago, but after Emmy's badgering, I had to go all-in.

The place was packed, bodies swaying and stomping in perfect rhythm, boots sliding and spinning across the room. The dance floor stretched wide, couples two-stepping like they'd been born with boots on. Light caught on the rhinestones of some woman's jeans as she spun, and for a second, I just took it all in. The whole room vibrated with life.

My gaze skirted over familiar faces from a lifetime ago, scanning the crowd for Emmy.

I'd been riding a high since that kiss in her kitchen last night, couldn't stop replaying it. The way she'd looked up at me with that mix of surprise and heat. The way her fingers curled in my shirt like she didn't want to let go.

She was coming with Stevie and Shannon tonight, both of whom had surprised the hell out of me last night.

"She's not here yet." Ty grabbed my shoulder and steered me toward a high-top along the edge of the room. "And I've been instructed to make you sit."

I chuckled, but took the stool he offered, glad to take some of the pressure off my hip. I was feeling better, but the night was young, and this was New Years Eve. I needed to last. "Who?"

Ty shook his head, then walked toward the bar. Several people stopped to say hi, asking after my mom or my healing, but tonight it felt less invasive and more genuine interest and concern.

The song ended and a line dance formed to Brooks & Dunn, everyone gathering in neat rows. I leaned against the high-top, letting my eyes sweep across the dance floor. There was something hypnotic about it—boots stomping, hips swinging, arms slicing through the air in perfect sync. It wasn't fancy, but it was tight, controlled chaos, not all that different from the way we moved in practiced patterns on the ice.

I didn't dance. Not well, anyway. But watching it now

made me itch to try. I chalked it up to anticipation, the buzz of knowing she'd be here any second.

Movement near the door caught my attention, and the crowd shifted like a spotlight shining right on Emmy.

Jesus, that green dress clung to her like a secret, short enough to show off toned legs that should've been illegal, and long-sleeved with a deep V that made my mouth go dry. Her brown hair curled in soft waves that brushed her shoulders, bouncing a little as she laughed at something Shannon said. Worn leather boots hugged her calves just right, making me want to do something reckless, like cross the dance floor and kiss her in front of half the damn town.

Stevie didn't give her the chance to get her bearings. She grabbed Emmy's hand and dragged her straight onto the dance floor. Emmy stumbled into the line of dancers, wide-eyed and already laughing, like she knew she was in over her head but wasn't about to back down.

Ty set a glass of water in front of me, taking a long swig of his beer, but I couldn't look away from where Emmy stood under the disco ball in the middle of the dance floor.

She missed the first step, turned the wrong way, then bumped into Stevie with a little squeak. Her head tipped back in a laugh as she tried to catch the beat.

One, two, three. Step, turn, slide.

She started to move with the crowd, her brow furrowed in concentration, but her hips swaying with more confidence every beat. She looked light and wild and completely at home.

Just when I thought I couldn't want her more, she looked up.

Her eyes locked on mine across the room, a little breathless, a little surprised. Her smile curled slow and wicked, like she knew exactly what she was doing to me.

I couldn't move. Could barely breathe.

That kiss last night had knocked me sideways. But this?

This felt like falling.

Ty's long sigh finally drew my attention, and I looked over at my friend. "I see we've moved past attempting to be sly about this. You could at least try not to eye-fuck my sister in front of me."

I grinned, loving that there was no malice in his tone. Reluctant acceptance I could work with. "She kissed me last night."

His dark eyes shot my way, even though his attention stayed firmly out on the dance floor. "You sound 15."

"Kinda feels that way too, man."

The song switched, and Ty's jaw worked like he was trying to decide what to say. Instead, he set his beer down and walked out onto the dance floor. His hand found his little sister's, and he swung her out onto the floor as couples began pairing off.

Somewhere along the line, I forgot Ty was an excellent two-stepper. He and Emmy floated across the floor in a fast pace, just like I'd seen their parents do once upon a time. They moved with this easy, inherited rhythm, Emmy laughing up at her brother as he spun her with a little flair.

"Alright, cowboy, looking a little lovesick there."

I turned to see Stevie grinning as she slid into the seat Ty vacated. She had on a black lace top and jeans that hugged her curves, her dirty blonde hair hanging in a perfectly curled ponytail down her back and gold hoops in her ears. A guy I hadn't met before followed, brown hair slicked back away from his face.

"Luke Sutton." He put the drinks he carried down then stretched out a hand to me. "I figured I should introduce myself before we get inducted into some weird husbands and partners cult."

I barked a laugh and reached across to shake his hand. "Beckett Conway. Good to meet you."

His grip was firm, the lean muscles in his forearms flexing beneath his rolled-up flannel shirt. "Huge fan, by the way. That shorthanded goal in game five of the Western Championship two years ago? Still gives me chills. My buddy and I watched it on repeat for a week."

"Appreciate it." I nodded, a little heat creeping up my neck. "Still hoping to get back out there once the hip's healed."

"You will," Luke said, like it was a fact. "The Yetis need you."

I liked him instantly.

Stevie took a long sip of whatever fruity thing she was drinking. "You should feel honored. I haven't been out two nights in a row since before the boys started sleeping through the night."

"You don't say," I replied, leaning back. "Girls' night was a good time."

Her smirk was pure trouble. "Until you crashed it."

"I didn't *crash*. I brought food, and she invited me in."

"Uh-huh. Because women frequently turn down hot men standing on their porch with a steaming cup of queso after said hot man anonymously brought her gifts all week." Stevie squinted her eyes, staring right at me. "Someone's cooked here."

I gave her my best innocent shrug, not willing to tell her it was my mom's idea. "Alright, but I have to ask—what was with the shirts? I can't stop thinking about how progressively *worse* they got."

Stevie grinned over her glass. "Wouldn't you like to know."

"I would, actually."

She leaned in like she was about to tell me a secret, then just winked. "Moms of Mayhem never tell."

Luke shook his head, laughing as he slung an arm around her shoulders. "I learned a long time ago not to ask too many questions."

"Smart man." I glanced back at the dance floor just in time to catch Emmy mid-spin, cheeks flushed, her smile bright and wild.

Shannon stood like a dark cloud on the side of the stage, talking to someone there. All black everything—ripped jeans, boots, a sleeveless top that showed off a tattoo sleeve of roses. Her dark hair hung long and straight, makeup sharp enough to cut. She looked like she'd been dropped in from an entirely different universe, and yet people kept greeting her like she was a regular.

I hated that I knew why.

Once upon a time, Ray and my dad closed this place down more nights than not. Best friends till the end, until the end came too early. It was easy to imagine her sitting outside in a running car, hoping the door would swing open soon.

The song faded out in a swell of whoops and clapping, and a second later, Ty and Emmy were weaving their way through the crowd toward our table. Her cheeks were pink from dancing, curls a little wild now, that green dress hugging every damn curve.

Emmy's gaze found mine instantly, and the smile she gave me went straight to my chest.

"Well, that was fun." She brushed a curl out of her face as she reached the table. "I forgot how much of a menace Ty is on the dance floor."

Ty elbowed his sister, then grabbed his beer off the table. "Me? You're the one who barreled into poor Betty Steinberg. Almost broke her brand-new knee."

Before I could jump in, Shannon appeared behind them carrying a whiskey for Emmy and a Diet Coke in her other hand.

"Here." She passed off the drinks with the practiced efficiency of someone who'd done this too many times.

Emmy took her drink with a grateful smile, chewing on the tiny plastic straw. "You're the best."

The three women clustered together, dancing along to the beat as Ty and Luke stood on either side of me. It was too loud to hear their conversation, but something Stevie said made Emmy cackle, her hand gripping her side to hold her upright.

I couldn't help but smile, watching her be so happy.

"Uh oh." Luke reached a hand across to clink beer bottles with Ty. "I've seen that look before. That's your sister, right?"

Ty grunted, and I grinned harder. "I always wanted a brother."

"You *have* one."

Luke laughed, a low, knowing sound, then turned his attention back to where Stevie swayed to the beat, her arms in the air like she didn't care who was watching. She said something over her shoulder to Emmy, who doubled over laughing again, and Luke's whole expression softened while he stared at his wife.

Not just admiration—*devotion*. There was a gravitational pull between them, like the two of them existed in a private orbit no one else could touch.

I felt it like a tug somewhere deep in my chest.

I'd seen couples like that before—on the surface, anyway. But this was different.

This wasn't just attraction or routine or staying together because it was easier than leaving.

This was *want*.

Even in the chaos and noise of a young family, Luke was attuned to her, like if Stevie so much as twitched, he'd be there to catch her.

I'd never had that.

Never even come close.

Now, watching Emmy light up like the world couldn't touch her, I found myself wanting it. Craving it. Not just the fun or the thrill of chasing someone new, but the pull. That deeper thing. The kind of connection that stayed with you through the storm life threw at you.

And it wasn't just that I wanted it. I wanted it *with her*.

The girls moved on and off the dance floor like a swarm of bees, moving together in every step. Sometimes they dragged Ty and Luke with them, and others they danced just the three of them.

Minutes turned to hours, and I contentedly watched from the sidelines, loving the sleepy, dopey grin that was spreading on Emmy's face. Somewhere along the line she'd switched from alcohol to Diet Coke right alongside Shannon.

She bounced back toward our table mid-song, cheeks

pink and curls looser now from all the dancing. Without a word, she plucked the cowboy hat off my head and shoved it onto her own. It was too big, slanting low over one eye, but damn if it didn't suit her.

"Hey," I called after her, half-hearted, because watching her spin back onto the dance floor wearing my hat and that wicked smile? I wasn't stopping that.

She looked unbelievably beautiful.

And not just in the way her legs caught the light, or the sway of that green dress, or how she wore my hat like that's where it belonged.

It was the light in her eyes.

The way she laughed with her whole body.

The way she kept one hand near Stevie's elbow when the beat got fast, and how she always knew where Shannon was, even if Shannon pretended not to care.

She was good. Not just gorgeous, but *good*. A ride-or-die friend, the kind of woman who showed up without needing to be asked. A mom who somehow balanced strength and softness so well it made my chest ache.

And she was happy tonight. That deep, in-her-bones kind that didn't come around often.

Stevie threw an arm around her, pulling her into a ridiculous slow sway that didn't match the beat. Emmy leaned her head on her friend's shoulder, both of them cracking up as they moved in lazy circles like they were the only two people in the room. Shannon lingered near the band again, peeling a few bills off a crumpled wad and handing them to the guy on guitar with a pointed look.

Whatever she said must've landed, because the next second she was weaving back across the floor, that signature Shannon smirk curling her lips.

The lights dimmed a little more. The music faded, and the DJ's voice came over the speakers, low and smooth.

"Alright, folks, this is our last song before the countdown. Grab your someone, because this one's a slow burn."

Sugarland's *Want To* started up, soft, sultry, and familiar. About two people trying to decide if they were ready to jump in.

Shannon passed me on her way to the table, patting me on the chest. "Go get 'em, tiger."

I didn't need to be told twice.

I stood, heart already hammering, and crossed the floor toward Emmy. My hip didn't dare to so much as twinge, knowing I'd keep going as if nothing was wrong in this moment. She spotted me a second before I reached her, eyes wide and warm beneath the brim of my hat.

I offered my hand. "May I?"

She didn't answer—just took it.

The moment she stepped into my arms, the rest of the world dimmed. The sticky floor, the neon buzz, the low hum of conversations—all of it slipped into the background.

She fit against me like this was exactly where we belonged, her hands sliding up around my neck, my palms settling on the curve of her waist. We swayed slow, letting the song do the heavy lifting while she rested her cheek against my chest.

"Took you long enough," she murmured.

I smirked. "Yes, well my PT keeps telling me to save my energy for the things that matter most."

The chorus wrapped around us, sweet and aching, and I held her like I already knew how she kissed. Like my body remembered it from last night and wanted more.

The crowd counted down in the distance—

Ten.

Nine.

Her eyes found mine, and I swore I saw my whole life ahead in them.

Eight.

Seven.

Neither of us looked away.

Six.

Five.

Four.

She smiled, small and certain.

Three.

Two.

And then, without hesitation, I kissed her.

One.

The room exploded into cheers. Confetti rained down from the ceiling, someone popped a bottle of champagne too close to the speakers, and people whooped and hollered like the world had just been reborn.

But all I felt was her.

Warm and steady in my arms, kissing me back like the rest didn't matter, because we were already exactly where we were supposed to be.

24

Emmy

I fumbled with the keys in the lock, Beckett's body pressed against my back. He dropped kisses to the side of my neck, his big hands resting on my hips.

"Pretty sure I'd move faster if you stopped doing that," I whispered, breath hitching when his lips brushed the sensitive spot just below my ear.

"Pretty sure I might be incapable of keeping my hands off you," he murmured, voice low and rough. "Unless you tell me to."

But that was the last thing I wanted.

The door finally gave way, and we stumbled inside, the quiet hush of the house a sharp contrast to the chaos we'd just left behind. The only light came from the streetlamps filtering through the front windows, throwing long shadows across the floor. I barely got the door shut before he had me pinned gently against it, one hand braced beside my head, the other skimming up my thigh.

"This dress." His hand gripped the fabric and slid it up.

"All night, I've wanted to know what it would look like on the floor."

My head hit the door behind me as his hand slid up over my hip, fingers trailing the line of my panties. I gripped his shirt, holding him to me, trying to remember a time I'd ever felt this desperate for anyone.

With my neck exposed, his head dropped, tongue licking and kissing across my skin. A wash of heat spread through me, trailing from everywhere he touched directly to my core.

The hand not teasing along the edge of my underwear slid behind my head, guiding me into the kind of kiss that stole the air from my lungs. Last night's kiss had been an awakening—soft, sweet, a promise. The midnight kiss had sparked a fire.

But this?

This was an inferno. A fire I couldn't put out even if I wanted to, and I did *not* want to.

He caught my bottom lip between his teeth, just enough pressure to make me shiver, then soothed the sting with his tongue. I opened for him without hesitation, and when our mouths met fully, it was slow and deep—like tasting something I'd been craving for far too long.

Our tongues tangled, not in a rush but in a rhythm, like we'd already memorized each other. My hands slid around his waist, pulling him closer until the hard line of his body pressed against mine. He groaned into my mouth, the sound guttural and raw, then dropped his forehead to my shoulder as his hips rolled into me with aching precision.

"Upstairs," I whispered, breathless, grabbing his hand and sliding out from under him.

His boots thudded heavy behind me on the steps, and I felt him watching me—watching the sway of my hips, the way my dress clung to my legs as I climbed up the dark stairs to my bedroom.

"Still think I should've carried you," he said behind me, his voice low and full of that familiar challenge.

I glanced over my shoulder, the heat in his eyes evident even in the dim light. "You're seven weeks post-op with a hip held together by sutures and stubbornness."

He grinned. "So, you're saying there's a chance."

"I'm *saying* I'd have to write up my own incident report, and that's not how I want to spend tonight."

By the time we reached the top, his hands were back on me—sure, steady, hungry. And I was already his for the taking.

We tumbled our way into my bedroom, clothes leaving a trail from the doorway to my bed until I was laid out under him in just my boots, bra, and panties. I held one foot up, and he gripped it by the heel, gently tugging until it slid free. It fell to the floor with a thud, followed by the second one.

"Fuck, you're stunning," Beckett said, reaching behind his head to pull off the henley he wore in one swift movement.

I sat up on my elbows, hips almost to the edge of the bed as he stood between my legs, His arms flexed as his hands slowly undid the belt at his waist. After weeks of working out together, I was fully aware of the muscles lining every inch of Beckett's body. But nothing prepared me for the way the moonlight streaming through my windows hit just right, emphasizing every cut, every line.

"Not so bad yourself." My voice was rougher than usual, not even kind of hiding how badly I wanted him.

He smirked, his head shaking lightly as his hands slid up

my calves and to my thighs, gently pushing them apart to make room for his hips.

My eyes dropped to his open belt, his jeans sagging just enough to show the waistband of boxer briefs. There was still a faint bruise on his hip, and I knew the surgery scars sat just below. "How's your hip? Maybe we should stop."

Beckett shook his head, then lightly slapped the inside of my upper thigh. "You're not in charge here, Emmy. I'm fine unless I say I'm not."

My breath came out in a little gasp, and I tried to squeeze my thighs together, but he didn't let me.

His hands slid across my thighs, then settled on my hips. Between one breath and the next, he lifted me and moved me further back on the bed, making room for himself.

The feel of his shoulders pushing my hips apart, my hips lifting under his hands, was enough to make my head drop back on the mattress. His nose ran over my seam, then his tongue laved over my hip bone, leaving a trail of kisses along my waistband.

"Beckett," I moaned, my hands sliding through his dark hair, searching for purchase. "Please."

"Please, what?" His head came up enough for me to see the heat in his blue eyes, shining bright in the dim room. "Tell me what you want, Peach."

"God, anything." I sounded desperate, but I didn't have it in me to be embarrassed when he chuckled at my answer. "All of it."

He rose to his knees, then climbed over my body, kisses trailing over my stomach and between my breasts. By the time he made it up my neck and to my mouth, I was a puddle of want. Of *need*.

My back arched into the kiss, and he reached behind me,

unhooking my bra. I moved my shoulders to slide it free, then flung it across the room, needing to be free of anything keeping his skin off mine.

The chill air in the house had my nipples pebbling instantly, but before goosebumps could erupt over my skin, Beckett's warm mouth covered one. He sucked gently, his warm hand kneading the other until I gripped his hair again, holding him to me.

My breaths came in short little gasps, warmth pooling in my belly with each passing second until I was on the verge of shaking, I needed him so bad.

"Touch me," I said, hardly recognizing my own voice.

He released my nipple with a little pop, his head coming up to smile at me. I couldn't look away from him, hands trailing over the muscled ridges of his broad shoulders, the planes of his back. A hand dropped down between my legs, moving under the hem of my panties until his fingers slid down my center.

I inhaled sharply, my chest rising off the mattress.

"Like this?" He glided his fingers through me, then circling over my apex. Over and over, he did it, the touch just barely enough to satisfy the bone-deep craving I felt. "Is that what you want?"

"More," I groaned, my fingers digging into the meat of his shoulders.

His lips came down over mine again, and a finger slid inside me. I gasped into his mouth, loving the way it curved upward just right, wiggling against where it felt best. He withdrew his finger, sliding back up over my clit, then down again. Over and over, until I was an absolute mess, needing way more than this.

I must have said that, because suddenly he added another

finger. The stretch was more, in the best way, and I squeezed my eyes shut as the wave of ecstasy built inside me.

"Do not stop," I said between panted breaths, my body buzzing with electricity.

"Wouldn't dream of it." Beckett curled his fingers just right until everything inside of me squeezed. "You're going to come for me, aren't you Peach? Show me what I've been picturing for weeks. Let me hear you so every time I jack off thinking of you, I know exactly how you sound."

The moan that came out of me was something I'd never heard before. When his thumb pressed down on my clit, I exploded. My body shook with the tremors, coming so hard I squeezed my eyes shut.

Beckett's mouth crashed back down on mine, swallowing the sound, and I looped my hands around his back, holding him to me as I rode the wave of ecstasy.

I could feel his heart thundering under my palm, matching my own. When my body finally sagged into the mattress, he rested his forehead on mine, arms flexed on either side of my head. "Well, that was fun."

A low laugh rumbled out of my chest, and I dropped my arms to the side of the mattress. "You're not even undressed yet."

He rubbed his jeans-clad hips across my thigh to prove my point, and I felt how hard he was beneath the fabric. "Good thing I'm nowhere near done with you."

I pushed on his shoulder until he fell to my side. The moonlight hit him even more so as he splayed out on his back, and I climbed up on my knees to take in the view.

"My eyes are up here." He put his hands behind his head, a cocky smirk on his face as he watched me watch him. The pose made every single muscle in his tattooed arms flex, and he knew it. I shook my head but couldn't stop my smile even if I tried.

"Who said it's your eyes I'm interested in?" My hands slid under the waistband of my panties, and I slid them off my hips, throwing them onto the pile across the room.

His nostrils flared, staring at where I was now completely bare to him. It took several seconds for his eyes to meet mine again, and I couldn't help but smirk just the way he had before.

"My eyes are up here."

"And what pretty eyes they are." His hand reached out and settled on my ass. Fingers dug in as he pulled me down over his chest, bringing my mouth up to his in another searing kiss.

His hand followed mine down to his waistband, freeing him of his jeans and boxers until he laid bare next to me. My heart raced as I stared down at his cock, watching his hand circle the thick shaft then slide up to the head, squeezing gently.

"I don't bite," he said when I'd stared a beat too long. "Hopefully you don't either."

I laughed, then let my hand drift down to his. He let go of his shaft to give me room, and I closed my fingers around him.

"How do you like it?" I asked, suddenly unsure I knew how to do any of this, even though I'd been married for 16 years. My entire sexual history sat with Ryan, who would've already flipped me on my back, finished inside me, and been in the shower by now.

Beckett's arms went back behind his head, his eyes closed and nostrils flared. "I like it when you're touching me. As simple as that."

My hand moved up and down him, running across the silky-smooth feel of his skin, and my mouth watered. "Can I taste you?"

A stuttered laugh came out of Beckett's mouth, and his arms dropped to the side. "I don't know, want to marry me?"

I grinned, then moved between his legs, my mouth hovering just over him. He grabbed a pillow and put it behind his head, his eyes half-lidded and focused intently on me. My tongue snaked out, licking just under the head in a teasing taste, and Beckett's fingers tightened in the sheets.

I did it again, and he inhaled so sharply, I couldn't help but chuckle. "Put me in your mouth, Emmy."

A wave of heat washed through me at the bossy tone, my eyes finding his in the dark.

"Slide my dick across your tongue as far as you can go. Let me feel how badly you want me to fuck you."

It was my turn to pant, but I did as he said. My lips opened, and I slid my mouth down his shaft, my hand sliding down to cover what I couldn't get into my mouth.

"*Fuck yes,*" Beckett said, his fingers resting gently in my hair. He didn't guide my movements, but held my head, as if he couldn't help but touch me too.

When I slid him to the back of my throat, taking him as deep as I could, we both groaned until he pulled out of my mouth. I stared up at him, worried I'd done something wrong, until he dropped his feet off the bed and grabbed his jeans.

Seconds later, he was back, a little foil packet gleaming in the low light. He put it in between his teeth and ripped, pulling out the condom inside.

Beckett slid the condom down his shaft. "On your back."

I scrambled to comply, my chest rising and falling as I

gave into the wave of lust hitting me so hard, I had no choice but to obey. "Spread those thighs for me so I can see your pretty pussy glistening for me."

My legs fell apart, and Beckett's hand reached forward to touch me again. Between sucking his dick and coming once, I was drenched. His fingers slid around my clit, then two plunged inside me, spreading me wide.

"You're gonna take my cock so good, aren't you Peach?"

I can neither confirm nor deny that the words that came out of my mouth were English, but I nodded my consent.

He moved forward on his knees, pulling my hips up until I sat against him. I rose up to my elbows, desperate for this depraved view. His hand rested on his cock, stroking once before he tapped it on my clit, then slid down.

The moment he pushed inside, my head tipped back. My breaths came in little gasps, the stretch as good as anything I'd ever felt, and he was barely inside.

"Holy shit." Beckett's hips stilled to hold him in place.

"Move, dammit," I said between gritted teeth, needing it more than I ever had before. My legs rose to bracket his chest, giving him more room to move, and he took it.

My hands rested on his stomach, feeling him move in and out of me while my gaze drifted to the ceiling, everything blurring out but the feel of him inside me.

"Look at you," Beckett said, a warm palm resting on my belly before sliding down to rub over my clit. "Taking me so good. No wonder you made me do so many fucking bridges."

My laugh transformed into a moan when his thumb circled just right, hips moving in a perfect rhythm until my body was just a blur of energy, ready to explode.

"More." My fingers dug into his back, that wave cresting in my again. "Make me come."

"That's it," Beckett said, a hand slapping gently on the side of my ass when I started to clench around him. The little zap was enough to shatter me. "Oh, fuck, Emmy."

His hips picked up the pace, and I held on, loving the feel of him losing himself to the same unrelenting pull. I couldn't look away, watching his head drop back, mouth hanging open, hands wrapped around my hips using me to find his own release.

The moment he did, his body slumped down over mine, sweaty forehead resting between my breasts.

"Not bad," I said once my brain came back online.

A stuttered laugh shook through Beckett's body, and I grinned up at the ceiling.

"Not *bad?*" His mouth slid over to my nipple, then bit down gently. I let out a little yelp, then burst out laughing. "Maybe I should have bitten you after all, you little brat."

He fell off to the side of me, splayed out naked and spent, but his head tipped toward me. I shifted onto my side, one hand under my head and the other lazily tracing over the muscles in his chest.

His hand came around mine, then pinned it to his heart. "Feel that, Peach? Feel my heart racing?" He waited for an answer, so I gave him a little nod. "That's because I've never come so hard in my life."

I looked up at him, feeling his fingers lace between mine. We stared at each other, long enough that something unspoken settled between us—something heavier than sweat and sated bodies. His eyes didn't flicker away, and mine didn't try to hide the way I felt it too.

He swallowed hard, like he was about to say something else, but instead he pulled in a sharp breath and rolled away.

"I need a shower," he muttered, voice rough, almost hoarse. He pushed up off the bed and padded naked toward the bathroom, his muscles rippling with each step.

I propped my chin on my hand and watched him go, pretending I wasn't completely exposed—heart, body, all of it. He was halfway to the door when he slowed, like he could feel my eyes on him.

Then he turned, but I didn't snap my gaze up from his ass fast enough.

That slow, cocky grin tugged at the corner of his mouth. "You keep looking at me like that, Peach, and we're both gonna need a second shower."

My cheeks flamed, but I didn't look away. "Maybe I like being dirty."

He chuckled, deep and low, then disappeared into the bathroom with a shake of his head.

The door clicked shut, steam already beginning to curl under the crack, and I lay there in the quiet aftermath, staring at the ceiling like it might have answers I didn't want to hear.

Because something had shifted, all right. And no amount of sass or shower steam was going to rinse it away.

25

Emmy

The morning light slipped through the blinds, soft and golden, painting streaks across Beckett's bare back. His arm was heavy around my waist, our legs knotted together like neither of us could bear to let go.

I'd spent my entire adult life worried about something, all the time. Since the moment I saw those two pink lines, doubt crept in, painting a picture of every single thing that could go wrong.

In those newborn years, I worried I was too young and incapable of giving everything I wanted Jace to have.

Then, I worried about milestones—was he talking soon enough? Growing fast enough? Sleeping enough?

And all the while, I was doing it alone.

Even when I was married, I was alone. Ryan was there in the way a guest was there—dropping in, smiling for pictures, then disappearing when it mattered.

When Jace had night terrors, it was me crawling into his bed with lullabies and whispered reassurances.

When the pediatrician mentioned potential hearing loss from too many ear infections, it was me scouring Google at 2 a.m., spiraling into worst-case scenarios.

When Jace had his first heartbreak in middle school, it was me who held him while he cried, feeling each of his tears like my own.

I carried the weight of being the parent. The comforter. The provider. The rock. Even when I felt like sand.

As a mom, I never got to rest. Not in the bone-deep way we all need every once in a while. I lived in a constant state of readiness, always waiting for the next call from school, the next argument with Ryan, the next crack in the foundation I was trying so damn hard to hold together.

But here, wrapped in Beckett's arms with the world muted around us, I felt peace. Real, bone-deep, unfamiliar peace. For once, my mind wasn't racing. Just the steady thump of his heart against my cheek, the heat of his breath on my forehead, and the quiet hum of a world that felt perfectly still.

I didn't know what the future looked like. Jace was fifteen—on the cusp of everything beautiful and terrifying about growing up. Ryan would still find ways to make things complicated. There'd still be fights and fear and moments I'd second-guess every decision I made.

But somehow, I knew I'd weather it. Because I always had, but also because maybe I wasn't so alone anymore. Between Ty and Shannon and Stevie, and now Beckett, my life was completely transformed from a year ago. Fuller, in the best way.

I shifted slightly, lifting my chin to look up at Beckett. His face was relaxed in sleep, lips parted, dark lashes brushing his cheeks. He looked younger like this. Softer. He'd been through storms of his own, yet here he was—curled around me like he'd found shelter, too.

Something warm curled in my chest, not so much butterflies or lust, but something steadier. Like roots beginning to grow.

I ran my fingers lightly down his spine, and he didn't stir. In this quiet morning light, wrapped up with a man who saw me, I didn't feel like I had to be on high alert. For the first time, I could just *be*.

"Good morning," Beckett said, his voice all gravel and groggy with sleep. "What time is it?"

I lifted my head to look at my phone on the nightstand, but it sat unplugged and dead on the tabletop. "No idea."

Beckett's arms wrapped tighter around my back, pulling me flush against him. "Someone tell my PT I'm busy this morning. I'll do my cardio at home."

I grinned into his chest, tracing my fingers across his smooth skin. "It's New Years Day. I think she can let it slide."

He nodded, his eyes still closed, and I settled in his arms. Everything about last night had been perfect. More than I ever could have imagined, and exactly what I needed.

"What time does Jace come home tonight?" Beckett said, and I melted a little more into his chest at the mention of my son. "Should I come with you to pick him up?"

That made my mind stutter-stop, imagining every possible scenario of how this could go. "What would we tell him?"

Beckett's eyes opened, shining bright blue in the morning light. "I don't know. What would you like to tell him?"

"Nothing," I said before I had fully thought through the idea. "At least, not now."

He frowned, then loosened his hold on my waist, putting some distance between us. I wanted to pull him back to me, to explain that it wasn't because I was ashamed of this. To reassure him with how I felt about him, this, all of it.

It wasn't Beckett I was afraid of, but the change, and everything it would mean to my son.

Already, I could tell how much Jace idolized Beckett, and I loved that for him. If I introduced Beckett into even more of our lives than he already was and that all imploded, I wasn't sure Jace would recover.

The moment I opened my mouth to explain, a quick *honk-honk-honk* sounded outside.

I sat up so fast, the world spun for just a minute, then scrambled to the window and peeked through the blinds.

Ty's truck idled outside, the blue paint sparkling in the sunlight. He sat in the driver's seat, Rowdy in the middle, as Jace climbed out of the passenger side with a duffel slung over one shoulder and a scowl on his face.

"Oh shit," I hissed under my breath. "Why the hell is he—"

Panic surged. I spun around, already halfway across the room, snatching a pair of pajama pants and Beckett's hoodie hanging off the back of the chair in the corner.

"Beckett!" I whisper-shouted, even though he was already sitting on the edge of the bed, looking at me like I'd lost my mind. "Jace is home!"

His eyes went wide, and I shoved a pile of his clothes into his chest. "Get dressed. Now. Stay in here and do not come out unless the house is on fire."

"Peach, what—"

"Shhh!" I pulled the hoodie over my head as I raced toward the bedroom door. I got it shut just as the front door opened.

Footsteps pounded up the stairs, heavy and annoyed.

"Jace?" I called, forcing my voice into something resembling casual as I stepped into the hallway. "I'm so glad you're back! How'd you get home so early? Your flight wasn't until tonight!"

He didn't even glance at me, beelining for his room. The duffel thudded against the floor when he dropped it. "Got on an earlier flight. Called Ty when your phone went to voicemail."

As panicked as I'd been at the sight of him in the driveway, a new kind of panic surged, making me sick to my stomach when I turned the corner and saw my son laying face down on his bed, body splayed out.

I followed, heart hammering like I'd just run a marathon. "Everything okay?"

"No." His words were muffled by the pillow he'd shoved his face into.

I lingered in the doorway, nerves frayed, glancing back at my room where Beckett was, naked and hiding inside. This was not how I imagined introducing my son to the idea of me and Beckett, not even close.

"Did something happen with Dad?" I sat down on the edge of the bed, reaching across the mattress to slide my hand across his back, mourning the days when I could just scoop him up and hold him tight.

Jace turned his face, the pillow scrunched up tight under his cheek. His eyes were red-rimmed like he was holding back tears, and my heart broke into a million pieces.

"Don't make me go back there."

My nose scrunched, eyes burning as I held back my own tears. "Tell me what happened, and I'll see what I can do."

Jace sat up, his back to the doorway, the pillow in his lap, and told me about how Ryan had taken him to film a podcast. "At first, it was cool—this big studio, lights everywhere, a whole setup dedicated to talking about hockey and father-son bonds. Dad was hamming it up for the camera, cracking jokes, name-dropping like it was a sport of its own."

I nodded, all too familiar with just how good Ryan was at winning people over. Tugging at the too-long sleeves of Beckett's hoodie I'd had for weeks now, I pulled my hands inside, needing to do something other than reach across and touch my son.

"He said all this stuff about how proud he was of me," Jace muttered, picking at a loose thread on the pillow. "Talking about how he's been there for all my biggest moments. First hat trick, first travel team tryout... even my fight at the beginning of the season."

My head jerked back as if I'd been slapped, anger building in me until I felt like a match to gasoline, seconds from going up in flames.

Ryan wasn't at *any* of those things.

"It caught me off-guard," Jace continued, voice tight. "But then he kept going. Talking about how we train together every summer, how we talk on the phone every night after games. Mom, we *don't*. I didn't even correct him at first, I was so surprised. I just... sat there."

My jaw clenched. I could practically hear Ryan's voice, smooth and smug, weaving his carefully crafted fiction. All for the optics. All for his brand. My hands balled into fists under the sleeves, wishing I could lash out at something, but I kept my mouth shut, wanting Jace to finish his story.

"Then the podcasters brought up the Mayhem. Asked if it was true Beckett's been helping coach me while he's on IR." Jace finally looked at me, eyes shining. "I said yeah, and said how cool it's been working with him and how much I've learned. And then Dad—he cut me off."

I couldn't breathe.

"He said I wouldn't be on the Mayhem much longer. That he got me into this elite prep school in Canada. Said it like it was already done. Like he was doing me this huge favor." Jace's voice cracked, tears gathering on the edges of his eyes. "But he never even asked me."

My heart shattered.

"Then he started bashing Beckett, the way he always does. Said I needed real coaching. Said I'd never make it to Juniors if I stayed here under some has-been." Jace's voice dropped. "But Beckett believes in me. He actually shows up. And Dad made him sound like a joke."

Silence stretched between us. The kind packed with heartbreak and fury and helpless love.

I swallowed the ache in my throat and put my hand on Jace's chin, lifting his face until he saw how serious I was. "Over my dead body are you going to Canada. Even if he did get you in, our custody agreement is crystal clear. He cannot decide anything without me, and I'm not afraid to fight your father. Not anymore. You're not going anywhere you don't want to go."

He nodded once, then tipped over on the bed until he laid in a little ball, his head resting lightly on my knee. "Did you find the dirty socks I left in the couch cushions for you?"

I brushed my fingers through his wavy hair, then leaned down and kissed his forehead. "Yes. You're disgusting. Don't ever leave me again."

Jace smiled, then wiped at his cheeks with the sleeve of his hoodie.

Guilt twisted in my gut, sharp and unrelenting. How many times would I let Ryan fool us into believing that things would get better? I'd told Jace time and time again that it was important to spend time with his dad, even when he'd said he didn't want to. I'd hoped that Ryan was trying, that it would be good for them to reconnect.

God, I'd handed him over like it wouldn't cost him anything.

But it had.

Anger surged next, hot and choking.

Ryan didn't take Jace to that podcast to bond. He took him to use him, to put on some polished, father-of-the-year performance for an audience that didn't know any better. And when the cameras rolled, he didn't care if his lies hurt the one person who still wanted to believe in him.

Then came the fury.

How *dare* he. How dare he sit there and rewrite Jace's memories for the sake of his image, speaking in absolutes like Jace was just another line in his resume. Like my son was a prop, not his *kid*.

And then—God help me—the hatred. For the man who had the audacity to mock Beckett. A man who didn't know the patient way Beckett coached Jace for no reason other than he wanted to. Who didn't see the pain he pushed through just to show up every day, the heart he poured into every second he spent mentoring a kid who wasn't even his.

Beckett wasn't some washed-up has-been—he was clawing his way back from hell and doing it with more grace and grit than Ryan could even fathom.

I was done playing nice.

Let Ryan think he had the upper hand. Let him believe his spotlight made him untouchable.

Because I would do anything to help Beckett rise. To help Jace see the truth. And to make damn sure Ryan Meyers choked on his own arrogance.

26

BECKETT

Emmy snapped the door shut as she rushed out to meet her son in the hallway. I stood there holding my jeans and shirt to my chest like I was 17, about to be caught with my best friend's sister. But this house was old and nothing was square; the door swung back open just enough for me to hear Jace and Emmy's entire conversation.

"He's cheating on Meredith, too," Jace's voice drifted through the half-cracked door. "Had a woman pinned against the bathroom wall when I went to find him. Then he asked me to lie for him."

I stopped with one leg in my jeans, fists clenched on the waistband as fury turned my vision red. This fucking asshole.

"That—" Emmy started, then cut herself off. The ache in her voice twisted something deep in my chest. "He is a grown man. That is a completely unacceptable thing to ask of you, *his child,* and I am so sorry he put you in that position. I will speak to him about this and make sure we're on the same page moving forward. He cannot ask that of you."

Jace sniffed, and I finished dressing, shrugging into my

henley, even though I was missing a sock and my boxers. I scanned the floor around the bed, then swiped a hand under the bed for the missing items but couldn't find them anywhere.

"I didn't do it anyway," Jace said, and my head popped up listening intently. "She picked me up from the studio after the podcast since he had to record Hockey Tonight, and I told her he was having a meltdown while trimming his nose hairs in the bathroom."

I choked.

A sharp, involuntary laugh punched the back of my throat, and I slapped a hand over my mouth.

Emmy let out a startled snort before catching herself. "Jace," she warned, but there was zero heat in it.

"What?" he said, deadpan. "He does have weird nose hairs now, so she bought it. I hope I don't inherit that."

I crouched again, one boot on, the other forgotten as I scanned for my sock with renewed urgency. My hip protested the movement, a sharp zing that reminded me of every way I'd tested my hip last night.

Glancing toward the door, still ajar, I listened to the voices drifting through it like echoes from another life. One I knew better than I wanted to admit.

I'd been the kid making cutting jokes to cover the fact that it hurt. That the people who were supposed to show up didn't. That you had to laugh or else you'd crack wide open.

Giving up on the missing items, I crept across the room, trying not to let the old wooden floorboards creak beneath me. Everything smelled like her—lavender and vanilla and something fruity. Her bed was still rumpled from the night we spent tangled in it, and her green dress was splayed across the floor like some kind of forgotten evidence. I should've felt smug. Satisfied. Maybe even amused.

But all I felt was heavy.

Jace was talking about Ryan, but without knowing it, he was describing my dad too. Different flavor, same poison.

Mine hadn't been flashy or well-dressed or on national television. He'd just been gone—buried in the bottom of a whiskey bottle most nights, yelling about things I didn't understand and forgetting he even had a wife and kids.

He didn't make excuses. He didn't even try. Like we never even mattered enough to disappoint.

Before I could drown in a past I'd spent the last 20 years running from, I looked toward the window, considering the worst possible plan: open it, swing my good leg out, lower myself carefully down the porch overhang, and—

Yeah, no. Not happening.

I could still hear Frankie's voice in my head like a tiny drill sergeant: *Do not overload the joint. No sudden impact. No unnecessary stress. And do your fucking clamshells.*

Jumping out a second-story window for sure qualified as "unnecessary stress."

I sighed and ran a hand through my hair. Fantastic. That left the hallway, stairs, front door, and a high probability of getting caught like some idiot sneaking out after a high school hookup.

Cracking the door a little wider, I listened to Emmy and Jace, voices quieter now. They were still in his bedroom, so maybe I could make it.

I took a breath and eased out into the hall, one careful step at a time, my boots in hand to keep the noise. Each creak of the floorboard sounded louder than a gunshot, but I kept going.

Down the hall.

Past the bathroom.

Past the open door where I could just barely glimpse Jace laying with his head on Emmy's knee, one hand in his hair. A picture of stability. Of effort. Of a mom who showed up, even when it hurt.

And then I was at the stairs.

They groaned under my weight like a tattletale.

I froze.

No one called out. No one moved.

I made it to the bottom and exhaled slowly, gripping the banister like I'd just completed an Olympic event. My hip throbbed, reminding me that I was not, in fact, invincible and had spent the night fucking the woman of my dreams in any position I could get us into pain-free.

But I was down.

I straightened up and glanced around the quiet living room, the remnants of Emmy and Jace's life everywhere— shoes by the door, books on the side table, and that peachy coral throw blanket half off the couch.

It was domestic and real and terrifyingly perfect, and I didn't want to screw it up. Not for her. Not for Jace.

Because if I was going to be in their lives, I needed to be more than just a warm body in the night. I needed to show up, too. Even when it hurt. Even when it was hard.

I needed to show them what stability looked like. To pick up the pieces when they were falling apart.

The lock turned quietly, and I snuck outside onto the front porch. A soft beep sounded, and I turned to look up at the little red light of the security camera I'd been dodging all week. Emmy had been delighted by all my gifts, but I knew just what Jace needed this time.

Yanking on my boots, I fished my car keys out from my pocket and made my way down the street to where I'd parked my truck. Last night, I'd been annoyed by the number of cars blocking the street near her house, but in the light of day, maybe it was a good thing I'd had to park so far away.

I made it to my truck and climbed inside, letting the heater warm up the cab until it felt like it would after a drive from my place to his. With a quick glance in my mirror, I pulled out into the street, and right into her driveway.

I pulled on a spare Yeti hoodie from the back and slapped a Mayhem hat over my head, then walked up to her front door, truck still running behind me.

Emmy's neighbor stood on their front stoop, staring at me with a shovel in hand. I hadn't noticed him when I'd left her house a few minutes ago, but the imagery of this situation was comical.

My hands shook as I reached forward to knock on the door, unease getting the best of me. Emmy and I hadn't talked about what was going on between us, and she seemed hesitant about telling Jace we were anything more than family friends.

But there was a kid upstairs devastated that his father was a piece of shit and didn't care about him, and I was here, standing outside, very much caring about him.

With one last exhale, I reached forward and rapped on the door, then backed up enough they'd be able to see me from Jace's window.

The curtains parted, and Emmy's face stared out in confusion seconds before Jace's appeared next to hers.

"Wake up, sleepy head. Time to skate."

The front door swung open a minute later, and Emmy stepped out onto the porch, her hair still a little wild from sleep. My hoodie swallowed her frame, the sleeves covering her hands, and I had to force myself to look her in the eyes instead of letting myself remember exactly what she looked like splayed out for me to devour.

She looked up the stairs, then back to where I stood on the stoop. "How are you outside?"

"I flew," I said, straight-faced. "You liked that bat-boy book, right? Thought it might give me a better chance."

She pulled her lips into her mouth, holding in a laugh, but just shook her head.

Before either of us could say more, Jace appeared behind her, ruffling his wavy hair. "Dude. What are you doing here? I told you I wouldn't be back today."

I shoved my hands in my pockets and did my best to play it cool, even though I was sweating under the hoodie like I'd just run a damn marathon. "Oh, really? Must have gotten my days mixed up."

Emmy's eyes narrowed. Jace didn't look convinced either, but he shrugged.

"It is New Year's, though, so I thought I'd let you sleep in. You want to come skate or not?" I nodded toward the truck idling in the driveway. "Pond's waiting."

Jace lit up like someone had flipped a switch, and I could practically see the tension drain from his shoulders. "Yeah, give me two minutes."

He disappeared inside, and suddenly it was just Emmy and me. The wind bit through my hoodie, but I didn't mind. Not when she looked at me like that—still a little stunned, like she hadn't decided whether she wanted to kiss me or kill me.

"Good morning," I said, smiling just enough to keep things light.

She folded her arms across her chest, probably more for warmth than anything else, but it gave her a look of wary suspicion I'd seen that first night back in town, and it was still just as adorable.

"Beckett..."

"I know," I said quickly. "We need to talk about this, whatever it is. But I could hear him talking, and trust me, that boy just needs someone to show up. I may not be able to do it every time, but today I can. Today, he can see with his own eyes just how much he means to me. Just how much I care. So"—I held my hands out to the side, hoping she knew I wasn't talking about just Jace—"here I am. If you'll have me."

Her expression softened a little, and I threw in my last-ditch effort. "Come with us. I know you don't want to leave him after this morning, and Mom would love to see you."

Her brows rose. "Skate? With you two?"

"Yeah. Come hang out. We can have lunch later. And maybe it'd be nice for Jace to see he's not the only one with complicated parents. That having a mom who shows up every single time is pretty fucking cool, even if your dad suffers from excessive nose hairs and an inflated ego."

Emmy smirked, bringing the sleeve of my hoodie up to her mouth. When she didn't answer right away, I kept going.

"Ty's coming too. You can sit with him and silently judge me together. He lives for that kind of thing."

That earned a reluctant snort from her, the corner of her mouth pulling up. "Ty's going?"

"Wouldn't be a proper public shaming without him," I said. "But seriously, come. You don't have to skate. Just be there."

Her eyes met mine, and there was something soft and

searching in her gaze, like she was measuring the cost of saying yes.

"I'd like that," she said quietly. "Just let me get dressed."

And just like that, I breathed a sigh of relief.

She was coming.

I didn't know exactly what that meant for us yet, but for now, it felt like something solid. Something real.

27

Emmy

Lori Conway's house was cozy in the way that only an older home could be—dated, yes, but lived in. The walls had been recently painted a soft blue, and the new sofa in the living room still had the faint smell of plastic wrap and delivery-day excitement.

Signs of her progressing Parkinson's Disease were everywhere, from the safety bars in the hallway to the line of pills on the side table, but this house still looked like a home. I could see why she didn't want to leave.

I stood near the window, hands wrapped around a steaming mug of tea, watching the snow blanket the quiet landscape outside. A line of evergreens bordered the back of the property, their limbs heavy with white. The pond stretched out just beyond the porch, its surface solid and shining in the soft winter sun.

Jace was out there now, gliding across the ice in a practiced rhythm, making me realize just how often he and Beckett had done this lately. His cheeks were flushed from the cold, hair curling at the edges from sweat beneath his beanie, and even from here I could tell—he was happy. Not faking it. Not trying to cover anything up with a joke or a shrug or some sarcastic jab.

Just happy.

My heart swelled, thick with a warmth I hadn't let myself feel in a long time.

Beckett sat on a stump to the side of the pond, one boot propped up and hands buried in his coat pockets. I couldn't hear what they said, but they were talking. Beckett's face was lit with easy focus, and Jace gestured animatedly with his stick, something clearly important being explained or re-enacted. And Beckett... he just listened.

Not waiting for his turn to speak. Not brushing him off. Just there. Present.

I wanted to show up for him, he'd said. And he had, in every possible way.

I pressed the mug to my lips, letting the steam drift up and warm my face, as the fullness in my chest spread out like sun melting the thickest ice.

So much of the last 15 years, I'd done alone, Ryan only showing up when it was convenient or made him look good. Beckett, on the other hand...

This was anything but convenient.

The weight of everything he'd put aside to stay here in town with his mom hit me like a truck, realizing how much more difficult he'd made his recovery path for himself. If he'd stayed in Denver, he would have doctors at his disposal, not ones he had to drive nearly an hour to see. He'd have Frankie breathing down his neck, and a far more experienced staff than me. He'd have teammates cheering him on, reminding him how much they wanted him back.

But instead, he sat down on a crooked stump, breath

fogging in the air as he gestured for what he wanted my son to do next.

He hadn't asked to take over. Just quietly and deliberately *showed up,* choosing his mom and my son over his own life.

I blinked hard, trying to clear the sudden sting in my eyes.

"Everything okay?" a soft voice asked behind me.

I turned to see Lori, a trembling hand light on the back of a dining chair, her expression kind. She had short blonde hair tied in a low ponytail that was more than a little uneven, but she looked far better than I'd anticipated, knowing where she was at in her Parkinson's journey.

I smiled. "Yeah. Today has just been a lot. Jace was so upset this morning, and now"—I gestured to the window, where my son and hers stood together on the side of the rink — "Do you ever get over thinking you're just royally fucking up your kids?"

Lori let out a sharp laugh, her eyes crinkling with amusement. "Unfortunately, no. But I was sure he was a lost cause after everything we went through, and look at him."

She came to stand beside me, following my gaze out the window. "He really is good with him." Her fingers bumped my elbow, and I lifted my arm in invitation. She slid her hand through, leaning on me for support. I could feel the way her body shook with a near constant energy, the tremors uncontrollable now in Stage 3. "That's not new, either. Beckett's always been the kind to make space for people when they need it."

I didn't answer, afraid that if I opened my mouth, too much might spill out.

"How are *you* doing?" I changed subject, looking over at

the woman at my side. "Beckett told me you got the all-clear for occupational therapy, and that they suggested someone come live here with you after he's gone."

She scrunched her nose, then looked behind her at the house. "This was my parent's house, you know. Every one of my good days was here. The bad ones, too. I just don't want to leave yet, not if I don't have to."

That was fair, and maybe someday I'd feel the same. She sighed, and I squeezed her hand resting on my arm.

"I'm not dying yet," she said, the grit in her voice sounding so much like her son. "Despite what everyone seems to think, I know I'm never going to get better. If I get to choose where I spend my last years, I'd like to do it right here, preferably with boys skating out on that ice again."

As if summoned by her words, Ty pulled in the driveway, Rowdy hanging out the passenger window. "Thank you for letting Jace and Ty use it. It means more than you know."

Lori patted my arm, like she felt how emotional I was. "Come and sit. Beckett had all this food delivered, and if we wait to eat until those boys come inside, there will be nothing left."

I laughed, and something loosened in my chest. The sharp edge of fear over whatever was going on between Beckett and I dulled a little.

Maybe this wasn't a fluke. Maybe this was the start of something, and not just a fleeting moment in time.

I looked back out the window one more time and let myself hope.

"Mom, did you see that wrist shot?" Jace said as he tumbled in off the porch, my brother and Beckett in tow. "Pinged off the crossbar so hard, you could hear it echo through the mountains."

"Too bad you still lost." Ty stood in the doorway to take off his coat and boots by the back door. All three men in my life did the same in unison, like they'd done this a thousand times before, and I barely bit back my amusement.

"By *one*."

"Still lost," Beckett chimed in, and I snorted a laugh when my son's eyes shot daggers at him.

"I thought you were rooting for me."

"Oh, I definitely am." Beckett came into the kitchen, leaning over to kiss the top of his mom's head and swiping several chips off her plate in the process. "But that doesn't mean you didn't lose."

Jace let out a *humph* and slid into a chair at the table, the wood creaking beneath him. His arms crossed over his chest, but any of the heartache I'd seen in his body this morning was gone.

"Next time, kid." Ty leaned down to hug Lori too. "Smells delicious in here, ladies."

"I can give you the recipe." Lori gestured at the many plastic containers with lids tucked underneath. "Grab your keys, head out the door and into your car, get on the highway, take two exits, and stop at the barbecue joint on the corner. Tell them you're here for the Conway Special, and it'll taste just the same."

We all laughed, then grabbed plates.

Lori was right—it was a good thing we'd eaten first, because the mounds of food disappeared far faster than I imagined possible.

Jace threw pieces of pulled pork to Rowdy, and we all chuckled as the three-legged dog leaped into the air, snagging each piece like he had no idea he was disabled.

The sun set early, and we moved to the couch, settled in to watch the Yeti play. I listened as the boys discussed how the season was going, and who had a chance to make a run for the Stanley Cup.

"How much longer until you go back?" Jace tossed a piece of popcorn up into the air, catching it in his mouth from where he sat on the floor in front of Lori's recliner.

Beckett wiped his hands on his jeans, his attention glued to the TV. The Yeti were up 1-0 against Las Vegas, their division rivals. "I'll find out more tomorrow, but I want to be back with the team and on the ice in February, if everything goes right."

The second period ended, and he sat back on the couch, an arm resting across the back. With all five of us in the living room, it was a tight fit. I sat on the new couch between Beckett and Ty, Rowdy resting on Ty's feet.

Beckett's hand brushed against the back of my neck and his gaze shot my way for only a second, but the attention was enough to have my heart racing.

February.

That was next month.

I chewed on the inside of my cheek, already mourning the loss of *this,* the feeling of family my son and I had never really had. My parents were great, but they were living the retired life they earned and weren't around much. I didn't blame them for that, but it didn't mean I didn't miss it. And Ryan's parents were even less involved than he was.

The broadcast switched to commentary, background

noise to my beating heart, until a familiar voice cut through the room.

"I still don't like the Yeti's chances for a Cup run this year," Ryan said, and the room went silent. "Even if Conway makes his return like they keep saying he will—and that's a big *if*, in my opinion—he's not the type of player that makes a difference. Maybe once upon a time he was, but now? He's old. His time has come and gone, and I just don't think he matters anymore."

Beckett's hand slid down and rested heavy on my neck, like he needed to be grounded in the moment and sought me out. We all looked at him, gauging his reaction as they began to discuss him like he wasn't a person with emotions, but a chess piece in someone else's game.

Beckett didn't flinch.

His gaze stayed on the screen, jaw tight, expression unreadable. The kind of practiced composure you develop after years of swallowing your pride and listening to everyone discussing your every move.

His hand remained on the back of my neck, warm and solid, and I didn't dare move, even though I wanted to throw myself in his lap and block his view.

The analysts didn't linger—maybe 30 seconds of dissecting his rehab schedule, another mention of his age—but it felt longer. They pivoted to trade rumors and the Olympics break, and the tension in the room slowly dissolved. But it was too late; the damage had been done.

I stared at the screen, my cheeks burning with a mixture of secondhand embarrassment and anger. Anger for Jace, who had to hear his father degrade Beckett once again. Anger for Beckett, who'd shown nothing but kindness and steadiness to me and Jace. And anger at myself, because no matter how far I ran, Ryan still had this uncanny ability to ruin perfectly good things.

Beckett's thumb brushed along the back of my neck once—barely there, but the gentlest reassurance, as if he sensed *I* was upset and wanted to soothe the ache.

Tears pricked my eyes that this man who had just been cut down to the quick still saw me even in his weakest moments.

I didn't look at him. *Couldn't.* Not with everyone so close.

Jace shifted on the floor, his back a little straighter. I didn't miss the flash of protectiveness in his eyes as he glanced at the TV, then at Beckett.

"He's wrong," Jace said, voice flat but certain. "You're the best player on that team. He's just jealous because it turns out he sucks and couldn't make it out of the minors."

Ty gave a low grunt of agreement. "Ryan's a blowhard. Always has been."

Rowdy gave a soft, affirming bark from under Ty's feet, like he needed to voice his opinion too.

Beckett finally smiled, small but real. "Appreciate that," he said to Jace. While his tone was calm, there was something tighter in it. Something buried. "But it's a team sport. I don't need to be the best. Just need to do my part."

It was the kind of answer that made you respect him more, and also want to punch someone for making him feel like he had to say it at all.

Beside me, Ty shifted, then muttered, "What a dick."

I exhaled through my nose, then took a long sip of the hot cocoa in my hands. *What a dick* didn't even cover it.

The game came back on, but the atmosphere had changed. The air was heavier now.

Beckett sat forward again, his arm returning to the couch cushion behind me, not touching this time but still close. His knee brushed mine once, but he didn't pull away and I didn't move.

For all the ways we couldn't be obvious, for all the things we weren't ready to name yet, I couldn't deny whatever this was between us. It was more than just sex, more than just attraction. It was starting to feel like bone-deep *need,* not even just a want. One I wasn't sure I had the power to say no to.

And what a terrifying thought that was.

28

BECKETT

The rest of January settled into a rhythm I hadn't expected, but one I started to look forward to.

Most mornings kicked off on the pond with Jace and Ty. The kid laced up before sunrise, the cold biting at our cheeks while his skates carved fresh lines across the ice. He talked a big game, chirped me every chance he got, but the kid had talent. Ty let him think he was keeping up. Maybe some mornings, he actually was.

After that, it was straight into PT to keep my hip on track, then Pilates at Emmy's studio. I kept telling myself it was just part of my recovery plan, but truth was, I liked being there. The way she quietly checked on everyone, her voice low and even, the kind of calm I didn't know I needed until it wrapped around me. How she made every single person in the studio feel like they held her whole attention, I didn't understand, but I could see why she had such a loyal following at the studio.

It didn't take me long to figure out Shannon controlled the playlists, and each one got a little more pointed. The first class after New Years, every single song had the word *kiss* in the title. Emmy blushed, I laughed, and the ladies snickered like they knew exactly what was happening. This was a small town, and I'd kissed her right in the middle of the dance floor, so chances were high they *did* know.

Afternoons were a carousel of doctor's appointments—some for me, some for Mom. Since Emmy had mentioned red light and oxygen therapy, I'd bought everything I needed for both of those, trusting her completely. Turned out that was a great decision—both my doctors and Frankie were shocked by how quickly I was progressing.

Mom started occupational therapy, tackling each new challenge her Parkinson's diagnosis gave her with more grit than I could wrap my head around. It was so good to hear her cracking jokes, still telling me to call Emmy, as if I didn't already see her every day. Still asked about the Mayhem boys like she was our assistant coach.

Gavin still hadn't heard anything from the Yeti about my contract renewal for next year, assuring me the best thing I could do was get back on the ice.

At night, I either watched Yeti games or coached the Mayhem. The high school team was coming alive, game by game. Passes were sharper, their skating cleaner, and they were finally starting to trust each other. We had a real shot at playoffs by the end of February, and I was continually shocked by how much I loved coaching, especially with Ty at my side.

I felt good. *Really* good, actually. But this was a different kind of busy than anything I'd known. The NHL schedule was chaos and cameras, hotel rooms night after night. This was both slower and faster, focusing on so much more than myself.

The only thing I hadn't figured out was how to get five uninterrupted minutes with Emmy without Jace or my mom popping up.

After a string of away games with the Mayhem, we were back home for a Friday night game. Like that first night back in town, the stands were packed. Everyone stood shoulder-to-shoulder in the bleachers, decked out in green and black.

New speakers hung above the score board courtesy of my brother, even though we hadn't come to a business agreement with Tate yet. She kept putting us off, saying we could meet about it after the season. That hadn't stopped Mason from sending vendors to install new things, one after the next.

The locker room had undergone a complete renovation, including an exhaust fan that made it smell less like twenty teenagers who were in the height of puberty lived here. It wasn't *good,* but it was less bad, and that counted for something.

I stood in the doorway of the locker room as the team finished gearing up, the sound of hockey tape stretching across stick blades as familiar as my own heartbeat.

"Ready, Coach?" Ty said as he walked by, Rowdy a step behind. The dog had spent so much time behind the bench, he'd become something of an unspoken mascot.

Scanning the stands one more time, I saw Emmy, my mom, and Ty's little neighbor sitting in the last row at center ice. That I could find her so easily in the crowd only spoke of how deeply obsessed I was becoming with the woman.

I gave myself five more seconds to watch her laugh at something my mom said, then turned back to the room. The kids were geared up, some bouncing their legs like they had caffeine in their blood instead of nerves.

Stepping into the middle of the room, I waited. They quieted, eyes on me, the weight of the moment sinking in like they could feel it just under their skin.

"All right, listen up."

My gaze swept the group—Jace chewing on the inside of his cheek, Molly adjusting her helmet strap, Miles blinking too fast.

"We're over halfway through the season. You've come further than anyone thought possible back in December. You're playing like a team now, not just a bunch of idiots who skate fast and chirp too much. If you keep doing that, if you stick together and play smart, you've got a real shot at the playoffs. Not because anyone handed it to you, but because you earned it."

A few heads nodded, and someone thumped their stick on the floor.

"But let me be clear: no cockiness. You haven't won anything yet. You show up humble. You play clean. No fighting." I pointed at Jace, and he gave me a little salute. "I don't care if their forward hip checks you into the glass—take the hit and get back up. If he talks shit about your sister? Beat him to the puck and don't let him touch it. Let the scoreboard throw the punches."

Rowdy gave a soft woof like he agreed.

"And shoot the damn puck," Ty added, sweeping his gaze across the room. "I want shots from every line, every angle, every chance. We don't score if we don't shoot. You see a lane? Take it. You see a body in front? Go *through* them."

I turned to Miles. "And you—contacts in?"

He nodded, looking a little green. "Yeah, Coach."

"No clamming up halfway through the second this time,

all right? Track the puck, stay square, and breathe. Trust your instincts—they know we have a hot goalie."

He lifted his gloved fist, and I bumped it with mine.

I clapped my hands once. "You've got this. Let's give this crowd something to get loud about."

Ty whistled and banged his hand against the wall. The team let out a war cry that echoed down the tunnel. Rowdy barked once and trotted after them as they poured out toward the ice.

I let the wave pass me, heart thumping with the kind of anticipation I hadn't expected to feel on this side of the ice. It wasn't my game anymore, but damn did it feel good to be part of it.

"Tonight's game is brought to you by Hudson Hardware," the announcer said as we took the ice. "Because where else are you gonna go?"

I chuckled, looking over at Ty. "That was the best you could come up with?"

He shrugged. "They asked me for a tagline."

With a shake of my head, I turned back to the ice. The puck dropped, and the game exploded into motion.

I'd been keeping track of the other teams we'd play this season, watching film of previous seasons. Going into it, I knew the Comets were both bigger and faster than mine. More disciplined than anyone we'd faced this season.

They played like a unit, tight formations and surgical passing that made my jaw clench and my legs itch to jump over the boards to get on the ice. It was going to be a grind, the kind of game where every shift counted and a single mistake could flip the scoreboard.

But our kids didn't back down.

We hustled. Hit hard. Chased every puck like it was the

last shift of our lives. It was messy in moments, giving the Mayhem name a new meaning, but we held our own.

Back on the bench, things got loud.

"Yo, number 12 skates like he just learned physics yesterday," Delgado yelled over the boards, squinting at the opposing center like he was trying to solve a riddle.

"What does that even mean?" Ty muttered beside me.

"No clue," I chuckled. "But I'm stealing it."

"Hey!" Grady shouted next, waving his glove in the air. "Tell your goalie his mom called—she said he left the ferret in the washing machine again!"

"What?" Ty asked, baffled.

"Add chirping to our skills worksheet for this week," I said. "That kid has a C in English and it's showing."

The next chirp came from Molly. "Hey 17, your stick handling's so bad, even Google Maps couldn't help you find the puck!"

I choked on a laugh. Ty just shook his head, and the rest of the bench howled with laugher when 17 turned around and missed the pass headed his way. "We're coaching a team of full-blown idiots."

"Yeah." I smiled as Jace laid out to block a shot. "But they're *our* idiots."

And somehow, we hung on.

By the end of the third period, my voice was hoarse from both coaching and laughing at the progressively worse chirping coming from our bench. We were tied 3-3 with two minutes left in the game, and Jace's line was up next.

"Watch number 9. Don't let him touch the puck." I patted him on the helmet before the shift change. "Get me one more goal."

He nodded, and I glanced up in the stands. Emmy stood

in the last row, high above the other people around her. The pom-pom on the top of her beanie bounced as she held her hands steepled over her mouth. Juniper stood right next to her, splitting her focus between the ice and copying everything Emmy did next to her, right down to the hands in front of her mouth. My mom sat next to them wearing a grin that spread from ear to ear.

"Line change!" Ty opened the door to the bench. Jace hopped over the wall as the others came off and sprinted across the ice.

Damn, seeing him explode like that, just like we'd been working on for weeks was something else. My whole body broke out in chills, my breaths coming a little quick as he raced toward the puck. His stick slid out to the side, scooping the puck out from number 9's control, just like I'd told him.

A scramble broke out behind the net, everyone fighting for the puck. Molly snagged it, then snapped it out to where Jace waited in front of our goal.

In a split-second, he shifted directions, taking off down the ice with two defenders on his heels. He was so smooth, so calm, a surge of pride like I'd never known welled in me. I leaned forward, my hands resting on Delgado's shoulders as I craned my neck to watch him race toward the goal.

"SHOOT!" Ty yelled, and Jace launched the puck. The goalie dropped, glove hand out, and the puck flew just over the top, crashing into the back of the net.

Jace's arms shot in the air, and the bench screamed, slapping their sticks on the boards. I clapped my hands, then looked across the rink to see Emmy bouncing up and down, having just short of a full-blown meltdown she was screaming so loud.

My mom grinned at me, looking as proud as the day I'd been drafted to the NHL.

The music died down, and the kids met once again at center ice. The ref dropped the puck, and 20 seconds later, the final buzzer sounded.

"On the line," Ty said, and we all filed off the bench and onto the ice. My feet were a little unsteady as I walked toward the opposing team's coach, but it felt good to be out on the ice, even in shoes.

The two teams went down the line, fist bumping each other, and I did the same. At the end of the line was the Comets' coach, an old friend of Coach Mikaelson.

"You know, I heard you boys were back." He gripped my hand tight. "Didn't know what to believe."

I let go, and he shook Ty's hand next. "Once a Mayhem, always a Mayhem, right Conway?"

"That's right," I agreed with Ty. "Great game, Coach. See you in the playoffs."

The older guy shook his head, then waved us off, following his team off the ice.

By the time I made it to the locker room, chaos had descended. Gear was everywhere, gloves and elbow pads thrown on the floor. Someone had already spilled a Gatorade, and another kid was using a practice jersey to mop it up. Rowdy barked twice and jumped up on the bench, tail wagging like he'd scored the game-winner himself. Someone started banging on a locker in a victory drumbeat rhythm, and, of course, the rest joined in.

Jace sat on the bench, helmet off, cheeks red, hair soaked with sweat and pride.

I gave him a quick nod as I passed. "Hell of a goal."

He grinned, flushed and lit up from the inside. "Thanks, Coach."

I turned to hang the clipboard on the wall when he said, "You think we'll have a shot at State in March?"

I paused.

The question wasn't complicated, at least not on the surface. But it hit somewhere deep, settling in a place I hadn't realized was soft yet.

March.

I'd assumed I'd be back on the ice in Denver by then—rehab complete, hip ready, back in a Yeti jersey, chasing the Cup. That had always been the plan.

But now?

I looked at Jace, this kid who'd grown into something more than just Emmy's son. I looked around at the chaos, at the stink and the noise and the locker room that felt more like home than any rink had in years.

I thought about Emmy up in the stands, her eyes shining, her voice hoarse from cheering. My mom beside her, smiling like she belonged there too.

And suddenly, the plan didn't feel so solid anymore.

"How about we win the next game first," I said finally, resting a hand on his shoulder.

He nodded, satisfied, already pulling his jersey off.

But I was still thinking about it long after the game, still feeling the shift under my feet. Because for the first time in a long time, I wasn't sure what I wanted.

29

Emmy

We'd hardly made it through the door before Jace sprawled across the couch, controller in hand, the last slice of pizza from the after party at Slice and Spice dangling from his mouth.

I nudged a plate under his chin to catch the piece of pizza before it fell on my sofa. "Nice game, bud. You didn't even get a penalty. Who are you?"

He didn't take his eyes off the screen. "Growth."

"Mmhmm. Don't forget to put your gear in the laundry machine. It reeks."

"You say that like it's a bad thing."

"It is, Jace. It absolutely is."

I left him to his digital war zone and headed upstairs, undoing my ponytail on the way to my room. The second I walked in, I beelined for the black hoodie hanging on the back of the bathroom door.

Technically, it was Beckett's. Realistically, I was never giving it back. Way too big, soft as sin, and smelling faintly like whatever bodywash he used. I slipped out of my bra and sweater then pulled it over my head, letting it swallow me whole. Without meaning to, I sighed like some lovesick teenager who couldn't get enough.

As it settled over my skin, I heard it.

Thud. Thud.

I looked over my shoulder at the window, confused as to what the sound was at 11PM on a Friday.

Thud-thud.

Crossing the room, I peered out the window and grinned. Beckett stood below in the snow with a handful of snowballs, smiling up at me like some sort of Hallmark hero.

I yanked the window open, a puff of freezing mountain air smacking me in the face. "Why didn't you just text me, you doofus?"

He shrugged, teeth flashing in the dark. "Seemed more like something one of those book boyfriends of yours would do."

I bit the insides of my cheeks, trying to contain my laugh, even as my heart fluttered at the sweet gesture.

"I'm just excited. We coached a win tonight, Peach. And I need a victory kiss."

My face heated, despite the bitter cold breeze. "Give me a sec," I whisper-shouted down, then shut the window.

Downstairs, Jace was mid-match, headset on. I grabbed my keys off the counter, heart racing as I thought of an excuse.

Tapping my son's shoulder, I said, "I need to run to the store for some coffee creamer. I'll be back in a few."

He gave me a quick nod, then went back to his game.

Beckett's truck idled at the curb, already warm inside when I climbed in. The moment the door closed, he reached across the center console, grabbing me by the back of the neck. Our mouths collided like it had been years instead of hours since the last time I'd kissed him just this morning.

By the time I was ready to combust, he pulled back, his gaze still heated like he couldn't get enough. With a quick glance up at the house behind us, he handed me a travel mug.

"Hot cocoa, with those little heart-shaped marshmallows you always liked."

"Are you trying to seduce me with childhood nostalgia?"

"Is it working?"

I took a sip, savoring the sweet taste. "Disturbingly well."

He pulled away from the curb, snow crunching beneath his tires as we left Linwood and headed up a familiar winding road. It took me a second to realize where we were going.

"You're kidding me."

Beckett glanced over. "What?"

"Beckett Conway, are you taking me to Makeout Point?"

"I believe its official name is *Elkhorn* Point."

"Oh, was that your game? Convince them to come lay under the stars and bore them with elk trivia? I mean, once they hear bull elk pee on their own legs to impress a mate, hockey smell seems not so bad, right?'"

He pulled to the overlook and threw the truck in park, doing his best to bite back a smile. "Well, it worked, didn't it?"

I laughed as he hopped out and opened the tailgate, hauling out a whole pile of thick blankets like he'd done this a time or twelve.

I climbed up beside him as we laid the blankets down. "You've had practice here."

He flopped down on the pallet we made and laced his hands behind his head, eyes fixed on the inky-black sky freckled with stars. "Guilty. But not in about 20 years. Some moves stand the test of time, though."

I settled in next to him, resting my head on his chest. His arm came around my back, holding me to his side as I listened to his heart beat a steady, calming rhythm.

"I made out with one guy here my sophomore year. We got to first base before Ty pulled up beside us and honked the horn. Scared the guy so bad, he cried."

Beckett barked a laugh. "I forgot you dated what's-his-name. Brian something. Ran track. Real sweaty."

"That's the one," I chuckled. "Needless to say, I never kissed anyone up here again."

"Well." Beckett rolled onto his side to face me, his nose brushing mine. "Allow me to change that."

"Oh, smooth," I teased, but my cheeks flamed, despite the cold night air.

"Was it? Because I feel like I'm struggling to hide the fact that I'm completely, hopelessly, stupidly into you. And I can't stop wondering if you feel the same way."

I wiggled my head back and forth, doing a shitty job of containing my grin. "Maybe a little bit."

"Just a little bit?"

His fingers tangled in my hair, cradling my head as he hovered his lips just over mine, waiting for me to answer.

"Yeah."

"Good."

His lips touched down on mine in a featherlight kiss, one after the next, testing and teasing.

And then we were all in.

It was the kind of kiss that made your toes curl and your fingers itch to tug someone closer. The kind of kiss that felt like a livewire had been pressed right against your skin and lit up every nerve ending from the inside out.

Beckett's hand found my waist under the blanket, fingers splayed wide over my skin. "Hope Ty doesn't come honk at us," he murmured against my lips.

I shook with laughter, even as I pulled him closer. He climbed over top of me, pinning me to the blankets beneath us. His hand slid under my hoodie, pushing the fabric up and leaving a trail of goosebumps in his wake.

He paused enough to look at me. "You cold?"

"No," I said, my lips swollen and voice breathless. "You?"

He shook his head, dipping to kiss along my neck. "Not even a little."

My fingers raked through his hair as his hands roamed my body, touching and stroking everywhere that felt good. His hips settled between mine, fully clothed as we kissed and groped, like we really were two desperate teenagers sneaking up to Makeout Point past curfew.

His lips slowed against mine until the kiss softened into something quieter—less heat, more ache. With a sigh, he rested his forehead against mine, breath mingling in the sliver of space between us.

"I keep wondering what it would've been like," he said, voice low and gravely, "if I'd done this 20 years ago. If I'd realized how amazing you were and swooped you up before you even met Ryan."

My heart thumped, sudden and sharp. "And?"

Beckett exhaled through his nose, rolling to the side and bringing me with him, eyes fixed on the night sky above.

"And I would've screwed it up. I was a mess after my dad died. A huge part of me was glad he was gone. Like... at least all the pain his addiction caused was over. He couldn't berate

Mom anymore. He couldn't hurt us with his silence. He couldn't ruin the good stuff just by existing in the room."

He swallowed hard. "But then I'd think—what kind of son feels relief when his dad dies?"

I ran a hand across his chest, remembering that night all too well. "I don't think that makes you shitty. He hurt you. And he couldn't anymore."

Beckett leaned his head against mine. "It wasn't all bad. When I was little, when he worked the mill, things were okay. But after it shut down... he just gave up. Crawled inside a bottle and dragged us all down with him."

"I'm so sorry." I snuggled closer, hating the weight in his voice. "I bet making Juniors after he died felt like a kind of freedom."

He let out a bitter laugh, arms tightening around me. "It was. I left and never looked back. I've spent over 20 years running, afraid that if I came home, the only things waiting for me would be ghosts."

"Are they?" I asked, my voice quiet.

He shook his head. "No. I don't see him anymore. I see Mom. I see Ty and Mason and me on the pond, freezing our asses off until our fingers didn't work. I see Coach believing in me when I couldn't even look in the mirror. At 16, all I could feel was the bad. But now? Now I see everything I walked away from. Everything I missed."

His words settled over me, heavy and honest.

After a moment, I whispered, "I don't know if we'd have made it work back then."

"Yeah." He nodded slowly. "I think about that too."

I let out a breath, my chest tight. "Back then, I was naïve. A little too brave. Not broken yet, but also... not me. Some days I'm still figuring out who that is."

He pressed a kiss to my forehead, smoothing back the fly-aways. "And if you'd never met Ryan, Jace wouldn't exist."

That landed like a stone between us.

I nodded, grateful he understood. "Even knowing everything I know now—I'd still go through it all again if it meant I got him. Every heartbreak. Every mistake. He's worth it." Tears welled at the edges of my eyes, but I didn't blink them away. "He's worth *everything*."

Beckett leaned in and kissed me again, thumb trailing across my cheek to wipe away the tears. "Absolutely, he is."

We lay there in silence for a few moments, tucked under layers of flannel and starlight, snowflakes drifting slow and soft past the open tailgate like the universe had decided to take its time.

"I thought you were bringing me up here to have sex," I said, and Beckett's chest shook underneath my cheek.

"I mean, I wouldn't say no. But this is pretty perfect, if you ask me."

"Careful, Conway," I murmured. "That almost sounded romantic."

"I can do romantic." He tugged me closer. "I just needed the inspiration. Needed to find the girl I wanted badly enough to sweep her off her feet."

"Well." I leaned up until our noses bumped. "Consider me swept."

He kissed me again, slow and sure and full of promise.

The drive back into town was quiet, music drifting through the car as Beckett wove his way back toward my house, our fingers intertwined on the center console. My heart was still humming to the rhythm of Beckett's kiss, the intimacy of tonight seeming so much more than just sex.

Too soon, we were back outside my house, staring at the blue siding and the little porch light. Beckett lifted my hand to his mouth, kissing the back of it. "See you in the morning."

I nodded, the smile on my face feeling damn near permanent at this point. "Bright and early."

Snow crunched under my boots as I hurried up the front steps, only then realizing I forgot to ask him to stop for coffee creamer.

I cracked the front door open, hoping that Jace had gone to bed already. But no such luck.

He was still on the couch, legs up, controller in hand, the same battle game lighting up the TV screen. His head swiveled toward me the second the door shut behind me.

I froze like I'd just been caught sneaking in from Makeout Point, which was ridiculous because *he* was the teen, and I was the mother in this equation, even though that was exactly what was happening.

Jace raised an eyebrow. "So, where's the coffee creamer?"

I stared at him for a half-second too long, then slid my boots off. "They were out," I blurted. "All out. Not a drop of dairy in the whole place. Even the half-and-half was expired. Total cream crisis. I don't know what we're going to do."

He squinted. "You were gone for over an hour."

"You wouldn't *believe* how packed the store was." I bent to put my boots under the bench, then went to the stairs. "That post-game rush, you know? And then the dairy shortage just made it worse."

He didn't say anything, just stared at me with that same skepticism.

"Anyway." I flicked off the living room lights, washing us both in darkness aside from the TV, hoping it hid the blush creeping up my cheeks. "I'm going to bed. You should, too. Practice tomorrow?"

"I practice every morning."

"And that's why you should go to bed."

As I reached the landing, I heard him mutter, "Man, she's weird."

I closed the bedroom door, leaned against it with a dopey smile, and tried my best not to relive every second of those kisses under the stars.

Tried, and failed spectacularly.

30

BECKETT

Tuesday morning Pilates shouldn't have been sexy. But apparently, when Emmy Hudson was the one guiding my mom through modified stretches and mindful breathing, it was damn near erotic.

She was patient and encouraging, quick to help when Mom lost her balance, and somehow still focused enough to keep things professional—at least on *her* end.

Me? I was toast the second she bent down to adjust Mom's form. Game over. Heart racing. Pants suddenly too tight.

By the time Mom was finished and cleared to leave, I was hanging on by a quickly unraveling thread.

I walked her out to the little SUV Mason had given her. She was steadier than last week, moving with more confidence, but I still hovered just in case.

"Thanks, hon," she said once she was settled in the passenger seat. "That was a good session. I can feel it in my core already."

"Means you're doing it right." I smiled and closed her

door, then looked back at the studio. I hadn't said goodbye to Emmy, and I wasn't ready to leave.

I opened the car door again and said, "Forgot my phone."

She waved me off. "Go."

With hurried steps, I slipped back inside the studio, pulse ticking faster with every step. The lobby was empty, Emmy's staff gone for their lunch break. I moved between the reformers and found her still in the PT room, wiping down the table, her ponytail swaying with each motion.

She looked up, surprised. "Lose something?"

"Yeah." I shut the door behind me and locked it with a quiet click. "My mind, every time I'm around you."

Her lips parted just as I closed the distance—and then I kissed her.

No warning. No slow burn. Just pent-up tension crashing down as I grabbed her hips and backed her into the wall. Her body hit with a soft thud, breath catching as I pressed my hard length against her.

She gasped against my mouth, one hand fisting in the collar of my T-shirt, the other sliding under the hem to skim across my ribs. My hands were everywhere—her waist, her back, her thighs—and it still wasn't enough.

I kissed her like I'd been starved for it.

"Jesus," I muttered between breaths, forehead resting on hers. "I want you so bad it physically hurts. Stupid of me to only makeout on Friday night."

She tugged me back in, lips swollen, eyes wild.

"I wish I had time to fuck you right here," I whispered, voice rough. "Right up against this wall, hands in your hair, mouth on your neck, your legs around my waist, my cock buried deep in your pussy until you come all over me."

She let out a shaky laugh. "Yes. That."

"Between your teenager and my mother, we've got the privacy of a shared bathroom in a locker room."

That earned a snort and a grin that nearly did me in.

"But my mom is in the car," I added with a groan, fingers still curled tight around her waist.

"Terrible timing."

"The worst."

I kissed her again, slower this time—memorizing the taste of her, the feel of her hands on me—and forced myself to step back before I did something reckless.

"Rain check?" I asked, still catching my breath.

"God, yes."

I gave her one last look, every inch of me still humming, then turned and slipped out before I changed my mind and locked the door again.

Back at the car, I opened the door to find my mom sitting patiently, holding up my phone between two fingers like it was Exhibit A.

"You mean this phone?" she asked, one brow arched.

I stared at it, then took it with what little dignity I had left. "Yep. That's the one."

She smiled like she knew exactly what had just gone down. "Tell Emmy thank you for today. I felt strong."

I sank into the driver's seat, started the car, and muttered, "Yeah. Me too."

We were halfway down River Street when my phone rang through the car speakers and Gavin's name lit up the screen.

Mom raised a brow. "That's the agent who says you're his most frustrating client?"

With a sigh, I hit accept. "Hey, Gav."

"About time, Sunshine. I've been calling since sunrise."

"I've been at PT."

"Well, some of us have jobs that don't involve foam rollers. But speaking of, how's the hip?"

"Great. Strength and mobility are back where they should be. Getting on the ice any day now. Make sure the Yeti are paying Emmy well—she's fantastic."

"Good. One less excuse for the Yeti to stall out. Still nothing on the renewal paperwork, by the way."

I shifted in my seat, fingers tightening on the wheel.

"Beckett," Gavin sighed, already annoyed. "Do you want me to start making calls or not?"

"I don't know," I admitted. "I always thought I'd be a Yeti until the day I was done. I'm still waiting to hear something from them."

"I've been waiting to hear something from *you*. Do you want to play next season? Do I start shopping you around like you're on clearance?"

"I'm not on clearance."

"Then stop acting like it," he snapped. "They've had your file open for three weeks and haven't made a move."

I didn't say anything— didn't know what *to* say.

Gavin sighed again, this time more tired than pissed. "Look. Just think about it. But don't wait too long. There's only so many teams with room for an old winger with a rebuilt hip and a habit of ghosting his agent."

"You're a real light in my life, Gav."

"That's why you keep me. Don't screw it up." He hung up before I even said goodbye.

The silence in the car stretched all of three seconds.

"So," Mom said, her voice calm but probing. "What do *you* want to do next year?"

I kept my eyes on the road. "Before the injury? Easy answer. I wasn't done. Not even close. But now..."

She nodded, not pushing.

And that was the problem. I didn't know.

I could see it now—staying in Linwood. Coaching Jace. Helping Mom. Waking up next to Emmy wearing that oversized hoodie I never intended for her to give it back. Sunday mornings. Pond skates. A quiet life.

It wasn't the life I'd planned, but it didn't feel like giving up, either.

"It's something to think about," Mom said, her voice soft. "Just make sure it's what *you* want."

"Yeah," I murmured.

By the time we pulled into the driveway, Mom was nodding off in the passenger seat. I helped her inside and guided her to her new bedroom off the foyer. She barely made it to the bed before flopping back against the pillows and mumbling something about brain fog.

"Love you," she said, eyes already closed.

I leaned down and kissed her forehead. "To the moon."

She was snoring within minutes.

I went back to the kitchen and cracked open a cold Gatorade right as the back door swung open.

Ty and Rowdy stepped in like they belonged here, a greasy brown paper bag in one hand.

He lifted it like a trophy. "I bring tacos."

"You're a good man." I grabbed two plates and handed him a bottle of Gatorade while he dropped the tacos on the already-chaotic kitchen island.

"How did she do at Pilates?" he asked.

"Great, actually. Emmy is awesome with her." I tipped

my head toward her room. "It wore her out though. She didn't even heckle me about my driving today."

"Miracles do happen."

He jerked his chin toward the explosion of practice plans and player notes spread across the counter. "So? How are we feeling about this weekend?"

I took a bite of my taco, then gestured at the board. "Pickles is a wall now that he can actually *see*. Great goalie. Turns out, proper prescription lenses do wonders."

"Wild concept," Ty said, already unwrapping his second taco. "Kid played for years like Mr. Magoo."

"Smash is still trying to figure out how to stop without hitting someone or something, but he managed a whole drill yesterday without bouncing off the boards."

"Look at Delgado. Proud of him," Ty said, deadpan. "Did he celebrate with a body check?"

"Into the bench. Progress, not perfection."

We both laughed.

"Molly?" he asked.

"No notes. She's a menace. Quick, smart, aggressive— honestly, she might be coaching *us* by the end of the season."

"Wouldn't even be mad."

I tossed my taco wrappers in the trash and leaned against the counter. "And Jace... he's leveling up every week. He found the juice. His speed's unreal lately, and he's getting better about reading the ice. Did you see that cutback pass yesterday?"

Ty nodded, chewing slowly. "He looks happy out there."

"Yeah." I smiled before I could stop myself. "He is."

There was a pause—just long enough for me to feel it coming.

"And Emmy?" he asked, not quite casually.

I cleared my throat, glad I'd finished my lunch already. "We're good."

He gave me a look. "That vague answer brought to you by someone who's fully whipped."

I huffed a laugh. "Yeah. I am. I'm in deep."

Ty didn't say anything right away, just gave a small, resigned nod. "Well. As long as you keep showing up for her and Jace like you have been, we're good."

"They're happy," I said. "And so am I."

"Then that's what matters."

He popped the last bite of taco in his mouth and washed it down with a swig of Gatorade, then set the bottle next to a clipboard covered in penalty kill notes.

"So." Ty wiped his hands on a napkin. "What happens to the Mayhem when the Yeti call you back for team practice in a few weeks?"

I exhaled slowly. "We haven't talked about that yet."

Ty arched a brow. "Bit of an oversight, don't you think? Considering *we're* the ones coaching the team?"

I gave a sheepish shrug. "Honestly, the day I volunteered us to help, it was pure panic. A knee-jerk reaction when it looked like Mayhem was about to fold. No one else was stepping up, and I couldn't let it die on my watch."

Ty snorted. "So, you dragged me down with you."

"Pretty much. I didn't think we'd be able to turn it around like this though. We're headed to playoffs if they don't fuck it up. Are you sure you want to keep this going, even without me?"

He glanced down at the kitchen island—practice plans, game notes, and Gatorade bottles scattered between half-eaten tacos and a notebook covered in chicken scratch.

"Are you kidding?" He lifted his hat, then set it back down on his head. "This is the most fun I've had in years."

I held out my hand, and he clapped his against it. "Same, brother. Same."

"You have your next physical this afternoon, right?"

"Yeah, heading out once Mom wakes up. There's a chance I'll get cleared to skate today."

Ty nodded. "Good. Then I can start kicking your ass again."

I chuckled, a weight lifting off my shoulders. "Can't tell you how much I've missed you over the years, Ty."

He waved me off. "That's enough mushy talk for now. Let's talk PKs."

We fell back into a rhythm discussing our players and how we could change up lines to make the most impact on a penalty kill. It was casual, and, in the grand scheme of things, unimportant.

But as we stood there—two guys in a cluttered kitchen, empty taco wrappers pushed aside, scribbled drills spread out like blueprints to something bigger—I realized I didn't care about the grand scheme.

This? Coaching a ragtag group of teenagers, arguing strategy over Gatorade and game notes?

This mattered.

And it felt like exactly where I was supposed to be.

31

Emmy

Girls' night moved back to the Pilates studio after New Years, and sometimes we even did Pilates. It had become so integral to my weekly schedule, I now closed the studio at 5 on Tuesdays, the front lights off so everyone knew this was a private event by invite only.

Once the last class filtered out, Shannon reached under the desk and pulled out a blender, then several mason jars of what looked like lemonade. Stevie had shown up right at 5 with Harper on one hip, and a small Crockpot on the other.

"Emmy, did you remember the chips?" she asked as the door closed behind her.

"Did I remember chips," I mocked her, pulling two bags of tortilla chips off the top of the cubbies. "What a question."

"I'm confused what queso and Pilates have to do with each other." Tate sat on the first reformer behind me, her long red hair tied up in a ponytail. She was decked out in leggings, a Mayhem hoodie, and grip socks.

Shannon didn't even look up as she plugged in the

blender. "You're assuming there has to be a connection. That's adorable."

"It's called balance." I opened the chips with a satisfying crack. "Health and cheese can coexist."

"They must," Stevie said solemnly, stirring the contents of the Crockpot. "It's a cornerstone of the Moms of Mayhem. Our motto, if you will."

Tate blinked. "So, this is just... what, queso night?"

Shannon raised a brow. "Did you think we were going to do planks while discussing our feelings?"

"I did bring my water bottle," Tate muttered.

"That's so cute," Shannon said. "You're hydrated and full of hope. You'll fit right in with these two."

Stevie snorted, then dipped a chip into the queso. "Give her a break. She's new."

"I'm not new," Tate said. "I've known Emmy since I was a kid. I'm just selectively social."

I grinned as I put a few new toys in the playpen for Harper. "Well, I'm flattered to have made the selection, then. We're fun, I promise. I roped Stevie in with margaritas and moral support, and look at us now."

"I make a good margarita." Shannon poured the blender contents into mason jars. "And by good, I mean you will be admitting your deepest, darkest secrets by the time you leave."

"I'm breastfeeding." Stevie held up a hand. "So, I'll just have two."

We all laughed, and even Tate cracked a smile as she took a cautious sip from the jar Shannon handed her.

"Oh." She blinked. "That's... wow."

"Right?" I flopped onto a reformer and stole a chip. "Hits like a puck to the ribs."

Stevie pointed at me with the chip bag. "I'm going to add that to my Yelp review about your studio."

"I think you're supposed to actually take a class before leaving a review." Shannon climbed over the playpen fence to sit down with Harper. "Sleeping through them doesn't count."

Tate looked around at all of us—the mess of snacks, the baby babbling, the blend of sarcasm and soft friendship— and her shoulders relaxed. "Okay, I get it now."

"Good." Stevie scooped up queso with a chip, hand hovered under it as she brought it to her mouth. "Now tell us what the deal was with Mason Conway proposing to you at the rink a few weeks ago."

"He's still doing that?" Shannon said from the back of the room, her mouth full of chips.

"Oh, this is an ongoing thing." Stevie rested her chin on her fist, one leg crossed over the other. "I forget you're all locals, so give me the gossip. Tell me the story."

I laid down on the reformer next to Tate, putting my feet on the bar, and slowly pushing the shuttle away. Tate took the subtle invitation and did the same.

"Nothing to tell, really," she said, sliding back and forth on the reformer. "I've known him my whole life. He used to do it for attention in high school, just to make everyone laugh. It's not like it means anything. He's not serious."

Shannon let out a sharp laugh, and I leaned across the reformer to help Tate move into the next stretch. She did what I said, but Stevie wasn't going to let this drop.

"So, nothing's ever happened between you two?" She took a sip of her mason jar, then shook her head as it went down. "Shit, Shannon. You driving me home tonight?"

"Well, you know I'm not letting you drive if you drink

those." Shannon looked down at Harper. "What do you think, Harper? Should I drive you and Mommy home?"

Harper clapped her little hands on either side of Shannon's face, then leaned in to give her a sloppy kiss.

Sensing Tate's distress over discussing Mason, I switched gears. "Beckett took me to Elkhorn Point on Friday night."

Tate's movements stuttered, and her head swiveled over to look at me. "I didn't know anyone still went up there."

"Who cares where you went," Stevie said through a mouthful of cheese, then pointed a chip at Tate. "They're fucking, by the way. She's adorable. He's hot as hell. It's great for all of us."

A laugh ripped out of me, and I sat up on the reformer. "How is my sex life great for you?"

"Are you kidding me?" Stevie wiped at her chin with the edge of her T-shirt. "You're so happy, it's making me happy. And every time you tell me about it, I want to bang my husband. Luke is so happy with this turn of events, he started doing the *laundry*. He's making *breakfast*. He fixed the hole in the wall that's been there since Wyatt decided to attempt a slap shot in the kitchen. He even got a babysitter for Valentine's Day."

"It's me." Shannon raised her hand in the air. "I'm the sitter, since your new sex life has not, in fact, helped me. Tate, are you single?"

Tate looked Shannon's way, her brow scrunched. "Yes, but I am unfortunately attracted to men."

Shannon let out a dramatic sigh and collapsed on the padded mats like she'd just taken a hit to the chest. "God, same. Being straight is the worst thing that's ever happened to me."

I grinned as I refilled Shannon's bowl of queso. "That's

bold coming from someone who tore their ACL doing karaoke."

"I stand by it," Shannon said, dunking a chip. "Men are exhausting. Knees heal."

Stevie snorted. "So, what you're saying is, if you could choose, you'd be a lesbian?"

"Fuck yeah. If I could get a cute wife, a baby like Harper, and someone to take out the trash, I'd switch teams faster than you can say Subaru."

Tate choked on her sip, coughing into her hoodie sleeve.

I laid back on my mat, giggling like I was a teenager again. This right here—this weird, lactose-fueled estrogen bubble of oversharing and laughing until your abs hurt—this was something I hadn't known I'd needed until it became the best part of my week.

Harper let out a squeal from the playpen, taking a mini hockey stick to a foam puck like she was gunning for a starting spot on the Mayhem.

Shannon raised her Diet Coke. "To you lovesick idiots."

"To babysitters who make it possible," Stevie added.

I raised my mason jar. "To my gut. May it someday recover from all this cheese."

After a beat, Tate held hers up too. "To not hating this."

We all looked at her.

She blinked, surprised by her own admission. "I mean. This might be the weirdest thing I've ever done, but it's kind of nice."

"Careful," Shannon said. "You're one margarita away from a friendship bracelet with these two."

"I love friendship bracelets," Stevie said. "Should we braid them or use beads?"

I clinked my jar against hers. "Definitely beads."

Everyone left an hour later, and I grabbed my sage green sweatshirt, turning off the last of the lights and shutting down the computer at the front desk. The studio was quiet now, still warm from laughter and body heat, smelling faintly of disinfectant and limes.

I stepped outside and pulled my hands inside the sleeves. Streetlights lined the road, their glow pooling in soft halos over the pavement. A dusting of fresh snow made the world feel tucked in, like the town itself had pulled up a blanket and gone to bed.

I loved it here—this little town, this stretch of street, this new rhythm of my life that had crept in so quietly, I hadn't realized how much it had started to feel like mine again.

The cold bit at my cheeks as I stepped onto the salted sidewalk, each step scraping softly beneath my boots. The headlights flashed when I clicked the keys, revealing Beckett leaning against the hood.

His hands were tucked into his coat pockets, hood up, head down like he was just casually hanging out in 20-degree weather. When my gaze met his, my heart did that fluttering thing it always did around him.

He straightened up as I reached him. "I was wondering how long queso night would go." My breath fogged as a laugh squeaked out past my lips. "You knew it was queso night?"

"Stevie texted me a picture of Harper trying to eat a chip with her whole face." He shrugged. "Told me I should wait around."

I stepped closer, leaning into his chest. His arms looped around my back, holding me in place. "What if I hadn't come out for another hour?"

He kissed the tip of my nose. "Then I would've had some alone time with your windshield wipers."

I laughed, too tired to pretend I didn't like this. Like him.

"What are you doing here, Beckett?"

His mouth dropped to hover over mine. "Can't stop thinking about this little mouth, so I figured it was time to kidnap you again. Seems that's the only way either of us has any time."

His lips touched down on mine, once, twice, and I sank into his hold, not caring that we stood in the middle of the sidewalk.

The kiss deepened, slow and deliberate, like he had nowhere to be and nothing else to do except memorize the way I tasted. Like we hadn't done this earlier today.

His hands slid up my back, under the edges of my coat, fingers splayed wide like he needed to anchor himself. I felt it everywhere—his breath, his warmth, the way he kissed like he missed me even though we saw each other hours ago.

God, this man could kiss.

When we finally came up for air, I rested my forehead against his chest, trying to remember my name. Then a thought slid through the fog in my brain, sharp enough to cut through the heat of the moment.

"Wait." I pulled back just enough to look up at him. "Where's Jace?"

Beckett blinked, then smiled. "Relax. He's at Ty's working on some physics project. Something about medieval siege weapons? They're in full MacGyver mode. I texted Ty before I came here—he said he'd keep him as long as we want."

I raised an eyebrow. "As long as we want, huh?"

He smirked. "We'll test the limits of that later. For now..." He glanced down the quiet street, then back at me. "Come with me. I want to skate."

"Skate?"

He nodded, suddenly a little sheepish. "Doc cleared me this afternoon. First time back on the ice since surgery. I'm nervous as hell."

My heart thudded with something more than just affection—pride, awe, that soft ache that came from watching someone try hard things. And then more than a little panic that we'd reached this next milestone so fast.

"And you want me there?" I asked, already knowing the answer.

"Of course I want you there." He kissed my knuckles, then opened the car door for me. "I don't want to do it alone."

I stared at him for a beat, then grinned. "My skates are in the garage at home."

"No, they're not." Beckett opened his truck door parked next to mine and held up the hockey skates I'd had since high school. "I already got them for you."

It was the smallest gesture, but the fact he'd thought this through ahead of time, planning to spend this moment with me, made me melt.

He tucked me into my car, then got into his truck, driving down the winding mountain streets to his house. Several trees around the pond were lit up with twinkle lights, and a soft glow came from inside.

Beckett opened my car door as soon as I parked, handing me a vest to put over my sweatshirt. My skates were slung over his shoulder, and his hand grabbed mine, tugging me into his chest for another kiss.

"I can do this, right?" he said, his voice far less cocky than his normal tone.

I reached up and smoothed a hand across his brow, easing the little crease forming there. "You absolutely can do this. The doctors think you're ready, and I think you're ready. And my phone is fully charged, so I can call 911 when we're wrong."

Beckett chuckled, his smile wide and shining bright in the moonlight. He dropped his forehead to mine, and for a long second, we just stood there, breathing in the quiet night.

He kissed me again, gentle and lingering, before pulling back. "If I fall and break something, promise you'll kiss it better."

"Only if it's entertaining," I teased. "Bonus points if I catch it on camera."

We walked the short path to the pond together, boots sinking into the new snow. The lights strung through the trees reflected on the ice, dancing across its smooth surface in shimmering patches. It was beautiful. Quiet. Like the whole world had taken a deep breath and let us have this moment to ourselves.

We sat down on the stumps near the pond to lace up. Beckett's fingers moved slower than usual as he tightened his skates. I could see the tension in his shoulders, the careful way he flexed his leg, testing its strength before even touching the ice.

"You good?" I nudged his knee with mine.

"Guess we're about to find out." He blew out a breath. "This is the longest I've ever been off skates since I was four. Feels weird."

"Well, I haven't sharpened mine in five years, and I think

one of my ankles is weaker than the other, so we can be weird together."

He grinned and stood, wobbling only slightly. I stood too, offering my hand. "Ready?"

Beckett nodded, then stepped onto the pond.

It wasn't graceful—not at first. His legs adjusted slow, his balance off by just a hair. But he moved, gliding forward a few feet, then stopping with a low, controlled turn. His eyes lit up with something I hadn't seen in weeks.

Not just relief. Not just joy.

Something deeper. Like he'd just remembered who he was.

He turned back to me and held out his hand. "Come on, Peach. Let's see what you've got."

I took it and stepped onto the ice, skating toward him with steady strides.

"You're not bad," he said, his voice full of wonder as we found a rhythm, skating side by side.

"You sound surprised."

"I'm impressed."

"You should be. I was unstoppable in gym class."

He laughed and skated ahead, doing a few laps before coming back to my side.

We skated like that for a long while, until our breaths puffed out in white clouds and my toes started to ache from the cold. I didn't care. Not even a little. I felt like a teenager again, heart racing, cheeks flushed, falling in love under a winter sky.

At one point, Beckett grabbed my hand and pulled me in close, our bodies still moving as he wrapped his arms around my waist.

"I missed this," he said quietly. "The ice. The cold. The way it shuts the world up for a while."

I nodded, resting my head against his shoulder. "I get that."

And I did understand. But as his lips touched down on my forehead, I realized I'd miss this. This exact moment. This quiet, stolen piece of something that already felt fleeting.

Because when he had to go back to Denver, how would I ever say goodbye?

32

BECKETT

Skating with Emmy was supposed to be just another PT milestone. A box to check, nothing more. But sharing that frozen pond with her cracked something open in me. How she smiled when I helped her lace her skates. How her laugh echoed across the ice. How she fit against me like we'd been built to glide through life side by side. It was supposed to be rehab, not a revelation.

By the time we got back to the driveway, emotions were running higher than I expected. My chest was tight with everything I couldn't say, everything I felt. It had been days of tension, of almosts and unfinished moments. And now— now I couldn't wait another damn second.

When she looked up at me with wind-chilled cheeks and kiss-bitten lips, I needed her. Right there. I needed her like breath, like gravity, like something primal I'd kept locked away too long.

I walked toward my truck, opened the back door, and climbed in. She followed without a word.

The doors shut. The world faded.

She climbed into my lap and her mouth crashed into mine like we'd been holding back for weeks, not days. Fingers hooked in the hem of my hoodie, her body pressing against mine with this desperate urgency that had my control unraveling by the second.

I unzipped her vest, then pushed up the sweatshirt, savoring the sound she made when I cupped her breasts.

"I think about this all the time," I murmured against her neck, tongue dragging along her pulse point. "You. Right here. Just like this."

"Yeah?" Her breath hitched when I pinched her nipple, head falling back. "You think about me in your fancy truck?"

"Fuck yes, I do."

She let out a breathy laugh, just before gasping when I lifted her, settling her across the back seat. Her leggings slid down easy, and I took my time pressing kisses along her chilled skin, pushing her thighs apart.

"I think about how you sound." My voice dropped. "How you taste. How perfect your body feels wrapped around me."

She reached down, popping the button on my jeans. "Then shut up and fuck me already."

I slid her underwear to the side, running a thumb over her slick heat. "So wet for me already. You been thinking about this too?"

"After you said you wanted to fuck me against the wall this morning?" she said, breathless. "God, yes. Now do something about it."

I groaned and grabbed the condom from my pocket, sliding it over my length. Not wasting any time, I lined up, pushing into her slow and deep. Her whole body arched, one hand slapping the fogged-up window, the other dragging me closer.

"Fuck, Peach," I bit out. "You feel so fucking good. So tight—goddamn."

"Harder," she whispered. "Don't make me beg."

"Oh, I *want* you to beg," I growled, pulling back before slamming into her again. "Want to hear you say how bad you want this. Want *me*."

"I do," she gasped. "Want this. Want you—*don't stop*."

I couldn't have stopped if I tried.

She clenched around me, thighs trembling, breath coming fast. Her name was a prayer on my tongue, and I worshipped every inch of her—quick and dirty and soaked in the kind of need that came from never having enough time.

But I was starting to think *no* amount of time would ever be enough.

"Come with me," she begged, eyes locking with mine. "Please, Beckett—right now."

And I did.

We shattered together, her body tightening around mine, my voice lost in the curve of her neck.

I stayed wrapped around her for a long moment, forehead pressed to hers, heartbeat finally slowing.

"Not exactly how I pictured it," I muttered, trying to shift so I wasn't crushing her. "You deserve better than ten minutes in the backseat of my truck."

She smiled, still breathless. "I'm not complaining."

I kissed her, slower this time, softer.

"I'll give you better next time," I whispered. "Promise."

She nuzzled into my chest with a satisfied sigh. "I'll hold you to that."

And for a second, I let myself pretend I could keep her

here forever. That this wasn't going to change when I went back to Denver soon.

She dressed slowly, with the kind of ease that made my pulse pick back up despite everything we'd just done. I helped her pull her vest on, kissed her one more time—lazy and soft, like neither of us wanted to leave this little bubble we'd created in the dark.

Then she slipped out of the truck with a whispered see you later, fingers brushing mine before she pulled away completely.

I stayed in the backseat, watching her taillights disappear down the road, my body still buzzing, my heart still lodged somewhere between *holy shit* and *please don't go*.

When I finally climbed out and shut the truck door behind me, the night felt colder than it had before.

The house was dark when I stepped inside. Mom had gone to bed, lights off in her room. The only sound was the soft hum of the fridge and the creak of the floor under my feet.

I stood there in the kitchen for a long time, coat still on, Emmy's taste still on my lips, and the ache of her body burned into mine.

And all I could think was, *how the hell am I supposed to leave this?*

Not just the house. Not the town.

Her.

That stupid hoodie she stole. The way Jace looked at me when something finally clicked in practice. Ty pretending he wasn't obsessed with coaching. Mom delighted with a full house around her.

All of it.

I'd left Linwood once, sure it was the right thing. The only way to become who I was supposed to be.

But now?

Now it felt like the best parts of me had stayed behind.

If Denver called tomorrow, I had no idea how I was going to walk away from this without tearing myself in half.

The heater clicked on with a low hum, and somewhere down the hall, the pipes groaned like the place was exhaling right along with me.

I stared at the island where our practice plans still lay scattered, next to a wrinkled Gatorade label and the pen Ty kept forgetting to take with him.

I didn't touch anything. Didn't move. Just stood there, soaking in the quiet and the weight of it all.

Eventually, I shut off the hallway light, hung up my coat, and headed to bed.

Sleep didn't come easy.

The next morning, I rolled over and blinked against the pale blue light leaking through my bedroom blinds. Jace had a test at school this morning, so Emmy insisted he skip morning practice. I'd slept in for the first time in two months, but rather than being relaxing, it was just weird.

Twelve weeks post-op, and I felt damn good.

Stronger. Looser. My stride was longer, my balance better. Still some stiffness in the mornings—and after a night spent with Emmy—but I'd never tell her that.

Once I got moving, I could almost forget what I'd been through.

Frankie was thrilled I was ahead of schedule. The graft

was holding beautifully, my range of motion was right where it should be, and the muscle tone in my hip flexors had come back quicker than expected thanks to Emmy's help.

I wasn't cleared for contact yet, but skating drills were back on the table, and the real stuff wasn't far off.

I sat on the edge of the bed for a second, bare feet on the cold wood floor, then reached for a hoodie off the top of my dresser. I pulled it on, grabbed my keys, and slung my gym bag over my shoulder.

Emmy would be waiting at the studio, clipboard in hand, hair up, smirk locked and loaded. And I couldn't wait to kiss the smile off her face.

I was about to lock up when a dark SUV turned into the drive. The doors opened, and two familiar figures stepped out.

"Of course," I muttered under my breath, grinning as they came into view.

Mikko Laaksonen, the Yeti's star defenseman and one of my best friends, shut the passenger door with a lazy thud. He had sharp Scandinavian cheekbones and short dark blond hair, complete with a look that said he'd rather be anywhere but suburban Colorado. "This house looks like a retirement home."

"I mean, he is old," said the guy next to him, tall and broad and unmistakably Canadian in the way he wore sandals despite the snow on the ground. Logan Parrish, full-time forward and occasional chaos goblin.

"Logan. Mikko," I said, stepping off the porch. "What the hell are you doing here?"

Logan grinned. "Road trip, baby. Frankie said you were starting to skate again. With the Olympic break, he said we should come check up on you."

Mikko rolled his eyes. "*Frankie* said. Like this wasn't your idea."

"You think the Yeti can survive without all three brain cells present? We're the holy trinity of shift changes and miracle goals."

I laughed and shook my head, letting them both in for a quick slap on the back. "You couldn't have texted?"

"And ruin the surprise?" Logan smirked. "Never."

Mikko just sighed. "I told him to text."

I shook my head again, heart lighter than it had been in weeks. With everything going on here in Linwood, I'd dismissed how much I missed my teammates.

"Where are you headed?" Logan pointed at my gym bag, then the keys in my hand. "To see this hot PT Frankie says you drool over?"

Mikko raised an eyebrow. "Is this the same one who made our starting winger cry during hip mobility drills?"

I sighed. "Her name's Emmy. I do not drool. And I only cried once."

"Sure, bud," Logan said, already heading my truck. "We're coming. I gotta see this for myself."

"You're serious?"

Mikko shrugged. "I didn't drive over Vail Pass to sit in your kitchen and talk about our feelings. Let's go."

"Fine." I unlocked my truck, trying not to think about last night. "But get changed. If Emmy sees you standing around, she'll rope you into Pilates, and I'm not saving you."

Logan grinned. "How hard can it be?"

I just laughed. "Tell that to your hamstrings when you're crying next to the senior citizens."

Mikko muttered something in Finnish that probably translated to how much he hated us both.

We got in the truck, and I pulled out of the drive, answering questions about my mom, Ty, and the Mayhem. I did my best to dodge questions about Emmy, but the more I avoided the topic, the more they badgered me.

I parked in front of the studio, and Logan hopped out, staring up and down River Street. "Well, this is adorable. Does it come with an oat milk latte and a dentist? I think I have a cavity from the sweetness."

Mikko squinted at the Elevation Pilates sign. "This is where she works?"

I clapped him on the shoulder. "This is where you die."

The door opened and several women filtered out, wearing colored leggings and high buns. Logan's gaze followed them, and I grabbed him by the hoodie to pull him back to me.

"She's in the back, waiting for you," Shannon said, not bothering to look up from the laptop resting on her thighs. She had her Doc Martens propped on the desk, legs outstretched, and the serious expression I knew meant she was studying.

"Oh, hello little Ten," Logan said, and I slapped him upside the head. He jerked forward at the impact, but his grin didn't falter.

Shannon looked up slowly, eyes flat. "I chew up guys like you and use their egos to line my trash can."

Logan blinked. "Honestly, that's not a turn-off."

Mikko, standing a few feet behind him, just shook his head and said something soft in Finnish. It was too smooth and too reverent to be anything but a compliment.

Shannon looked at him, one dark eyebrow raised. No smile. No expression. Just one long, measured stare like she was throwing down the gauntlet, waiting for him to back down.

I glanced between them, brows lifting. Mikko didn't break eye contact.

Logan turned to me and stage-whispered, "Should we book them a room by the hour or...?"

I wasn't sure what that was, but the thought of Emmy waiting had me headed down the aisle of reformers and toward the back room.

"Took you long enough." Emmy rose on her toes to loop her arms around my neck when I turned the corner. Her mouth was on mine before I had a chance to tell her we weren't alone, but *fuck*, she was too good to pass up.

Her lips moved against mine like she needed the contact as much as I did. Like the afternoons at her place when Jace was at school and long, lingering kisses behind closed doors at the clinic weren't enough. And, God, I felt the same.

I couldn't get enough of her, plain and simple.

Which was why I'd completely forgotten about the two idiots now standing frozen behind me.

"Uh," Logan said, clearing his throat. "Should we come back in ten? Or five, from the look of you horndogs?"

Emmy jerked back, eyes widening in a split-second flash of embarrassment. But just as fast, it vanished, like it had never been there at all. She recovered like a pro, spun on her heel, and turned those sharp eyes on Logan.

"I bet I can humble you in Pilates faster than that."

God, I loved that about her. The way she bounced back. The way she could throw a verbal elbow with the same precision she adjusted a hip joint.

Mikko smirked. "I'll take that bet."

I chuckled and held a fist out to bump against Mikko's.

"I *hate* both of you," Logan muttered.

Emmy crossed her arms, clearly enjoying herself now. "Nice to finally meet the infamous Yeti backup dancers. I hope you stretched."

"What the fuck just happened to me?" Logan said outside my truck, his hands on his knees and heavy breaths fogging the air.

Mikko slapped him on the back, nearly sending Logan to the ground. "You got shown up by a 65-year-old woman in a bedazzled muscle shirt. That's what happened."

"You can't tell anyone about this." Logan straightened, then arched his back, twisting side to side.

I chuckled at the video playing on my phone, then hit send to forward it on. "Too late. Shannon videoed it, and I already sent it in the team chat thread. Ruth powering through her moves when you bailed out needs to live on in infamy."

Logan grabbed the phone from my hand and *Macho Man* played through the speakers while Logan squealed like a pig with his legs in the air, stuck in some kind of twisted pretzel bridge while Ruth yelled at him to activate his deep core.

All three of our phones blew up with texts coming in, one after the next, but my favorite was one from Frankie.

FRANKIE

> Look at Conway's form in the back.
> You're welcome for all those clamshells,
> boy. Parrish, on the other hand. We didn't
> grind through three off-seasons building
> that glute shelf just for you to get folded
> like a lawn chair by Grandma.

Logan groaned and tossed the phone back at me like it burned. "Why am I friends with you?"

"Because you love the attention." I fished out my keys and unlocked my truck.

We stopped when Shannon stepped out of the gym's front door, dark hoodie pulled tight against the chill, her backpack slung over one shoulder and boots scuffing the pavement as she typed furiously on her phone, her face in a deep scowl. She moved toward the rusted hatchback beside my truck, jaw tight, eyes flicking toward us.

Her car looked worse in the daylight. More rust. More duct tape. The passenger door was a different color entirely, and the windshield had a crack spidering across the top corner.

Logan let out a low whistle. "That thing's still alive? Colorado winter hasn't put it out of its misery yet?"

She didn't say anything, which was more than a little weird. I expected a sharp comeback, but the silence was somehow worse. I watched as she opened the door, tossed in her backpack, and slid behind the wheel with a glance over her shoulder like she hoped we'd just disappear.

The door creaked on the hinges when she climbed inside and turned the key.

Nothing.

Tried again. Still nothing.

She smacked the steering wheel, then rested her forehead against it for a beat.

I stepped forward and tapped the window. "Come on. I'll give you a ride."

She didn't move. Just sat there for a second longer, staring at the dashboard like it might magically come back to life. Then she sighed, low and resigned, and opened the door.

"It's fine. I'll figure it out."

"It's cold," I said. "You're not figuring anything in that death trap."

She hesitated again, eyes flicking from me to Logan and Mikko, then back. "I don't need—"

"I know you don't," I said, gently. "But the offer's there anyway."

Her gaze lingered on me, unreadable. Finally, she grabbed her backpack, slung it over one shoulder, and walked over to the truck, eyes down, jaw clenched. She opened the passenger door and paused again before climbing in.

"No one needs to know where I live," she said, low and sharp. Her shoulders hitched up toward her ears, body language shut down.

I knew where she lived—probably the same run-down trailer on the edge of town. If her dad really hadn't changed, he was already drunk, maybe passed out in the living room with the TV blaring.

She didn't want us seeing that.

Didn't want anyone seeing that.

"They won't say a word," I promised, voice just as quiet. "Hell, Mikko hardly speaks English and Logan is so full of shit no one trusts anything that comes out of his mouth."

Her shoulders dropped just a little, but I saw the hint of

amusement hiding in her eyes. She nodded once, then got in, pulling the door shut with a little more force than necessary.

From behind me, Logan called out, "Play us some sad girl bangers, baby. I could use a good scream-cry."

Mikko leaned across the center console from the backseat and tapped on my truck's screen to control the music. "Anything is better than you crying on a reformer, Logan."

"It was intense!" Logan shouted.

Mikko snorted. "You were whimpering."

I shook my head and started the truck, the weight of Shannon's trust settling over me like something fragile and earned. She sat back in the seat, hood up, arms folded tight across her chest, and went back to the weird silence.

Amy Lee scream-sang over the speakers as I pulled out onto the road, headed toward what was once the Wilder Family Farm.

It was just past noon and the sun bounced off the snow like a mirror. Linwood looked deceptively perfect under all that light—quaint shops lining River Street, a couple of skiers grabbing burgers at The Lantern, the Eagle River flashing silver as it rushed past the edge of town. The mountains stood tall on either side, jagged and unforgiving, even under a cloudless sky.

We passed my place and Shannon didn't look. Just sat in the front seat, arms crossed, hoodie drawn up like armor while Logan belted every single word to the Evanescence song.

A few minutes later, the pretty parts of Linwood gave way to forgotten ones. The fences here sagged, broken boards leaning at angles that made my chest tighten. An old windmill creaked as we drove past it, the blades long stopped spinning. The big barn had collapsed into itself after years of neglect, its red paint faded to rust, like the bones of something that used to breathe.

The farmhouse sat like a ghost beside it. Paint peeled off the siding in chunks, the roof was buckled on the west side, the porch was rotted through, and all the windows were boarded over. A truck in even worse condition than her hatchback lay half-buried in the snow.

A trailer sat beside the abandoned house, looking not much better. It leaned slightly on its cinderblock supports with duct tape running along the seams like stitches. One window was patched with cardboard and black plastic. Midday sun made the whole place look worse—no shadows to soften the edges.

Shannon hadn't said a word the whole drive, but I felt her go still, like she was bracing for impact.

"Just drop me here," she said suddenly, her voice quiet.

I eased off the gas, pulling over to the side of the road just past the gravel drive. "Shannon—"

"I can walk the rest."

"You don't have to," I said gently, wishing there was anything I could do to help this burden. If my mom hadn't been an absolute saint of a human, my life might have looked pretty similar. But Shannon didn't have that support, only a shitty dad and shittier brothers.

"I want to," she bit out, then after a pause, quieter, "Thanks for the ride."

She opened the door before I could say anything else and slid out of the truck, not looking at any of us. Not even when Logan leaned forward like he might say something.

The wind caught her hoodie as she walked, making her look smaller than she already was. She didn't glance back.

Just marched toward the trailer with that same stubborn spine I'd seen in the studio a dozen times.

Logan let out a long breath. "Jesus."

Mikko watched in silence, eyes narrowed. Not judging. Just seeing.

"She doesn't need your sympathy," I said, more to myself than them. "Just space."

Logan nodded slowly. "Yeah. But it sure looks like she's running out of that too."

Shannon was halfway up the walk when the screen door banged open. Ray stumbled out onto the porch, one arm braced on the frame, a half-empty bottle clutched in the other. Even from the truck, we could hear her dad, slurred, loud, and mean.

"Where the hell you been, girl? You think you can come and go like you pay bills around here?" he barked, voice cracking at the edges.

"I do pay the bills."

"Don't you sass me. I needed a ride to the goddamn store hours ago! You think you're better than this family now? That it?"

Shannon flinched but didn't stop. Just kept walking like she could walk through it. Like if she didn't react, maybe it wouldn't count.

The man kept going, insulting her hair, her clothes, even gesturing at the truck when he called her a whore. All of it was spat so loud, we heard every single poisonous thing he said.

Mikko's door opened without a word.

He stepped out, calm and controlled. But I saw the tightness in his jaw, the way his fists curled. His eyes were locked on Shannon's dad like he already had a target.

"Mikko—" I said.

Too late. He was already moving.

Logan cursed under his breath and scrambled out after him. "Nope. Nope, nope. We are not making the news today."

I was right behind them.

Mikko picked up speed, long strides chewing up the frozen ground between the road and the porch. Logan reached him first, grabbing his arm, but it was like trying to stop a tank.

"We can't deck a drunk guy on his own porch. That's a lawsuit. That's jail time."

Mikko didn't answer. He just kept walking.

I came around the other side and stepped between him and the path. "Hey. Look at me."

Nothing. Just that icy focus he got when something snapped. I'd seen it on the ice more than once, usually right before he dropped gloves and broke a man's nose.

"Mikko," I said again, firmer now. "This isn't your fight."

His eyes flicked to me, barely a second of hesitation, but it was enough.

Behind him, Shannon's dad shouted something so nasty and venom-laced I felt it in my spine. She walked past him and went inside, her shoulders stiff, her head still down.

"Goddamn ungrateful brat," the man muttered, then seemed to realize three men stood on his driveway.

Mikko's hands were still clenched. Logan looked ready to tackle him if he took another step.

"Well, if it isn't Beckett Conway," Ray said, his words slurred. "I heard you were back but figured it couldn't be true. No way would Linwood's little favorite return, not even for his sick mother. Your dad was right to always be ashamed of you. Wasn't even sure you were his kid."

Ray stumbled, then grabbed the porch railing for balance. While my dad had never been kind, alcohol made him more indifferent than mean. Ray though, he was just as mean as I remembered.

He swayed slightly, shoulders hunched like the weight of his own bitterness was eating him alive. His words came out thick with alcohol and venom. "Nothing to say, Beckett? Thought you big-time NHL types didn't take shit from anyone. Or maybe you're still just that useless little bastard who ran off when things got hard."

I stepped up onto the porch, the wood creaking under my shoes. Ray didn't back away, but he didn't meet my eyes either. Cowards never did.

I got close enough to smell the booze on his breath. "You want to run your mouth at me, go ahead. But if you ever talk to Shannon like that again, I swear to God, I'll bury what's left of you in that barn and burn it to the ground."

Ray scoffed, eyes flicking up just long enough to catch the fury in mine.

"I'll press charges," he muttered, puffing up again. "You so much as touch me, I'll ruin you."

I took another half-step closer, and he flinched. "You've ruined enough already, I think."

Behind me, footsteps crunched over the snow-covered gravel. Mikko walked past, cool and quiet, like a shadow with purpose. He stopped just at the base of the steps and looked up toward the screen door.

"Shannon," he yelled, and the curtains over the nearby window pulled apart, Shannon's face behind the dirty glass. "Get in the truck."

She stood frozen, gaze looking back and forth between her dad and us.

Ray spun toward her. "Don't you move, girl. Don't you dare—"

"Get in the truck," Mikko repeated, eyes never leaving hers.

Shannon stared at him for a second. Then she disappeared from sight, and the screen door pushed open again. With steady steps, she walked past Ray, past all of us. Head up. No looking back.

She climbed into the truck and shut the door behind her.

Ray turned back toward me, mouth twisted like he still had something to say, but I wasn't interested anymore.

"You can finish that bottle or throw it through a window for all I care," I said. "But next time you want to tear someone down, you better hope I'm not in earshot."

I turned and walked off the porch without another word. None of us looked back. We got in the truck, and we drove.

33

BECKETT

The drive back to my mom's house was silent, like everyone was trying to figure out what to say and deciding against it. Shannon leaned against the window in the front seat, hood still up, her legs pulled up on the cushion like she was trying to make herself smaller. Mikko stared straight ahead, arms crossed over his chest. Logan fidgeted with the cuff of his sleeve like he was trying to unhear everything that had just gone down. I kept my eyes on the road, familiar turns blurring past.

After seeing the ruins of the Wilder Family Farm, I couldn't help but appreciate mom's house. The blue paint was peeling in spots, but it was cheerful. A wreath hung on the front door, and it looked like a *home.*

I couldn't help thinking about what it would've looked like if my dad had lived. If I'd grown up with the kind of love that broke instead of built. I didn't have a perfect childhood, but Mason and Mom were as good as it got. We were a trio, as solid as they came, even before Dad passed away.

In comparison, Shannon's life was just as broken as the

house she lived in, and I hated that for her. I needed to help, but I knew her well enough to know she'd shut down anything she saw as charity.

The truck rolled to a stop in the drive. Mikko and Logan climbed out without a word, the doors shutting softly behind them.

I didn't move. Not yet.

I turned a little in my seat to glance back. "Shannon."

Her hood still covered most of her face, but I caught the flick of her eyes in my direction.

"How long has it been this bad?"

"None of your business."

I nodded, but didn't let her shove me away yet. "Come inside."

She blinked. "Why?"

"Because Mom is standing at the window and can see you in the truck. She doesn't get out as much anymore, and if you leave without saying hi, she might cry."

Shannon didn't smile, not really—but her mouth twitched like she wanted to. Her arms were still crossed tight over her chest.

"You don't have to stay long," I said. "But she'll be delighted to see you, and furious if you don't at least wave. You know how much she's always loved you."

It was true—Lori had doted on Shannon since we were kids, back when our families used to spend holidays together, back before the sharp edges of our dads' drinking started slicing everything up. Lori never had a daughter, but if she could have picked one, it would've been Shannon. I wasn't sure what their relationship had been like after I left, but I was positive my mom would welcome her with open arms.

Shannon hesitated, like she was doing the mental math of risk versus reward.

Eventually, she let out a quiet sigh and opened the door.

"Five minutes," she muttered.

"Deal."

We walked up to the house, and I opened the front door to the smell of something warm and cinnamon-sweet baking in the oven, a plan crafting in my mind that would solve two problems at once.

Mom stood just inside the door, one hand on the railing we'd installed there and the other held up for a hug. "I thought that was you, Shannon! Oh, my sweet girl, I've missed you so much."

"Sweet?" Logan mouthed behind them, pointing at Shannon.

I just grinned, watching Shannon sink into my mom's hold. They hugged for far longer than I expected, like Mom knew exactly how much she needed it. Hell, maybe she did.

"You're staying for brunch?" she said when they finally pulled away. "Beckett won't let me cook anymore, but I can still put cinnamon rolls in the oven."

"Mom." I rubbed a hand over the creases in my brow. "Do you not remember this exact conversation at the doctor's this week? They don't want you trying to take anything hot in or out of the oven. You should have just waited."

"Well, hurry, then." She waved her hand toward the kitchen, and Shannon chuckled, walking into the kitchen like she still remembered exactly where everything was.

Once we'd all descended on the spread of food Mom set on the counter, everyone moved to the table. She'd met Logan and Mikko several times over the years, and like the angel she was, remembered everything about them. Even if her hands shook, her mind was still intact. Her doctors had warned me that dementia was probably in our near future, but not yet.

The entire time, she held Shannon's hand, and surprisingly, Shannon let her. Emmy's friend was quieter than I'd heard her since my return, but I couldn't imagine how fast her mind was racing, trying to figure out next steps.

"Mom," I said when the conversation lulled. "You can't just keep denying every single applicant for in-home care I give you."

Mom's exhale was long and exaggerated. "I'm not denying them. I'm *filtering*."

"Filtering?" I deadpanned.

She lifted her chin. "I didn't like the way that first one smelled like tuna salad."

Mikko stifled a laugh behind his napkin. Logan didn't bother trying to hide his.

"And the second one?"

"She said 'no cap'." Mom grimaced, like the phrase had physically offended her. "I don't even know what that means. That's not someone I want in my house."

Logan muttered, "Harsh," around a bite of cinnamon roll.

"And the one after that," I prompted, knowing full well what she'd say.

"She wore Crocs. In a snowstorm. They had holes, Beckett. *Holes*."

Shannon choked on her orange juice.

I gave my mother the most exhausted look I could manage. "So, to recap: you've rejected one person for smelling like sandwiches, one for using slang, and one for bad shoe choices."

"Exactly."

"Mom, you don't have to love them. You just need someone here who can help you cook, drive you to appointments, and make sure you're taking your meds."

She scoffed. "And live in my house. And touch my things."

From the corner of my eye, I saw Shannon's brow crease.

Then, soft but clear, she said, "What exactly are you looking for?"

Everyone stilled.

Mom turned toward her, surprised. "Are you interested? Please, tell me you're interested. You don't smell weird and are smart enough to use proper grammar."

I bit back my grin, afraid to do anything that made this seem anything but organic so Shannon wouldn't run. I leaned forward, grateful she hadn't already bolted. "She needs help with meals, getting to and from appointments, and the occasional pill reminder. Otherwise, she's still pretty independent. Just not supposed to be living alone anymore and I have to go back to Denver soon. The job comes with room and board plus a weekly stipend. Mason bought her a car too, so you can use that."

Shannon blinked. "What about my school schedule? I can still do that?"

"Absolutely," I said quickly. "And work at the studio if you want. We just need someone consistent. Someone she trusts. And you clearly already have that."

Mom beamed at this new idea, wrinkles framing her big smile.

Shannon still looked wary. "What's the stipend?"

I hesitated for just a second. "$700 a week."

Her jaw dropped. "That's—what? Almost three grand a month."

"Three thousand," I confirmed. "Flat. Plus, no rent, no utilities, and you can buy your groceries on my card when you get hers. I'll give you another couple grand as a signing bonus to get whatever you want for your room. New clothes, or whatever you need for the next semester. However you want to spend it."

She sat back, looking like she'd just been hit in the face with a cinnamon roll.

Mikko shifted beside her, watching her reaction like a hawk. Logan was wide-eyed, halfway through a second roll and looking like he'd take the job himself if she didn't.

Shannon blinked down at her lap. "I mean, yeah. Yeah, okay. I could do that. If you're sure."

Mom lit up like Christmas morning, grabbing Shannon's hand again. "Oh, I'm very sure. Can you move in today? I need some girl power in this house of boys."

Shannon swallowed hard, and for a second, I thought she might cry. But she just nodded and squeezed Mom's hand back.

I leaned back in my chair, satisfaction settling in deep. Two problems solved and a safe home for both of them.

Mikko met my eyes, giving me the briefest nod of approval.

We finished the meal, topic shifting to tonight's Mayhem practice and how excited the guys were to meet the team.

My first time out on the Linwood Rink ice was more exciting than I had anticipated. The cold hit me the second I stepped onto the ice, familiar and comforting. I'd spent the afternoon sneaking in as much ice time as I could on the pond, out of sight in case I embarrassed myself. The ache in my hip was barely a murmur, drowned out by the thrill of movement as I glided toward center.

Ty was already out there stretching, his stick tapping lightly against the boards. He gave me a lazy grin. "Took you long enough. I thought you young folk were supposed to be spry."

I shot him a look. "You're four months older than me."

"Which makes you the baby." He shrugged. "I don't want to know about your diaper rash though. That's a you problem."

Before I could come up with a good comeback, the doors at the far end of the rink opened, and a wave of noise came pouring out—sticks clattering, voices yelling, laughter echoing through the arena.

"Conway!" Molly was the first one on the ice, helmet unclipped, braid swinging. "Are the rumors true? You're not just here to stand around looking pretty today?"

Delgado followed, adjusting his elbow pads. "You cleared to skate or just ignoring doctor's orders?"

"Can't be both?" I called, grinning as I started toward them.

Jace was right behind them, eyes flicking to my stride like he was assessing me. "How's the hip?"

"Good enough," I said. "You going to take it easy on me, Juice?"

"Nope."

"Didn't think so."

Miles skated out last, his helmet tucked under one arm. "I was told there'd be blood today."

"Relax, psycho," Ty called. "It's a skills skate, not the Octagon."

Jace skated a slow lap around me, then stopped, eyebrows raised. "You sure you're not going to embarrass yourself?"

"Not planning on it," I said.

"That's what old people say before they break a hip," Delgado chimed in.

I gave him a deadpan look. "You're, what, five foot seven?"

"Five nine *and a half*," he shot back.

"With skates on," Molly added under her breath.

The chirping continued, loud and fast, everyone talking over each other. I grinned so wide it hurt.

Then the doors to the rink opened again, and the second Mikko and Logan stepped out onto the ice, every single kid went *silent*.

Mikko glided effortlessly, calm and collected, eyes sweeping over the group like he was already breaking them down by line.

Logan, naturally, was the opposite.

"Well, well, *well*," he called out, dragging out the last word. "Is this the mighty Mayhem I've heard so much about? I expected more. I mean, half of you look like you still nap after cartoons."

Delgado's eyes went huge. "Is that *Logan Parrish*?"

Molly nodded, starstruck. "That's Mikko Laaksonen."

Jace looked from Mikko to Logan, then to me. "What the hell kind of practice is this?"

"A special one," I said, trying not to laugh at their faces. "They're running drills with us today."

Logan gave an exaggerated bow. "Try to keep up, kiddos. And no crying when I dangle you into next week."

"I'm not crying," Miles said immediately. "You are."

Mikko skated up beside me, deadpan. "You sure they're ready for this?"

I grinned. "They're ready. You?"

His eyes tracked the group of suddenly nervous teenagers huddled by the boards. "Definitely."

Ty blew the whistle, and the fun began.

34

Emmy

The sound of barking and shouting and overlapping voices hit me as soon as I stepped onto Beckett's porch. I pushed the door open and stepped inside to the unmistakable *whump* of pizza boxes hitting a table, followed by Ty yelling something about pineapple on pizza being a war crime.

Rowdy slid a little on the hardwood while he hopped over to me, tail wagging wildly. I knelt to scratch behind his ears as the rest of the chaos unfolded around me.

"Emmy!" Logan yelled when he spotted me, holding a slice of pizza in one hand and a soda in the other.

Lori popped her head out from the kitchen. "You made it! We have pizza in here, and Shannon made a salad because good babysitters make their kids eat their vegetables."

"You're hardly a kid, and I don't think I can qualify as a babysitter anymore."

I was more than surprised to see Shannon here. She was perched on a barstool at the island, looking slightly overwhelmed. She met my eyes with a cautious kind of smile and gave a tiny wave.

I glanced toward Beckett, who had just emerged from the kitchen, a bottle of root beer in hand.

"Babysitter?" I asked quietly.

He came up beside me, then tugged me down the hall, just out of sight. The moment we were alone, he backed me into the wall, and his mouth was on mine. I sank into the kiss, incapable of saying no, even though my kid was just around the corner.

"Hi," he said when he pulled back. His forehead rested on mine for a second before standing up. "I missed you."

I chuckled, pushing him slightly back from me so I could see him better. "I saw you seven hours ago."

"I know." Beckett leaned in for one more kiss. "Too long."

I pointed toward the kitchen. "What's this about Shannon?"

He looked over his shoulder, smiling at where Shannon and his mom stood together in the kitchen. In hushed tones, he told me about what happened when he dropped her off after Pilates, and how she'd ended up back here. Anger ripped through me at everything her father had said, and that she hadn't told me how bad it was.

"It all happened kind of fast." His hand found mine. "But she needs somewhere safe. And Mom needs someone she trusts."

Tears gathered in the corners of my eyes; a mixture of hurt for everything my friend had been going through, and a new level of adoration for this man I was not prepared for. "Did you steal my employee?"

He grinned, then ducked down to kiss me again. "Nah.

Just offered her room, board, a stipend, and a car. She can keep doing her schoolwork and working for you around Mom's appointments. We'll work it out."

"And Lori's okay with it?"

"Thrilled," he said. "Honestly? So am I. Mikko and Logan seem to think Frankie's going to call me back to Denver any day now, so I feel better about leaving, having a plan in place for her."

I nodded, because that made perfect sense, and it was a perfect solution for everyone. But each mention of our time being nearly up made my chest tight, panic sinking in.

He tugged me back into the chaos in time to see Lori bustling around with the confidence of someone determined to out-stubborn her own diagnosis. Her hands trembled, and one foot dragged slightly as she moved. Despite it all, she was warmth and light as she carried a bowl of popcorn the size of a small child to the coffee table.

"I told them the kitchen closes when the game starts." Lori set the bowl down with a grin. "But no one listens to me anymore."

"*We* don't listen? *You're* the one who tried to make cinnamon rolls earlier," Beckett muttered as he passed by. "Could have burned down the house. We're lucky to be alive."

"I heard that," Lori called sweetly.

Jace had already claimed one corner of the couch, socked feet propped up like he owned the place. "Come on, Mom. It's hockey night."

"Oh, pardon me." I stepped around Logan's legs, who was laid across half the rug like he was posing for a beach calendar.

Ty and Mikko were near the TV discussing the paninis

they'd had for lunch, while Shannon slipped into the kitchen behind Lori, like she'd done it a hundred times before.

My friend reappeared and pressed a paper plate into my hands. "There's pepperoni and supreme left. Go fast—Logan eats like someone's chasing him."

"Thanks," I said, searching Shannon's face for her feelings on the day's events.

She nudged me with an elbow. "I'm good, I promise. Better. This is good. A lot, but good."

I looked around. At my brother, enjoying himself with friends. At Lori, battling a degenerative disease with more grace than I knew possible. At Rowdy, currently stealing pizza off the coffee table. At Jace, wearing the biggest grin as he casually chatted with some of his idols. At Shannon, somehow fitting in among the chaos.

And finally, at Beckett, leaning against the kitchen counter, bottle of root beer in hand, baseball cap turned backward like it had been all afternoon. His eyes were on everyone, quietly observing, checking in without needing to speak.

Every single person in this room was here because of him.

Every piece of this little puzzle fit because of him.

The realization I was in love with him hit me like a punch to the chest.

Not just the man who was kind to my son or who made me feel seen. I loved this version—this messy, beautiful, deeply loyal man who'd made it his personal mission to make everyone around him feel his love, even when his own heart was barely hanging on.

And he was leaving.

I felt the crack of it splinter through me—quiet and sharp and unavoidable. The NHL would call him back at any minute, and the whole point of this recovery stint had been temporary. Get better, get cleared, and go. That was the deal.

But this wasn't temporary. Not to me. Not anymore.

He caught me staring and tilted his head, a question in his eyes and the barest hint of a smile on his face. I gave him one back, just enough to mask the ache. Because what else could I do?

"Yeah," I said softly, barely more than a whisper. "It's kind of perfect."

Beckett grinned. "That's what I said."

And I wished, more than anything, that he meant it in the forever kind of way.

Lori came in again, waving her hand at the TV. "Alright, game's starting. Get your butts in seats. If I can't fly to Italy to watch Mason play in the Olympics, I'm sure not missing even a second of this. Jace gets the floor because he's a child. I get the recliner because this is my house. Logan—"

"Gets the couch because I'm the fan favorite," Logan finished, tossing popcorn in his mouth.

"Fan favorite of who?" Jace slid onto the floor in front of Lori's chair. "Your mom?"

"And also, God," Logan replied, dropping onto the couch.

He hadn't even settled in before Mikko shoved him back onto the floor next to Jace. "You heard her. Children on the floor."

The first game started—Sweden vs USA—and the heckling began. Logan argued that neither team stood a chance against Canada, while Mikko just seemed to hate on anyone from Sweden. Ty didn't say much but sat on a barstool behind the couch with his arms crossed, eyes alight with happiness. Beckett's leg bounced, leaning forward on the couch, pointing out plays to Jace, coaching even now. Lori had tears in her eyes, glancing between her son on the TV and the room of boys around her.

I stood in the kitchen, feeling too fragile to be a part of it all.

"Absolutely never repeat this," Shannon said around a celery stick smothered in ranch, her words quiet enough so only I could hear it, "but hockey isn't that bad."

I huffed out a laugh, barely audible over the roar of the TV and the boys shouting at each other from the floor.

"I mean, it's still mostly overgrown man-children skating around chasing a rubber disk," Shannon went on. "But occasionally, it's tolerable. When there's good snacks and no dads throwing bourbon bottles."

My stomach twisted. Her voice was too flippant, too light.

I leaned my hip against the counter, arms crossed tight to keep from hugging her. "You okay?"

Shannon shot me a look that was all dry disbelief. "Of course. I'm living my best life. Two kinds of dip, a whole functioning family I didn't genetically come from, and a boy band of hockey delinquents fighting about geography. What's not to love?"

I didn't answer. Just watched as Jace tilted his head toward Beckett, absorbing every word like gospel. His legs were stretched out long in front of him, one socked foot nudging Logan in the side as he laughed at something on-screen. For a moment, it looked like everything I wanted for him. Steady, safe, easy.

But Beckett was leaving soon, and I didn't know how to soften the blow that the man he'd come to adore was headed back to the world that had taken his dad from him, too.

Different circumstances, same outcome: an empty seat in the bleachers.

I swallowed the lump in my throat. "He's going to be wrecked."

Shannon didn't ask who. She knew.

"Yeah," she said softly. "But look on the bright side. At least he's not going to be devastated alone. You'll be sobbing into your puzzles, and I'll be upstairs drowning in my own abandonment issues. We can form a support group. Cry into carbs. Trade trauma like Pokémon cards."

I let out a watery laugh that cracked halfway through. "God, you're so messed up."

"The good ones always are." She bumped my shoulder with hers. "Don't cry in the queso. I just got it the right amount of spicy."

But my eyes burned. Because Beckett was going. Because I couldn't ask him to stay, not when I knew how badly he wanted to prove he could still play. Because my son had found a new version of family, and I was about to watch him lose it again.

And most of all, because I loved Beckett, and I had no idea how to say it without making it harder for both of us.

I wiped the corner of my eye before the tears could fall and crossed the room, sinking onto the barstool next to Ty. He didn't say anything, just wrapped one arm around my shoulders and let me lean my head against him, solid and steady like always.

Between the second and third periods, the game cut to commercial, and the room broke into chaotic conversation. Shannon shouted something about snack refills and made a dramatic exit with the veggie tray. Ty handed me a fresh soda without asking. And then Beckett's phone rang.

He glanced at the screen and stiffened, mouth tightening.

"It's Coach," he said, already swiping to answer. "Hey. You're on speaker."

The room quieted instantly. Even Logan stopped mid-popcorn toss.

Frankie's voice came through first, cheerful and direct. "You passed your post-op movement tests this morning, Conway. Coach and I just finished your file review with Dr. Carter. You're cleared to return to practice on Friday."

For a beat, no one moved.

Beckett's voice didn't waver. "Friday's perfect."

He hung up, then looked up at the room, his smile faltering when he looked at my son. "Shit. That's the last regular season game for the Mayhem."

My eyes flew straight to Jace. He didn't say a word—just looked at the floor and nodded once. He was trying to act cool, like it didn't matter. Like it hadn't meant the world to him. But the way his shoulders curled inward made my chest ache.

Ty shifted beside me and leaned forward, raising his voice just enough to cut through the quiet. "I've got the rest of the season. We'll make you proud."

Jace looked up, surprised, and Ty locked eyes with him across the room.

"Promise," he added. "You're not losing us."

That one word—*promise*—landed like a stone in my chest.

Jace gave a tight nod, and this time, his shoulders didn't sag quite so far.

Then the room erupted.

Logan whooped and tackled Mikko in a side-hug that was half full-body takedown. Lori clapped, then held her hands out for a hug from her son. Even Ty gave Beckett a solid clap on the back.

And Beckett—God, he turned around glowing, grinning like a kid at Christmas, and strode toward me like he was going to kiss me right then and there. I saw it coming. The lean, the look, the way his eyes dropped to my mouth like he couldn't help it.

But then his gaze flicked just past me to my son, still sitting cross-legged on the floor, eyes on the TV, trying a little less hard now to pretend he wasn't paying attention.

Beckett's steps faltered. He caught himself, masked it with a grin, and pulled me into a quick, one-armed hug instead, his cheek brushing mine, his voice low and warm in my ear.

"Later," he whispered. "I'll come over tonight."

Even though my heart ached from the weight of good-bye, I couldn't deny him anything.

35

Emmy

After the chaos of Lori's house, my own felt far too quiet.

Jace had gone to bed almost an hour ago, exhausted from practice and pizza and trying not to let the weight of the world show on his shoulders. I'd lingered in his doorway after saying goodnight, watching the soft rise and fall of his chest, committing it to memory like I always did when life started to shift around us.

And things were shifting, fast.

Beckett was going back to Denver, back to the NHL. Back to a life that had never included us and might not again. At least, not like this.

In all our time together over the last three months, we hadn't talked about what came next. I told myself it was because I didn't want to distract Beckett, didn't want to add pressure when he was already trying to rehab his way into a miracle recovery. But, deep down, I was terrified.

What if this was only ever meant to be temporary?

The TV hummed across the living room, volume low, some old romcom flickering like a ghost of something just out of reach for me. The water I'd poured myself after we got home was mostly untouched on the coffee table, condensation pooling in a perfect ring beneath it.

I glanced at the clock—11:46 p.m.—and curled my legs beneath me tighter on the couch. I didn't know why I was so nervous. He'd been here dozens of times. Kissed me breathless in my kitchen. Even slept in my bed on New Years Eve. But something about tonight felt heavier, knowing it might be the last time.

My phone lit up on the armrest beside me, showing motion at the front door.

I didn't even look at the feed. Just stood, smoothed my hands over my worn pajama pants and his oversized hoodie, and tiptoed barefoot across the hardwood.

When I opened the front door, Beckett was already grinning at me, holding out a handful of flowers.

"They're a little wilted," he whispered, glancing down at the flowers with an arched brow. "Hope that's okay."

I smiled as I reached for them. "They're my favorite."

He leaned forward just enough to kiss my cheek, the faintest brush of his lips against my skin. "God, you look like trouble."

"And you look like you snuck out of your mom's house at midnight."

Beckett chuckled low in his throat. "That's because I did."

I closed the door quietly behind him and slid the deadbolt home. "Come on." I took his hand. "Try not to wake the teenager."

We crept up the stairs like teenagers ourselves, my heartbeat kicking up with each step. He was warm behind me, close enough I could feel his breath near my neck.

By the time we reached my bedroom, I was barely holding it together.

I turned, meaning to say something, but the moment the door clicked shut behind us, Beckett stepped in and kissed me.

No hesitation. No space between.

Just his mouth on mine like he'd been waiting all night. Like he needed this as badly as I did.

I clutched the front of his hoodie and kissed him back, letting the weight of everything we weren't saying fall away.

Maybe we couldn't name what this was. Maybe we didn't know what came next. But he was here, and I wasn't ready to let him go.

His hands slid under the hoodie I'd never returned and he'd never taken back, pushing the thick fabric over my head. I hadn't bothered with a tank underneath, hoping my evening would end like this.

"Fuck," Beckett muttered, his palms sweeping across my skin to cup my breasts. "You have the perfect tits."

The warmth of his touch made my stomach twist, not just with arousal, but with something deeper. His thumbs brushed across my nipples, drawing a gasp from my lips as my head tipped back against the wall.

"You've seen them almost daily," I said, voice uneven as he closed his mouth over one nipple, his hand kneading the other. "Figured you'd be bored by now."

He answered with his mouth—biting gently at my skin, enough to make me shiver. "Never," he whispered.

I dragged my nails up his back, feeling the way his muscles flexed beneath my touch, and it made him groan— deep and low. He leaned away just enough to yank his tee over his head in one rough pull, baring all that inked, golden skin I'd traced so many times.

The moonlight poured in over his shoulders, casting him in silver and shadow as he pressed his chest to mine again. His skin was warm, his heartbeat steady, unraveling me with every beat.

Our mouths met again, slower now. Softer. Like we were trying to say everything we were too scared to say out loud. I looped my arms around his neck just as his hands gripped my waist, tugging me tight against him before lifting me off the ground entirely.

I wrapped my legs around his hips, clinging to him like I never wanted to let go. He carried me across the room and lowered me gently onto the bed like I was something precious. Like I mattered.

He hovered over me for a second, eyes searching mine. I almost told him then. Almost whispered *I love you*, but the words stuck behind the fear.

It was all too much—his hands, his mouth, his weight against mine. But it still wasn't enough to hush the ache in my chest. The one that whispered, *This can't last. This isn't yours to keep.*

I blinked hard, willing the tears away. He kissed down the side of my neck, slow and reverent, and it took everything in me not to break.

"Hey," he murmured, lifting his head, voice gentler than I deserved. His breath brushed my cheek. "Em."

I tried to smile. Failed. "I'm fine."

"No, you're not." He didn't pull away. He just stayed there, watching me. Patient. Present.

"I wish this didn't have to end," I said finally, the words

pulled from that aching space behind my ribs where the hope lived—and the fear right beside it.

Beckett froze.

"I tell myself I'm protecting Jace," I went on, the words tumbling faster now. "That it's better to wait, to be sure, to not turn his world upside down unless we know this is real. But it *is* real, at least for me. It has been for weeks. And he's not stupid. He's 15. He sees everything, and still I've got us sneaking around like we're something temporary."

Beckett sat back on his knees, his hands warm and steady on my hips. "You think we're temporary?"

"No." I shook my head, tears sliding silently down my cheeks. "God, no. I wish we could be everything. I wish I could have all of this, out loud and forever. But I can't. Not yet. Because Jace comes first. And if this ever fell apart..." I swallowed hard. "I couldn't put him through that. And I can't make you choose us."

Beckett's expression softened, pain flickering through his eyes. "What do you think I'm going to do, Em? Walk away? Leave you hanging when it gets hard?"

"No," I whispered. "That's the worst part. I believe you. I believe in *this*. And that's what terrifies me."

He exhaled, slow and steady, like he was feeling the weight of every heartbreak I carried. "I've stopped trying to be subtle about it," he said. "Ty knows I'm in deep. My mom knows. Anyone paying attention probably knows I'm so fucking in love with you, I'd do anything to be with you. I'm not hiding this, Emmy. I don't *want* to."

My breath caught, eyes finding his. "You love me? Even when I'm sneaking you up the stairs like a teenager with a curfew?"

His thumbs brushed away the tears, and his voice

dropped into something rough and tender. "You're protecting him. I know that. But Em, you don't have to protect him *from me*. And you don't have to protect *yourself* from me either. Because yes, I love you so fucking much I don't know what to do with myself. You're way too good for me, and I don't deserve you even a little bit, but I've always been selfish. I can't let you go. I can't let either of you go."

The dam broke. A fresh tear rolled, and I let it.

My hands brushed through his dark hair, holding him close. "I've seen how you are with Jace. How careful you are. How much you already *care*. That's what terrifies me the most. Because it means this isn't casual. It never was."

"Fuck no, it's not casual," he said with a quiet fire that went straight to my chest. "You're not some temporary fling I'm passing time with. You're *it*. Maybe you always have been."

I let out a breath that felt like a release, and then I kissed him.

Not out of lust, but out of *hope*. Out of the aching truth that I didn't want a single night more without letting him fully in.

He kissed me back with a kind of reverence that stole the air from my lungs.

When I leaned back on the bed and pulled him with me, it wasn't desperation. It was surrender.

We undressed each other slowly, like we had all the time in the world. Every brush of skin, every kiss, was a quiet vow I wasn't ready to speak aloud.

His fingers slid down my body like he was memorizing every inch. My thighs parted for him, breath hitching as he stroked over my clit, then lower, slipping inside me with gentle precision.

My hand flew up to muffle the sound threatening to rise.

"Quiet." Beckett's blue eyes sparkled in the dim light. He removed my hand and covered my mouth with his. One kiss turned into two, then his tongue slid between my lips just as he added a second finger, curling them just right.

I moaned into his mouth, and Beckett pulled his hand free, leaving me empty and on the edge of an orgasm.

"What?" I whispered when he sat back, rising up on my elbows to chase him. "Why'd you stop?"

His hand slid over his cock in slow strokes, staring down at me. "Gotta keep you quiet, don't I?"

His free hand wrapped around my wrist, tugging me toward him until my mouth was right in front of his cock.

My breaths came in quick bursts, staring up at him towering over me.

"Open that pretty mouth, Peach." His thumb traced over my bottom lip, prying my mouth open. "Show me how good you suck my cock so you're all I think about on the road."

I pulled his thumb into my mouth, swirling my tongue over the pad, until his head tipped up toward the ceiling, nostrils flared. He pulled his hand from my mouth, and I opened wide, my tongue out.

He closed the distance between us, the smooth skin of his cock sliding between my lips. My hand gripped his thigh, tugging his hip toward me, then easing back with each stroke.

"Oh, fuck," Beckett groaned, his hand resting on my knee. I spread my legs wider, and he slid his hand back down to my center.

With his cock in my mouth and his fingers in my pussy, I hummed with need. We moved like we'd done this a thousand times, chasing each other's pleasure down. My legs shook, I was so close to the edge, an orgasm hovering just out of reach.

My mouth slipped free with a *pop*. "Need you, now. You can skip the condom—I'm on the pill."

Beckett's nostrils flared, and he pulled his hand free. I hardly had time to feel the emptiness before his cock was there, sliding home.

We both groaned in unison, bare skin feeling so good with each stroke. His mouth crashed down on mine, teasing and tasting in time with his movements. My nails scratched across his back, digging in as I tried to hold on. Tried to keep this moment from ending.

But everything felt too good. His head dropped down to my shoulder, kissing there. "Tell me you're going to come. I don't know if I can hold out any longer, you feel so good."

I nodded, afraid to open my mouth, afraid of the noises I wanted to make.

"Come for me, baby," he said against my skin. "Let me feel you."

My body tightened around his, pulsing and squeezing tight, and Beckett swore into my skin. His hips picked up the pace, growing erratic, until he shuddered above me.

He dropped his weight down on me, and I wrapped my arms around his back, holding tight. Skin to skin, breaths mingling, hearts pounding, I let myself *feel* the love pouring off him, even if I hadn't said it back.

In that moment, I wasn't just afraid of losing him. I was afraid of how deeply I needed him. Of how badly I didn't want to let go.

36

BECKETT

The room was still wrapped in shadows when I woke, the faintest thread of light just beginning to stretch across the horizon.

Emmy was beside me, half-tangled in the sheets, her face turned toward mine, lips parted in sleep. One hand rested on my chest, her fingers curled just above my heart like she'd been holding on even in her dreams.

My breath caught somewhere between awe and ache.

I *had* to go.

Training started on Friday, which meant I had to drive down today.

Returning to the ice was everything I said I wanted. Everything I'd worked toward since the day I went under the knife, since the moment the surgeon said *if* instead of *when*.

And yet, lying here, with her tucked against me in bed, it didn't feel like victory.

It felt like heartbreak.

I brushed my knuckles gently along her arm, tracing the line of her shoulder, careful not to wake her. I wanted to freeze time, stay wrapped in this quiet dawn with her forever.

She shifted slightly, letting out a soft sigh that hit me square in the chest.

This wasn't supposed to happen.

I wasn't supposed to fall for her. Not like this. Not so fast or so deep that the thought of leaving her made my stomach twist into knots I couldn't untangle.

I'd spent my whole career chasing the next level, the next win, the next shot to prove I was good enough. And now that it was finally in reach again, all I could think about was what I'd have to leave behind to take it.

Who I'd leave.

Emmy had changed everything.

Not just my recovery or my routines, but the way I saw my future.

Of course, I wanted to be on the ice. I missed it. But not like I knew I was going to miss this—the early mornings at the pond with Jace. The sound of my mom's house full of love and laughter. The late nights with Emmy's body wrapped around mine.

I never thought the hardest part of going back would be walking away from home, because that's what this was. Her, and Jace, and this messy, beautiful life we'd somehow stitched together.

I didn't know how to leave.

Didn't know how to stay, either.

But I did know I'd never be the same again. Not after her.

I brushed the hair out of her face, leaning forward to kiss her. Her lashes fluttered, and her hands tightened on my chest, snuggling closer into my chest.

"Good morning," she murmured, voice thick with sleep.

"I love you," I said, the words tumbling out before I could stop them.

Her eyes snapped open like I'd yanked her straight out of sleep and into freefall.

She hadn't said it back last night, but that wasn't what this was about. I didn't say it to get something in return. I already knew how she felt. I felt it in every glance, every touch, every time she looked at me like she wasn't sure how we got here but was damn glad we did.

Still, I said it again, slower this time. Clearer. "I love you, Emmy Hudson."

She stared at me, breath catching, her gaze flickering between mine like she was trying to make sense of the words.

"Beckett," she whispered. "You can't say that. Not when you're leaving today."

I brushed my thumb along her cheek, gently pulling her back into the moment. "That's exactly why I'm saying it."

She sat up, the sheet falling to her waist, panic creeping into her voice. "You have to go back. And I can't go with you. I won't ask you to stay—I would never—"

"I know." I sat up with her, cupping her face in my hands. "You'd never ask. That's why I needed to say it. So there's no confusion. No gray area."

She blinked fast, lips parting like she wanted to argue.

"I'm not giving up my dream," I said quietly. "But see, my mom has this theory about dreams. The moment you realize there's something better out there, they change. Still the same, still mine, just more."

Her lips parted, and I could see the moment the words landed. The way her whole body stilled like she was afraid to believe me.

"You were always part of the plan," I continued. "I just didn't know it yet."

Tears welled in her eyes, spilling over before she could stop them. She pressed a hand to her mouth, then reached for me like she didn't know what else to do.

"I love you too," she whispered into my shoulder, voice breaking on the last word. "I didn't mean to fall so hard. God, I didn't mean to, but—"

"But you did," I murmured, wrapping my arms around her and holding her like I'd never let go. "And so did I. So, let's figure out how the hell we do this."

Her arms tightened around my neck, her face buried in my chest.

"I want you to chase it," she whispered. "I want you to get everything you've worked for, everything you deserve. I just..."

"I don't want to do it without you." I finished the sentence for her. "So, we won't."

She pulled back just enough to look at me, eyes rimmed red. "Now, if only you'd quit stealing my parking spots, you'd be the perfect man."

A laugh stuttered out of me, and I leaned in to kiss her, hope for tomorrow filling my chest. I didn't know what it would look like, but I knew it would be with her.

I went home to pack, said goodbye to my mom and Shannon, then got Mikko and Logan on the road. Gravel crunched under my tires as I rolled to a stop outside Copper Ridge. Ty's ranch on the outskirts of town was my last stop, and then I would be following my teammates back down to Denver.

Unlike the Wilder farm, Ty kept everything at Copper Ridge in pristine condition. Fresh red paint coated the barn, neatly kept fence posts lined the property, and the chicken coop practically glowed it was so clean. The only thing that wasn't perfect was the one-eyed llama staring at me over the fence when I climbed out of my truck.

"That's Uno," a little voice said from across the driveway. I turned to see Juniper sitting on Ty's porch swing in her snow gear. "We got him at an auction last week."

I chuckled at the name, smiling when Ty stepped outside with a carrot in hand. Rowdy bounced behind him, tail wagging at the sight of me.

"You headed out?" Ty handed the carrot to Juniper. She jumped off the porch, then ran across the snow-laden front yard toward a snowman in progress.

"Yeah." I pulled at the back of my neck, not sure how to say everything I needed to get out. "Couldn't leave without saying goodbye though."

Ty nodded, then walked off the porch. He leaned against his blue truck, one ankle crossed over the other. "Emmy and Jace okay?"

I nodded, smiling down at my feet. "Yeah. I think so. We're going to figure it all out as we go, but I'm so fucking in love with her, Ty. With both of them."

"I know," he said, like it was just that simple.

My nose tingled in the cold air, emotions too close to the surface this morning. "It wasn't supposed to be like this. I was supposed to come back to town, spend some time with Mom, and repay you for everything you've done for me. But, like always, I'm just leaving a pile of my own shit in your lap and leaving again. You didn't even want to coach—I *made* you—and now I'm leaving it in your hands alone. I'm so fucking sorry."

Ty pointed out to the barn where a car sat parked in the snow. "See that Jeep?"

I nodded, not following.

"It's Emmy's. She showed up on my doorstep unannounced nine months ago in a car that was basically smoking, divorce papers fresh off the printer, a kid who wouldn't talk to anyone, and a frown so deep-set, I thought she'd never smile again."

I rubbed at my eyes to keep my emotions in check, imagining them so broken.

"For months, I tried to convince her to let me buy her a new car, but she refused. Insisted on doing everything herself. Probably some misplaced notion that she needed to prove she could do this on her own. I had to cut the fucking oil lines for her to even agree to drive my car instead of hers, knowing my stubborn little sister would come over to the hardware store to ask me how to fix it."

I bit my cheeks to hide my smile, imagining the scene. "How'd you get her to take the Land Rover?"

"Told her the parts were backordered, and I'd tow it here until we could get them."

I arched a brow, a grin spreading. "Have you ordered the parts?"

"Nope." Ty slapped the hood of his truck, then looked out over the field where Juniper was busy positioning sticks into the arms of her snowman. "And I have no intention of it. The only way Emmy is letting anyone in is if they break in with a sledgehammer. And apparently, you did just that with the whole coaching thing."

"It was more of a crutch and a pathetic whimper than a sledgehammer, but I get what you're saying."

Ty leaned his elbows on the truck, and I went to stand next to him. "Either way. She let you in, and even more importantly, so did Jace. I'm not mad you volunteered me to coach. I love it. I just knew she'd never see it as anything but me trying to fix her life, yet again."

"Well, you're welcome, I guess." I laughed, then slapped him on the back. "It's been a blast doing this with you."

Ty looked over at me. "It really has."

I pointed at the girl, then the llama. "You saving everyone who will let you now? Is that what this is?"

He sniffed, then turned toward me, the humor of moments before gone. "Violet, Junie's mom, is dying. She has brain cancer. Junie knows it, but everyone is afraid to speak it aloud. Afraid of what comes next. Despite Junie spending every free moment here, I actually don't know Violet very well, so it's not like I can walk over and ask to see a copy of her will. So, I went and got certified to be a foster parent, just in case."

"Shit, man." My heart constricting at the thought of everything they were going through. "I'm so sorry to hear that."

"If that little girl needs me and some misfit animals to feel at home in this terrible time in her life, then I'll buy whatever the fuck she wants."

"You truly are the best man I've ever met," I said, meaning every word. "You know that, right?"

His mustache twitched with the hint of a smile. "Way better than you, that's for damn sure."

I laughed, then wrapped my arms around his shoulders,

hugging him tight. "I'll be back this summer. Keep them safe for me, will you? Give that boy a chance to win State."

Ty slapped me on the back, then pulled away. "You know I will."

"If you need anything," I said, gesturing at the farm, the girl, the town, all of it. "Call. Doesn't matter where I am."

"I know," Ty said, then glanced toward my truck. "Now get out of here before anyone sees me having emotions. It'll ruin my whole image."

I grinned and turned toward the truck. Junie waved from the barn, arm flailing wildly.

"I'll see you soon," I called.

"You better," he shouted back. "She might have me bottle-feeding a possum in a baby sling next week."

I laughed, climbing into the truck, heart heavier than I expected, and fuller than it had been in a long, long time.

37

BECKETT

By the end of February, I was skating with the team again. Running drills, crashing into the boards, feeling like myself. Between Frankie's routines and Emmy's suggestions, all of my rehab had paid off.

But my apartment was too empty, too quiet.

I talked to Jace every morning while he and Ty drove to the pond before school. They kept me updated on practice schedules and the team's group chat drama, and once sent me a video of a locker room dance-off that made me snort coffee through my nose. The Mayhem were on fire, headed straight into the finals for playoff season, and I was living vicariously through them.

Emmy called every night, sometimes for five minutes, sometimes for an hour. Just hearing her voice settled something in me, but the silence after I hung up always came louder.

I was grateful to be back in Denver, healthy, and on the verge of a comeback. I wasn't taking any of it for granted. But each time the Yeti notched a win, each time the guys made a play that lit up the rink, it wasn't the same. Not when I knew what I was missing to be here.

Over the last few weeks, I'd managed a few stolen nights —quiet getaways on my rare off days when the travel schedule lined up and nobody was watching too closely. I'd hit the road before sunrise, make the mountain drive to Linwood just to be there for one practice, one dinner, one night where I could fall asleep with Emmy curled against me. Then I'd wake up to sneak out of the house, and come back in to Jace grumbling about breakfast cereal, unaware I'd slept just down the hall. It wasn't sustainable, but it kept me sane.

By mid-March, those chances disappeared. I was traveling with the team again, the calendar was packed, and expectations were mounting. My ability to sneak away slipped through my fingers, and the distance stretched wider by the day.

Going weeks without seeing Emmy and Jace wasn't just hard—it felt like losing parts of myself I'd only just gotten back. As much as being off the ice had killed me, being away from them was almost worse.

"You should have seen it," Jace said the night after they won the semi-finals, his voice buzzing with adrenaline and eyes alight with excitement even through the video call. "Molly got checked so hard she flew straight into their bench and took out three players. She's so fucking good its criminal, and yes, I swore. Shut up."

I chuckled, loving his enthusiasm. "So, how'd you score then?"

"That's the craziest part. Somehow, she still managed to keep control of the puck. Got it to me, and I nailed the top shelf like it was nothing. Everyone lost it. I think Ty even smiled."

I laughed as I leaned back against the headboard in my hotel room. "That's gotta be a sign of the apocalypse."

"Seriously. It was the best game of my life," Jace said, a little breathless as he flopped back on his bed, holding the phone above his face. "I wish you could have seen it."

His face softened, not angry, just honest.

I rubbed the back of my neck, throat thick. "I know, bud. I wanted to be. The whole Yeti locker room was watching the clips your mom sent over my shoulder. Logan put the end of the game on in the locker room so we could all see it. I even wore my Mayhem hoodie. Doesn't matter if I'm a thousand miles away—I'm still your biggest fan."

"I know," he muttered, his cheeks pink with a blush at the idea of all my teammates rooting for him. "It was just fun when you were on the bench."

"It really was, huh?"

We sat in silence for a second, letting the ache settle between us. Then I cleared my throat.

"You ready for State?" I asked. "You nervous?"

"No," he said instantly, but his gaze drifted to the side. "Yes. Maybe."

His cheeks puffed out, and I gave him the time he needed to figure out what he wanted to say.

"Dad says he's going to try to come to the game. Think you can be there, too?"

I squeezed my eyes shut, hating that I didn't know. "I'm trying my best, bud. There's nowhere I'd rather be."

Not until the words were out of my mouth did I realize what I'd said, and how deeply I meant it.

There was *nowhere* I'd rather be.

Not on the ice at Mile High Arena, not racking up points in the NHL, not chasing a comeback that had driven me so hard through recovery, not even a Hall of Fame induction ceremony.

Just *there*. With him. With Emmy. With the people who didn't care about the number on my jersey or the highlight reel on ESPN. The ones who'd celebrated my smallest wins like they were monumental. Who showed up, every time, no matter what.

We hung up shortly after, and I stared at the ceiling, phone still clutched in my hand. Something loosened in my chest—something I hadn't even realized was wound tight.

For so long, I'd thought making it back to the NHL was the only path forward. That if I couldn't get back on the ice, I'd lose the best parts of me. But watching Jace become the player he was, watching Emmy rebuild a life from the ashes of everything she'd sacrificed... maybe it wasn't about getting back.

Maybe it was about being present.

The Mayhem bench didn't come with an arena spotlight but it came with Jace. With pride. With joy. With something that felt a hell of a lot like purpose.

Maybe the comeback I was meant to make wasn't to the NHL.

Maybe it was to them.

Shortly after, Ty called.

"She's holding it together," he said, without preamble. "But barely."

My stomach twisted. "What happened?"

"Nothing." My best friend sighed. "Everything. Ryan says he's coming, but she's afraid he won't show and Jace will play like shit again. I have more faith in him than that—Jace is playing like he's got something to prove—but she's feeling all of it."

I scrubbed a hand over my face, wishing I could do anything to help.

"Have you heard from the team yet?"

Staring down at the stack of papers on the bed next to me, I said, "Today, actually."

"And?"

"One-year renewal. It's a good deal. Gavin thinks I should take it."

"What do *you* think?"

I thumped my head against the headboard, at a loss for how to explain that everything I'd fought so hard for wasn't that appealing anymore.

"She's not going to ask you for anything," Ty said after I didn't answer. "You know that, right?"

"I do know that."

"But if she did?" Ty asked, voice low, serious.

"Maybe you have the right idea, walking away from it all."

"Whether it's today or next year or five years from now when your bones are nothing but dust as the oldest fucker in the league, home will be right where you left it."

Ty hung up, not bothering with a goodbye, which was so very *Ty* of him.

As if summoned by the weight of it all, my phone buzzed again. Emmy.

I answered before the second ring, grinning at her beautiful face staring at me.

"Hey." The words were soft and tired and somehow still the best sound in the world. She had on my hoodie, snuggled in her bed, and I'd give just about anything to be there next to her.

"Hey, Peach."

"You talked to Jace?"

"Yeah. That kid is bouncing off the walls. Said it was the best game of his life."

"He is," she chuckled, her eyes alight with happiness. "And it was. He played out of his mind."

"Damn, I'm so proud of him," I said, meaning every word. "It's killing me to miss it."

"I hate that you're not here," she whispered. "But I love that you're doing what you were born to do."

"Got a morning skate in with the team this morning," I said, needing to make all of this pain I was putting us through worth it. "Playing like my hip is brand new, like I had this super hot, really talented PT that kicked my ass back in shape."

She grinned, her smile watery. "I'm so proud of *you*. It's killing me to miss it."

I ducked my head, savoring her words, and wishing like hell I could kiss her. "What am I doing, Emmy?"

"Showing my kid how to work your ass off to chase your dreams, even when the odds are against you. Getting back on the ice before the end of the season, proving everyone wrong. Teaching Jace and I that physical distance is a sham excuse for lack of attention, *that's* what you're doing. So, go win that Cup for me, yeah?"

I nodded, barely holding my emotions in check. "Then I'm coming straight home to you. All summer, we'll do this for real."

Emmy smiled. "I like that plan."

We stayed on the line, not saying much. Just breathing. Just holding onto every little moment together.

"Conway." Coach Tremblay tapped my locker as I pulled on my hoodie after practice the next week. "My office."

"Ooh," Logan drawled from the next stall, half-dressed and already halfway into a protein bar. "Dead man walking. Should I start a GoFundMe for your funeral or just make a eulogy for the boys?"

"Make it a slideshow," I said dryly. "Include my greatest hits."

"Can I be in charge of the soundtrack?" Logan asked, deadly serious. "I'm thinking dramatic violin over your hip injury montage. Or maybe some super sad Celine Dion."

"Don't let him do that," Mikko muttered, taping his stick with methodical calm. "You remember the birthday video."

Logan grinned, all too proud of the cinematic master-piece he'd created—a slow-motion montage of our rookie goalie Nate Kozak housing ice cream after every win, set to emotional indie ballads and ending on a close-up of him licking a Drumstick like it was the meaning of life. "That was art."

"That was cruel and unusual punishment," I grabbed my water bottle. "For both him and everyone who had to watch it."

Logan gave me a mock salute as I passed. "Godspeed, Cap'n Comeback."

I smirked and shoved open the office door.

Coach Tremblay stood with arms crossed, that hard-to-read expression of his somewhere between approval and suspicion. Frankie was perched backward on a chair, spinning a dry erase marker between his fingers like it was a dagger and he was about to challenge someone to a duel.

"Sit," Tremblay said.

I sat.

Frankie pointed the marker at me. "So. Any phantom hip pain? Ghosts in the joint? Spooky cartilage spirits?"

I shook my head, barely holding back a laugh. "You're so fucking weird."

Coach didn't blink. "How's the body, Conway?"

"Strong," I said. "Stable. I feel better than before the injury."

He nodded once. "Good. Because the plan is to play you in the last regular season game next week. Ease you in before playoffs."

That electric jolt of adrenaline hit my chest—but behind it came that familiar tug. The one that always pointed somewhere else lately.

Coach studied me. "You ready?"

I nodded, maybe a little too quickly. "Yeah. Absolutely."

"You sure?" he asked. "Not just your body. Your head. You've done the work, but I've been around this game a long time. I can tell when a player's carrying something off the ice."

I stared down at my hands, trying to come up with what to say.

Frankie leaned in like he was about to whisper some ancient wisdom. "You constipated? You've got the look of a man who hasn't shat in three days."

"Frankie," Coach warned, and this time I did laugh.

"I'm good," I said, forcing a breath. "Focused. Grateful. And shitting normally, thanks Frankie. Just want to make it all count."

Tremblay narrowed his eyes. "You haven't signed your contract extension."

Shit.

"I know," I said, carefully neutral. "Gavin's looking it over. Nothing weird, just making sure it all makes sense."

"It's a good offer," Coach said.

"I know." My heart raced with every passing second. The silence was heavy for a beat.

"Jace is in the state playoffs tomorrow, right?" Coach shifted gears like he knew he wasn't going to get more out of me on that today.

"Yeah." I couldn't hold back my grin. "They play tomorrow at 3 in our arena. Logan's planning a watch party in his hotel room."

"You've been watching film like it's your job," Frankie said. "Which it isn't, by the way."

Coach gave me a long look, then nodded once. "Well, tell Logan you have to miss his little soiree. Your plane leaves after our game tonight. Go see your kid play."

My head snapped up, meeting his gaze. "You sure?"

"I have you booked back out Sunday morning to meet up with us in Edmonton," he said. "But yeah. Go be where you need to be. Then come back to me, head in the game."

I stood, emotions clogged in my throat. "Thank you, Coach. Really."

He held his hand out to shake, and I put my hand in his. "Make it count, Conway."

38

Emmy

Mile High Arena pulsed with noise—skates carving into ice, pucks thudding against boards, the low hum of anticipation building to a roar. It vibrated in your chest, all adrenaline and edge, and it had my heart racing before the puck had even dropped.

State finals. We were really here.

The lower bowl was filled with far more spectators than I'd anticipated, our little town and the neighboring ones in the Vail Valley showing up in support. Stevie stood in the front row against the ice, her sons each holding up painted posters—one read *Meyers on Fire!* complete with a sparkly stick figure holding a flaming hockey stick. The other said *Mayhem? More like Slay-hem.* The "Y" in Mayhem had googly eyes glued to it, and there was a sticker of a smiling moose because why not.

Shannon and Tate stood in the row behind them, decked out in green. Luke held Harper on his shoulders, wearing little green ear protectors and clapping along to the music.

I stood just to the left of the rink entrance, hands curled

around the railing, heart thudding like I was about to step onto the ice with the Mayhem.

Ty was behind the bench tapping helmets, clapping shoulders, and getting his kids ready during their warmup skate. His expression was all business—brow furrowed, jaw set.

But I knew that look. It wasn't pressure. It was *purpose*. Coaching had lit something up in him I hadn't seen since his early NHL days—before the injuries, before the grind wore him down. This was a different kind of fire. A steady one.

And watching my brother pour everything into these kids, watching him *thrive* in this next chapter of his life—it made my chest ache in the best possible way.

Ty wasn't out there coaching to do me a favor—he was out there because he loved it.

Before I could get carried away by my emotions, I looked back out at the ice. The Mayhem looked loose, confident even. No signs of the team who'd been demolished 6-0 in their first game this season.

Jace adjusted his gloves and tilted his head toward the rafters to count ceiling lights, a pregame superstition he'd had for years.

I bit my cuticles, nausea bubbling up in my throat for my son, but he looked calm. Focused.

"I don't like how he was carrying his stick," Ryan said as he walked up beside me, leaning over the railing. "He's dragging it. Lazy posture."

I stiffened. The tension rolled through my shoulders like a slow wave at the sight of my ex-husband.

I wasn't sure what I expected to feel, seeing Ryan again for the first time since I walked out of that glossy

Connecticut house last summer. Dread? Anger? That slow, familiar ache of betrayal?

But none of that came.

All I felt was a sharp, focused protectiveness for Jace—fierce and blinding. The man beside me had messed with our son's heart in ways I was still helping him recover from.

All the damage Ryan had done—every lie, every backhanded compliment, every moment Jace spent second-guessing himself because of it—rose like a tide in my chest.

There was no heartbreak left. No sadness. Just clarity.

Ryan hadn't broken me. He'd taught me exactly what I would never allow again.

"He's too far back in the line." Ryan was in full-on commentator mode now—blond wavy hair perfectly coiffed, cuffed slacks too pressed, and a deep green quarter-zip that just barely nodded at team colors. He looked like a man who'd walked off a golf course and into a boardroom, not one standing next to the rink at a high school state championship. "He needs to be more aggressive, not waiting for a cue."

I clenched my jaw and looked back toward the ice.

While Ryan listed flaws, I saw a kid who'd gotten up early every morning to skate, who'd pushed through losses and doubt, who earned his way here. A kid who didn't need perfection—he needed support. And I wasn't about to let anyone take that from him.

"Ryan," I warned, but it came out softer than I meant.

"I told him he needs to get his head up," Ryan added, tapping the metal railing like it was his own personal telestrator. "We've talked about this. Every video you send me, he's looking down when he's carrying through the neutral zone. That's how turnovers happen."

I saw the moment Jace noticed him in the stands. His shoulders twitched, that familiar tightening I knew all too well. Not fear. Not doubt. Just the slow clamp of trying to be too much at once. To perform, to please, to carry weight that didn't belong to him.

Ryan cupped his hands around his mouth, yelling, "Head up, Jace! You're dragging already!"

Jace deflated, snapping the practice puck off his stick in a slapshot that went wild, nowhere near the goal.

I gripped the railing so hard my knuckles ached. "Ryan. Stop."

"This is why we need to get him up to Canada," Ryan said, not listening to me. "Get him some real coaching, not just your little has-been team."

I saw red.

It wasn't just the arrogance or the jabs—it was the way Jace's shoulders hunched, like all the air had been sucked out of him by the person who was supposed to build him up.

Fury surged through me, hot and wild, my pulse beating so loud it blurred the crowd into background noise. My hands trembled with the need to shove Ryan back from the railing, to rip into him for every word, every years-long dig that had carved doubt into our son's confidence. I wanted to scream. To call out everything he'd failed to be.

But I didn't.

Because Jace would see. Everyone would see. And the last thing my kid needed on the biggest game of his life was a front-row seat to his parents going to war in the stands.

Out of the corner of my eye, I saw Shannon cutting through the crowd, her jaw tight, eyes locked on me like she could sense the explosion brewing.

I forced myself to breathe, then turned to Ryan, voice

low and lethal. "Say one more word like that about my son and I swear to God, you'll regret opening your mouth."

He smirked, the same condescending twist of his lips he'd used in every argument we'd ever had.

"And no one is taking my kid anywhere," a voice said below me.

My breath caught, head snapping to watch Beckett walk down the tunnel toward the ice.

He strode forward in slacks and a Mayhem quarter-zip, his gait steady and sure, like he hadn't just flown across the country to be here.

"Excuse me?" Ryan said.

But I couldn't look away. Couldn't breathe when Beckett's eyes locked on mine the second he cleared the hallway. His eyes held a giddy smile, but his body language told a different story.

His jaw was clenched tight, fingers curled around the duffel bag strap on his shoulder. His pulse hammering in his neck, just above the collar of his shirt.

He'd heard Ryan. Every smug, dismissive word, and he was just as furious as I was over the way he talked to my kid.

My kid. The words echoed in my head, making my heart race with each repetition.

And just like that, I went from rage to pure, aching adoration. It was whiplash. Heart-splitting, breath-stealing whiplash.

Of course, Beckett was here.

Because when it mattered, he showed up. Not out of obligation or for appearances. Not to criticize or make himself look good. But because he loved us. Because he meant it when he said he wanted to make this work.

Ryan had shown up today because it lined up with his

schedule, and it looked good to have a son playing in the state finals. Nothing was ever really about us, always twisted to how it could make him look best, and only when it was convenient.

But Beckett... Beckett showed up *despite* the miles, the pressure, the playoff race waiting for him in Denver. He came because his priorities weren't cloudy—they were crystal clear. And he'd just claimed my kid as his own.

He dropped his duffel bag on the rubber floor, walked past the players coming off the ice and back to the locker room, and grabbed the railing, hopping up until his face was level with mine.

And for the first time all day, I could breathe again.

"You're not in Seattle," I said, barely able to get the words out through the lump in my throat.

Beckett shook his head, eyes alight with that quiet joy that never failed to wreck me. "Nah. I heard there was a team of has-beens about to win the State Championship. Figured this was the place to be."

My heart flipped, and if we hadn't been in front of half the state and my seething ex-husband, I might've launched myself into his arms right then and there.

"*Your* kid?" Ryan snapped, his voice sharp and shrill enough to cut through the noise of the arena. His face had gone crimson, lips pinched like he was holding back a full-blown tantrum. "What, you think you can fuck my wife and suddenly claim my kid now too?"

With perfect timing like the universe had planned it, Jace skated off the ice, eyes scanning the stands as he tugged his helmet off. He froze mid-step when he spotted Beckett, then seemed to take in what Ryan had just said.

Beckett hopped down off the railing and met him at the

base of the ramp, calm as ever. He clapped a hand on Jace's shoulder and gave him that grin that always made my kid stand a little taller. Then he looked back at Ryan, gaze steady, voice low.

"Yeah. *My* kid," he said, like it was the most obvious thing in the world. "How can you not love him? He's got more heart and hustle than half the NHL, and the mouth of a seasoned locker room vet. He's sweet to my mom and his. And when life punches him in the gut, he just skates harder."

Then Beckett's eyes flicked to me, warm and sure and absolutely devastating.

"And his mom?" He gave a low whistle. "She's not your wife. You lost the right to call her that a long time ago. So yeah, I'll claim them both, every chance I get. If they'll have me."

Jace's head snapped toward me, brows raised in surprise. But Beckett didn't flinch. He turned, meeting Jace's gaze dead on.

"We were going to wait until this summer to talk to you properly," he said, voice steady. "But I'm all in, Jace. With her. With you. With this whole messy, wonderful life. I love her, and I think you're the best damn kid I've ever met. I'd be proud to call you my family, if that's something you'd be okay with."

Jace blinked. A beat of silence stretched—then my arrogant son shrugged, the barest flicker of a grin tugging at his mouth.

"Dude. You think I didn't already know?" He jerked his chin toward me. "She hasn't smiled this much in a decade, and I have access to the doorbell camera, dumbass. You've been toast since New Years."

I let out a laugh-sob that broke straight through my

chest, hand flying to my mouth. Every nerve in my body buzzed with love for both of them.

"You can't just stake claim on my kid," Ryan said.

Beckett turned back to him, that glacier-calm composure hardening into steel.

"Sure I can," he said. "His biological dad is a real dick and left the position of 'decent man worth looking up to' wide open, so I'm stepping in. Gladly."

Jace smirked, tilting his head toward Ryan. "Fine by me."

Ryan sputtered, nearly tripping over his own fury when he pointed a finger at me. "You did this. You turned him against me. This is parental alienation, and it violates our custody agreement. I'm calling my attorneys."

"Cool." Jace adjusted his elbow pad. "Can they skate? We could use one more defenseman."

Beckett let out a low laugh, and I saw the corner of his mouth twitch like he was barely holding back pride.

Stevie reached me just in time, slipping a calming hand on my arm while Tate looked on with her phone suspiciously angled like she was filming the whole thing in case we needed it in a future custody battle. Shannon stood a row in front of me, directly between me and Ryan like my own personal guard dog.

"Let's go," Ty called from the end of the hallway, giving his best friend a little nod of approval. "Locker room, kids."

Jace gave me a look—a mix of apology, resolve, and something stubborn and fierce—and jogged down the tunnel with Beckett right behind him.

And just like that, the storm moved on.

But the aftershocks? Oh, I felt those in every part of me.

Shannon eyed me like she was assessing damage. "Do I need to walk you to the bathroom so you can scream into your hands for 30 seconds? Or is this more of a hot pretzel moment?"

I let out a shaky breath, blinking fast. "Honestly? I might need both."

Ryan turned toward me, mouth already opening, jaw flexing like he was gearing up for a monologue I didn't ask for.

But Shannon cut him off without even glancing in his direction. "Read the room, Vineyard Vines. Unless the next words out of your mouth are 'you can have full custody and a big, fat check', keep it to yourself."

Ryan's jaw snapped shut like a trap, color still high on his cheeks as he glared at us, but, for once, said nothing.

Stevie tugged on my arm, pulling me back toward where Luke sat with the kids. "Let's go before she gets banned from this arena for homicide."

I leaned my head on her shoulder, grateful I'd honked at her in that stupid parking lot and found my people.

39

BECKETT

The Denver Yeti locker room felt different today, and not just because it was full of kids rather than grown men. It was quieter, almost reverent.

The Mayhem shuffled inside like they were stepping into church, wide-eyed and buzzing with the kind of nervous energy that only came with state championships and dreams that suddenly felt real. Their voices bounced off the walls, soft and awed. A few of them trailed fingers along the edges of lockers, like maybe just being in this space would turn them into the players they'd always wanted to be.

And there, dead center of it all, was Jace.

Sitting in my stall.

I swallowed the lump in my throat, staring at the *Conway* nameplate emblazoned over his head in that same spot I'd claimed for years. His elbows rested on his knees, chin tucked like he was trying to stay cool, but I saw him scanning the room. He leaned back just a little, like the weight of the moment was pressing into his spine, trying not to freak out.

I was barely holding it together, because seeing Jace

sitting there wearing my number and sitting under my name was him claiming me right back.

I cleared my throat, the sound sharp in the stillness. Every head turned my way.

"I've been in a lot of locker rooms," I said, voice steady even though my chest was tight. "Stanley Cup qualifiers. Olympic trials—"

"Okay, showboat." Delgado cut in, loud enough for the whole room to hear.

A ripple of laughter broke through the nerves. I grinned and rolled my eyes.

"Just trying to establish my street cred, kid."

"Pretty sure coaching a bunch of hormonal teens did that," Molly said. "Takes some real bravery to put up with these losers."

More laughter followed, and I raised my hands, encouraging them to settle. "Some of the biggest games of my life started right here, in this room."

I paused, letting my eyes sweep the space—these kids, this team, *my* team now.

"But standing here today, with you guys? This is the proudest I've ever been to wear a team's colors. When I came back to Linwood, I thought my career was over. I didn't know what came next, and I was lost. But watching you push through every practice, every loss, every early morning skate —you reminded me why I fell in love with this game in the first place."

"You crying, Coach?" Jace asked, then threw a towel at me. "Here's a towel for your feelings."

The room lost it, howls echoing off the walls.

I laughed too, throwing it back at him and shaking my head as I fought off the ridiculous sting in my eyes.

Ty stood just off my shoulder like always. He gave a sharp nod, voice quieter but no less firm.

"You've earned this." Ty pointed a finger at the floor. "You've fought tooth and nail to be right here, in the finals. Now go show them why no one wants to face the Mayhem in March."

The room exploded in shouts, sticks slapping on the floor in a rhythm. Every single one of them was fired up, and so was I.

Hell, I might've been the only NHL player who felt more purpose coaching from behind a youth bench than chasing glory under stadium lights. But with this team? With this kid?

Yeah. This was the most important game of my life.

The first period hit fast and hard.

I stood at the end of the bench beside Ty, arms crossed tight over my chest as the Mayhem hit the ice like they had something to prove. The Kodiaks were no joke—big, disciplined, and sharp as hell on the breakout. But our kids met them stride for stride.

Jace was locked in from the first face-off. Head down, skates blazing, he chased every puck like it owed him money. But he wasn't just fast; he was controlled and focused. He took a hit behind the boards on his first shift, and I held my breath, waiting for the temper that used to flare up and cost him time in the box.

But it didn't come.

He popped right back up, shook it off, and got into position like nothing happened. No chirping. No slamming his stick. Just pure composure.

Ty leaned in. "He's not fighting himself anymore."

My throat was too tight to answer, my chest feeling like it might crack wide open.

Molly ripped a shot just wide early on, and Delgado flattened a Kodiak forward in front of the crease like he'd been waiting his whole life for it. Miles made a glove save so slick it had the whole crowd on their feet.

But the Kodiaks were relentless, and with two minutes left in the first, they capitalized on a rebound and slid one past Miles. 1-0.

I didn't flinch, and neither did our bench.

Ty muttered, "We're fine."

And he was right.

The second period belonged to us.

We came out with teeth. Delgado pinched hard at the blue line and kept the puck in, swinging it across to Molly, who deked her defender with a move so clean the stands erupted. She passed it straight to Jace, and my kid—*my kid*—didn't hesitate. Quick wrist shot, top shelf, blocker side.

Tie game.

The bench exploded, but Jace didn't even celebrate. Just turned and skated back like it was routine. Like he expected that goal.

"That's new," I muttered to Ty.

He smirked. "Damn, he looks like you out there. Uncanny what a good role model can do."

I grinned, then looked up in the stands and found her.

Emmy was on her feet, clutching a soft pretzel like it was a lifeline, cheeks puffed out like a damn chipmunk. Her eyes were locked on the ice like her whole soul was down here with us.

I laughed under my breath.

Ty caught me staring and groaned. "God, she's still the same. Stuffing her face mid-heart attack like snacks will ward off stress."

"She's perfect," I said without thinking, still grinning like an idiot.

Ty gave me a long-suffering look, then went back to the game.

The rest of the period was a war. One shot after another, bodies crashing into the boards, sticks clattering on the ice. Miles made a series of saves that had the Kodiaks' fans groaning in disbelief.

At the horn, it was still 1-1, and every single player on our bench looked hungry.

Ty clapped a hand on my shoulder. "You good?"

I gave a slow nod, heart thudding, eyes still on the ice.

"I've never been this proud of anything in my life."

The locker room was buzzing when we stepped inside— sweaty, hyped, half-shouting over one another as skates squeaked against rubber floors and sticks clattered into racks. The scoreboard read 1-1, but the energy in the room felt like we were already winning.

I waited a beat before stepping in front of the white-board, letting them burn off that adrenaline.

Ty followed me in, already unzipping his jacket, eyes sweeping the room like he was cataloging every bounce of the knee and crack of knuckles.

"Alright," I said, loud enough to cut through the chaos. "Kodiaks are big, but they're tired. Watch their line changes

—second line's gassed and late getting back. If we can catch 'em on transition, they'll fold."

Heads nodded. Molly wiped sweat from her forehead, looking anything but tired.

"Delgado, keep doing what you're doing on the blue line. Miles, you're dialed in. Keep your glove hot."

He gave a sharp nod from his stool, sipping water like it was rocket fuel.

"And Jace," I said, catching his eye. "Their left defenseman's falling for your outside move every time. Next shift, fake wide, cut inside, and take it to the net."

Jace smirked. "You got it, Coach."

Ty stepped up beside me, arms folded. "Stay smart. Stay aggressive. You've earned this. Go take it."

As the team started to rise and regroup, I caught Jace's shoulder and pulled him aside. His cheeks were flushed, hair slicked back, eyes still burning from the second period.

"Hey," I said quietly, hand still on his shoulder. "No matter what the scoreboard says when this is over, I am so damn proud of you. Not because you scored. Not because you're flying out there."

His brows lifted, waiting.

"You're playing with control. With purpose. You've earned every second you play out there by being the biggest hustler on the ice. I'm so fucking proud."

His mouth twitched like he wanted to crack a joke but didn't quite get there.

"I'm lucky to know you," I finished, voice rough. "Lucky as hell to be part of this."

Jace looked down, then back up with a grin I'd know anywhere.

"Cool." He dropped his helmet down over his head and

buckled the chin strap. "But if number 6 takes a cheap shot at Molly one more time, my gloves are coming off."

I huffed out a laugh and slapped his helmet. "Just don't get thrown out of the damn game in the third period."

He walked out with the rest of the team, fire in his veins.

I stayed back for one extra second, just breathing it in.

This team.

This moment.

This kid.

Game on.

40

Emmy

I couldn't sit down. Couldn't breathe.

"Is it normal to be sweating this much just from watching hockey?" Stevie whispered beside me, fanning herself with a program while balancing Harper on one hip. "I feel like I'm going through something. Like, emotionally."

"You're not," Shannon deadpanned, eyes still locked on the ice. "But Emmy is. She's in her final form. Behold: the Mother of Mayhem."

"I hate that it fits," I muttered around a mouthful of hot pretzel.

Wyatt and Reid were draped over Luke's lap, shrieking in tandem every time the Mayhem touched the puck. Harper whipped a foam finger around, hitting everyone and totally unbothered by the chaos around her.

Shannon sat one row down next to Lori, both of them wrapped in blankets like they were just here for a cozy night out—if cozy involved full-body screaming and a mutual vendetta against the refs.

"That was offsides, you blind trout!" Lori yelled, surprisingly loud for someone with advanced Parkinson's and a cane tucked beside her seat. Her voice might have wobbled, but her aim was sharp as ever.

Shannon leaned over, handing her half a Twizzler. "Subtlety is dead. I love it."

Tate was just behind us, arms folded, eyes tracking every line change with surgical precision. "The Kodiaks are rotating their first and second D-pair to try and double-team Jace's line. It's going to leave an opening on Molly's side if we get a clean zone entry."

Stevie blinked. "Tate, that meant nothing to me, but I'm so proud of you."

Meanwhile, I was vibrating in place, chewing tiny bites of the second pretzel I didn't remember buying and trying not to launch myself over the seats every time Jace skated past.

Every time he hit the ice, I stood. Didn't even notice until Luke gently tugged at the hem of my jacket.

"You're blocking Harper's view," he whispered.

"She's 18 months old."

"She's very invested in Uncle Jace's success."

I snorted but didn't sit. My heart was lodged in my throat, pulsing in sync with every pass, every shift, every damn move he made.

And then there was Beckett.

I kept looking down at the bench, like some invisible magnet was pulling my gaze there. He stood next to Ty, both shouting encouragement and calling lines, focused and locked in, and somehow still managing to check the scoreboard, the refs, and the kids' body language all at once.

My eyes burned.

Last year I was sitting in a cold, sterile house with a husband who hadn't looked at me like I mattered in years. I was exhausted, hollowed out, trying to hold myself together for Jace while slowly falling apart. I had no plan. No peace. Just a broken heart and more resentment than I knew what to do with.

Now? I sat surrounded by friends who'd become family, watching my son chase his dream. Sitting in the crowd with a woman who'd raised the man I loved, screaming just as loud as I was.

Beckett was everything I didn't believe I deserved back then. Steady and fierce, loyal and present. Unmistakably *ours* no matter where he was.

I took another shaky bite of pretzel, trying to blink back tears.

"You okay?" Stevie asked softly.

I nodded, hand pressed to my chest.

"I'm just…" I swallowed hard. "Really freaking happy."

Shannon pointed at the ice. "I'll be happy when that ref grows a spine and makes a fucking call."

All heads turned toward her.

Even Tate blinked.

"I thought you hated hockey," Stevie said, half scandalized, half impressed.

"I *do* hate hockey," Shannon snapped. "I also hate injustice, and that was a damn trip."

Lori cackled beside her and raised a mittened fist. "Amen, sister."

"I don't care what you say, we're friends now," I muttered, wiping a tear off my cheek.

"Fine." A hint of a smile tugged on Shannon's lips as she looked over at me. "I guess."

A whistle blew and the tension surged like a current through the stands. I gripped the arm rests, forgetting the pretzel entirely as the puck dropped at center ice for the final minutes of the third.

Back on the ice, the Mayhem were locked in.

Jace's line came out again with under three minutes left on the clock, and from the moment the puck hit, he was hunting for his opportunity, sharp and focused.

Delgado took the breakout and threaded it up the boards to Molly, who barely touched it before flipping it cross-ice to Jace. He caught it in stride, powering past the Kodiaks' defenseman like he'd been waiting all game for this one opening.

The arena rose around me, a wall of noise I barely heard.

Jace deked left.

The goalie bit.

He dragged it back right and buried it—clean, quick, right between his pads in the five-hole.

I don't remember screaming. I just know I was suddenly three rows down from where I'd started, arms in the air, tears streaking down my cheeks, and Stevie was screaming right along with me.

The bench erupted.

Beckett slammed a fist against the boards, yelling so loud I could practically hear it from here. Ty was shouting, hands cupped around his mouth, then fist-pumping the air. Even Miles skated out of the crease to tackle Jace into the corner where the team mobbed him.

It wasn't the end of the game—not yet. There were still 52 seconds on the clock, but the Mayhem never gave the Kodiaks another look.

Every pass, every block, every save from Miles in those final moments was a statement: *This is ours.*

And when the final horn blared and the score held at 2–1, I lost it.

Hot tears, hysterical laughter, the kind of release you can't even explain unless you've spent your life loving someone that hard.

Lori sobbed next to me, like she felt every one of my emotions too. Shannon had her face in her hands, probably trying not to cry. Tate was smiling a full-on, teeth-showing grin. Even Harper looked excited, flailing her foam finger at no one in particular.

On the ice, my son was buried in a pile of teammates, gloves and sticks flying as they celebrated together.

Beckett met my eyes from across the rink, his grin enough to melt any lingering doubts that this was forever. For one perfect second, everything else fell away.

The parking lot outside the arena had turned into a full-blown party. There were no grills or folding chairs anymore, just a sea of parents, siblings, friends, and a level of emotional wreckage that only a championship game could deliver.

We all huddled near the buses, bundled in jackets and team sweatshirts, still vibrating from the win. Stevie had a giant Mayhem blanket draped around her shoulders like a cape, her face still flushed from all the screaming. Luke was next to her, wearing Harper in a chest carrier, her chubby arms waving around like she knew exactly what we were celebrating.

Wyatt and Reid had commandeered someone's cowbell and were alternating between ringing it and sword-fighting with the foam fingers.

"They've been doing that for ten minutes," Luke said, rubbing his temple. "I think I'm concussed."

"Same," I murmured, heart still trying to climb down from the clouds.

Tate stood next to me, arms folded, her smile subtle but steady.

Shannon leaned against the Mayhem's bus, looking equal parts bored and elated. "I swear to God, if I see that ref in a grocery store, I'm slashing his tires."

Lori chuckled from the folding chair someone had offered her, cane resting across her knees. Her Mayhem beanie was slightly crooked and her face lit up with pride.

And then the doors opened.

The kids poured out, gear bags slung over shoulders, dress shirts half-untucked, cheeks still red from the locker room. Parents erupted into cheers and applause, a tidal wave of celebration.

Molly and Delgado were smiling like they'd won the lottery, leading the players down the line of celebrations. Miles gave high-fives like a pro, pausing only to hug his little sister. Every single one of them was glowing.

Jace came out last, hair wet from the shower and grin so wide it lit up his whole face. He looked up, found me in the crowd, and waved. Not just a *hey mom* wave—a full arm pump, like he knew I'd been ready to storm the ice myself.

I waved back, laughing through tears.

Ryan was nowhere to be seen. He'd left before the final buzzer, too proud or too petty to stick around and face everything he'd lost.

I hated that for Jace's sake. Some part of me had always hoped Ryan would realize his mistakes and try harder, rather than pass blame. Not for me, not to fix what couldn't be repaired, but to at least show up for his son when it mattered most.

But he didn't. And as much as that still stung, the ache was softened by the man who chose to show up not out of obligation, but because he wanted to be here.

As if summoned by my thoughts, Beckett walked through the crowd, his eyes locked on mine like I was the only person that existed in the world.

Still in his Mayhem pullover, sweat-damp hair curling at the edges, walking like nothing and no one could keep him from me. Ty was a step behind him holding the giant State trophy, letting him go ahead like he knew exactly where Beckett needed to be.

He didn't hesitate. Just walked right through the chaos, past the noise and the crowd.

Beckett pulled me in like gravity itself had written this moment into existence. One hand on my waist, the other curling behind my neck, and then his mouth was on mine—firm, warm, and full of everything we'd held back while the world watched.

My hands fisted in his shirt, my feet barely remembering how to stay on the ground.

Someone wolf-whistled, and we broke apart.

Shannon crossed her arms and muttered, "Finally, the world's worst-kept secret is out."

Stevie gasped like she hadn't been in on it for months. "Okay, *but still*! Public kissing? This is officially official."

Luke snorted. "They kissed in public in December. That seemed kind of official."

"Please." Tate shook her head. "Have you seen how lovesick he is?"

"He came to girls' night with queso," Shannon said flatly. "That was basically a proposal."

Lori leaned over from her folding chair, eyes glinting with feral grandma glee. "I'm taking out a *full page* in next week's paper. Right next to the obits and the fire department spaghetti dinner."

Beckett pulled back just enough to look over his shoulder, smirked, and called, "Make it a two-page spread, Mom. Front and back. I look good from every angle. Everyone needs to know she's mine."

Lori cackled. Shannon groaned. Stevie, misty-eyed and clutching her heart, whispered, "I love love."

Beckett rested his forehead on mine, still holding me against his chest.

"Hi, Peach," he said, softer now.

"Hey," I murmured, still breathless.

Behind us, the Mayhem hoisted the trophy into the air, the crowd roaring one more time.

Ty clapped Jace on the back, then caught my eye and gave me a nod that was quiet, proud, and all heart.

I just leaned into Beckett's arms and held on, buoyed in the moment. Because the life I'd been terrified to want—the love, the family, the hope I thought I'd lost—was here.

Loud and messy.

Real and earned.

And finally, *finally* mine.

41

Emmy

"Hell yeah, fuck yeah," Delgado said, looking up into the packed stands around us.

Ty slapped him over the head and Delgado ducked out of his range. "Language."

"If being at game six of the Stanley Cup championships doesn't earn a swear or two, my name's not Molly," Molly said. "Because *hell yeah, fuck yeah.*"

Delgado held a hand up for a fist bump, and I chuckled at my brother's exasperated head shake.

The sound inside Mile High Arena was absolute chaos, so much louder than a few weeks ago when the Mayhem had played here.

Music pulsed. Lights strobed. Fans screamed like their lives depended on it. The Yeti were up 3-2 in the series, and the Cup was in the building. One more win tonight, and it was over.

I stood at the glass, clutching an emergency pretzel and doing my best not to pass out.

It had been a grueling two months of playoffs. Beckett

had given body, mind, and soul to this run, and we'd been at every single home game. His own little cheering squad, loud and proud and aggressively decked out in Conway gear.

I thought I was used to the nerves by now, that after a decade of standing on the sidelines for Jace I'd learned to handle it. But watching Beckett warm up for what could be the biggest game of his life felt like I was back in the stands at Mayhem games, clutching the bleachers like it was the only thing keeping me upright.

Ty leaned over, voice raised above the roar. "You going to breathe anytime soon, or should I start Googling CPR instructions?"

"Not helping," I muttered.

Around us, the Mayhem pressed against the boards, eyes wide, practically vibrating with excitement. Delgado was narrating everything like a broadcaster. Miles had already dropped half his popcorn. Jace looked cool on the outside, but I could see the twitch in his jaw, the excited energy in his stance.

All our players were wearing new Mayhem jerseys with *Coach Conway* printed on the back, excited to show them off.

"Man, this is so cool." Jace grinned. "He's going to lose his mind when he sees us."

I fidgeted with my new custom jacket, the leather fabric emblazoned with his name and number that said I was far more than just a fan.

Ty eyed me sideways. "Feeling exposed there, sis?"

"I look like a groupie."

"You look like a WAG."

Before I could argue, the team took the ice for warmups, and the volume inside the arena somehow doubled.

The Mayhem kids exploded in cheers as Beckett skated

out, laser-focused. He did a loop, practiced a shot, exchanged glove bumps with a teammate, and then he saw us.

I swear, I felt that subtle shift in his stride. The way his head lifted just a little. His eyes locked on ours, and then directly on me.

I froze. "Oh God."

Jace leaned in with a wicked grin. "Brace for impact."

Beckett coasted toward our section, slowing as he neared the glass. A few fans waved and someone banged the glass next to us, but he didn't look away. As one, the kids turned, showing off their new jerseys, and I watched his eyes light up with glee.

"Did he see it?" Molly shouted, looking over her shoulder.

I grinned back at him, feeling every ounce of his joy. "Yeah. He saw it."

Beckett skated right up to the glass, braced one glove on the boards, then he pointed to my chest, and mouthed, *Turn around.*

I shook my head, cheeks heating. He mouthed it again, slower, one brow raised: *Turn. Around.*

"Do it, Emmy!" Molly yelled. "Let him see!"

"She's blushing!" Delgado cackled.

"Don't faint, Mom," Jace added, clearly delighted.

Groaning, I turned around and spread my arms so he could get a full view of the jacket, peeking over my shoulder to watch his reaction.

He nodded, smiling like a smug bastard, and tapped his chest right over his heart.

Ty chuckled. "Well, that was subtle."

I turned back around, heart hammering, trying and failing not to grin.

Beckett skated off to resume warmups, and I turned to watch the kids enjoy themselves.

Above us, I spotted Shannon, Tate, Mason, and Lori already settled in the suite. Shannon waved her phone in the air like she was recording everything. Tate looked like she was trying not to smile. Mason blew me a kiss and immediately turned to Tate, saying something that made her roll her eyes.

"Ten bucks says he just told her if the Yeti win, he's proposing on the Jumbotron," Jace said.

"If the Yeti win, I'll propose to Molly on the Jumbotron too," Delgado said.

She shoved him hard in the chest, sending him reeling backward over the row of chairs, and I snorted a laugh.

"Hey," Ty said beside me. "You okay?"

I looked up at my brother. At his warm eyes, his steady presence, the way he'd carried me through every broken moment over the last year without asking for anything in return.

Then I looked back at the ice. At Beckett, still watching us between drills like we were his entire world.

I took a shaky breath.

"Yeah," I said. "I'm okay."

Ty raised a brow. Waited.

I smiled. "This is it, isn't it? This is forever."

He didn't say anything for a second. Just nodded, clapped a hand to the back of my neck, and pulled me in for a quick hug.

"I know," he said, like he'd known it all along.

The buzzer sounded for warmups to end, and Beckett gave us one last grin before skating off toward the tunnel, tapping his stick to the glass again on the way.

Ty rounded up the kids, steering them toward the nearest

stairwell. "Let's go find our seats. We've got a championship to win."

I followed after them, walking toward my seat in a jacket with Beckett's name on it, surrounded by the best people I'd ever known, in the place where I'd found everything I didn't even know I needed.

Two hours later, the Yeti did it.

Stanley Cup champions.

Beckett scored two goals—one of them the game-winner—and I was still trying to remember how to breathe.

Logan played like he was powered by spite, chirping the entire opposing bench and still managing to log two assists and a breakaway goal that sent the arena into a frenzy.

Mikko was a wall on defense—blocking shots, clearing the crease, and leveling a forward so hard in the third that the guy had to be helped off the ice.

But it was Beckett who sealed it. Against every odd, he skated like he had something to prove, and someone to come home to. When that final buzzer sounded, he didn't throw his gloves, didn't celebrate with the team. He turned, found us in the crowd, and smiled like the only victory that mattered was right here.

The roar in the arena was deafening, but I barely heard it. My whole body buzzed as I made my way down to the ice with Ty and the kids. They were practically bouncing out of their shoes, shouting, hugging, tripping over each other in their excitement.

Security waved us through as the on-ice celebrations

began, and just as we stepped onto the carpet leading toward center ice, I saw him.

Beckett was grinning like a madman, helmet off, hair damp with sweat, hugging teammates left and right. The Cup hadn't been presented yet, but the joy in his face was pure, unfiltered, and victorious.

Then a reporter stepped in front of him, holding out a mic.

"Beckett Conway! Two goals tonight, including the game-winner in what is rumored to be your final NHL appearance. The fans want to know if the rumors are true— are you coming back next season?"

I froze, reaching out and grabbing Jace's hand. Every cell in my body went still, like the world had narrowed to this one fragile, impossible moment.

Beckett's eyes found mine through the chaos, through the lights and the noise and the swirl of celebration.

His smile wasn't the triumphant look of a man who'd just won everything. It was the look of a man who knew exactly what he wanted.

We'd talked about this for weeks, after games and in the quiet early mornings when we drank our coffees together on speaker phone.

I'd told him I didn't need him to walk away for me. That I loved him in the NHL or out. That if he had more to give to this game, I'd stand beside him every step of the way.

And still, this was the choice he made.

Not for me. Not for Jace. For *him*.

He turned to the mic and said, loud and clear, "This was my last game in the NHL."

A ripple moved through the arena. The reporter blinked. "You're retiring?"

Beckett nodded, eyes still on me. "As much as this game has meant to me, I met a kid this year who reminded me why I started playing in the first place. He's got more talent and heart than most of the guys I've ever played with, and he's the future of this game. I can't wait to coach him."

The reporter chuckled. "Sounds like a special kid to give it all up for."

Beckett's smile deepened. "You have no idea how special he is. And hopefully, I can convince his mom to marry me, too."

The crowd erupted, the kids lost it, and the reporter clutched her chest like she had no idea how to process the bombs Beckett dropped left and right.

I burst into tears, laughing as Jace yanked on my arm. "You're going to say yes, right?"

I nodded, unable to find the words. Beckett held out his arms as I reached him, the chaos of the championship erupting around us, and pulled me into him like he never planned to let go.

And I knew, without a single doubt, that he never would.

Up Next: Ty Hudson

He's a grumpy coach and brand-new foster dad.
She's Junie's aunt—and the one woman he never forgot. Now she's living next door and turning his quiet life upside down.
Preorder Mayhem Book 2 today!

BECKETT

Two Years Later

We stood in the driveway of a familiar white ranch-style house on the edge of Coldridge, an old basketball hoop in the driveway and a hand-painted "Welcome Hockey Families" sign in the flower bed. Jace unloaded his gear bag, tossing it over one shoulder like it weighed nothing, even though I knew damn well it was packed with almost everything he owned.

This was his host house—his home for the season as he started Juniors playing for the Coldridge Thunder. He'd be sharing a house with another 17-year-old kid from Minnesota and Coach Granger, the now retired coach who'd taken me from Juniors to University of Michigan to the NHL.

Granger stepped out onto the porch, still broad-shouldered and sharp-eyed despite the gray in his hair. He nodded once at me, that silent approval that always said more than words. I'd played for him at 17, and now here we were. Full circle.

I handed Jace a container of protein powder like it was some sacred parting gift. "Don't eat like an idiot."

Jace smirked. "I'll do my best. Chicken and veggies, right?"

I tried to laugh, but it caught somewhere behind my ribs. My whole chest was tight with pride, but also something raw and sharp. I'd only just figured out how to be Emmy's husband and his dad, and now he was leaving.

Together, the three of us got his room set up, and before I was ready, it was time to go.

Emmy stood next to me on the porch, composed and calm. Warm hand in mine, steady smile on her face, like she was the one holding me together.

"You okay, old man?" Jace asked, clearly enjoying this far too much. "You need us to walk you to the car?"

Emmy snorted, leaning into my side. "Don't tease him. He's doing his best."

Then she looked at Jace, voice steady, eyes misting. "I'll wait to cry in the car on the way home, like a *professional*."

Jace hugged her first, then turned to me. One of those shoulder-clap, eye-contact moments that hit like a puck to the chest.

"You two are soft," he said with a shake of his head. "But I love you."

"Yeah," I muttered, blinking hard. "I love you too, kid."

We watched Jace head inside, a bounce in his steps. Coach shook my hand, promising to take good care of our kid, and then shut the door behind him.

Emmy squeezed my hand as we sat in my truck in the driveway. "You okay?"

"Not even close," I said quietly, afraid to back out of my spot, to say goodbye.

She smiled, soft and secretive. "Well, since you're nailing this dad thing, I guess it's a good thing we're starting over."

I turned to look at her, not sure I'd heard her right. "What?"

"Well, you're about 6 weeks closer to being a dad again."

Not until she grabbed my hand and rested it on her belly did her meaning truly sink in. "You're pregnant?"

She nodded.

And just like that, I was gone. I kissed her like she'd just handed me a new dream in a baby-sized Mayhem jersey.

Jace was thriving, headed for greatness. Back in Linwood, Ty and I were coaching the Mayhem, running the team we loved. Mom's Parkinson's was getting worse, but I was where I needed to be—for however long we had.

After all, it turned out my mom was right: just when you thought your dreams were big enough, another one came along that was even bigger and better than the last one.

Mine used to be about the spotlight, the roar of the crowd, the chase for glory.

Now it was Emmy's laughter echoing down the hall. Jace's excited whoops after a play. A new heartbeat waiting to meet the world.

And for the first time in my life, I didn't want to chase anything—I was right where I was meant to be.

WANT MORE MAYHEM?

There's more to come in Mayhem Country! Join Aimee's newsletter at aimeevancebooks.com to be the first to know!

Mayhem Hockey Club

Moms of Mayhem

Mayhem Book 2 - Coming Spring 2026

Deadlights Cove

Small Town Cozy Paranormal Rom-Com Series

Smoke Show

Deja Brew

A Very Merry Christmoose (Novella)

Wing and a Miss

Pier Pressure

Karma is a Witch

Foxing Day (Novella)

Timber Creek

Small Town Cozy Paranormal Romance Series

Wild Wild Wolf

Love Bites

Call of the Norns

A Viking Time Travel Fantasy Trilogy

Fates Illuminated

Fates Promised

Fates Defied

ACKNOWLEDGMENTS

Goodness gracious, y'all. This one got me right in the feels. Motherhood is the most demanding, most natural role I've ever stepped into. Pouring my heart into the tiny humans I created? That part comes instinctively. But holding onto the parts of me that existed before them? That's where the challenge lives.

It's not hard to give them everything—but in the process, it's far too easy to forget ourselves. This story is a love letter to that messy, magical middle season of motherhood. To the women fighting to find themselves again, and the friends who steady us when the ground feels shaky.

To the readers—thank you for picking up this book, for cheering on Emmy and Beckett, and for letting my words find a home in your heart. You are the reason these stories exist, and I'm endlessly grateful for every message and review. You make the mayhem worth it.

To my editor Brit—thank you for going on this journey with me, time and time again. You make my writing stronger, my characters sharper, and my ideas so much more coherent. But even more so, thank you for doing this motherhood thing side-by-side with me. I love you times infinity.

To Britt, my assistant and chaos wrangler—you keep me organized and laughing when I want to curl up under my desk and hide. Thank you for making this author life feel possible and fun, even on the wildest days.

To B, Becky, Sarah, and Vanessa—thank you for every bit of encouragement, every brainstorm session, every "what if..." idea that helped shape this book into what it is. Your support means more than you know.

To Chelsea—I'm endlessly grateful to you for creating the *most* beautiful cover art—my favorite one yet.

To Michael—for making me giggle through hundreds of Pilates classes. I could barely walk out of class today, but I forgive you. You're still my #1.

To my brother, Eric—who knew the decade-plus I spent as a rink rat would lead here? Buddies forever.

To my girls—every moment spent in the stands and on the sidelines for you made this story so much more fun. I love being your #1 fan.

And last but never least, to Chris, Mr. Aimee Vance Books, the Bookmark Guy—you believe in me more than anyone, and I love you forever.

ABOUT AIMEE VANCE

Fueled by peach tea and chaos, Aimee Vance writes heartwarming and hilarious romance stories. She holds a B.S. in Public Relations from Texas Christian University and has always been an avid fantasy reader.

Residing in Texas with her husband, two young daughters, and Labrador Retriever, Aimee loves to transport readers to worlds hidden between the pages where magic and love intertwine. She prefers sassy heroines, grumpy heroes, and enough humor to keep you chuckling with every page.

facebook.com/aimeevancebooks

instagram.com/aimeevancebooks

goodreads.com/aimeevancebooks

amazon.com/author/aimeevancebooks

bookbub.com/authors/aimee-vance